M000194988

THE MAGI MENAGERIE

BOOK ONE

KALE LAWRENCE

Content Warning

The following work contains elements that some readers may find uncomfortable. These include active scenes of religious and ethnic hate crime, bullying, death, and physical parental abuse. One character is a survivor of past sexual assault, though the actual events are implied and not explicitly shown on page.

© 2021 Kale Lawrence

All rights reserved. Published in the United States by EnchantFire Books.

This is a work of fiction. Names, characters, places, and incidents are either product of the author's imagination or are used fictitiously. Any resemblance to actual persons, living or dead, events, or locales is entirely coincidental.

First Edition

ISBN: 978-1-7365125-3-1

Cover design by MoorBooks Design
www.moorbooksdesign.com

www.kalelawrence.com

For Sara,
who showed me I could do impossible things.

THE ORDER OF BABYLON

With precise graphite strokes, Ezra Newport constructed his dreams.

Like an ancient tower piercing the clouds, Ezra manifested buildings beyond the likes of the European cities that had served as his backdrop over the past decade. But none of them could ever compare to the municipalities of his mind. Carefully, as if he were building the monument from tangible things, he assembled shapes, lines, and archways until they spilled from the parchment. Illuminated by the soft amber glow of the wall sconces, jarred only by light vibrations from the locomotive's journey along the tracks, Ezra's creations breathed a life of their own. A life reminiscent of his former Ottoman home, basking in the Constantinople sunlight.

Satisfied with his work, Ezra signed his name beneath the structure's foundation.

Ezra Newport. March 2, 1906.

Ezra glanced upward, grinning at his mother who had long since given in to sleep. Her head rested against the compartment window. A section of long, dark hair spilled from her headscarf, twisting downward around her golden broach pinned above her heart.

The sharp call of the train prompted her eyes to flutter open. Leyla drew in a deep breath and righted herself in the seat.

"Get good sleep, *Anne?*" Ezra asked.

"As decent as one can get on a train," his mother drowsily replied. Her brown eyes scanned the compartment. "Where is your *baba?*"

Ezra shrugged, setting his pencil bag and notebook on the empty cushion beside him. "He said he wanted to speak with someone several carriages down."

"Oh?" The inflection in her voice contradicted the uneasiness in her eyes. "That's curious."

Ezra studied his mother's face as she retrieved the timepiece she wore around her neck. Leyla consulted the hour and tucked it away into the high collar of her blouse. He knew the crease between her eyebrows only appeared simultaneously with troubled thoughts. But the façade she wore like a mask could only obscure so much for so long.

"How close are we to Belfast?"

"We're nearing Portadown Station," his mother stated. Refocusing her attention, Leyla smiled when she noticed the sketches beside him. "I see you've finished another masterpiece."

Ezra proudly surveyed his work and handed her the notebook. "Belfast Royal Academy better have an engineering program in the curriculum."

Pride glimmered in his mother's expressions. She handed the sketches back to him. "Yes. Your talent is bound to turn a few heads."

His sense of accomplishment faded. "Will this be the last?"

"The last what, *canım?*"

"The last move."

A heaviness pulled at her weary features. Perhaps the façade was lifting.

"My love, you will be eighteen in seven months. When you are a man, you will decide for yourself the direction of your steps."

Ezra smiled in understanding and allowed Leyla to take his hands in hers. He wasn't certain whether the jostling of the train or unspoken emotion caused her fingers to tremble.

"Your *baba* and I will always have a…a *desire* to keep moving," she continued. "But I promise you, no matter what, we—"

Her voice trailed off, distracted by a flutter of motion behind the window's condensation. After squeezing his hands, she rose at attention from her seat. "Stay here, *canım*. I shall return."

Ezra nodded obediently as his mother approached the compartment door.

When time itself screeched to a dreadful halt.

A blinding white light illuminated the compartment then faded just before a concussive shockwave sent the scene around them into oblivion. Reeling in confusion, Ezra found himself lying prostrate in a barely conceivable jumble of his former surroundings. Splintering glass shattered around him. A warm stream of a substance—oil? Blood? —trickled down his forehead and along the corner of his mouth. Ezra wiped it away with the sleeve of his coat, cringing at the crimson trail left behind. His equilibrium— as much as he tried to control it—spiralled in a vicious vortex, rendering it nearly impossible to get his bearings.

"*Anne?*" he croaked in Turkish. His voice, hardly louder than a whisper, was drowned out by the infernal ringing in his ears.

Reaching for the compartment door handle to pull himself to his feet, Ezra recoiled when he noticed the door had been smeared with cruel red streaks. Smoke billowed throughout the walkway, choking him as he navigated on hands and knees through the devastation.

"*Anne?*" he called again.

"Ezra!"

His mother was within arm's reach, but the look in her eyes seemed dangerously far.

Ezra crawled to her side where she lay gasping for air. His stomach contorted into knots at the sight of a dark, liquid halo surrounding her headscarf.

"Let's get you out of here," Ezra insisted, attempting to prop her up into a seated position. He frantically looked around for any sign of his father. "We need to find *Baba*!"

"Shhh," she insisted, shakily reaching up to her son's face. "Don't worry about us. Flee. Get as far away from here as you possibly can."

"What are you saying?" Ezra said, wondering if somehow his brain had lost all ability to comprehend language.

"Your *baba* and I knew this day would come," she whispered, tears swimming in her eyes. "They have found us. They have found *you*."

"Who? Who has found—" Ezra began but was silenced when her complexion faded to a ghastly white. He hesitantly followed her gaze over his shoulder.

Distorted by smoke, an inky black shadow materialised at the end of the walkway. The figure plodded toward them with an uneven gait, accompanied by ominous, mechanical whirring. But when the being finally stopped, and the smoke cleared just enough to expose his anamorphic features, Ezra could not bring himself to move.

"By the Order of Babylon, you are hereby commanded to follow and obey," his deep voice warbled through some type of amplification apparatus. His breath's condensation—or rather, steam—fumed from the steel grates around where his mouth should have been.

Ezra's own breath faltered as the orange light from nearby flames illuminated the figure's head. Slits in his mask revealed rugged skin and dark shadows beneath an organic eye, but the other portion consisted entirely of an intricate web of gears and piping. While at one time, the figure might have been an ordinary person, whoever now stood before him was nothing close to being human.

"We shall not!" his mother barked defensively, feigning a physical strength Ezra knew she lacked. "We will *never* yield."

"Hmm," the shadow mused. "So be it, Magus." A snap of his fingers sent ruby sparks into the haze and, upon deteriorating, revealed a massive cobra. Its thick body slithered across the wreckage and advanced straight for Ezra.

"Ezra, go!" cried his mother as a deluge of glass fragments rained upon them.

Crab-walking backward, Ezra manoeuvred as fast as he could away from the serpent, but it navigated the debris as if nothing stood in its way. The reptile snapped its jaws centimetres from his leather shoe, a fierce wrath in its eyes.

"Leave him alone, devil!" yelled Leyla, summoning what strength remained to kick at the snake with her boot.

Almost in slow motion, the cobra turned its fiery eyes toward his mother and bared its fangs as if overjoyed to set a course for its new target.

"No!" Ezra screamed in terror. "No, no, no!"

The cobra paid no attention to his pleas. It struck in one sickening flash, almost too fast for the eye to comprehend. As it withdrew, Ezra choked back arduous smoke—and a wave of tears—as his mother reflexively reached for her neck.

Narrowing its eyes as if perversely satisfied by the work of its venom now coursing through her veins, the cobra turned back to Ezra.

Trembling, Ezra tried to move but could not persuade his petrified limbs to cooperate.

"Go, my love!" Leyla rasped. "Go!"

Using his elbows to help pull him down the corridor, he furiously attempted escape. If the half-man, half-machine could grin or show any form of expression, Ezra imagined he was elated beyond measure at the persistence of his pet. The mysterious being advanced, his boots ravishing the ashy remains of pencil-sketched architecture.

"Where is your father, boy?" demanded the figure. "Tell me!"

Ezra could barely breathe as the figure hovered above him. A true vision of the Grim Reaper. The last thing Ezra saw before his vision faded was the cruel twinkle behind the mask of the stranger.

Visions of the Magi Master

Jonas van der Campe awoke with a start.

Heaving heavy breaths, his fingers fumbled for the key on the oil lamp mounted to the wall above his nightstand. Golden light bathed the bedroom in a soft essence, shedding a momentary sense of relief over his heightened nerves.

"Just stay calm," Jonas muttered to himself as he untangled his limbs from his bed linens. With every panicked heartbeat, vexation set in. He never had to talk himself down from a proper nightmare. As a child, perhaps. But as a thirty-year-old Magus? He was stronger than this. "Pull yourself together, now."

The horrific carnage of the train accident troubled him more than any dream typically would. Jonas could feel in his bones this nightmare was *real*. And it wasn't the first time he had witnessed cruelty at the hands of the Watchers.

Without wasting a second, he pulled a robe around his night clothes and hurried from his cellar flat up three flights of stairs to the rooftop garden. The moment the glacial March air washed over his face, he sighed in relief and closed his eyes to bask in the clarity of daybreak.

"You're certainly up early, Cousin," spoke the soothing voice of a young woman sitting underneath a vine-covered trellis. Still in her nightdress, Kierra

McLarney's bare feet grazed the rug beneath her as she allowed the swinging bench to sway in the morning breeze.

Jonas swallowed the trepidation forming in his throat.

Kierra waited for his reply but turned when silence answered instead. Her features morphed from complacent to uneasy.

"What's wrong? Bad dreams?"

"The whole thing. Ghastly. All of it," he stammered, searching for his usual voice of reason. "Kierra, I feel the tides are shifting."

"How do you mean?" She motioned for him to join her on the bench.

Jonas sank beside her and stared at the purple glow crowning the horizon. The images burned across his consciousness were not the only things troubling him. The timing—

God. The timing could not be any worse.

With worrisome storms brewing in his mind, Jonas reached into his robe pocket and retrieved a small logbook, right where he had left it after the previous evening's stargazing. Flipping toward the centre, he ran a fingertip over the pages and froze, his fears confirmed by the hasty ink.

"What, Jonas?" Kierra asked, her features becoming increasingly troubled.

"The State of the Stars at the turn of the new year hinted at something concerning in our near future," he summarised, his eyes racing across the penmanship. "When I observed the stars the evening of January first, I noted a strong planetary presence within Aquarius. Both Saturn and Mars battled for dominance within the Great Water Bearer."

"Concerning, indeed," Kierra admitted. Strands of light red hair obscured her face, rippled by the wind.

Jonas closed the book, his palm caressing the soft leather cover. Such disturbances within the Magi's constellation suggested more than a mere harbinger. It sang of transformation, an irreversible shift in destiny. "It did not make sense then, but now…" his voice trailed off, battered by internal tempests. "We will undoubtedly find ourselves challenged by fiery aggression from our enemies. And I think I might have just witnessed the igniting spark."

Kierra remained silent, anticipating his explanation.

"In my dreams, there was a boy," Jonas said, his voice distant.

"A boy? One of my students at the academy?"

"No. At least, not yet. He's an immigrant," Jonas recalled. "All I know is that he—or his family—are important to them. Beyond the usual means. I cannot explain it, but I know they are important to us, too. Crucial to the Magi's existence. Right now, at this very moment in time."

Kierra's eyebrows knitted together while she digested the information. "So, this is not just about the Order of Babylon?"

"Something even darker than that."

Kierra hesitated as Jonas folded his hands together in nervous contemplation. "What should we do? Should we alert the Magi Administration?"

Jonas lowered his eyes from the horizon to the oil lamp sitting on the floor beside them, completely bewitched by the dancing flame. Even with the Gift to control fire, the flames taunted him with their flickering movements. It was far too similar to the ones he had just witnessed devouring a vulnerable passenger train only minutes before. Letting the scene dissolve into a fading echo, he met his younger cousin's gaze.

"I shall send them a telegram this morning," Jonas insisted, drawing his robe closer around himself for warmth. "We must wait for further instructions from the Council. They will know what to do."

Despite the confidence in his voice, the flame inside the oil lamp teetered on the edge of extinction.

NEW BEGINNINGS

"Your final destination, Mr. Newport?" came the voice of the magistrate.

Staring into the depths of his teacup, Ezra did not even notice the anticipatory look on the Irish official's face. Two days had come and gone in a whirlwind of whispered condolences, medical evaluations, and an onslaught of questions for the reports. Foreign memories and phrases tumbled from his lips, about mechanical beings and serpents. Despite his insistence, the authorities wrote it off as the ramblings of a weary mind. Every conversation began with sympathy and ended with a statement of pure astonishment that he had even survived the ordeal.

But just *how* he survived, how he escaped the horrors of that night, confounded him. In fact, it haunted him.

It was just another unshakable moment in time to add to his collection.

"Mr. Newport?"

"Apologies," Ezra muttered morosely. He shifted in his seat. "Belfast."

"Belfast," the magistrate continued, traipsing behind his desk. "For family matters, I assume?"

"Immigrating. I have no other family."

"Not even back in London?"

"Not London, sir. Not Budapest. Not even Constantinople."

"Constantinople?"

"Where I was born."

The magistrate stopped his incessant pacing to examine Ezra. Every vociferous tick of the wall clock evolved with the uncomfortable silence that overtook the office. Finally, he produced a pipe from his trouser pocket and plucked a match from the fountain pen holder on his desk. "As you are undoubtedly aware, your father's body was never recovered from the wreckage. At this point, the authorities have no leads to go on, so you are essentially a ward of the courts until he reappears," the man explained, only pausing to draw from his pipe. "And as that seems unlikely, we have no other choice."

Ezra's eyes snapped up. "Sir?"

"It means you go where we put you," said the magistrate with the air of someone who had to do this far too often. "Because of your age—seventeen, is it? —the orphanage is hardly suitable. I believe it would be wise to have you continue with your parents' plans of enrolling you at Belfast Royal Academy." The magistrate scrounged through a file cabinet and produced a book adorned with a trio of crests and a rose, a thistle, and a shamrock woven within its borders. He let it fall with a thud into Ezra's lap.

"Belfast Royal Academy does not come free, of course, so you will be employed as a custodian while enrolled to pay your room and board..."

Whatever the magistrate said afterward had been completely lost to eternity as his head spun with infinite questions. Uncertainty had never been a welcome companion to Ezra Newport. And the uncertainty—of how exactly he got to safety that night on the train, of where his father disappeared, of what would happen now that he was assigned to stay at the academy— gnawed at his insides.

The idea that he would live out the rest of his secondary education days in a foreign institution did not scare him. Instead, the terrifying image of a figure born from the shadows kept him vigilant, even as he made the miserable journey to school grounds.

A tremendous splash echoed throughout the boys' lavatory as Ezra flung the sponge to the floor.

The porous pillow oozed soap bubbles much too readily, too sanguine for the task at hand. As awful as it was cleaning the facilities, the work was not simply a chore. It was Ezra Newport's currency.

He traced the tile floor in wide, sudsy arcs, careful not to disturb the shattered ceramic fragment near the first urinal. The fresh gash across his knuckles served as an adequate reminder of more forgetful times. He moved across the expanse on his knees, groaning in disgust over the state of the stall.

Belfast Royal Academy had been his new home for less than a week, but in that short time, Ezra had deduced the Irish were the most outlandish individuals he had ever met. While some displayed abounding hospitality, others glared at him like he was a personification of the plague. A shadow besmirching the emerald glimmer of the isle.

He was an immigrant. Not a criminal.

Of course, the coastal city was a far cry from any of his former homes. Belfast's docks lacked the vibrance of the Constantinople harbours. The Irish municipal buildings failed to hold themselves with the same elegant posture of Budapest's skyline. And the streets—while abuzz with brand new electric trams—fell short of the enchantment of London's busy thoroughfares.

No matter where he had lived, his heart longed for his former home. In Constantinople, the sun glimmered just a little bit brighter. His future—of perhaps one day being an architect—seemed a tad more achievable. But with every jarring move, every departure from normalcy, Ezra often found himself wondering if he'd ever be able to settle down into a comfortable life. After the train incident, that hope seemed more intangible than ever.

Ezra wiped his brow against his rolled shirt sleeve and wrung the sponge into the bucket. Evening chores: complete. Perhaps he would spend the last hour before curfew taking in the night air on the roof ledge outside his dormitory window.

Unfortunately, the moment of respite was shattered by the lavatory door flying open on its hinges and thudding shut behind the room's newest occupants.

"Thought we'd find the new servant here," sneered the sing-song voice of Dennis Kearney. His two cronies, Martin and John, were at his heels and—as Ezra was quickly learning—were never up to anything constructive.

Ezra said nothing but glared darkly at the threesome. He knew their type. And he knew they were not there to chat pleasantries.

"Hmm. Immaculate," Dennis mused as he ran a single finger over the edge of a sink. "Much unlike yourself."

John and Martin snickered.

Ezra's face contorted in confusion. "What is that supposed to mean?"

"It means that you are a despicable orphan from Timbuktu," Martin interjected, "and we don't want you here."

"First of all, I am not an orphan," Ezra said defensively, rising to his feet. "And secondly, I am not from Timbuktu."

"Unnecessary detail, Ezzie," Dennis chided. "We actually do not give a damn."

Ezra narrowed his eyes, picked up the pail, and hastily made for the door. On cue, John and Martin crossed their arms and stood shoulder-to-shoulder, blocking his only escape.

Wrong. *One* of his escapes.

Leaving not a second wasted, Ezra dropped the pail and bolted for the window across the lavatory. The squeals of leather soles against freshly cleaned floors pursued him. He nearly had the window unlatched before they rendered him immobile.

"What is your problem?" Ezra growled, struggling to break free from the grasp of Dennis' sidekicks.

"Well, now that you mention it, there is one thing." Dennis' voice curdled with evil.

Ezra watched in disgust as the bully proceeded to unfasten his belt and relieve himself all over the tile. Golden rivers trickled in hastening torrents along the grout, edging closer to his shoes.

"I have a problem with the cleanliness of this place," Dennis exhaled. "You missed quite a bit in this area." He re-adjusted his belt and tucked in his crisp, white Oxford shirt. "It's a crying shame the school servants cannot even get a simple task right."

Obnoxious laughter ricocheted across the lavatory as Martin and John shoved Ezra into the mess. And if that was not enough, a forceful kick from Dennis knocked the wind—and what was left of his dignity—out of him. Without any further discourse, the trio disappeared just as quickly as they had arrived, the door squealing to a close behind their elated chatter.

For a long, excruciating moment, Ezra forced himself to hold back his emotions. A nauseated shiver quaked through him as he lifted himself out of the cooling yellow pool. The haunting images came back in tumultuous waves—flashes of crawling through blood, ash, and debris that fateful night on the train. Most of those memories were as blurry as the bathroom scene around him. Ezra got to his knees and dragged the wash bucket across the floor, once again slamming the sponge down to viciously scrub the watery remnants of urine.

But the voice that haunted him with every stroke was not that of Dennis, Martin, or John. It was the gruesome timbre of a strange mechanical figure, whispering a foreboding phrase that echoed relentlessly in his mind:

"By the Order of Babylon, you are hereby commanded to follow and obey."

The Order of Babylon.

QUIETUS

Diego Montreal could view Past Time like a newsreel.

Since the beginning of his training with Jonas, Diego had become well acquainted with the rarity of his Gift. History—in all its opulent glory—was his for the taking. Just to explore, of course. To observe and learn. Changes were strictly prohibited by the Magi Code, but many regarded such an act as a great impossibility. In the five-thousand-year history of the Third Order, the worst a Magus had ever done was accidentally ripple Time during his travels, resulting in a moment of *déjà vu* for nearby Past Subjects. Permanent changes in history had never been done. Despite this, the Administration had made it quite the egregious offence if a Time Manipulator ever accomplished such a feat.

If Diego had his way, he'd be the first to make more than just a ripple in the fabric of Time. But until then, he was stuck carrying out his commitments as a fully licensed Magus.

In the eyes of the Magi, not using one's innate talents for the betterment of society meant grounds for expulsion. Not to mention the heinous fate of being severed from the Celestial Lifeforce altogether. In the eyes of the Royal Irish Constabulary, Diego's Gift for time manipulation allowed them to accurately apprehend criminals. While they didn't have the authority to strip away his powers if he chose not to assist, the officers had been known to be quite enticing.

Diego had lost count of how many times he'd graced the corridors of the RIC Belfast division since becoming an Irish resident. Despite being one of the department's most valued consultants, every pedestrian in the vicinity assumed otherwise. Apparently, being of Mexican heritage made one seem notoriously suspicious.

Slouching in the uncomfortable chair of the reception room, Diego's concentration roamed his surroundings. When that became too obnoxious to bear, he glanced at his pocket watch as the minute hand philandered the ninth numeral in favour of the tenth.

Early.

Again.

The clacking of heels across the floorboards snapped Diego to attention as the receptionist approached her post. Stella's vivid red hair had been swept into an updo, with elegant ringlets gracing her face. Her wide grin, framed by lovely dimples, spoke a different story than simple greeting.

Ay, Dios mio. How desperately he wanted to kiss those rosy cheeks.

She gathered her skirts and perched behind the desk, beaming pleasantly at him.

"Chief Constable Norman says he will be with you momentarily, Mr. Montreal," announced Stella, her green eyes never once leaving his. "He also mentioned how early you are and wants to know if you have overwound your pocket watch again."

Diego smirked. "Now, why would someone do that?"

Stella returned his sly mannerisms. "Well, perhaps he is excited to get along his daily routine," she paused, boldly dropping her gaze toward his trousers. "Or perhaps, he's just heavy-handed when screwing things."

He sputtered helplessly and squirmed in his seat. "Miss Stella, do you always talk like that in the workplace?"

"Only when you're here," she confirmed.

"It is not very lady-like," Diego reminded her. Truly, Stella could talk like that to him all day if she wished. Every word drove him wild.

"Neither are my daydreams, my sweet," she replied, leaning over the desk. She propped her chin upon a delicate hand as she stared him up and down. "Of you and me, removing article upon article of—"

A wordless exclamation sent them both into frozen panic.

"Newspaper clippings!" Stella finished swiftly, embarrassment flushing her cheekbones at the presence of the chief constable. "Lord knows I keep too many editions of *The Telegraph* lying about. Blast those articles."

Thoroughly amused, Diego chuckled but was silenced by the sharp look brewing behind Norman's enormous moustache.

"If you would be so kind, Mr. Montreal, would you please stop flirting with my secretary and accompany me to my office?" the chief constable requested. "The Royal Irish Constabulary does not consult with Magi just to have them morally degrade young ladies like Miss Stella Birch, even if she *is* your beloved."

"No, you are quite right, sir," Diego apologised, following him down the corridor. The last thing he wanted was for word to get back to Jonas about his bold behaviour. He'd never hear the end of it. "I am sorry; it won't happen again."

"You bet your lucky stars it won't," Norman growled. He gestured inside his office. "In you go, young man."

Without another word, Diego complied. He removed his tweed coat and flat cap, hanging them on the rack while Constable Norman arranged several files upon his desk.

"What will it be today, sir?" Diego changed the subject, rolling up his shirt sleeves and cracking out his knuckles. "Another bank robbery? Vandalism? Drunken pub fight resulting in setting the building ablaze, yet it looks like arson because no one remembers burning the place down?"

Lifting his gaze from the files, Chief Constable Norman shot Diego a questioning glare. "What on earth do you eat for breakfast, kid? Sugar cubes? No. Today, I have something legions more concerning."

The constable flopped a stack of newly developed photographs on the desk. Dreadful crime scenes frozen in time splayed before him like a hunter's trophy catch. Despite being illustrated in shades of sepia, the disturbing scenes bled crimson across Diego's vision. Prying away his attention, he looked to the constable for explanation.

"Two nights ago, the Bowen family from Strandtown was discovered murdered in their beds," Chief Constable Norman remarked after taking a swig from his coffee cup. "My investigators are theorising it has the makings of a murder-suicide, due to Mr. Bowen's known gambling addiction and ongoing financial woes. There were no signs of forced entry and absolutely no weapons on the premises."

"But I'm assuming murder-suicide is not your gut reaction?" Diego guessed, folding his arms over his chest.

"Not in the slightest. Especially since last night, an adolescent was found dead near the River Lagan in Dunmurry," Norman continued, depositing even more photographic evidence before him. "The boy had been chopped up into pieces, and my best men still haven't found his head."

Diego cringed and forced himself to divert his eyes from the pictorial proof of the mangled corpse. "Do you think both incidents are connected?"

The chief constable nodded solemnly, rummaging about the pile of photographs. He edged two of them forward with his index fingers. Bleak and foreboding, each snapshot captured a single word, written in what Diego could only assume was some sort of tar or paint.

Quietus.

"Quietus?" Diego questioned, staring at the dripping letters. "Written in—"

"Blood," the chief constable finished for him. "Some sort of threat, no doubt. It's a checkmate. A final warning."

"A final warning for what?" asked Diego.

"I'm inclined to believe violence like this can mean one thing: The Irish Republican Brotherhood extremists are making a comeback. More likely a reprise of the Invincibles," Norman answered. "I can only imagine this is some sort of twisted way to get attention on a national scale. Don't get me wrong, I certainly understand the passion behind Home Rule, but if history has proven one thing, it is that these fellows won't think twice about murder."

"Huh," Diego mused, unconvinced.

"Anyway, that is why you are here," Norman remarked. "I need you to assess both events and tell me who we're *really* looking for."

"Of course," Diego complied, instinctively searching for any physical evidence he could use for his quest. Besides the photographs, Norman's desktop looked rather sparse. "But you know the routine, sir. I need something from the scene to navigate to those moments in Time."

"Yes, yes," the chief constable muttered, seemingly annoyed by his request. He rummaged through a bag at his feet and produced two trinkets: a wedding ring and an electric torch. While Diego examined the items, Norman scribbled two sets of numbers on a piece of parchment. "Hopefully this will suffice?"

"That'll do," Diego affirmed. He fished around in his waistcoat until his fingertips became acquainted with the cool metal of his pocket watch. Flipping open the cover, he lay the timepiece beside the Souvenirs and retrieved his pointed quartz from his back pocket. At Diego's silent beckoning, the crystal erupted into light, illuminating the dingy office with unadulterated brilliance. Diego traced an invisible Star of David in the air over the items, leaving a residual trail of light energy behind. Referring to the dates and times Chief Constable Norman had provided, Diego held the crystal over his watch and flashed his boss a mysterious grin for good measure.

"Well, get on with it," Norman groaned in exasperation.

Time bowed before him and within seconds, the Past was at Diego's command.

The Headmaster

The unfortunate thing about escapes is that they didn't exist at Belfast Royal Academy.

According to whisperings of gossip that Ezra managed to overhear, a Year 10 student—Nathaniel Marcussen—had attempted a breakout after the prefects finished their nightly rounds. Some said he had been deeply unhappy while others said he had a taste for rebellion. Nevertheless, Nathaniel did not even make it to the front gates before he was hauled back to Headmaster Evert Willigen's office.

Not long after Nathaniel's attempt, another group of students from House Pottinger tried to see how far they could get and have their names permanently etched into Belfast Royal Academy history. Enacting a brilliant plan to divert attention, they had nearly gotten to Great Victoria Street Station before an army of faculty caught up. Unfortunately, the students were introduced to the academy's corporal punishment program and never spoke of the historic escapade in the days following.

With these events still fresh on the minds of his classmates, it became clear to Ezra that leaving the academy—even for a moment of respite—would not be an easy feat. So, with a heavy heart and even heavier steps, he plodded into his Friday morning history lecture.

"Oh, look, the servant boy cleaned up nice," came a snide whisper from behind him. "Last we saw, you were covered in piss."

Ezra did not have to turn around to know his nemesis had reprised his sadistic quest.

"*Siktir git,*" Ezra remarked bluntly in Turkish. They were all alike, bullies. Every country, every school. Every. Single. Time.

"Oooh, he's muttering his mumbo-jumbo Timbuktu language again," laughed Martin, from one row of desks over.

Ezra rolled his eyes just as Miss Kierra McLarney entered the room.

"Lovely morning today, isn't it, class?" Miss McLarney chirped cheerfully as she glided toward the oak desk at the front of the classroom. Her light red hair was piled atop her head in the same manner as the ladies of Great Britain, but her tailored grey dress had definitely seen better days.

Everyone rose to their feet and returned the greeting in a monotonous unison. "Good morning, Miss McLarney."

"Blimey, dears, where is your fire—your *passion*—for learning?" Miss McLarney joked as she unloaded books from her leather bag and stacked them onto her desk. Ezra caught his teacher's gaze but disregarded the hawklike look in her eyes as his imagination. He sunk back into his seat. The young teacher chewed on the inside of her lip and redirected her attention back to her desk.

"Open to page 373, please," Miss McLarney instructed, rummaging through her bag for a new pack of chalk. "You will absolutely love this lesson. There's plenty of drama, death, and destruction which, apparently, you kids love to learn about these days." Miss McLarney shook her head in humour and scratched out a diagram on the slate in arcs of dusty white. "We're starting a new unit on the Black Death."

While she was distracted, a wad of notebook paper grazed Ezra's ear. He glared dangerously over his shoulder at Dennis.

"*What?!*" Ezra hissed.

"Lordy, someone's irritable this morning, " Dennis whispered, grinning at Martin and John. "Clearly you need to turn in earlier."

"Yeah, Ezzie, what could possibly be keeping you up at night?" snickered Martin.

"Life as a gong farmer must be rough," John chimed in, referencing a medieval history lesson from earlier in the week, "especially a dim witted one who can't get anything right."

"I believe you mean zounderkite."

Ezra clenched his jaw but forced his concentration toward his notebook. Squeezing his pencil between his fingers, Ezra furiously sketched the outlines of an ocean liner.

"Our lesson on the Bubonic Plague begins in 1347," Miss McLarney said. "In October of that year, those working the docks in Messina, Italy were met by a gruesome surprise; of all 12 of the ships that had arrived at the dock that fateful day, most of those aboard were already dead. Those who still clung to life were gravely ill."

"Personally, I think Ezra started the Black Death," Dennis said in a hushed tone.

His cronies snorted into the back of their hands to keep from laughing aloud.

"Would you idiots stop talking?!" spat a nearby student. If her dark gaze had been any stronger, Ezra was certain it would have sliced through the very desks they occupied like a hot knife through butter.

"Of course, Aja," Dennis complied with a grin. "Anything for you, dearest."

The Indian girl scowled at them and returned her attention to the front of the room.

Much to Ezra's annoyance, Dennis began kicking the back of his seat. The point of Ezra's pencil disintegrated deeper into the surface of his notebook with every jerk of the chair. *Just ignore him,* he told himself. *He's not there. He doesn't exist.*

"You know, forget the Plague," Dennis continued to his mates, his voice barely above a whisper. "I'll bet my ten pound note he killed his own parents."

That was it.

In one swift motion, Ezra launched himself from his desk and decked the sorry git across the face.

All at once, the entire room of students leapt to their feet in a mix of astonishment and excitement. History class never saw this much entertainment in one sitting. Cheers and chants escalated as the two of them wrestled against each other for physical dominance.

"Boys!" squeaked an alarmed Miss McLarney as she pushed through the throng of students. "Boys, stop this at *once!*"

"Get off me, you miserable scamp!" commanded Dennis. An unfortunate blow collided with Ezra's nose.

"Do not *ever* speak about me like that again, and I will," promised Ezra, blood trickling over the ridge of his lip.

"Sorry, I can't give you my word on that."

"STOP THIS AT ONCE!" Miss McLarney yelled. Ezra choked when his teacher yanked him from Dennis by his shirt collar. "Ezra Newport! Dennis Kearney! Headmaster's office, *now!*"

Every student fell into petrified silence at the mention of the headmaster. Whatever fate Ezra and Dennis were about to receive would be legions ghastlier than the fury in Miss McLarney's eyes.

"Students, please remain seated as I escort your belligerent classmates to the office," Miss McLarney instructed as she grasped both of them by the arms. "If you move even a toe out of line, you will join them."

The treacherous journey from the academic wing to the headmaster's office seemed like a trek across the world. Each footfall became more burdensome with every turn of the corridors, as if gravity itself could not escape the misery of Willigen's headquarters. All sounds of daily activity faded into non-existence except for the ticking of a grandfather clock. Its pendulum swung in perfect synchronicity with their sullen footsteps.

Tick. Tock. Tick. Tock.

Ezra swallowed his remorse and wiped the blood from his nose on the sleeve of his uniform. Whatever waited for them beyond the ornate wooden doors might render them completely mad, if the rumours housed a shred of truth. With a sigh, Ezra knew that could not possibly be true for him. He had already seen hell.

Miss McLarney pushed open the double doors to the headmaster's wing. "Come on, you two," she spoke, ushering them inside. "In you go."

At first glance, the room looked like any other in the school: spacious, orderly, and decorated in accents of brass and stone. Where the forest green walls weren't lined with framed portraits of the namesakes of the academy's houses, dark stained shelves held leather-bound volumes and golden trinkets. Every side of the hexagonal room—save the one they had just come through—housed a window that overlooked the trimmed hedges adorning the front lawn of Belfast Royal Academy.

No wonder the headmaster always knew what was going on, thought Ezra. *He's got a bird's eye view.*

The abrupt sound of Miss McLarney clearing her throat snapped Ezra to attention just as the chair behind the stately desk swivelled around.

Headmaster Evert Willigen did not seem like the type of man who took well to interruptions. His unforgiving gaze was slightly obscured by a monocle over his left eye and a cloud of smoke from his pipe. The large man stood, checked his pocket watch, and removed the pipe from his mouth.

"Whom do we have here?" the headmaster asked, without any sort of emotion in his husky voice. "Two ninnies who can't pay attention in class, eh?"

Ezra felt the heat of his teacher's gaze searing into the back of his skull.

"Two young men who cannot seem to get along, more like. They decided a brawl was in order during the middle of lecture."

"Hmph." The headmaster chomped on the end of his pipe as he looked the boys up and down. "I don't have time for dunces. Especially *you*." He prodded the mouthpiece of his pipe into Ezra's chest. "Who started it?"

"Ezra did, sir," Dennis cried, feigning a tearful display. "One moment I was listening to Miss McLarney and in the next moment, he attacked me. I was only trying to defend myself, sir. Truly, I was."

Headmaster Willigen stood dangerously close to Ezra, so close that he could see every yellow ember in the fire of his hazel eyes. "And what do you have to say for yourself, Mr. Newport?"

Ezra remained silent, diverting his line of sight away from the headmaster's. Even if he opened his mouth, no words of defence could adequately douse the cruel intensity in the air. Nothing—not even a miracle—could change a mind already committed to labelling him as the wrongdoer. He could see it within every fibre of the headmaster's being.

Pardon and overlook.

"Well, boy?" Willigen barked.

Ezra swallowed and shook his head.

"Very well," the man replied, motioning toward Dennis. "Off you go, Mr. Kearney. Shape up or the next time will be your last."

"Yes, sir. I promise, sir," exhaled a relieved Dennis. The bully made sure Ezra caught a glimpse of his devilish smirk when he turned to leave the room.

The headmaster returned to his desk and yanked open the top drawer to reveal a thick leather strap. He toyed with the three tails at the end, revelling in the chance to discipline yet another student. "Twenty lashes should do the trick, yes?"

Miss McLarney frowned. "That seems excessive. Besides, I'm almost certain Mr. Newport did not start it."

"Then why didn't he say that?" A ruddiness saturated the boundaries of the headmaster's shirt collar, a sure mark of one not used to being challenged. And from a woman, no doubt.

Still, Ezra dared not meet his teacher's line of sight. If he took the punishment, then perhaps Dennis would leave him alone.

"The last group of children to misbehave received five lashes!"

"Do not tell me how I should punish my pupils!"

"Sir, if you could please reconsider that punishment, I—"

"Miss McLarney, you are dismissed," spoke the headmaster in a dangerously low tone.

"Y-yes, sir," she finally relented. She hesitated, as if she wanted to speak again, but reconsidered and rushed from the office.

When the door latch had clicked back into place, the headmaster grabbed Ezra's wrist and slammed his hand on top of his desk, palm facing the ceiling. A porcelain teacup in the immediate vicinity clinked in distress within its saucer and nearly toppled its murky contents.

"Let's just get this over with," growled the man as he raised the strap above his head.

Ezra shut his eyes and gripped the edge of the headmaster's desk with his free hand. His palm stung as if bitten, over and over. With every snap of the leather, the headmaster gained momentum while Ezra's tenacity deteriorated.

Each strike painted a vision of a deadly cobra in his mind. Slithering ever closer, through the wreckage of his life, with a mechanical figure towering over him.

"...four, five, six..."

The night on the train, the deafening explosion, the halo of blood.

"...thirteen, fourteen, fifteen..."

All-consuming fire, his mother's last moments, the resolute nature of death.

"...eighteen, nineteen, twenty."

32

Follow and obey the Order of Babylon.

When the headmaster had finished, he released his death grip on Ezra's forearm. Ezra recoiled, lifting his shaking hand only to see thick lacerations crisscrossing the natural lines of his palm.

"Don't *ever* cause a ruckus in my school again, boy," spat the headmaster as he tucked the strap away in the drawer. "That's the problem with your type. You think you can get away with anything you damn well please. Well, Ezra Newport, be reminded of this: Our world does not need you in it if that is how it's going to be. Shape up and maybe one day you will fulfil your destiny cleaning muck out of stables for a living."

Trembling from the fortitude it took to restrain cries of pain, Ezra bolted from the office and collided with Miss McLarney. The tears brimming in her eyes suggested she had heard the whole thing.

Of course she had.

"Oh, Ezra, I am *so sorry*," the young teacher apologised. "You did not deserve that."

Ezra stared at her, cradling his bleeding hand to his chest.

His teacher pursed her lips as she tried to hold back a sob. "I heard what the headmaster said—"

"With all due respect, ma'am, I really do not wish to talk about it," Ezra muttered as he pulled away from her. "I understand, all right? You people do not need to remind me *every waking moment!* I—" His breath caught in his throat. "I already know I am worthless."

Miss McLarney looked as hurt as he felt. "You are far from worthless, Ezra Newport."

Without another word, he shook his head and retreated toward the dormitories.

He had to get out of here.

The Courier's Message

After a week of bothersome silence, Jonas started to wonder if the Magi Administration had turned a blind eye to his telegrams.

It wouldn't have been the first time his colleagues at Administration headquarters wilfully ignored his communications, as if somehow their saintliness would be tarnished by speaking to him.

Yes, I made a few blunders, Jonas often thought to himself, whenever memories from the trial rose from the ashes. *But my actions should not have amounted to half of this treatment.*

Members of the Magi Council—the nine leaders ruling the Administration—behaved as if he had murdered someone in cold blood. Burned a city to the ground. Denounced the ways of the Magi to study dark sorcery. Jonas had pleaded guilty to several minor offences, but he knew those offences paled in comparison to what the Council *really* held over his head: his former relationship with someone he truly loved.

As if love could ever be a reason for reprimand.

Attempting to suppress the uncomfortable recollections, Jonas navigated the morning High Street traffic toward the docks. Perhaps today, the Magi Courier Service would deliver some modicum of advice from the Administration. The smallest hint that they still trusted him. Anything.

Blue dawn flooded the avenue, fragmented by the grand Albert Memorial Clock Tower. The piercing cries of gulls heralded his approach to Queen's Square. Hands draped casually in his coat pockets, Jonas sprinted across the street. Horse-drawn merchant carts clattered over the tram rails behind him and made enough racket to startle a flock of pigeons in his path, leaving a clear route to the harbour's edge.

A glance up at the clockface prompted him to increase his momentum. The courier never waited a second longer than necessary. And today, Jonas had a strong intuition he could not be late.

Salty wind tinged with the stench of fish and earthworms welcomed Jonas to the River Lagan. A light mist draped over the water, obscuring a small craft docked beneath the dying glow of the electric streetlamps.

"Morning, Mr. van der Campe!" called a jubilant voice from the boat.

"Good morning, Henry," Jonas answered, leaping down the stairs two at a time. Even in the dim light, Jonas could plainly read the elegant script along the side of the vessel, announcing it as *The Epiphany*. "Easy waters, I hope?"

"Nothing I couldn't handle," responded Henry the Courier. The older man finished tying a sailor's knot, almost losing his Phrygian cap in the murky Lagan as he tethered the boat. "Now, the seagulls I can live without. I swear upon the Famed Three that I witnessed one eating a pigeon on the way in. Do they do that?"

Jonas grinned and shrugged.

Henry wiped his hands on his colourful robes and reached into the craft to retrieve a knapsack. "Let's see here. I know the Magi Administration had something for you."

Heart pattering against his ribs, Jonas watched as Henry fished through the bag.

"Wouldn't it be nice if we went back to Dream Messaging?" Henry mused. "It certainly worked for the Famed Three avoiding that Herod fellow."

"Until the Administration finds an efficient way to regulate it, I assume we're stuck with good old-fashioned post," Jonas replied. Not that he minded, of course. There was something comforting about tangible communication.

"Ah, yes. Here we are." The courier procured a golden envelope and handed it to him. "You better not be in trouble again, young man."

Jonas clutched the envelope, grimacing at Henry's comment. "Let's hope not."

"Give the Irish Chapter my regards," Henry instructed.

"I shall," said Jonas distractedly as he retreated to the wharf. His fingertips traced the edges of the thick, linen paper. After a brief wave back at the courier, Jonas ran his thumb under the seal, tearing open the envelope. His eyes devoured the official document with untamed ferocity.

THE MAGI ADMINISTRATION

March 4, 1906

Dear Mr. Jonas van der Campe,

By the time you receive this, it will be well into next
week and you will most likely be aware of an incident
taking place near Portadown, Ireland on March 2. This
horrific tragedy involved a Magi family immigrating from
London, England. The Magi Council has been notified that
Leyla Newport is among the dead and that her husband,
Ibrahim Newport, has not been located. Additionally, the
Council has discovered that the Newport's son, Ezra, is
alive and assigned to Belfast Royal Academy until
graduation.

At this time, your services are not required for the boy's
ongoing safety. The Council has already despatched agents
to Ireland to monitor the situation. Do not engage.

We sincerely appreciate your cooperation and hope you are
well. Any questions may be directed by telegram or post to
the Department of Transmissions.

Respectfully,

Clarence Westerfield

Clarence Westerfield
Executive Secretary to
the Magi Council

Disappointment trickled from Jonas' chest into his gut as he stuffed the letter back into the envelope. Of course, the Administration could not trust him with something as simple as keeping watch over an adolescent. No matter the extent he had gone to prove himself over the last six months, the Magi Council continued to overlook his accomplishments in favour of his shortcomings.

Jonas scoffed. They had always been incredibly gifted at that.

Tucking the communication inside his jacket, Jonas shoved his hands into his pockets and trudged back toward High Street, with discouragement weighing down every step.

A Broken Vow

Constantinople, 1895

The small room twinkled with an other-worldly ambiance.

Leyla watched apprehensively as her six-year-old son jumped to reach the dazzling lamps strung from the ceiling. "Careful now, Ezra. Those were your babaanne's decorations."

"Well, they are old," a young Ezra replied, "and Allah wants me to take them down."

"I am quite sure he does not," laughed his father. "Besides, we want our house to look somewhat presentable for when Taylan and Kiraz arrive."

Ezra made a face. "Are they bringing Yonca with them?"

"Perhaps," Ezra's mother said, ruffling his dark hair. "And perhaps you will be taller than her this year."

Young Ezra narrowed his eyes. "I had better."

A steady knock sounded at the door.

"Ah, that must be Taylan, right on time as always," Ibrahim remarked, rising to welcome their guests.

"Mutlu Bayramlar, Ibrahim!" came Taylan's festive voice as he and his wife stepped across the threshold and slipped off their shoes. Yonca timidly followed her parents, clutching fistfuls of their tunics in her small hands.

"Eid Mubarak, *my friend*," answered Ibrahim. He exchanged friendly greetings with the newcomers. "Why, look at how you have grown, Yonca!"

With a heavy sigh, Ezra folded his arms and made a dramatic show of disappointment at his mother.

"Oh, Leyla, it smells so good in here!" exclaimed Kiraz as she offered a plate of baklava to Ezra's mother.

"Thank you," Leyla replied with a polite nod. "If you think it smells great, wait until you've tasted it. I have got all of your Eid favourites, coming right up!"

In almost no time at all, the six of them tucked in to the glorious, heaping piles of food. Finally. This was what the night was all about, the long-awaited celebration of Eid al-Fitr.

Without considering the consequences, Ezra stuffed a whole piece of pide in his mouth.

"My love, take smaller bites, please," insisted Leyla.

"Why?" young Ezra replied with his mouth bursting at the seams with the flat bread. "It is good."

Yonca grinned, displaying the prominent absence of her front teeth.

That figured, Ezra grouched. Yonca was taller and she would be getting all her grown-up teeth before him.

"Remember what Ramadan is all about, son," said Ibrahim.

Ezra met his father's eyes upon feeling his strong hand grip his shoulder.

"Self-control is just one of the many lessons Allah teaches us during this time."

"Did Allah ever have a huge plate of pide in front of him?" Ezra remarked with a grin. "No."

Kiraz snorted into her teacup while Leyla shook her head in amusement.

"Well, what about you, Ibrahim?" asked Taylan. "What did Ramadan teach you this year?"

"Many things," Ibrahim answered. He put his arm around his wife's shoulders and drew Ezra into a half embrace. "I made a promise to myself—and a vow to Allah—that I would be the best husband and father I can for as many days as I have left on this earth.

I would sacrifice everything for the safety of these two. Life simply would not be worth living without them."

While not as vivid as they once were, Ezra's early memories of celebrating the end of Ramadan lingered in the dusty corners of his mind. This memory had haunted him from sunrise to sunset ever since the fateful evening on the train.

If Baba *was so intent on protecting us,* Ezra speculated, *then why did he disappear the very moment we needed him? Why did he abandon us to face evil alone?*

The more he mentally repeated his father's sovereign vow, the more apparent it became that recent events did not add up. Confusion gave way to exasperation, and exasperation transformed into bitterness with every passing minute. That evening, Ezra's anger festered more than usual—an unfortunate side effect of Dennis and the academy's disciplinary tactics. The disturbing combination was just strong enough to ignite something drastic. Like oil to flame, a notion of sweet escape flared into life, crooning with the promise of uncovering what *really* became of Ibrahim Newport.

Cursing his classmates' stories and ignoring the voice of rationality, Ezra's undaunting decision solidified.

He was going to break out of Belfast Royal Academy.

Ezra set his jaw in determination and gripped the strap of his travel bag with his un-marred hand. At this hour, his stealthy trek through the school corridors would likely go unnoticed as students and faculty had turned in for the evening. However, it was also the route with the highest chance of failure.

Remembering the fearless students who had paved the path before him, Ezra snuck through his dormitory window and carefully felt around for footholds in the uneven brick. If he did this right, if he somehow dodged the all-seeing eye of the headmaster, he would be free. Free from Dennis and his cruelty. Free to find his father and discover once and for all why his vow lay broken before *Allah* and man.

—
41

Just get past the front gates and take the alleys to Great Victoria Station, Ezra coached himself as he scaled the walls. *One step at a time.*

Triumph tingled in his ears when his shoes finally met the ground. The taste of freedom danced along his tongue when he clambered over the iron fence. With the brilliance of the full moon to guide him and the accompaniment of an owl's song to cover his footsteps, Ezra sprinted down Cliftonville Road, mentally charting his southern route as he ran.

Ezra dodged the circumference of light from the streetlamps and darted his way through alleyways and gardens. His heart thumped a hopeful rhythm, pounding in time with his footfalls.

Weaving through red brick buildings just past Carlisle Circus, Ezra slowed when the scraping of gravel echoed throughout the otherwise still air. A gradual exhale rippled a Union flag draped from the window of an upper level flat. Ezra tensed, drawing in a breath of his own. He gripped his bag tighter and edged along the side of the building, eager to escape whatever lurked in the night.

Yet, the sound came again, louring and formidable.

Scritch. Scritch. Click.

With anxiety crashing through him like an icy wave, Ezra whirled around just as a pair of ragged boots stepped into the moonlight. What followed next nearly stopped his heart.

An all-too familiar mechanical humanoid came into full view, toting a weathered crossbow. The figure ominously stomped forward, then motioned for whomever was following astern to step in line. With three frightening beings now lumbering toward him, Ezra tried to move, but fear restrained him.

"Ah, we meet again, Ezra Newport," jeered the leader of the group, his finger stroking the crossbow trigger. "And this time, we're very much eager to see you join your mother in death."

ℙREMONITIONS

The piercing cry from the tea kettle rattled Jonas from his thoughts.

Since receiving the official letter from the Magi Administration earlier that morning, Jonas urged his mind away from the typeset words and the warnings beneath them. But the more he mentally recited the letter, the more his intuition wavered in the winds of apprehension. It wasn't merely the fact he was instructed not to interfere. The Magi Administration had said nothing about the larger threat looming in the shadows. Something was still off. The alignment of the stars, the balance of the Celestial Lifeforce. Something.

Jonas stirred milk into his tea and welcomed the hot liquid to his lips. Meandering toward the fireplace, he lowered himself into an armchair and stared into the dying flames. His fingertips reached toward them, sparking the logs back into life.

"Evening, Mista Jonas."

Jolted from his internal musings, Jonas almost spilled his tea but steadied the cup at the last second. He hesitantly raised his eyes to Zaire, who stared at him with a wide, humoured grin.

"A lil' on edge, I see?"

Jonas forced a smile and sipped from the cup. "Mm. You could say that."

His fellow Magus took a seat on the settee, leaning forward in concern. "Miss Kierra told me about your dream last week. Has the Administration recommended a course of action?"

"According to the letter I received this morning, they've got everything under control," Jonas replied, watching as his friend raised an eyebrow. "But I can't shake the feeling that it is not over just yet."

"Dark Watcher raids are nothing new, though," Zaire reminded him. "They've done ravaged everywhere from India to America for centuries looking for people like us. What makes you think this is any different?"

"This time, the stars tell a more sinister story," Jonas whispered, glancing at the fireplace. "I'm highly convinced—"

The teacup crashed at his feet, fragments of porcelain skittering across the floorboards. Jonas grasped his head and shut his eyes against a sudden, painful assault. Lightning streaked across his retinas. Flashes of blurry scenes transmitted throughout his mind: Fear, running down alleys, the twang of crossbows...

"Mista Jonas?" Zaire said, abandoning the couch to put a steadying hand on his shoulder. "What's going on?"

"Go—go get Kierra," Jonas groaned. He clutched the armrests, willing the pain to cease. Instead, it wormed its way further through his being. "She's upstairs in her flat."

"Right away."

When Zaire returned, Kierra was at his heels, her face pale and contorted with worry. She knelt at his side, clutching his forearm.

"Cousin, what's wrong?"

"I don't know," Jonas replied, his voice cracking. "One moment I was speaking with Zaire and the next moment—"

He cried out as another burst of discomfort made him double over in the chair.

"Should I go get Ms. Annabelle?" Zaire offered.

"No," Jonas gasped. His breaths came sharp and heavy. "No, I think this is some sort of...Celestial Message. A forced vision. Memories—"

Kierra furrowed her eyebrows. "If they're memories, I can attempt to see whose they truly are," she offered. "I need you to relax."

Jonas closed his eyes, digging his fingernails into the fabric of the chair. "I believe it—it might be Ezra."

"What makes you think so?" Kierra asked, holding her palm centimetres from Jonas' skull.

"Infallible intuition," he answered as his cousin mentally scanned his memories. While Kierra rarely used her Gift to wade through the fibres of his own recollections, Jonas knew the experience exerted quite the toll on a person. Thank the Universe she wouldn't have to dive in too far.

A flag rippling in the breeze, boots stepping into the moonlight, a black arrow with red feathers—

A black arrow with red feathers.

Kierra yanked her hand back, returning Jonas' terrified expressions. "Ezra is in danger."

Jonas lost no time in leaping to his feet. Reeling from the sudden motion, he collected his jacket and fedora from the coat rack. "The Watchers are back," he explained aloud, mostly for Zaire's sake. "We don't have much time."

"But Mista Jonas, what about the Magi Administration's letter?" Zaire reminded him. "Didn't they say they had everything in order?"

Jonas hesitated near the door, his fingers stopping short of the steel handle.

"They *did* tell you not to interfere," Kierra added.

Jonas let out a slow, calculated breath. If he took one step out that door, one step with the intention of going against the Council's orders, then the entire last six months of winning back their favour would be for naught. His license, his status as a Magi Master, his apprentices, everything he had worked so hard to reclaim would be lost.

But Felix...

Swallowing unspoken misery, Jonas shut his eyes and bowed his head. Of course. Felix would want him to do the right thing. Boldly. Unapologetically. Steadfast in every way.

I am already walking a tightrope, Jonas considered, gripping the door handle. *What's another step into the spotlight of scrutiny?*

Jonas confidently turned to face Kierra and Zaire. "As Magi, our duty is to our community and right now, a boy needs our help."

Surely, the Administration would understand.

ARROWS OF THE WATCHERS

Ezra blindly darted through backstreets but whenever he thought he had lost the nightmarish trio, the ringleader was already waiting around every corner, his weapon aimed at his chest.

"In the name of *Allah*, most gracious, most merciful!" prayed a panicked Ezra as he retreated uptown.

There had to be a way to get them off his trail. If only Ezra could remember how he accomplished survival the first time. Maybe then, he'd actually have a chance.

Fear drove him further into unknown territory. Endless brick buildings, meandering roads, and identical lampposts disoriented him. At times, the footsteps in pursuit would hasten and other times, the echoes from their pattering would cease altogether. Relying on an idea borne from desperation, Ezra sprinted into another alley off Donegall Street and leapt into a large rubbish receptacle. He lowered the lid onto the container and shrunk back in the putrid darkness.

And the world fell into silence.

So did his heart.

After what seemed like ages of this, Ezra's pulse assaulted his ears as he lifted the lid to steal a glimpse of his surroundings.

Three sets of glowing eyes glared back at him, full of undying hunger for his blood.

"Nice disappearing act, boy," chastised the ringleader. He signalled for the other two to haul Ezra out of the rubbish bin. They roughly deposited him on the concrete, stomping their boots upon his back to keep him from escaping. "But the thing about hiding is that your own fear always betrays you in the end."

Trembling, Ezra lifted his eyes to meet the leader's edacious expression. "What do you want?" he yelled, voice breaking in emotion. "You already took my *anne* from me! What do you want!?"

"For you to follow and obey the Order of Babylon," answered the figure, cocking his head menacingly to the side.

"I will *not*!" replied Ezra. "I don't even know what that is supposed to mean!"

"Most unfortunate," uttered the ringleader. "I would have hoped your parents shared at least *something* important with you."

A burst of courage inspired Ezra to squirm out from under the boots of the hunters. He had almost reached the end of the alley before the click of the crossbow heralded a piercing agony in the tissue of his thigh.

Crumpling to the cement in anguish, he conjured what strength remained to pull himself out of their firing range, but they effortlessly kept pace.

"This will be so much easier if you tell us where your father is now," sighed the figure, reloading his weapon with another black arrow.

"I—I do not know where he is!" cried Ezra. A strange prickling sensation emanated from where the arrow protruded from his thigh. Within mere moments, his entire leg and midsection burned as if his insides had been set ablaze.

The arrow must have been poisoned.

"Lies. Tell us and perhaps we will spare your life tonight," the ringleader asserted.

"I already told you!" Ezra growled through clenched teeth, trying not to look at the blood collecting beneath him. The more he fought against the poison coursing through his veins, the faster his surroundings spun around him. Sweat brimmed along his forehead and traced the curvature of his nose. "I—I don't...know," he panted.

"Hmm," the mechanical human noted, watching him struggle. "You are thoroughly more entertaining to watch than your mother."

Ezra let out another cry of pain, grasping at the ground as if that would stabilise him. His eyes sank again to the growing pool of blood, and he quickly shut them, trying to ward off visions of his dying mother on the train.

"Please," Ezra begged, his entire body shaking from a combination of rapid blood loss and the wretched arrow. "Please."

"Please, what?" chirped the mechanical voice of one of the beings. "Show you mercy?"

Ezra struggled to keep his eyes open as the three brutes loomed over him.

"This one is a fighter," one of them said. "Usually, they cannot make it past the first minute."

This is it, Ezra contemplated, letting his heavy eyelids fall. *Anne, I'm coming...*

His world succumbed to blackness.

NOT ENOUGH TIME

"We're close," Jonas told Kierra and Zaire as they sprinted down Donegall Street. Deep within his gut, he worried it was already too late. Yet, an inexplicable buoyancy carried him further into the heart of Belfast, despite his previous reservations about overstepping the Administration.

Gripping his crystal quartz wand, Jonas crept along the perimeter of St. Patrick's Church, his ears trained on any noise that would give away Ezra's location. Besides the buzzing of the streetlamps and a distant boat horn blasting in the harbour, all was silent.

Except—

Jonas homed in on brutish laughter several blocks away. Nodding toward Kierra and Zaire, he welcomed the Celestial Lifeforce into his being, causing his wand to respond with warmth and luminance. Pure white light spilled out before them, leading the way to a back street.

The first thing Jonas saw when he turned the corner were three silhouettes armed with crossbows. But when his eyes adjusted, Jonas gasped when he noticed the form of a boy crumpled on the ground.

"Back away from him at once!" yelled Kierra, charging into the alley without any sort of plan. "I swear to God above I will unleash hellfire if you do not comply this instant!"

The three Watchers turned and guffawed at the woman in their presence.

Jonas chased after his cousin and stood beside her. "I would take her seriously if I were you," he advised.

"I take her as seriously as I would a butterfly with a vendetta," chuckled one of the brutes.

"Back up, you filthy Watchers!" commanded Zaire, clearly annoyed. "You done messed with the wrong people tonight."

"Ahh," came the voice of the ringleader. "Three Magi here to join the soiree! What—no gifts for the host?"

"We only bring gifts to royalty," replied Kierra, her brows creasing above her blue eyes, "not talking rubbish heaps."

"Your kind always were arrogant," jeered one of the Watchers.

All at once, Kierra channelled a beam of energy through the quartz crystal pendant around her neck and directed it toward the ringleader of the group.

He squealed in terror as the ethereal light penetrated his industrial armour and cut through flesh, causing him to collapse lifeless to the ground.

"And your kind always were despicable," Kierra mocked him.

Jonas nodded in approval. "Nice work," he commended. He had always admired Kierra's incredible ability to harness the Celestial Lifeforce. If it weren't for her being family, Jonas would have been absolutely terrified of her.

Following Kierra's lead, Jonas formed a globe of fiery energy in his hands and propelled it toward the closest Watcher. The magic exploded into a resonating shockwave, slamming the figure forcibly against a brick wall before he crumpled in a heap.

Take that.

"I been waiting too long to try this one," exclaimed Zaire. He fanned a deck of black playing cards and blew over top of them, causing them to spark and crackle as if electrified. Acting on their own accord, the cards lifted from his hands, arced over his head and with a flick of his finger, flew like daggers toward the remaining mechanical bounty hunter. Each card met its mark, slicing into the Dark Watcher with alarming accuracy.

"Very impressive!" praised Jonas with a grin. "Americans never cease to surprise me."

"Why thank you, Mista Jonas," Zaire said, stooping into a theatrical bow. "Learned that from my maw maw back in New Orleans."

All three of the Watchers had been defeated, but Jonas did not waste a moment on celebrating the victory. Instead, he rushed to Ezra's side and placed a hand over his face to check for signs of life.

"He's alive, but just barely," Jonas remarked in a panic. His frantic eyes scanned the alleyway for anything that would suggest the protective presence of the Magi Administration.

No agents. No remnants of the Celestial Lifeforce. No protective enchantments. Nothing.

Where were they?

Kierra knelt beside Ezra. "The arrow must have severed an artery; I've never seen so much blood from a puncture wound like this," she surmised. Her voice trembled as she placed her palm over her student's forehead.

Zaire removed his jacket and bent to the boy's level. "We need to act fast, Mista Jonas and Miss Kierra," he spoke, knotting the fabric just above where the arrow stuck out from Ezra's leg. "He needs professional medical help. I don't even think Ms. Annabelle could mix up an elixir to save him now."

"Perhaps not, but he *does* need an antidote to the Watchers' poison," Jonas commented, digging through his jacket pockets. After a frenzied search, he drew out a small vial of sapphire liquid, holding it up to his eye.

"Ah. I knew carrying this stuff around would pay off one day. Remind me to thank Diego later."

Jonas cradled the young man's head with one hand and poured the liquid into his mouth with the other.

"That should do the trick."

Kierra stared sympathetically at Ezra and brushed hair away from his eyes. "Hold on, sweetheart. You'll get through this; I know you will."

"And if he doesn't?" asked Zaire.

"If he doesn't, every Magi on earth should fear for their lives," replied Jonas. "I do not know how, but everything changes from this point forward. The writing is already on the wall."

"Then let's run like hell," said Zaire as he and Jonas worked together to lift the boy. "We ain't got enough time in the world to mess with destiny."

BEYOND THE BEND

Ezra stirred in a half sleep. Every time his brain nudged him to wake up, he fought against it—especially since waking life was accompanied by an overwhelming ache in his left leg. After what seemed like hours of this, he groaned and finally gave in to consciousness.

As his eyes fluttered open, he jumped in surprise upon seeing a stranger perched in a rocking chair next to his bedside.

"Oh, darling, you have the most beautiful eyes," cooed the elderly woman. "Like honey in a terra cotta vase."

"Er, thank you?" Ezra replied, completely out of sorts as to where he was and how he had gotten there. He shifted awkwardly under the quilted covers and ran his fingertips over the texture of the linen. Instead of his school uniform, he now wore unfamiliar, freshly laundered night clothes. "Who are you?"

"Annabelle Jane Chicory, but you can call me Mum," answered the woman in a compassionate voice. Her blonde hair had been pulled into a sweeping updo, held in place by braids. While her facial features seemed somewhat intimidating with her long, sharp nose and piercing blue eyes, the lines along her forehead and mouth convinced Ezra she had nothing but kindness beneath her exterior. Her lips—dressed in a subtle shade of rouge—

curled into a grin as she waited for a reply. She patiently folded her gloved hands over her lap.

"Hello," Ezra said, thoroughly baffled.

"Hmm. I think it would be wise to bring in someone to which you have already been introduced," Annabelle said and rose from her chair. "Just a moment, my dear."

The door thudded shut. Ezra gulped and eyed his surroundings. A sliver of mid-morning daylight filtered through a grimy window so high up on the wall that Ezra figured he had to be in a cellar somewhere. If he were at Belfast Royal Academy, he had never seen this section of the institution before. And, seeing as he had cleaned nearly every square inch of the grounds, he was almost certain he was nowhere near the school. The small room housed a cot—in which he currently resided—and a bunk bed perpendicular to it. Red damask patterned wallpaper adorned the walls and wooden bookcases full of vials and glass bottles decorated the spaces in between.

Just as Ezra entertained the idea of getting up, the door swung open again, revealing a weary Kierra McLarney.

"Miss McLarney," Ezra gasped, not sure where to start. "I—I am terribly sorry; I know my custodian duties were not completed last night, and I should not have been off school grounds. I can explain—"

"Ezra, dear, you do not have anything to explain. I'm just glad you are safe," said Miss McLarney as she sank into the chair. The dark shadows under her eyes suggested sleep had not visited last night. "Now, I'm sure the headmaster would beg to differ, but I wouldn't worry about that. How are you feeling?"

"Not the best." He winced as he sat up and propped himself against the wall. "What happened?"

Miss McLarney studied his face. "How much do you remember?"

Ezra shut his eyes, reaching back into his harrowing memories. "I remember these strange mechanical people, but this is not the first time I've seen them. They killed my mother last week, and I think..." Ezra opened his eyes again, looking straight into his teacher's blue ones. "I think they are after my father now."

Miss McLarney nervously played with the hem on her sleeve. "Do you know why?"

"I don't. But this is the second time they have tried to kill me." The words felt strange as they left Ezra's mouth. Only a fortnight ago, he had not the slightest idea anyone would ever want to harm his family. Now, it was all too real.

"I am so sorry," Miss McLarney whispered in sympathy. "That is awful."

"What were they?"

"They're called Dark Watchers," she answered without missing so much as a beat. "They are undead beings brought to life through sorcery."

Ezra stared at her, his mind racing in endless circles. "Excuse me?"

"Your parents never told you?"

"Told me what?" Ezra responded, heart racing so fast he thought he might faint. What could they have *possibly* kept from him all these years? The longer he stared at his teacher's startled expression, the more debilitating the pang of panic became in his chest.

"Oh my," sighed Miss McLarney. "In that case, there is quite a bit to explain, and I'm not sure—"

"I can handle it," Ezra interrupted, eager for an explanation. "I have endured much worse."

Miss McLarney forced a weak smile. "That you have. However, what I mean is that I am not sure I'm the proper person to tell you."

As if on cue, a tall man who looked to be around thirty years of age entered the room. His combed brown hair shone with a golden hue in the light permeating the cellar window. He sported a thin moustache and a sparse, yet neatly trimmed beard. Dressed in a white button up shirt, black pinstriped waistcoat and matching trousers, the man looked incredibly too cheerful—and dapper—for the hour. He grinned and offered his hand to Ezra.

"Ezra Newport? It's a pleasure to officially meet you," he said, shaking his hand. "I'm not sure if my cousin here has mentioned me at all, but the name's Jonas van der Campe."

"Nice to meet you as well, Mr. van der Campe," Ezra replied, admiring the man's Dutch accent.

"Please, call me Jonas. Say, let's go for a stroll, shall we?"

Ezra looked toward his teacher for approval, and she nodded in the affirmative.

"Yes, certainly," Ezra agreed, sliding off the cot. However, the twinging soreness in his thigh reminded him of his recent confrontation with danger, and his leg inadvertently gave out. Ezra managed to catch himself by grabbing a hold of Jonas' arm.

"Easy there, chap," Jonas said kindly. "You took quite a nasty blow to your leg last night. Not to worry, we'll take a tram."

"But first, let's get you something appropriate to wear," Miss McLarney insisted, collecting a pile of clothing and Ezra's travel bag from the lower bunk. "It doesn't seem like you had much in the way of proper attire in your bag, so I gathered some of Jonas' spare items that I think would fit you nicely until you get back to the academy."

Ezra gratefully took the apparel without question. "Thank you."

"Take care, Ezra. I will see you at dinner, Cousin," Miss McLarney said as she left the room.

After Ezra had changed into a pressed pair of trousers and a dress shirt, Jonas led him up a musty staircase framed by brick, through an alleyway, and into brilliant daylight. Ezra blinked, encouraging his eyes to adjust to the brightness. When they finally did, he could not help but stare in wonder at his surroundings.

They stood in the heart of downtown Belfast; the gritty hustle and bustle of the city sparked a renewed life into Ezra's veins. It was almost as if he were seeing everything for the first time through a new lens. City dwellers crossed the main thoroughfare on foot, darting around horse-drawn retail carts and over the inlaid tracks within the street. Electric wiring for the passenger trams was strung above the streets by ornate poles, about nine meters in height, giving pedestrians plenty of clearance to make their way about. Men wore their finest suits and bowler hats while women, outfitted in high-necked blouses and long skirts, shaded themselves under parasols. Everyone seemed to be in a hurry, even the pigeons flying between the buildings.

The rumble of an imported automobile startled nearby horses into giving a wide berth for the motor vehicle to pass. Ezra figured only the extremely wealthy in Ireland could afford that type of transportation. He had heard they were quite popular in America but hadn't seen many in his lifetime to validate a similar claim for Europe.

Jonas signalled to a red and white passenger tram, and the driver halted the transport just long enough for them to board.

"Mornin', sirs," said the driver with a tip of his hat. "How's about ye? Lovely day, inn'it?"

"Most certainly," Jonas replied. He guided Ezra into the enclosed body of the tram and gave him a compassionate smile when he sat on the bench across from him.

At once, the tram accelerated forward. Ezra uneasily cleared his throat and for a few moments, lost himself in the distraction of the scenery flying past. The whirring of the inner mechanics and the click-clacking of the wheels over the tracks made the awkward silence between himself and Jonas van der Campe just a tad more bearable.

"Well, Ezra Newport, it seems as if the Universe has been desperate for us to make each other's acquaintance."

Ezra turned away from the window. "What?"

"Surely you must be wondering how Kierra, Zaire, and I knew where to find you last night, swooping in at just the nick of time to save your life."

"Well, yes," Ezra admitted. "That amongst other things."

Curiosity sprang from the shadows under the brim of Jonas' fedora. "To be quite frank, so am I."

Ezra frowned. "Sorry?"

"Even in my line of work, it is not—shall we say—*typical* for one to be able to suddenly look through the eyes of a complete stranger, no matter how brief," Jonas placidly stated. "Especially as I have not been Gifted with Sight."

"I'm sorry, sir—er, Jonas," Ezra squeaked, suddenly confused beyond measure. "I have no idea what you are talking about."

Jonas smiled but Ezra noticed it looked forced, perhaps hiding internal conflict. For only knowing him a few minutes, Ezra concluded it seemed quite out of place in someone with such a cheerful demeanour.

"What I'm saying is that I should not have been able to see—in vivid detail, mind you—what happened to you the night of the train wreck in Portadown," Jonas explained. "Similarly, I should have not been able to see your exact steps as you fled through Belfast. But I did."

Ezra dropped his gaze toward his hands. The scars across his left palm seared an angry red in the midday light and with a rush of embarrassment, he turned his hand over against his trousers.

"You are quite the anomaly." Jonas leaned forward in his seat, resting his forearms on his knees while folding his hands together between them. "The events that unravelled last night should have killed you, but they didn't. How do you explain that?"

Ezra stared at the man. "I—I can't," he apprehensively began. "I feel as though in the past week, I have been living in a nightmare and no matter how hard I try, I cannot wake up."

Sympathy glinted in Jonas' eyes. "You have battled demons most seventeen-year-olds could not even imagine."

Ezra allowed quietness to consume them while he fought a bothersome tingle in his throat. "It all happened so fast."

"Mm. Yes. The inevitability of life," Jonas commented. "Tell me, Ezra, what made you decide to leave school grounds?"

Chewing on his lip, Ezra broke his gaze away from the man. Guilt churned in his stomach, leaving a sour taste upon his tongue. "I—I wanted to see if I could find my father."

"You believe he's alive?"

"He must be," Ezra asserted. "Those *things* are still searching for him."

"Dark Watchers," said Jonas, intrigue on the edge of his voice. "All right, let me ask you this: Do you believe in the supernatural?"

"You mean like God and angels?" Ezra questioned. He wasn't quite sure what Jonas was getting at. "I was raised in the ways of Islam. So, yes."

Jonas nodded and adjusted a small, golden pin on his suit jacket. Before Ezra could delve into the familiarity of the design, the man continued.

"Yes, a bit like that." Jonas paused, as if considering his words carefully. "Besides the last week, have you ever witnessed anything you could not explain?"

Ezra shrugged. "Not that I am aware. Besides moving from country to country my entire life, I would say things have been relatively normal up until recently."

He studied Ezra. "Is that your conscious or your subconscious speaking?"

"Er...conscious, I guess?" This Jonas fellow certainly was a man of many enquiries.

"Did your parents ever tell you why?"

"Why we moved?" asked Ezra, uncomfortably shifting in his seat under the weight of Jonas' questions. "All my parents said is that we *had* to relocate for 'better opportunities.' I had assumed it was financial."

"And why do you say '*had* assumed?'"

"Because there was a moment on the train—just before one of those Dark Watchers killed my mother—I wondered if we were running away from something." Ezra swallowed the emotional pain and stared at his shoes. "But I cannot say for sure."

Jonas drew himself up into a confident posture. "Never discredit your intuition, Ezra," he whispered. "You'll come to find that's one of your strongest defences."

Ezra pondered his words, wondering just how tightly to hold onto them. So far, Jonas had not shown any indication that he was a dishonest crook, so he persisted.

"The Dark Watcher called my mother a Magus. I'm not sure what that means."

An unexpected sparkle in Jonas' eyes lit up the entire interior of the tram. "Luckily, I know all about that."

Ezra jumped at the abrupt hiss spewing from the tram's breaks.

"Ah, Albert Bridge. This is our stop," Jonas said as he patted Ezra on the shoulder. After he had paid the fare, Jonas tilted his head in the direction of a stone walkway that snaked alongside the River Lagan.

"Are you familiar with the story of the Magi?"

"The Magi? Only a little," Ezra admitted, recalling the snow embellished nativity scenes he had seen during Christmastime in London. "I think they have something to do with the birth of Jesus Christ?"

Jonas casually placed his hands in his suit jacket pockets as they strode along the pathway. "Precisely. The western world knows the Magi's story from the account given by Matthew in the Bible. But the story goes back further than that. Much further. The Magi's origins can be traced all the way back to the height of the Babylonian empire, thousands of years ago. They were revered by kings, respected by the commoner, and made quite a name for themselves in the process."

Ezra snuck an incredulous look in Jonas' direction. "Okay. So, what does that have to do with my parents?"

Jonas grinned, hardly able to contain his excitement. "The word 'Magi' comes from the Greek '*magos*,' which is where we get our word for 'magic,'" he explained. "See, the Magi are not simply wise men, as most people believe. They are descendants in a long line of dream interpreters and astronomers. They excel in supernatural talents, talents that defy scientific explanation."

"Talents," Ezra noted aloud, reminded of Miss McLarney's mention of sorcery. "So, they're sorcerers?"

"Oh, no, no," Jonas hurriedly replied. "Not sorcerers. The magic channelled by the Magi is strictly used to help others. Never for selfish or destructive purposes."

Ezra glanced sideways at Jonas. "How do you know all this? Are you a history teacher like Miss McLarney?"

Jonas stopped in his tracks, turned toward Ezra and with all seriousness answered, "I know these things because I am one of them."

"You're a Magus?" replied Ezra. "They actually exist?"

Jonas chuckled at Ezra's remarks and looked out over the River Lagan. "Yes, even today."

"And my mother?"

"Both of your parents were Magi," Jonas responded confidently.

Really?

Perhaps Jonas was a dishonest crook after all.

"But that cannot be," Ezra remarked as he waded through his turbulent thoughts. The mental dam holding back his stream of consciousness had split apart, and he tried not to drown in the deluge. "How could I have *not* known something like that? Why would my parents keep that a secret?"

"Ah. Well, that is where it gets interesting," Jonas said with a tinge of darkness in his voice. He guided Ezra toward a wooden bench, and they both took a seat. "As you know, the threat against people like me and your parents is very real. That's why the Third Order of the Magi operates in secrecy. Our identities and abilities are our most precious possessions. Save for governmental entities, elected officials, and royalty, no one knows we exist. But if you look hard enough, you'll find us. We are the volunteers of the town, the vigilantes in the streets, the educators and guardians of knowledge in the libraries."

Ezra considered his words in silence, staring out at the River Lagan's muddy waters. "Why are you telling me all this if you do not want to be discovered?"

Jonas squinted in the sunlight. "Because, Ezra, I am highly convinced you are *also* a Magus. Not just anyone can survive being shot by a Watcher's poisoned arrow."

Ezra's jaw dropped open. He attempted to form words, even the most basic of grammatical structures, but could not utter anything more than primitive grunts of confusion.

"Now, as for your other questions, those will be answered in time," Jonas promised. "Right now, all you need to know is that you are safe with us."

"Us?"

"The Irish Chapter of the Third Order of the Magi," Jonas replied as if the matter were as simple as explaining the sun in the sky. "There are seven Magi residing here in Belfast, but our backgrounds are from all over the world. My cousin, Kierra, is one of them. Two others attend Belfast Royal Academy."

Oh no, thought Ezra as his stomach somersaulted unpleasantly. *I swear to Allah if those two students are Dennis and one of his awful sidekicks...* He absentmindedly ran his thumb over the fresh scars on his opposite palm. The wound still prickled and burned with inflammation, a physical reminder that he wasn't wanted in Ireland.

But Jonas wasn't like the others, and that was the problem. His genuine nature seemed too good to be true. The whole story, as oddly timed as it was, seemed too good to be true. There could not be an alternative explanation: Jonas' grand tale about the Magi *must* have been fabricated.

"Look, I appreciate your kindness, but I am no one special," Ezra spoke resolutely as he stood. As much as he wanted to hold onto the fleeting hope of a better life, he could not accept this was the answer. "I had better return to school before I have another disciplinary session with the headmaster."

"Do you know why I brought you here?"

Ezra stared blankly in response.

Jonas gestured toward Albert Bridge and the River Lagan. "This river doesn't look like anything special. In fact, it appears rather dirty and unimpressive as it winds through our city. This bridge—though it has a wonderfully designed exterior—collapsed twenty years ago and had to be rebuilt. But just beyond these imperfect landmarks, only six kilometres due northeast from where we now stand, the river opens to an inlet and merges with the vast and beautiful North Atlantic. There's a world of wonder just beyond the bend, Ezra. You only have to be willing to take the first step of faith around the corner."

Fire Signs

A bombardment of early spring rain pounded against the storefront windows as Jonas hung his drenched coat near the register. Leaning against the counter, he exhaled a defeated breath. Recruiting those with exceptional skills had always come easy, but his latest attempt with Ezra left him wondering if he should strictly focus on his day job.

The Emporium of Exotic Trinkets stood vastly different than any other shop in the vicinity of High Street. While other retailers focused on finely tailored clothing and high-end jewellery, Jonas preferred to carry more peculiar items. Polished ametrine from Bolivia and various archaeological artifacts from Mexico City were encased behind glass. A myriad of magnifying glasses, leather-bound books, and telescopes adorned tabletops near the storefront windows while intricately threaded scarves hung from coat racks. Faded Tibetan prayer flags crisscrossed along the ceiling rafters and an assortment of maps, logbooks, ink pens, knapsacks, and compasses sat upon the shelving that ran the length of the store. All in all, the shop seemed to be the precise personification of Jonas van der Campe himself.

While the Emporium invoked the sense of adventure in its customers, Jonas knew it had far greater value than a mere hobby shop. Instead, it was an unusual—but altogether perfect—façade for what lay *underneath* street level.

Jonas referred to the secret lower quarters as "Elysium"—a safe haven for the local members of the Third Order. While Kierra lived in the flat above the Emporium, Jonas occupied the extravagant cellar, along with Zaire, Diego, and Annabelle. The Freemasons might have had their lodges and temples, but the Third Order hid out of sight and out of reach from prying individuals. And that was just the way Jonas liked it.

He lifted the folds of his damp jacket and unfastened the golden star-shaped pin on the lapel. His thumb traced the grooves within its confines. The sign of Aquarius within a blazing compass rose, the symbol of the Magi, had always given him hope when he had none. But now, it only seemed to mock him.

Jonas placed the pin on the counter, rolled up his sleeves, and grabbed a rag to polish the glass displays.

"Someone looks as if they could use a hug."

Jonas forced a smile and scrutinised the impossibly soaked young man who had just entered the Emporium.

"You know, Diego, you should really take an umbrella with you," Jonas suggested as he continued wiping down the displays. "You're not in Guadalajara anymore."

"No kidding," Diego replied. He wrung out the excess water from his flat cap. "I've been on this earth for twenty-two years and in all that time, I still have not figured out how the Irish aren't horrendously shrivelled prunes by now."

"What an impeccable visual," laughed Jonas. A nagging annoyance clawed at him, causing his humour to fade. Not even bothering to look Diego in the eyes, Jonas tossed the rag behind the cash register and flipped the sign on the entrance to signify the end of operating hours.

"Closing already?" asked Diego.

"Indeed," said Jonas. "We have matters to discuss."

"About what?"

Diego's question went unanswered as Jonas descended the spiral staircase leading to the cellar. Every echoing clamour of the steel rungs awakened the sea monster within Jonas' stomach. Despite the Magi Administration's strong warning to steer clear of Ezra, their mysterious absence from Belfast continued to fuel his anxiety. Jonas expected them to be beating down his door by now, demanding an explanation as to why he had disobeyed orders. And yet, nothing ever came. No telegrams. No transmissions over the transponder. Nothing.

Besides that—and the uncanny connection he still maintained with Ezra—Jonas had another reason for uneasiness: Diego himself.

By the time he and Diego had reached the lower landing, Jonas forced a deep cleansing breath to squelch his irritation before it contorted into something altogether horrifying.

The ruby door flew open as if on its own accord.

"I had a feeling you would be closing up shop early today, my dear," said Annabelle as Jonas rushed through the doorway. "It is a good thing, too; we have only a few moments before the Administration transmits."

"Excellent. Round up the crew, Mum," Jonas instructed, making a circular motion with his index finger. "Diego and I will be right there."

Annabelle nodded but gasped when she caught sight of the young man. "Diego Javier Montreal! You are soaked to the bone! What did I tell you about taking an umbrella with you? You are going to catch cold!"

"¡Ay, dios mio, Mamá!" he grumbled as Annabelle yanked him along by the shirt collar on her frantic journey to find him a towel. "That is an old wives' tale!"

"Well, I happen to call it an old *wise* tale," Annabelle remarked. She located a quilt and wrapped it over his shoulders. "Now, have a sit in front of the fireplace and warm up. I'll gather the others."

"Come with me," Jonas requested, grabbing Diego by the forearm. He led him down the corridor to his bedroom and shut the door firmly behind them.

Diego stared at Jonas for a moment, an eyebrow arching in curiosity. "What? Why are you acting so strange?"

Of course, Diego could see right through him. He had quite the knack for doing that.

Frowning, Jonas folded his arms. "I am not acting strange."

The young man's mouth curled into a smirk. "A Sagittarius can detect lies from across the galaxy while blindfolded. That, and you are a terrible liar. You, *mi amigo Holandés*, are acting strange."

Jonas observed Diego in silence. Waves of dark, wet hair curled underneath the edges of his flat cap and elegantly graced his cleanly shaven jawline. Barely into his twenties, he appeared just as charming, just as vibrant, as he had three years prior when they first met in Mexico. A breathtaking enthusiasm blazed throughout Diego's aura, and that was merely one of the things Jonas admired about him.

But his dress shirt had been buttoned hastily, half-heartedly. Wrinkles traversed over the fabric of his trousers. The remnants of lipstick smudged his neck. Redness in his eyes suggested sleep had been interrupted by more vigorous activities.

Diego's heart had been unequivocally claimed by another.

"I figured you stayed at Stella's flat last night," deduced Jonas. His words sounded lifeless and indignant.

Jealous.

Diego's light-hearted demeanour faded. "So? I was with her all day, too, at the Royal Irish Constabulary. Arrest me."

Jonas blinked away his exasperation and picked at a fraying thread on his shirt sleeve. "You have been slacking in your duties. As a Magi Insigne, your responsibility now that you are a full-fledged member of the Irish Chapter is to serve your community. To help those in need. Gallivanting around Belfast with Stella is hardly a priority, especially now when times are rapidly changing."

"I *am* doing my duties!" Diego retorted, "or need I remind you that I work with the police?"

"Well, Chief Constable Norman tells me you often leave consultations early once Stella's shift ends," Jonas shot back, "and he mentioned just last week he caught the two of you in the alley—"

"Jonas, that is irrelevant."

"No, that is *highly* inappropriate while you're on duty! Not to mention it infringes on public decency. What were you thinking?"

Diego drew in a sharp breath. "You are just—"

"Don't," Jonas warned, fire prickling in his chest. "Don't you *dare* say it."

The young man chewed on the inside of his cheek, challenging him with a dangerous glare. Several times, he opened his mouth as if to speak but thought better of it. Eventually, he worked up the nerve to release what yearned to break loose from his lips. "Am I not allowed to move on from...from what we had? Is *that* what this is about? Remember, it was your decision to call things off in the first place."

Jonas clenched his fists with white-knuckled ferocity.

Yes, because I was forced to end it.

"Not at all," Jonas managed to state calmly, though he could feel his blood pressure pounding in his ears. "What I am saying is that you need to become serious about being a part of the Third Order. You swore an oath, Diego. That oath must be upheld. 'Good thoughts, good words, good deeds,'" he quoted, "'forever be the life I lead.'"

"*Si*, I know the Magi's Creed."

"Then follow it."

A formidable stillness cast a spell over the entire room. Irritated, Jonas ran his fingers through his hair while Diego attempted to suppress his temper by clenching his teeth. They glared at each other, fire and frustration blazing within their auras. The longer the silence reigned, the thicker the barrier between them grew. But as with any structure standing on shaky ground, it was only a matter of time before the foundation crumbled into dust.

"You sound just like the Magi Council," Diego seethed in disappointment. "Indoctrinated, unforgiving, and hopelessly stuck on the rules. The Administration would be proud."

"You know that is not true," Jonas responded, hurt. His voice cracked from the restraint it took to conceal his distress.

"Congratulations, *Señor* van der Campe," Diego said, sarcasm dripping from every syllable as he mock applauded him. "I do not know how, but you have made everything worse." While Jonas grappled for a response, Diego scoffed, yanked the bedroom door open, and stalked off down the corridor.

Jonas' lungs deflated with regret in the deafening silence that followed.

Touchy subjects should be left for calmer times, he scolded himself. *And this was definitely not the time.*

TRANSMISSIONS

Still stewing from the heated conversation with Jonas, Diego flopped in front of the fireplace, drawing the quilt around his shoulders.

If Jonas wanted to be a bothersome fool, then so be it. Two could play at that game.

Now actively preparing a pot of tea, Kierra had arrived in the short time Diego had been absent from the common room. Zaire busied himself with fluffing the couch cushions while Annabelle diligently worked on her knitting project in the armchair. Every time Diego tried to make eye contact with any of them, their eyes skirted away in awkward haste.

"What?" Diego asked, though it came out more aggressive than was necessary.

"Diego, my darling, Jonas means well," spoke Annabelle, her needles crisscrossing over her blanket. "After all, he is the leader of the Irish Chapter. If nothing else, you owe him respect for his position in the Third Order."

"Yes, well, I get the feeling his arguments have ulterior motives," Diego grumbled.

Of course, the damn walls in this place are excruciatingly thin, he thought. *No wonder everyone always knows our business.*

"Just give him some grace," suggested Kierra, handing him a steaming cup of tea. "He will come around."

"Doubtful," Diego muttered as he sipped on the beverage. "Leos are the most stubborn sign of the Zodiac." His tone signalled he wanted nothing more than to end that conversation.

"No children this evening?" Annabelle enquired to Kierra after a glance around their current company.

Kierra shook her head and sat on the couch next to Zaire. "Aja and Oliver are studying for upcoming exams," she explained. "They will be here tomorrow for their apprenticeship lessons."

The melodic chime of the transponder prickled through the atmosphere. Standing at a height of twelve centimetres, the golden pyramid-shaped device atop the mantel flashed royal blue. As it did so, it emitted the first eight notes of *We Three Kings,* signalling the beginning of a message over the electromagnetic air waves.

"Mista Jonas!" Zaire hollered. "The Administration is broadcasting!"

"Greetings to all members of the Third Order of the Magi," came the disembodied voice of a man through the transponder. "The Council sends their brightest regards to every Chapter, from the nearest field and fountain to the farthest moor and mountain. Everyone in our Constantinople headquarters has been hard at work, fulfilling the duties we strive to uphold."

Finally, Jonas sauntered into the room, ignoring Diego altogether as he leaned against the mantel. Diego narrowed his eyes at his presence but turned his attention back to the broadcast before he could slosh around in his anger.

"As for our announcements bulletin: Due to several recent events under investigation, the Magi Travel Bureau has temporarily changed the requirements for logging travel with the Administration. Beginning April 1, all licensed Magi must document travel with the Bureau for trips 100 kilometres or greater. Last week, the Council voted to decrease the requirement from 500 kilometres to 100 kilometres in a measure to more adequately ensure Magi safety."

"In other words, they keeping us on a shorter leash," Zaire pointed out.

"I wonder what that's all about," remarked Annabelle.

"The Department of Abilities and Mastership welcomed 33 newly sanctioned members last month," the jubilant voice continued through crackling static. "Congratulations to the Rio de Janeiro Chapter for cultivating 20 of those 33. Your training programs continue to be a shining example to Magi Chapters around the world."

"Hooray for Rio," Diego replied without enthusiasm as he waggled his fingers in mock celebration.

"The Commission on Gift Giving reminds all Chapters that resources are available for providing meaningful gifts to governmental leaders and royal families," the announcer persisted in his grand manner. "Please telegraph the Administration if you wish to receive a pamphlet in the Magi Post.

"And lastly, the Department of Transmissions thanks you for tuning in to our program today. May the Famed Three and the Yonder Star guide you as you go about your moral obligations. Celestial blessings to you all."

The transponder's twinkling blue luminance faded as the voice dissolved into silence.

Jonas raised his eyebrows, sharing a concerned glance with his cousin.

"Well, that was dreadfully enigmatic," Kierra noted. "'Events currently under investigation?' Do you think they mean the Portadown train incident?"

"Perhaps," Annabelle mused. "But why would they restrict all Magi's travel due to a single occurrence? Unless—"

"Unless there's more at work than what they are letting on," Jonas said, crossing his arms over his chest.

"Are you suggesting the Magi Administration is hiding something or are you just sore that you are on probation with them?" asked Diego, not even bothering to hide his irritability.

Jonas shot him a warning glare.

"You don't think," Kierra began, cupping her hands around her tea, "the Legerdemain Brotherhood is somehow involved, do you?"

The atmosphere in the cellar went cold at the very suggestion.

Like a persistent viper, the Legerdemain Brotherhood excelled at slithering in and out of the world spotlight long enough to snuff the life out of hope and retreat into darkness. Besides their undying commitment to building their army of Dark Watchers to hunt Magi and uphold the Order of Babylon, Diego knew the sorcerous society had been rather silent over the past century. While at one time the Brotherhood and the Third Order of the Magi were one and the same, differences of opinion on how to wield the Celestial Lifeforce drove them apart. The schism between those who wished to use magic for the betterment of the world versus those who wished to use their abilities for their own selfish ambitions grew deeper over the years. But apart from insignificant quarrels in the political arena and vying for the same consultancy positions as the Magi, the Brotherhood had vastly kept to themselves.

Bitter. Brooding. Venomous.

Diego urged himself to meet Jonas' sightline. If anyone had even a fraction of knowledge of what might be on the Brotherhood's agenda, it was Jonas.

The Magi Master traced the grains of the wooden mantel with his fingertip in quiet contemplation. A brewing darkness dampened the usual sparkle in his eyes. "I am sure it is a possibility."

"They been quiet for a while," said Zaire, "hiding in the shadows while they let their Dark Watchers do their dirty work. I even heard rumours the Legerdemain Brotherhood is disbanding completely. Lack of support and funding, I guess. Well, that and the lack of Magi wanting to comply with the archaic Order of Babylon."

"Don't let their quiescence fool you," Jonas warned. "Remember, predators often lurk in the darkness before attack."

"Your interpretation of the stars from January might have been heralding something like this," Kierra reminded her cousin. "Perhaps this really is a larger issue coming to fruition."

Diego turned an incredulous stare toward Jonas. "Interpretation of the stars? What did they say?"

Jonas slid his hands into his trouser pockets, trying to appear casual and relaxed, though Diego knew he only did so to hide his trembling fingers. With a profound seriousness confiscating his features, Jonas struggled to meet Diego's eyes. "Some stars aren't meant to be followed," he said, slow and deliberate. "And if we are to dig deeper into the meaning of these signs, I truly believe we may find ourselves on a journey we're not prepared to confront."

Chewing on his lower lip, Diego redirected his attention to the fireplace. A damp chill having nothing to do with his rain-soaked clothing crawled down his spine. While he might not have wanted to listen to Jonas' relationship advice, these words were something he couldn't dismiss so easily.

Their world was changing.

In more ways than one.

THE SHAHMARAN

When Ezra had returned to Belfast Royal Academy earlier that Saturday afternoon, he immediately dove into his cleaning tasks. The busier he could keep his hands, the easier it was to stave off his wild speculations. But no amount of dusting or scrubbing could adequately douse the panic. Even though Miss McLarney had assured him she would speak with Willigen on his behalf, Ezra knew he had an imminent disciplinary hearing waiting. He ruminated over the confession he would be required to provide the headmaster. As Ezra rehearsed his discourse, he realised it bordered more on a frantic plea to refrain from physical discipline and not so much an explanation of why an audacious escape had been necessary. As if being injured by half-dead bounty hunters fuelled by sorcery wasn't enough.

The very idea caused Ezra to scoff with disbelief. Perhaps he had finally gone insane with bereavement. He had not even had a chance to properly mourn his mother. Every moment since the train wreck blurred together in his memories. The dizzying momentum pushed him forward, not allowing him a spare second to breathe.

Ezra's weary mind swirled in confusion well into the evening hours. So, he escaped to the one place he could actually think.

Perched upon the roof gables outside his dormitory window, Ezra scanned the grounds for anything out of the ordinary. Not even a blade of grass bent out of place. But that did not stop the icy fingers of anxiety from gripping his throat. Dark Watchers seemed to excel in materialising out of nowhere.

They would be back. He was sure of it.

However, his disquieted fears were slightly dampened by Miss McLarney's promise, a promise that involved placing some sort of protective, magical barrier over the school.

"No more off-site excursions," she had stressed upon his return to the academy. "You'll be protected from Dark Watcher attacks as long as you stay on school grounds."

While Ezra trusted her wholeheartedly, he still could not believe magic existed. It couldn't. It was absolute ludicrous. Instead, just the idea that Miss McLarney would be watching out for him calmed his racing mind.

A chilling wind from the north blew Ezra's dark hair into his eyes, blocking the evening view of the school grounds. While the earlier rainstorm had given way to overcast skies, the bitterness of the Irish air tingled in his nostrils.

Ezra wound his Turkish scarf around his neck for added warmth, and he took in the scent of the well-worn fibres. His fingertips grazed the snakelike embroidery winding its way across the fabric. The design sang the story of the Shahmaran, a mythical half woman, half snake born from Turkish legend. Of course, the scarf and the story had always reminded him of home, even when the very word felt like a foreign concept. He closed his eyes, pretending the very action could transport him back to Constantinople. The call of the boats in the harbour, the smell of food in the marketplaces, the glorious Hagia Sophia mosque ornamenting the skyline. All of it came flooding back the moment he sank into the scarf's comfort.

Suddenly prompted by an earlier memory, Ezra rummaged in his coat pocket for the calling card given to him by the mysterious man named Jonas. In the dim light, he could just barely make out golden lettering:

THE
EMPORIUM OF EXOTIC TRINKETS

JONAS VAN DER CAMPE - SHOP OWNER
40 HIGH STREET BELFAST
HOURS MAY VARY

As much as Ezra wanted to belong to something even remotely resembling a community, he found Jonas' tale difficult to believe. Yet, he was not quite sure how to justify the presence of the Dark Watchers—or why they were after his family—if Jonas' claims were false. Perhaps they owed money and were running from debt collectors? Perhaps they had issues with immigration papers and needed a quick getaway?

Just not magic. *Anything* but magic.

Ezra returned the card to his pocket, hugged his knees to his chest, and buried his face in his arms.

"Subconscious or conscious, Ezra? Which one speaks the loudest?"

Ezra jumped in surprise at the sound of a woman's voice and squinted around the vast darkness.

Miserably dank, with a curious stench of honey and rotting things, the cave in which he now found himself began to pulse with bass-like resonance. Starting soft and building in fervour, the vibrations felt oddly salubrious and if it were to stop, Ezra feared the life might drain from his body.

"Is—is someone there?" his shaky voice called out. Nothing answered besides the resounding tickle in his eardrums.

Stalactites dangled from the cathedral ceiling, spiralling downward into a glassy black lake. A purple glow enchanted the space and refracted off dust fragments descending like snow into the water. All the while, Ezra kept his attention trained on the shadows, as if at any moment, he might see something horrific emerge from the depths. Ezra had never been fond of caverns, but this one in particular chilled his soul.

"Subconscious or conscious? Wasn't that what the Magus asked you?"

It took him several moments to comprehend the voice spoke of Jonas.

"I don't understand," Ezra responded to the darkness. "Why is that so important?"

"Because they are not the same," the woman's voice replied. Her silky vocal timbre skimmed the surface of the water. "So, which one speaks louder?"

Emerging from the blackness, the figure of a woman glissaded amongst the rocks in his direction. Eyes glowing gold, with long brunette hair slithering over her shoulders, her human hips melded into the smooth, muscular body of a serpent. The closer she approached, the more Ezra's face flushed in embarrassment. Convicted, he turned his eyes away to avoid her nude torso.

The Shahmaran.

Ignoring that he had not answered her last question, she persisted. "Why are you here, boy?"

"I—I don't know," Ezra said. His parched throat caused his words to come out cracked and subdued. "I am lost."

The creature eyed him curiously. "Do you want to be lost?"

"No," Ezra felt himself choke on his emotion. "I just want to know where to go next."

A flicker of something dangerous twinkled in the Shahmaran's eyes. Her sweet breath caressed his face. "I think you already know the truth."

"I don't."

"You do," she insisted, raising her eyes toward the cave ceiling. "You do."

Ezra's eyes sprang open. At least a half minute had come and gone before he realised how close he was to teetering off the roof's edge. Heart pounding in his temples, he let out a shaky breath and leaned back against the gable.

Curtains of clouds had become thin wisps, allowing several diamond specks to shine through. He studied the twinkling pinpoints of light, as each one tried their hardest to penetrate the cosmos. Ezra envied the stars; every ball of fire had been appointed their place, their meaning in the universe. Destiny fuelled them. Guidance was unnecessary.

And then, there was him: Alone. Confused. Lost.

Life would be so much simpler if the stars revealed their secrets, he reflected, wiping away the sting of tears from the corners of his eyes. *Perhaps then, I'd know where to go.*

On the wind, Ezra could almost hear the words of Jonas and the Shahmaran, each syllable intertwined with the next:

"Never discredit your intuition…"

"I think you already know the truth."

A Blemish in Time

Not very many things had the power to piss off Diego Montreal.

Disloyalty? Naturally.

Being held back? Of course.

Jonas' embitterment toward his relationship with Stella? Without question.

Failure?

Failure had to be the worst offender. Nothing could make him feel more incompetent than defeat, especially if that defeat had anything to do with Time Manipulation.

Diego screwed up his face in concentration, squeezing the edges of the quartz wand into his palm. Usually illuminated with natural light, the chief constable's office was now shrouded in shadows, too tenacious for the weak desk lamp bulb and the evening gloom. The Souvenirs—the ring and the electric torch—had been laid out before him, alongside Norman's heavy scrutiny.

This time, it *had* to work.

"Forgive me for my lack of understanding, but I honestly don't see why this situation is different than the rest," the constable grumbled as he lit a cigar and propped his feet upon the desk. "This should have worked the first time. After all, you've managed to view crime scenes before."

Diego lifted his burning gaze to his boss.

Despite his flagrant tone, the constable spoke the truth, as much as Diego hated to admit it. Previous attempts had gone without a hitch. But for some unknown reason, these crime scenes proved resistant to his abilities. What seemed like the simple work of a madman with a fondness for the word "*quietus*" had an impenetrable exterior. Every time Diego turned back Time to view these events, a thick darkness cloaked whatever evidence remained. He had never seen anything quite like it in any of his Time Excursions.

Either his abilities were somehow being drained or someone was erasing history. Both scenarios did not sound particularly thrilling.

"Yes, well, I wouldn't expect you to understand the technicalities of it," Diego muttered.

"No, I don't," huffed Norman, "but there's something I *do* understand, and it is that now, we aren't the only ones dealing with this madness." The constable reached into his top drawer and dropped a newspaper on the workspace, further disrupting Diego's focus.

His eyes skimmed the recent headline but backtracked when he realized it was in French. What Diego could not ascertain from the print, he translated from the front-page photograph.

Plumes of fire and coal dust disrupted what once was a mining operation. Lifts, splintered planks, and glass fragments littered the work site, while flocks of ravens dotted the chaotic skyline. While the photograph neglected to show any of the dead or injured, it *did* provide a glimpse of something far more impactful: the painful emotion in their comrades' faces, streaked amongst the grime.

Whatever had just taken place not only rattled the northern French countryside. It had shaken survivors to their cores.

La catastrophe de Courrières.

"They're saying more than a thousand people are dead," said the chief constable. "What they are not saying—in the papers, at least—is that authorities discovered the word *quietus* painted in red across one of the communal shacks. I suppose you can understand why this is a bit higher of a priority now that it has crossed international boundaries."

Diego gritted his teeth and pushed the newspaper away from the Souvenirs. "So, the Irish Republican Brotherhood is out of the question, I assume?"

Norman narrowed his eyes. "Most likely."

"Right. Well, there's only one thing we can do," Diego began, once again tracing the Star of David in the air with his quartz wand. "Pray my theory will hold strong enough for me to bring something back."

"Best of luck, kid," Chief Constable Norman said through a puff of smoke. "Do me proud."

Diego saluted him and pressed the crystal tip to the face of his pocket watch. Focusing on the time and date written on the scraps of paper beside its corresponding Souvenir, Diego internally beckoned the power of the stars to navigate to the exact moment when the Dunmurry boy lost his life. The clock hands wound backward in a savage spiral. The present world faded away, like streaks of paint drowned in torrents of water. He was now a sailor amongst the Sea of Time, directing the helm toward imminent disaster.

Within moments, Diego found himself standing in a vast void, dark and shapeless. His feet caught on invisible brambles. The wind's wary whisper nudged tree branches. A dank earthiness enveloped his nose and tongue. Yes, the scene certainly *existed*, but the black veil aptly hid reality from sight.

While his astral projection explored what remained of the past, his physical body stayed grounded in the present, meaning anyone in Past Time would not see or hear him. Instead, he would be rendered invisible, a complete blessing for moments like these when secrecy mattered.

Diego reached into his back pocket for a small compact mirror Stella lent him. If his theory held correct—and this really was some sort of magical charm, not simply operator error—then a reflection should show some insight.

Flicking open the mirror cover with his thumbnail, Diego held it eye level and gasped when hazy trees reflected within the glass.

"*O!*" he said, his chest puffing with pride. "*Dios*, I knew it! A cloaking spell."

Sneaky bastards.

Diego's feet stepped in a wide arc, panning around so he could get a better view of his surroundings. Besides the babble of the Lagan and the roaming shadow of a night bird crossing into the path of the moon, all seemed eerily still.

The proverbial calm before the storm.

Yet, something seemed dreadfully wrong.

Cursing his limited viewpoint, his eyes searched for anything suspicious: a broken branch, a flash of an electric torch, torn fabric. Yet, nothing seemed out of place.

Diego rotated again and nearly dropped the compact mirror when the apparition of a man wearing a hooded cloak appeared behind his shoulder.

Recovering just in time, Diego embarked on a backwards pursuit, not wanting to take his eyes off the figure's reflection within the looking glass. Not once, but three times, he had to steady himself from tripping over downed trees or sloping terrain. Eventually, the hooded figure came to a halt, joining two others in front of a sizable oak tree.

"We must hurry," whispered the latecomer. "The woods grow restless."

No matter the angle, Diego failed to get a glimpse of their faces. For all he knew, they were featureless creatures of the night. He was so preoccupied in solving their identities that he hardly noticed them dipping their fingers into a sack at their feet and smearing a tar-like substance across the tree bark.

Each stroke formed what was becoming the most formidable word in Diego's linguistic repertoire: *Quietus*. Each time they reached into the bag, a putrid stench assaulted Diego's senses. He knelt at the trio's feet, holding the looking glass above his head and tilting downward to get a better look at what lay at the base of the tree.

That was no sack…

Lifeless eyes of a freshly decapitated head stared back at him.

Disoriented, Diego fought the urge to vomit.

"Do not forget the Time Blemish," instructed one. "One for every site, remember?"

"We cannot be too careful," agreed the next.

"Indeed," replied the last. Diego detected the shape of a grin beneath the shadows as he scrounged for something under his cloak. A glint of gold attracted his eyes to the figure's belt, adorned with the triangular badge of the Legerdemain Brotherhood. "Woe to any fellow who gets caught up in one of these."

Frozen in terror, Diego could not do much more than tremble as the figure slammed a small hourglass to the ground. The black vapoury contents wafted on the breeze, electrifying the molecules of the evening air while the fog quadrupled in size.

Diego retreated but underbrush caught his ankle. He lost his footing, colliding with the forest floor. Frantically, he fumbled for his quartz pendant and pocket watch.

"Take me back to Present Time!" Diego commanded aloud.

Nothing happened.

Panic shocked his insides. Time *never* disobeyed his orders. He tapped the clock face with his crystal, attempting to spark the hands back into life.

This wasn't Cloaking magic. It was an Entrapment Spell. Someone knew he'd be there, poking around through the events of the past. Why else would they go through such lengths to hide them?

Diego squirmed against the invisible hold of the velvety mist. The more he fought, the heavier the darkness pressed upon his chest.

"*¡Darse prisa!*" Diego gasped, shaking his timepiece. "*¡Vamos!*"

Again, nothing.

Suddenly, the world around him began to lose all sense of spatial integrity. He chanced a glance in the now shattered compact mirror. Transparent apparitions of the figures appeared several meters above where they originally stood before jolting to another place entirely. The trees became abnormally fluid, fluttering in the March wind. Even the ground beneath him flickered in and out of existence.

Help! he beckoned. He could only pray that the chief constable could see he was in trouble from Present Time and disconnect the magic before it was too late. Diego had never been trapped in the past. Before that moment, he did not even think it was possible.

Get me out, please!

White bursts of pain inside his head intensified. His muscles writhed and twitched, jolted by some sort of electrical current. Numbness crept up his legs and into his torso. All around him, the scene erupted into cyclonic madness while the heavy fog threatened to suck the air from his lungs.

"Mr. Montreal!"

Abruptly, the roar of activity around him faded. When his limbs relaxed and he opened his eyes, Diego found himself on his back against the floor of Norman's office. Judging by the constable's horrified expressions, Diego had a feeling that once the shock wore off, he'd soon find himself in a firing squad of questions.

"Are you all right, kid?" Norman asked, just as breathless. "What happened?"

Diego propped himself up on his elbows. "*Dios*," he whispered once the feeling came back into his legs. "I actually wet myself."

The chief constable's facial features did not lighten whatsoever. "You were having a fit. I was about to call for the medics."

"No need," Diego grumbled. He tossed his pocket watch and wand onto a nearby chair. His palms traversed his face and pushed back the matted hair clinging to the sweat on his forehead. "Just as I suspected, we're not dealing with anything…ordinary."

Norman gaped at him, baffled.

Diego fought the urge to roll his eyes. Usually, the constable was not this thick.

"People with Gifts," Diego stressed, articulating every syllable. "Magical abilities."

The chief constable moved his mouth as if he were struggling to find the right words. "Are—are you absolutely positive you're all right?"

"What? Yes!"

"It's just…you've never done something like that before. Had a proper seizure. In my office."

"I promise you, Chief Constable, I will not die on your watch," Diego insisted. "Now listen to me: We are dealing with dangerous criminals. Masterminds with foul intent as well as experience with magic."

"I see," Norman answered. Thankfully, the colour began to seep back into his face. He lent a hand to help Diego off the floor. "So, one of your kind?"

Diego scrunched up his nose. "You could say that. Nevertheless, this falls into the jurisdiction of the Magi Administration."

"They've got their hands full with this one. I will file the reports with their Investigative Division; you go on home and get some rest."

Drawing in a breath, Diego decided to abandon his retort when Norman glared daggers, clearly intent on his order. Instead, he collected his hat, coat, and trinkets, and nodded to his boss on the way out.

"*Buenas noches*, Chief Constable Norman."

"Good night, Mr. Montreal. Take care of yourself."

As soon as he left the station, Diego buried his hands deep into his tweed jacket pockets and bowed his head against the bone-chilling wind. Visual echoes of the mysterious trio ricocheted throughout his mind. Even the rustling bushes along the sidewalk made his heart flutter just a little more rapidly.

In the last few minutes, two things had become inherently clear: The Legerdemain Brotherhood had returned. And while they'd gone to great lengths to cover their tracks, their one-word message spoke volumes to its intended audience, which Diego could only assume were the Magi.

On the political stage, the Legerdemain Brotherhood had lingered in the wings far too long. Grasping at velvet curtains, eagerly observing their Dark Watchers in action. But whatever they had brewing behind the scenes, they weren't playing by the rules of their old game.

This was a new game entirely.

Perhaps Jonas was right: The Magi weren't prepared for a situation like this. Most in their society would not even see it coming. Nevertheless, Diego knew he needed to hightail it back to Elysium and give Jonas a detailed overview of what he'd gathered from the Time Excursion.

Diego stood at the corner of Victoria and High Street, shifting his weight from one foot to the other. The Emporium of Exotic Trinkets sat two blocks away, but something kept him from advancing further. Hesitating, he turned his eyes skyward. While the glow from the streetlamps vied against the stars for brilliance, the stars always won. Rising in the east, just beyond Albert Memorial Clock Tower, Virgo carried the moon under her arm. Wispy clouds draped over the maiden's alluring figure, inducing a hunger within Diego.

At this hour, Jonas would be deep into his training with Aja and Oliver. And honestly, Diego wasn't pining for another stiff conversation with him.

Dismissing responsibility, Diego set his course toward Cathedral Quarter. At least Stella would bring some relief and satiate the stirring within him.

Jonas could wait.

Lessons and Revelations

A bright blast of energy reverberated across the room, causing the lampshades to tremble.

"Excellent," Jonas commended, watching as his two apprentices squared off against each other in the Elysium common room. Sunday evening training sessions had always been a favourite of his, especially now when carefree moments came at a premium. "Remember: When channelling the Celestial Lifeforce to earth, Magi must be respectful of its power. Magi must also be respectful of their opponent and the environment, aiming only to disarm."

"Ah, but that takes all the fun out of it!" joked seventeen-year-old Aja Burman. Her long, dark braid whipped around her shoulders as she edged around the furniture, wand raised at attention. "What if I want to get back at Little Ollie for setting my star logbook on fire?"

"Oh, for the love of the Famed Three! It was an accident!" insisted fourteen-year-old Oliver Abberton in his posh London accent. A look of annoyance blazed behind his spectacles. "And don't call me little!"

Jonas shook his head at their banter. "Focus, now. Oliver, I have yet to see a decent shield from you this evening."

"That is because Aja keeps sending a barrage of blasts at me," the boy whined, "and she's being a distraction."

Aja laughed maniacally and aimed another orb of energy in his direction. The blast exploded light across his face. "Then come get me, Little One!"

"Argh, that's it!" replied Oliver. He stumbled over the bohemian rug, chasing her around the couch.

The Indian girl squealed with amusement as she dashed toward the row of potted plants decorating the south wall. Abandoning the defensive properties of the Celestial Lifeforce altogether, she held out her hands and closed her eyes. Without warning, the ferns began to grow at a voracious pace, their tendrils reaching out for the boy's ankles. Before Oliver could react, he had been knocked clean off his feet, hopelessly tangled in the foliage.

"Aja!" Oliver groaned. "That's not fair!"

Jonas stifled a laugh at his students' antics. "Unfortunately, Oliver, Gifts are not off limits when it comes to real life situations. Magi have the opportunity to use the physical energy of the Celestial Lifeforce alongside their natural abilities as Miss Burman so adequately demonstrated."

"Thank you, Jonas," Aja beamed and curtsied.

"Hmph," grumbled Oliver as he lifted himself to a seated position. The boy adjusted his spectacles back to their proper angle on his face. "It is still not fair. Aja can use her Gifts to manipulate plants. I can only see auras. What good does that even do?"

"Every Gift can be used for good," Jonas reminded him. "Maybe not so much for defence purposes, but you are still able to see things she cannot." He walked around the couch and held out his hand to assist Oliver in returning to his feet. "As someone who can see life signatures, you can detect locations of trapped or missing individuals, whereas Aja could not."

"Besides," Aja began, "I've had three more years of training than you. That does give me a bit of an advantage."

"And you'll go through the Rites of the Magi and get your pin before me," Oliver sighed.

Jonas smiled kindly at his student's enthusiasm. "The path of the Magi is not a race. Thank the Universe it isn't because there is much to learn. Even I am still learning."

"Yes, but you are a *Magi Master*," Oliver articulated. "Not an apprentice. Not a Magi Insigne. Not even a Magi Adept, like most. You're the highest rank of them all."

"And perhaps the most *eligible* of them all," Aja spoke boldly, twirling about the room in a frolicsome flurry. "Miss Irene from the flower shop down the street often gushes over you."

Blood tingled in Jonas' cheeks when his apprentice's words caught him off guard. "Aja—" he said at the same time Oliver said, "Ugh!"

"She really fancies you, Jonas," Aja smirked.

"Well, I am flattered but if she enquires about it again, tell her I am not interested."

Nor would he ever be.

Aja giggled. "You should tell her that yourself."

"And I shall."

"Or just tell her you are more interested in Diego," Oliver said in all seriousness.

"All right, this conversation is *quite* improper," reprimanded Jonas, hoping his face wasn't flushed beyond measure. He awkwardly cleared his throat. "And I am *not* interested in that, either."

"Mmhmm," Aja murmured with a grin, sharing a knowing look with Oliver.

"Perhaps I should remind you how dangerous distractions can be for young apprentices," Jonas cut them off. Just as he was about to delve into a detailed morality tale about Marcellus, the one-eyed Magus of ancient Rome, Aja gasped and hurried across the room to rummage through her school bag.

"Speaking of distractions," she said, unfurling a recent edition of *The Daily Telegraph*. "From time to time, my mum sends me newspapers from back home in London. This one caught my interest, and I thought you might like to have a look." Aja presented the publication to Jonas, who snatched his reading spectacles from the mantel and eagerly devoured the front page:

4
A.M.
EDITION

The Daily Telegraph

MAGIC KEYS
TYPEWRITERS
EAST LONDON
BEST IN TOWN

LONDON. THURSDAY. FEBRUARY 22. 1906

ARTIFACT'S MEANING REVEALED
NEWLY TRANSLATED CUNEIFORM TABLET BAFFLES HISTORIANS

BY ARCHER J. HAWKINS

Scholars at the British Museum are reeling today over the latest translation from an ancient Babylonian artifact.

Though first discovered in the 1850s at the Ashurbanipal dig site, this particular stone tablet, among countless others, sat untranslated in the British Museum archives. However, the museum's Board of Trustees say they have reinvigorated efforts to interpret the content of the tablets in their possession, especially after the accomplishment of translating the Mesopotamian creation myth, Enuma Elish.

"Finally understanding the content of this tablet is simultaneously a relief and a headache," said Nicolas Dixon, deputy chair of the board. "While we now know the text, the message it holds still eludes us."

After several weeks of work and research, cuneiform experts transcribed the following from the artifact:

When struggles crest
Kings crumble at the tryst
The Roaming Lion shall rise
And the Tribes he'll assist.

Locked within time
Where Destinies are viewed
The Lion's touch opens eyes
Immense power renewed.

Unite the Lion, Dragon, and Bull
At the mouth of Babylon's Gates
A circle of Twelve shall overcome
Hail the victors' celestial fates.

Experts do not believe the passage is correlated to the Seven Tablets of Creation, as the tablet dates to approximately 500 B.C., around 100 years after the dating of the Enuma Elish tablets. Instead, they suggest it most likely can be classified as Babylonian poetry.

"Well, what do you think?" Aja prodded, bouncing on the front edge of her shoes with excitement.

"Curious," Jonas whispered, lowering the paper. Desperately, he rifled through his recollections to determine why the text seemed so familiar. But as seconds faded, so did the hope of pinpointing anything helpful.

"It seems very reminiscent of Magi history, if you ask me," Aja replied.

Oliver—who had been reading the article around Jonas' shoulder—immediately perked up. "It sounds like a prophecy," he stated. "Would that have been written around the time of Balasi and Labynetus?"

"500 B.C.," Jonas said to himself, removing his spectacles. "Yes, that would be the correct timing."

Every student who had been trained in the ways of the Celestial Lifeforce knew about the two youngest Magi in King Nebuchadnezzar's royal court. While Balasi and Labynetus began their lives as friends, they ended them as bitter enemies, ravaged by the king's newest decree: The Order of Babylon.

It was not enough that Nebuchadnezzar's staff of dream interpreters and astrologists could provide intellectual guidance. Now, if his Magi wished for continued employment, they had to also fulfil other whims of the king: Revenge. Political coups. Murder plots. The only way to do so was by embracing sorcery—the unnatural enhancement of the Celestial Lifeforce. Conflicted by the predicament, half turned against the Magi Code to acquiesce to the King's wishes. The other half, led by a defiant Balasi, resisted.

While Labynetus had chosen the way of the newly established sorcerous faction, the Legerdemain Brotherhood, Balasi had chosen the way of the Light. Their actions carved the path of both societies, setting the stage for centuries of discord.

"Do you think Balasi wrote it?" Oliver theorised.

"Mm. No, I do not believe so," Jonas replied. "The Magi Administration keeps extensive records of his writings. I have read them multiple times and never once came across that passage."

"Ooh, mysterious!" Aja exclaimed, rubbing her palms together. "Well, what do you think it means?"

Jonas drew in a cautious breath. "I am not sure. But let's not get too distracted; we have other matters to worry about in the present."

Aja's shoulders fell. Oliver scrunched his nose in disappointment.

"In the meantime, I will reach out to the Administration to get their take on it but until then, I have a proposition for you both that will provide beneficial training experience," Jonas swiftly added, folding the newspaper and setting it alongside his spectacles on the mantel.

"A proposition?" asked Aja, her eyes widening with intrigue.

"A very important mission," Jonas confirmed, looking both of his students in the eyes. "Are you up for the task?"

The Magi Apprentices jumped up and down in unbridled excitement.

"I need you to help Kierra in keeping watch over a student at Belfast Royal Academy," Jonas explained. "While I have yet to confirm, I strongly believe he is a Magus."

"Oh, Miss McLarney mentioned that," Aja responded. "She said three Dark Watchers attacked him when he was off school grounds. The whole thing sounded dreadful."

"It certainly was," said Jonas. "Ezra Newport needs us right now. His life depends on it."

Oliver stood at attention and saluted Jonas. "Sir, yes, sir!"

Jonas chuckled. "At ease, cadet. You are both dismissed for this evening. Kierra will be wanting to get you both back to the academy at a decent hour."

The students retrieved their school bags and waved cordially as they departed through the red door of Elysium.

"Goodbye, Jonas!" called Oliver.

"Don't let Miss Irene fluster you into a corner!" shouted Aja.

"I won't," laughed Jonas.

Waiting until the door latch had clicked into place, Jonas frowned and retreated to the fireplace. The typeset words and high contrast photograph of the cuneiform artifact taunted him from the mantel. Whispers from the past tickled his ears as he traced a fingertip over the newspaper ink.

This was not the first translation to be unearthed from archaeological digs. If anything, the startling amount of insight that had been gleaned from artifacts over the last few decades bordered on the imbecilic. And, like every cuneiform tablet translated before it, the words painted stories of an ancient history once unknown to modern society. While intriguing, that's all they were. Stories.

This was just another artifact. Just another translation. Just another article in the paper.

Disregarding the fleeting curiosity as foolish, Jonas folded the newspaper and shelved it with the rest of his books in the Elysium common room.

An Unlikely Ally

The grandfather clock in the academy library had a way of taunting Ezra for always being up so early.

With every swing of the pendulum, a mounting restlessness accompanied the strokes of the mop as he attended to his morning cleaning duties. The otherwise sterile silence in the hours before classes did not help. For the quieter his surroundings, the more Ezra's thoughts could run rampant.

More than anything, Ezra missed his parents. He longed to hear his mother's laughter just one more time. He yearned to feel his father's embrace and bask in his encouraging words. He wanted them to come alongside him and promise that everything would shift back into normalcy. To offer explanations for every answer left unsaid. To tell him why they had stayed silent on so many things.

Anne *might be gone, but* Baba *is still out there,* Ezra concluded as he moved across the library's expanse. *I know it. I feel it.*

Ezra had always heard that time possessed healing powers. Beyond the abilities of doctors, beyond the likes of ordinary medicine. But in the days following the events that nearly claimed his life, he doubted time could do much more than strengthen his fears. It had been two days of incessant mental torture. Of why more Dark Watchers had not appeared. Of the supposed existence of magic. Of the fact that his parents might not have been who he once thought. Nevertheless, Ezra carried on. Or at least, attempted to go about his life as normally as one could after learning such things.

If only magic were like dust, Ezra thought to himself as he traversed the library with the mop. *If only it could be swept under a rug. Out of sight and forgotten.*

If only it were that simple.

Satisfied with the now gleaming floors, Ezra picked up the water bucket in his free hand and lumbered along in a sleepy haze. With dawn approaching, Ezra wanted nothing more than to spend the last peaceful minutes in prayer before the morning bell. As Ezra rounded the corner into the corridor, he collided with another body, sending them both—along with the mop and water bucket—tumbling to the ground.

"Ah! Just the bloke we were looking for!"

No. Not again.

Ezra hauled himself up into a seated position, watching as the outer banks of the indoor lake expanded across the library. While Dennis recovered his menacing stance, Martin and John loomed over Ezra, disturbing grins setting their eyes ablaze.

"I'm surprised you're not chanting your little Islamic prayers yet," sneered Martin. "We were really hoping to ambush you during them."

Ezra scooted backward but the boys pinned him down against the frigid, wet floors. A twinge of pain sparked the nerves in his thigh into life. "Honestly, you three need to find something better to occupy your time!"

"Why?" Dennis said, pressing his shoe into Ezra's belly while Martin and John held down his arms, "when it gives me so much pleasure to torture you?"

"You are mental!" Ezra spat, struggling for freedom.

"No," John said, pausing to consider the remark. "No, I don't think we are."

"Come on, boys," Dennis instructed his mates. "Let's see if *Allah* will save him."

In one swift movement, Martin and John hauled Ezra to his feet. Dennis slammed his fist into his gut, doubling him over. Every time Ezra attempted to fight back, sudden blows from behind caught him off guard. They only became stronger, more ruthless, and more excruciating as the minutes passed.

The longer they kicked and beat him, the harder Ezra found the simple act of breathing. Somehow, they had managed to wrestle him face down against the polished floors. The taste of metal swam along Ezra's tongue just before a significant blow to his back forced him to cough up crimson.

"Stop!" Ezra pleaded amidst choking sobs.

He wasn't sure how much longer he could take the beating before he lost consciousness. Judging by the prickling feeling in his head, it would not be much more than a few minutes.

"Look at him cry like a baby," Dennis laughed, using his shoe to lift Ezra's chin upward. "Pathetic, isn't it? Looks like even *Allah* can't be bothered to come to your defence, Ezra."

Inspired by Dennis' cruelty, Martin and John jeered and pushed Ezra face first onto the watery floors.

"GET. BACK."

The room fell into silence. Even Ezra held his breath.

"Or what, sweetheart?" he heard Dennis chide. "You'll rat me out to Headmaster Willigen?"

"That's too good for you," said the familiar voice. "No, I was thinking of tying you all up by your ankles to the front lawn tree branches. Call it a science experiment. I'm interested in seeing how long it takes for you to pass out from the blood rushing to your head."

A rigid stillness washed over the three bullies before they burst into laughter.

"That's probably the funniest thing I've ever—"

But Dennis did not have a chance to finish his sentence before a flash of light and whoosh of air blasted him backward into a bookshelf. Startled, three pairs of footsteps scurried over the wet floors and faded down the corridor until all Ezra heard was the pounding in his own ears.

"Are you all right?"

Groaning with pain and humiliation, Ezra rolled himself onto his side and squinted up at the young lady.

She sank to her knees, her House Cairns tie and long, black braid racing each other toward the pool of mop water. The ornamental bindi between her eyebrows glittered in the dim light of dawn filtering through the library windows. Deep empathy creased the skin around her mahogany eyes.

Shaking, he hoisted himself up but regretted the decision when his vision fuzzed along the perimeter. Ezra did not even realise he had grabbed onto her arm for balance until he felt her other hand reach out to steady his shoulder. He prayed embarrassment had not yet reached his cheeks.

"Easy does it," the student encouraged him, brushing his hair out of his face. "Are you okay?"

Ezra examined the state of his clothing. His uniform was in shambles, streaked with blood and soiled water. The bandage around his thigh had shifted and allowed moisture to saturate the dark fibres of his trousers. Eyes stinging and heart racing, Ezra seethed with anger once the shock wore off over what had just happened.

"Argh. I'm going to pummel them so hard—" Ezra began, but the House Cairns student shook her head.

"No, because I will make good on my threat before that happens," she promised, a slight smile brightening her worried features. "I'm Aja Burman, by the way. We are in Year 14 history class together."

So *that* was where he had seen her before.

"Oh. Well, Aja, I owe you all my gratitude for getting me out of...of *that*," he croaked, gesturing obscurely around them. "I'm Ezra—"

"Newport, I know," Aja finished for him. "Jonas told me about you. You have had a rough last couple days, haven't you?"

Taken aback for a moment, Ezra gaped at her. Her timely—and explosive—response to warding off the three bullies was starting to make more sense now. "Er—oh. You must be part of his group."

"I am," Aja confirmed, "along with my friend Oliver Abberton, Year 11 here at the academy. He's in House Currie."

"Ah," Ezra said, distracted. "Did you just do magic a few minutes ago?"

Aja grinned. "Technically, I 'summoned the Celestial Lifeforce to conjure a defensive energy blast.' But yes, you can call it magic."

For some reason, her response struck him as hysterical.

She eyed him sceptically. "What?"

"Headmaster Willigen will sure get a fright out of having to discipline a student with magical powers," Ezra laughed.

"Miss McLarney will talk him out of it," Aja said with striking confidence. "She's the master at redirecting attention away from feats that defy explanation. After all, who would believe whatever comes out of that little sod's mouth, anyway?"

Ezra shrugged and attempted to get to his feet. "Well, the headmaster certainly believed him last time."

Aja grabbed his wrist before he toppled over. "Are you sure you're all right? Should I walk you to the nurse's office?"

"I'm right as rain," Ezra insisted, though he wasn't entirely sure the truthfulness of the statement. He smiled until the widespread aftermath of the mop bucket arrested his attention. There would be no possible way he could clean it up before first bell. Not even with a second convenient miracle from *Allah*.

Aja must have noticed his anxiety over the library's disorderly state. "Don't worry about this. Allow me to help. It's the least I can do."

"You do not have to." Ezra moved his shoe about in small circles to disperse the water. "It is my duty."

"And *my* duty is to make sure you are properly looked after," Aja stated. "Go get changed. I'll take care of it."

Ezra sighed and, after a few moments of internal contemplation, met his classmate's gaze. "You are different than the others here."

"Oh, really?" Aja answered with a sly grin. She playfully folded her arms. "Did the matter of me being Indian give it away?"

"No, I mean...you are kind."

"Well, I strive not to be an ignoramus like Dennis," said Aja. "I have made it my sole purpose in life."

Silence overtook him as he studied her. The longer he stared, the more he narrowed his eyes in concentration, as if engineering the proper angle for a medieval flying buttress.

"What?"

"Why do you and the other Magi even care about me?" he whispered, not even positive Aja heard him. "Why risk your own safety for...for someone like me?"

Features softening, Aja laid a firm hand on his shoulder. "Because, Ezra, your life is important to us. You matter. And we fight for the ones whose voices need to be heard."

Ezra returned her friendly smile and began his watery trek toward the corridor.

"By the way," Aja called after him, "you have got quite the impressive right hook. I thought you were going to knock Dennis' lights out completely in class last week."

"Believe me, I tried," Ezra remarked with a short laugh. His diaphragm ached in retaliation. "Dennis and his mates are miserable halfwits."

"Well, if it happens again, I've got your back, Ezra Newport. There is no reason you should ever go into battle alone."

Her words stuck with him as he made the journey back toward the boys' dormitories. First Miss McLarney. Then Jonas. Now Aja. Every member of the so-called Irish Chapter of Magi twinkled like diamonds, radiating a light Ezra had not seen from anyone before.

Except his parents.

His stomach somersaulted with sadness, hope, and—

Sudden recognition.

Vivid mental portraits in shades of gold featured his mother's broach— her star-shaped compass rose broach. The very same symbol Jonas van der Campe had been wearing upon their first meeting.

The symbol of the Magi.

He *had* always known the truth.

Somewhere in the recesses of his mind, the faintest sound of a woman's laugh echoed across a black lake.

OFFICIAL BUSINESS

While the rest of the pub bubbled with effervescence, it failed to liven the usual embodiment of high spirits: Jonas van der Campe.

He drew a cigar and matchbook from his coat pocket and fixed himself a smoke. Normally, he would pass off the habit as a vice but these days, a cigar was the least of his worries.

Jonas studied his surroundings with his typical perceptive eye. Charles, the comedic bartender with a portly stature and a long, grey moustache, made small talk with a group of businessmen at the pub counter. Several fishermen in ragged overalls and wool caps gathered around a table by the street side picture window, placing bets on their game of cards. Meanwhile, a fellow sitting on a stool near the front entrance played a rousing tune on his violin, each note more jubilant than the last.

Oh, to be as unfettered as a Quotidian. Regular, non-Magi folk did not realise how blessed they were to have such ordinary lives. They weren't burdened with centuries of civil responsibility or the unfortunate connection to another's recent memories, whether or not it was desired.

That, and they were not at the mercy of the Magi Administration for advice on what to do about the appearance of Time Blemishes.

While Jonas would not call his recent conversation with Diego "cordial," *per se,* it was a step in the right direction. If by "right direction" one meant 'filled with hideous details of an entrapment charm, laid at the hands of the Legerdemain Brotherhood.' Clearly, the Brotherhood had trickery up their sleeves that no one—not even Magi—could even imagine. Jonas had not felt this encumbered since—

"Jonas! How about an ale, eh?" shouted Charles from behind the counter.

Forced from his reverie, Jonas urged a smile. "Make it a stout."

"Comin' right up!"

Expelling a mouthful of smoke, Jonas tapped the end of the cigar into a crystal ash tray.

"*Hola, mi persona favorita.* Is this seat taken?"

Jonas pulled out the chair next to him and gestured for Diego to sit.

"I hope you are in a better mood now," Diego said as he slipped out of his jacket and draped it overtop the chair. "You are, aren't you?"

Jonas drew several puffs from the cigar. "Mm."

"*Ay, dios mio,*" Diego replied under his breath as Zaire, Annabelle, and Kierra joined them at the table. "I don't even have to speak in Spanish around Jonas right now; he's not listening anyway."

Kierra took a seat at her cousin's other side. Fresh from her Women's Suffrage Society meeting, she still wore her green "Votes for Women" sash. "Have you heard anything more from the Magi Administration about the Time Blemishes?"

"If they'd even divulge such information," Zaire said darkly, clasping his hands together over the tabletop.

Jonas blinked and set his cigar down in the ash tray. Letting out the last of the smoke, he looked around the table into the eyes of his Magi family.

"I alerted the Administration as soon as Diego brought the matter to my attention. Additionally, I mentioned what I observed in the stars back at the turn of the year," Jonas confirmed. "I have not heard anything since."

"Well, they best get to it," Annabelle admonished, reaching over to draw Diego into a half embrace. "I don't want my poor little Diego dear caught up in another one of those traps."

"*Mamá*," Diego groaned, attempting to pull away. He cringed when she succeeded in planting a motherly kiss on his cheek.

"Neither do I," said Jonas. "I did not think something like this could even be in the cards."

"That was your first mistake," Zaire honestly remarked. "*Every* scenario is in the cards. It's just that sometimes, the dangerous ones linger in dusty corners for ages and just when you think you're in the clear, they're drawn."

At that moment, Charles plunked a pint in front of Jonas and surveyed the rest of the table.

"Blimey, this party needs some more drinks," he said jovially. "What can I get you all?"

"Tea for me, dearie," Annabelle said.

"A glass of red wine sounds nice," Kierra responded.

"Whiskey, my brotha," Zaire replied.

Charles nodded and pointed at Diego. "What's it going to be for you, Diego? Tequila?"

"Why do you *always* think that is what I am going to order?" Diego asked in exasperation and then cracked a smirk. "*Sí*, tequila."

"Right-o!" Charles said and disappeared toward the pub counter.

The entire table once again directed their attention toward Jonas.

"And yet, I am utterly bewildered."

"Oh, the great Jonas van der Campe is actually bothered by something?" Diego teased, elbowing him in the ribs.

Jonas allowed the slightest grin to transform his otherwise solemn features. "From time to time."

"What is it?" Kierra urged.

"Why now? My connection with Ezra and this increased activity from the Legerdemain Brotherhood," Jonas listed off. "Why is all of this happening now?"

"I supposed that's the question," noted Annabelle. "I wonder if the other eleven chapters have reported anything lately."

"My mother told me earlier today she received a letter from a friend of hers in the Salem, Massachusetts Chapter," said Kierra. "In it, Greta explained they discovered the word *'Quietus'* splashed across the exterior of a church, and shortly after, it burst into flames. Apparently, the situation has rattled the whole town."

Jonas pressed his back into the leather seat and folded his arms. "The Legerdemain Brotherhood is clearly trying to get a message across. I would say it's working, but I'm confounded as to—"

Charles brought a tray of drinks to the table and dispersed them. "Drink up, my friends," he encouraged in a cheery manner. When he deposited Kierra's glass of wine, he winked. "You know my policy: Suffragettes get my vote as well as drinks on the house."

"Oh, well that is very kind of you," Kierra responded. "We appreciate your support."

"You must be very proud of your cousin," Charles said to Jonas.

"Immensely proud."

The bartender offered a quick smile at the group before returning to the counter.

Jonas waited until the pub's musician began another tune before speaking. "I'm confounded as to what is fuelling this behind the scenes."

"Do you have any ideas?" Zaire enquired.

Jonas took a gulp from his stout and heavily plunked the glass upon the table. "Nothing concrete, but I have theories."

"As do I," Diego cut in, "and it is the theory that we *really* need to forget about this and have some fun tonight."

"You know, the kid is right," Zaire agreed. "What we really need is a moment to clear our minds. It has been the strangest March on record."

"I am not a kid," Diego mumbled.

"Yes, you is," Zaire sassily remarked. "If you half my age, you is *a kid.*"

"You are *all* kids to me," Annabelle said, sipping her tea.

Jonas sighed. "And just how do you propose we 'have fun' with this burden lingering in the shadows?"

Grinning, Diego slurped the rest of his tequila, sprung from his chair, and approached the violinist in the corner. After a brief exchange, the violinist stood up, elegantly poised his bow over the instrument, and erupted into the liveliest of songs.

Diego skipped back to the table and tugged on Jonas' shirt sleeve to get him up from his seat. "I think it's half past Irish Jig o'clock."

Jonas surprised himself when a chuckle escaped his lips. "All right! All right, you got me."

Kierra and Zaire also rose to their feet and danced alongside Jonas and Diego, stepping in time to the music. While Kierra, Zaire, and Diego were graceful in their movements, Jonas swayed and bobbed in an awkward manner.

"Come on, *Mamá*!" Diego encouraged Annabelle. "Show us your moves!"

"Oh, I thought you would never ask," the elderly woman replied, joining the fun. "Heaven knows I love a good Irish drinking song."

Jonas had become so caught up in gallivanting around the pub that he abruptly collided with another body at the counter. Recovering quickly, the stout little man stared in bewilderment from behind his wire-framed spectacles, as if completely offended by the interaction.

"Oh! I'm so sorry, I didn't—" Jonas apologised but stopped short when he noticed the golden Magi pin on his jacket lapel. A silver medallion rested beside it—engraved with the Star of Bethlehem—effectively heralding his status with the Magi Administration.

The man adjusted his spectacles and cleared his throat. "Out for a bit of fun tonight, Mr. van der Campe?"

By this time, the rest of the Irish Chapter had gathered behind Jonas. He could practically feel their gazes darting between him and the newest guest in their company.

"Oh, er…"

"You are a difficult man to track down," the official said, holding out his hand in greeting. "My name is Edwin Mears, Auditor of Affairs at the Magi Administration. I do hope that I can speak with you in private?"

Jonas swallowed. He had been expecting this for some time. But now? Here?

"Certainly."

"I had better be present for this conversation as well," Diego interrupted, squaring his shoulders to appear intimidating. His small stature worked dreadfully against him. "As a representative of the Royal Irish Constabulary."

Annoyance twitched at the corner of the official's mouth before he let out a high-pitched chuckle. "Ah. Our police consultant. Mr. Montreal, am I correct?"

"No," Diego replied, standing on the balls of his feet. "It's 'Your Royal Highness Hailing from the Radiant Kingdom of Mexico.'"

Jonas snorted but immediately tried to disguise it as a cough.

"Well, whatever you go by these days, I do not need your interference," Mr. Mears stated. "This shall strictly be a private conversation between Mr. van der Campe and myself, on direct orders from the Magi Council."

"But—"

"Mr. Montreal, if you do not wish for this encounter to go permanently on Mr. van der Campe's probationary record, I would suggest you hold your tongue."

A devious grin worked its way across Diego's cheeks but a warning look from Jonas made it retreat just as quickly as whatever questionable retort he had in progress.

Mr. Mears held up his hand, suggesting the conversation had ended. "This way, if you please, Mr. van der Campe."

Sharing a concerned glance at the Irish Chapter, Jonas obliged and followed the Magi official through the corridor. After climbing steep stairs to the second level inn, Edwin Mears shoved a skeleton key into the lock and held out his arm to invite him inside.

Dust curled its wispy fingers upon the entrance into the dingy room. Thick drapes blocked out the light from the streetlamps and any residual luminance from the waning moon. Besides a bed clothed in a patchwork quilt, small table, desk, wooden chair, and a tiny washroom, the temporary living quarters were rather sparse.

Jonas tentatively sat in the chair, watching as Edwin lit the oil lamp on the rickety bedside table.

"I appreciate you taking the time to speak with me," Mr. Mears remarked after he collapsed upon the edge of the bed. The furniture quivered under his weight. "But I'm sure you could say the very same, if I'm not mistaken."

"I have been waiting for proper responses from my telegrams," said Jonas. As soon as the words left his mouth, he hoped they did not come off as too eager.

"Yes, yes. I have copies of them here." Edwin reached into his jacket's interior breast pocket and brandished a short stack of official correspondence. "I had a chance to review them as well as your case file on the train from

Constantinople. Seems like the Council was rather harsh on you for not logging three months of international travel with the Bureau."

"I believe the Council based their sentence on something else entirely."

Mr. Mears glanced up from the telegrams. "Oh?"

Curse my contemptibly honest Dutch mouth, Jonas scolded himself.

"Er—they were not fond of my romantic interest at the time."

"Nor would any governmental establishment be very fond of that, I imagine," said Edwin, an astute smile curling beneath his moustache.

Jonas hesitated before speaking, lest his words let loose anything else to betray him. "Are you my probation officer? The Administration mentioned I should expect a visit soon from whomever was assigned—"

"Oh, no, of course not," Mr. Mears responded, fixing himself a cigar. "That would be Miss Atlantis Townsend, although she is still serving with me in the Investigative Division of the Magi Gendarmerie. Surely, you can understand how thinly stretched we've been as of late."

"Ah. Yes, I understand." Jonas allowed his gaze to descend to the gnarled planks beneath the man's leather shoes. "Can you tell me what is going on? How much does the Administration know about recent happenings?"

"That is confidential," Edwin admitted, "but trust me when I say we are facing some heinous times."

"And the Legerdemain Brotherhood—"

"Have seemingly risen from their ashy graves like a phoenix," finished Mr. Mears, puffing on his cigar.

Jonas bristled at the statement.

"Our society has quite the predicament on our hands, but the Council was hoping *you* would shed some light on the situation."

Channelling all the patience he could muster, Jonas struggled to keep his eye contact steady. "Sir, if you are suggesting I'd know something because of my family's involvement with the Legerdemain, I can assure you I have not the slightest idea."

"I assumed as much," Edwin sighed. Grey clouds seeped from his lips. "When was the last time you spoke with your father?"

"Not since I was eighteen," Jonas remarked. He watched through an unfocused haze as Mr. Mears tapped ashes into a tray, the flecks fluttering to their crystal coffin like blackened snow. "Not since he told me to never come back home."

Twelve years stood between Jonas and the moment he said goodbye to Amsterdam. Twelve years since he last saw the tears of disappointment in his mother's eyes. Twelve years since his father had banished his only son from his homeland. Twelve unbearable years.

And yet, it still wasn't long enough.

Digging under his bed, Edwin withdrew a briefcase and rifled through the paperwork inside. Finally, he procured a golden envelope and opened it ever so cautiously as if it would combust at any moment.

"Do you know what this is?"

Jonas shrugged, hoping his impatience had not become evident in his mannerisms. "Something to do with my probation?"

"Precisely," Edwin remarked, placing the memorandum down on his knee. "It has come to the Magi Council's attention that you have overstepped your boundaries. You do recall receiving a letter after the Portadown train incident, do you not?"

"Yes, I received it."

"And the contents of that letter urged you not to interfere with the Newport boy as the Administration had everything under control, did it not?"

"Yes, but—"

"And yet, you interfered."

Jonas cringed at the accusatory undertone in the official's voice. "Ezra was nearly killed under the Administration's watch!" he retorted, fighting the urge to stand to his full height. Some remaining shred of caution kept him rooted in place. "If it weren't for the Irish Chapter, he would be—"

"Mr. van der Campe, the fact of the matter is this: When the Magi Council gives you direct orders, you follow them."

"Even if you know those orders are flawed?" Jonas said, challenging him with a dark glare.

Edwin Mears studied Jonas for a moment before continuing. "It has also come to their attention that a protective crystal grid was placed over Belfast Royal Academy. You are under strict directions to take it down."

Jonas could not believe his ears. "Sir, that is preposter—"

"Was it authorised by the Administration?"

"Well, no—"

"Has the proper paperwork been filed for its creation?"

"No, but—"

"Then I suggest you remove it with haste," interrupted Edwin. "Mr. van der Campe, you know the rules of our Order. Yet you are treading into perilous waters by disobeying them during your probationary period. If you continue to defy these mandates, you will have your Magi license revoked. For good."

Vibrations from his words resounded for several seconds following their release. Jonas winced under their heaviness as if he'd been struck across the face.

"Did you know they were fugitives?"

"Pardon me?"

"The Newports. Both Ibrahim and Leyla had their Magi licenses revoked a decade ago for crimes they committed while working for the Administration," Edwin stated bluntly. "But I doubt you spent much time wondering why the Administration urged you to stay out of their complicated affairs in the first place."

An electric jolt violated Jonas' heart. "So, you're saying the Administration wanted to arrest them?"

"Lord, no," Mr. Mears said with a dismissive wave of his hand. "They are not a threat. However, we *do* want to understand why the Legerdemain Brotherhood is after them, because it is not the Order of Babylon."

"No?"

"Mr. van der Campe, why would the Legerdemain want to convert two former Magi who had their connection to the Celestial Lifeforce severed?"

Severed.

Just the way the words spilled from his lips invoked a chill down Jonas' spine. In fact, the entire room fell victim to a sudden onslaught of glacial air.

Severed. The Newports had received the worst possible punishment after their licenses were rescinded. And the very sentence was not at all out of the question for himself, either. Jonas forced himself to stay calm.

"Perhaps they sought Ezra?"

Mr. Mears shook his head at the hypothesis. "I doubt it. There is no evidence the boy is even a Magus. From what our team witnessed after the Portadown incident, it seems highly unlikely."

Jonas folded his hands over his lap, tightly interlacing his fingers. "I would not rule out his abilities just yet."

"Still, I would advise you stay clear of the boy," Edwin stressed. "At least during our active investigation. And for the love of God, please follow orders as requested."

"Yes, sir."

Mr. Mears scrutinised him for another moment as he drew one last puff from his cigar. "I will admit, I find you quite fascinating, Mr. van der Campe. So intelligent, yet so bereft of common sense."

"I beg your—" Jonas began, but Edwin cut him off.

"However, the Council is willing to overlook your recent offences in exchange for your assistance."

Jonas swallowed his nerves. "Assistance?"

"Frankly, we are desperate for intel. Now that we have evidence suggesting the Brotherhood is behind the *Quietus* ploys, this is more important than ever," Edwin explained. "It's really quite simple: The Brotherhood is up to something. You have an in with them, and we intend to use it. Either you work with us to provide the intel we need, or I can arrange for a probationary hearing to review your recent charges."

Jonas shifted uncomfortably in his seat. Edwin's fierce stare blazed through his spectacles with such intensity that caused Jonas to wonder how it did not melt the very glass he peered through. The fact of the matter was not that he did not wish to help. As part of the Third Order, this was his duty, his calling. But effectively doing so would require opening old wounds Jonas was not eager to relive. The very thought of it sent pangs of dread throughout his chest.

Nevertheless, Jonas straightened his posture, looked Edwin in the eyes and spoke softly, resolutely, "What must I do?"

According to the Stars

Constantinople, 1895

The girl emerged from the ocean with strands of seaweed in her hair.

Young Ezra whirled around when ripples lapped against his back and yelped at the proximity of the sea monster.

"Yonca!" Ezra gasped. "Don't scare me!"

"You were scared?" Yonca giggled, skimming her arms over the surface of the water. "Oh, Ezra. It is only me."

The afternoon sun had ripened her cheeks and shoulders. Freckles dotted her face like stars. But every time Ezra tried to get a closer look at them, he shied away and instead, found interest in a fish that flitted around his ankles.

"You are so jumpy."

Ezra smirked and splashed sea water at her. "Well, you look like a susulu."

"Because I am a susulu," joked Yonca. She arched her back and flipped her feet like a dolphin. "We are both water signs, you know. My anne says I am a Pisces, and you are a Scorpio."

Of course, Kiraz would say something like that about him. So would Taylan. Ezra had overheard one too many conversations between his father and Taylan, mostly centred on his strong will as a six-year-old. But this remark confused him. A scorpion? Ezra was positive he was a boy and not a scorpion. He squinted back at the shore, scrutinising Kiraz as she spoke with his mother under the shade of palms. Hopefully she was not convincing her of the same thing. "I am not a scorpion."

"A Scorpio," Yonca laughed. "It's part of the Zodiac."

Ezra raised an eyebrow.

"My baba says that stars paint the skies with stories," Yonca explained. "Every person has a story in the stars."

"All right, then," Ezra responded. "What does yours say?"

Yonca sank into the ocean until her chin grazed the surface. "Well, it says I'm creative and that I love the sea." She allowed the waves to carry her for a moment and then kicked her way back to him. "And it says I am very drawn to Scorpios."

Ezra chewed on his lip. How could stars be responsible for such things? Weren't they merely lights in the night sky? Lesser beings that circled the cosmos? "It—it does?"

"According to the stars."

"That cannot be true."

Abundant wonder sprang from the depths of Yonca's hazel eyes. "If you do not understand the meaning in the simplest things—the stars, the moon, the sun—how will you ever understand the Great Unknown?"

Belfast, 1906

With the dawn of the Spring Equinox set to enchant Northern Ireland in a matter of hours, a sense of renewal had already strengthened Ezra Newport.

The grounds of Belfast Royal Academy basked beneath the mid-March sun. While Ezra had only been enrolled at the academy for two weeks, it had become a vastly different place since he met Aja Burman. The hallways seemed brighter. His tasks felt lighter. Best of all, since their last run-in, Dennis and his mates had steered clear of him in favour of picking on a couple of younger pupils. Ezra knew how fast circumstances could change, yet he decided to welcome this new chapter of serenity with open arms.

But that was the extent of it. While he appreciated Aja's support and the hospitable gestures from the Irish Chapter, they would continue to stay at arm's length. Of course, they would always be allies, but he did not belong in their world. He never would.

On one especially sunny morning, Ezra meandered across the front lawn between classes. The crisp spring air invigorated his senses as it drifted on the breeze. He spotted Aja and another student sitting underneath one of the large oaks and navigated his way around the maze of hedges to join them.

"Ezra, hi!" Aja waved as he approached. "Come sit."

Beaming at his new acquaintance, he allowed his school bag to fall to the grass before planting himself beside the two of them.

"Ezra, this is my friend Oliver Abberton," Aja said, motioning to the young man sitting next to her. "He is the other Magus I was telling you about."

"It's a pleasure," Oliver said animatedly, holding out his hand toward Ezra. "I've heard so much about you."

Ezra shook Oliver's hand. "I don't know if I should be flattered or worried," he laughed.

Oliver adjusted his circular spectacles atop his small nose. "Considering your aura is a warm, rich orange today, I wouldn't worry too much at all."

"My what?"

Aja giggled. "Oliver is a Magus with a Gift for reading people's auras."

"Every living being emits light, ranging from any colour of the spectrum," Oliver explained, "and your dominant colour today just happens to be orange. That tells me you are feeling especially self-confident and optimistic."

"Ah," Ezra answered. "Interesting."

"What's mine?" Aja asked.

"You don't have one," Oliver stated in complete seriousness. "You must be a corpse."

"And you must be a blooming idiot," Aja replied, giving Oliver a friendly push.

"So, does every Magus have a special ability?" Ezra enquired.

"Most of us do along with the other specialties that make us Magi," Aja said. "Want to see what I can do?"

Without even waiting for an answer, Aja reached her fingers toward a tiny wildflower poking out amongst the tree roots. Suddenly, the plant flourished and burgeoned until it stood a foot off the ground, its purple petals splaying outward as it faced the sun.

Ezra's jaw dropped open. He craned his head around to ensure no one else had noticed the startling event. Thankfully, no one had.

Aja laughed at his response. "Being a Virgo, an earth sign, it is only natural that my Gifts are strongly connected to the environment."

"W-wow," Ezra stammered. "That really is quite fascinating." The authentic tone of interest in his voice prompted a stirring guilt within. He swatted it away.

"Jonas thinks you are a Magus, too," said Oliver, earning a look of chagrin from Aja.

Of course he did, but Jonas was wrong. While his parents might have belonged to the secret organisation, Ezra refused to accept they had metaphysical abilities beyond the realm of understanding. After all, he had never seen them do anything out of the ordinary in his entire life. No shred of evidence—besides his mother's golden Magi pin—existed to prove their affiliations.

Magic did not run in their veins, and it sure as hell did not run through his.

Ezra clenched his jaw and diverted his sight line away from the boy. "I am *not* a Magus, and I would appreciate if you didn't bring it up again."

Aja picked at the grass beside her ankle high boots. "Sometimes, the greatest gifts we possess are the ones buried the deepest within us. It takes time, effort, and a little bit of patience to unearth them."

The look on his face must have communicated something dangerous as Aja immediately backed down.

"Well, maybe you are not a Magus, but you still have a story in the stars!" Aja sifted through her schoolbag and procured a notebook, a leather-bound tome, and a fountain pen, arranging them in her lap.

Story in the stars? Why did that sound so familiar...

"Oh, don't bother poor Ezra with your astrological obsession," Oliver insisted.

She glared at him over the top of her book. "Hush, Little One."

"Aja," Oliver groaned, shaking his head. "I'm turning fifteen in May."

"You're still the youngest Magus in the local chapter, which makes you a *Baby* Magus."

"Ugh, please do not repeat that," Oliver remarked, turning pink in the face.

Their humorous exchange sparked Ezra's mouth into a grin.

"Speaking of birthdays," Aja remembered. She flipped through the pages of her notebook until she came to a fresh sheet. "The stars' story. I have you pegged as a Scorpio. Are you a Scorpio, Ezra?"

Of course. Yonca had told him the very same all those years ago.

"Er, yeah," he answered. "My birthday is October 31, 1888."

Aja smiled and scribbled a note. "I am just over a month older than you, by the way."

"Careful, Ezra," Oliver said. "She won't ever let you hear the end of it."

"Time and place of birth?"

"Constantinople. I think I remember my mother telling me I was born around three in the morning."

Aja nimbly leafed through the pages of her book. Her fingertip explored the tables of fine print while she made notations as she went about her research.

"What are you doing?"

"Compiling your natal chart," Aja simply answered. "Using the tables published in the *Ephemerides*, I can track the positions of the planets across the sky as they were at the exact moment of your birth. That positioning helps me unravel more about who you are as a person."

Ezra raised an eyebrow.

"Just wait until you hear how accurate your chart is," Aja noted with a sly grin.

Ezra watched as she drew a circle and divided it into twelve equal sections. Moving back and forth between the book and her notebook, she scratched out unfamiliar symbols around the circle as well as within the various slices. She drew straight lines between select symbols, creating a web of unexplained confusion in the centre of the diagram.

"Hmm, while your sun sign is Scorpio, your chart ruler is actually Virgo," Aja said matter-of-factly. "It's your ascendant."

Ezra stared at her.

"That means that you tend to favour order and control, with quite the dedicated work ethic," Aja responded. "You also have Mars in your fourth house, which illustrates your need for stability and security. But the moon in your twelfth house shows you favour solitude and don't make friends easily."

Okay. Definitely accurate.

"Uranus in your first house suggests you either have strong individuality or you are unstable and deceptive in nature," she continued. "But—oh! Here's an interesting bit: Neptune in your ninth house says you are open to mysticism, so perhaps that's a good sign you'll come to embrace the ways of the Magi. Now, your second house…"

Every syllable tumbling from Aja's mouth sounded more peculiar the longer she spoke. Her words intertwined with Yonca's, building upon the foundations of conversation at the beach.

"If you do not understand the meaning in the simplest things—the stars, the moon, the sun—how will you ever understand the Great Unknown?"

The Greatest Unknown had submerged Ezra in murky train horns, screaming smokestacks, and fiery blasts. The repercussions had done more than kill his mother and prompt the disappearance of his father. It had uprooted his entire world.

While he still had doubts about his parents' allegiances, perhaps meeting the Irish Chapter of the Third Order of the Magi had been a blessing in disguise. The more he could understand about them—their society, their abilities, their enemies—the better his chances of figuring out where his father might have disappeared. He might not have belonged in their world, but he needed them to reconstruct his.

With a renewed sense of purpose, Ezra leaned forward in interest, resting his head on his hand as he listened to Aja detail who he was according to the stars.

DOOMSDAY CONSULTATION

Legerdemain Brotherhood Headquarters, London, 1889

Diederik van der Campe had the uncanny ability to bewitch people with nothing but words.

From the local parish priest to the constable patrolling Herenstraat, Jonas' silver-tongued father could talk his way out of murder. As the newly elected leader of the Legerdemain Brotherhood, no one would dare stand against him.

Of course, smooth talking was not his only Gift when it came to supernatural abilities. Diederik's excellence in eidetic memory allowed him to remember almost anything he had ever seen or heard with incredible precision. Jonas would often watch in utter bemusement during his father's Division meetings as the man astonished his fellow Legerdemain with his recollections.

"Ah, yes. Paris. I've only graced the city once—this year, actually—during the grand opening of the Eiffel Tower. But ask me about any street, and I'll tell you about every shop along the way," Diederik would say with a wink and a raise of his glass, almost as if he were toasting himself. "Put me to the challenge, and I shall prove it to you."

His father's unapologetic ways as a braggart would prompt much scorn from Jonas' mother. Also Gifted in the ways of the Celestial Lifeforce, Sterre van der Campe kept her abilities contained to the home. Mostly, she limited her talent for psychic navigation to tracking her only son throughout Amsterdam, ensuring he wouldn't stray too far. Or—to both Mr. and Mrs. van der Campe's dismay—meet up with Felix, the Magus boy with whom he was completely infatuated.

To avoid times like these, Diederik would often bring fourteen-year-old Jonas with him to the underground facilities serving as the headquarters to the Legerdemain Brotherhood. Sheltered from the dreary London rain, the tunnels gave way to expansive rooms of alabaster and intricate stonework. Vines laced with emeralds traversed across stone bridges, and silver lanterns snaked their way throughout the corridors.

Certainly, the tunnels were far-reaching, but Jonas had no idea the extent of their grasp. According to fragments of conversation overheard before Assembly meetings, the tunnels' network extended to the catacombs of Paris, the Edinburgh Vaults, and even the Giza Plateau. No matter the validity, Jonas used every scrap of information to piece together rough maps of the Legerdemain World. What else was there to do whilst waiting for his father to finish with whatever it was a consul did?

On one particularly mundane morning, Jonas lounged on the marble floor, staring up at the high ceilings of the foyer. His folded hands rested against his belly while his eyes traced the curvature of the elegant designs.

Why would they put such bloody effort into a ceiling? he thought for what seemed like the millionth time. *Are they purposefully trying to make people stumble about like lunatics?*

Jonas had a feeling the architects might have been intoxicated. That, or they had a strange compulsion to make sober people act like fools.

"What are you doing?"

Jonas bolted into an upright position and smiled when he recognized Edison Bellinor standing at his feet. Also fourteen years of age, Edison shared yet another commonality with him: His father, Symon, served the Brotherhood as Consul Diederik's second-in-command. Whatever business Diederik had on his schedule, Symon was typically required to attend, meaning Jonas and Edison often found themselves at the mercy of whatever fun they could conjure within the Consulate's walls. Though, between the two of them, adventures in the underground realm were never sparse in the hours waiting for their parents.

"Admiring the ceilings again?" Edison enquired, extending his hand to help Jonas to his feet. "You know they change patterns, right?"

"I believe that is hearsay," Jonas replied. He dusted off his trousers, though not a trace of dirt existed. "They have not changed the entire time I've been staring at them."

Edison smirked and elbowed him in the ribs. "Yes, because you are distracted."

"By what?"

"By whom, more like."

Jonas flushed and turned away, hoping Edison did not catch the panic in his eyes. "Erm—I have no idea who—"

"Don't be daft. I overheard what Consul van der Campe told my father," Edison chuckled. "You've been possessed by a Magus named Felix."

"Shut your mouth," Jonas grumbled, tapping the toe of his shoe on a vine-strewn pillar as they passed. "Honestly. I don't want him to get in trouble."

Edison allowed their conversation's resonance to fade before continuing. "Associating with their kind is forbidden."

He was not wrong. By all accounts, Jonas should not have even entertained the prospect of a friendship with Felix. Yet, he couldn't imagine a world without him. Jonas understood their affiliations differed—both their families rivalled each other in everything from politics to magic—but Jonas accepted Felix, nonetheless. And he, him. Jonas just held out for the hope that one day, Felix would see eye to eye with him regarding the ways of the Brotherhood. As brazen and ill-advised as they were, the Magi still saw the Legerdemain as barbarians for amplifying the Universe's power for greater opportunities. What was so wrong with that?

"You know, we used to be part of the Third Order, Ed."

"To each their own. Besides, I could care less what you do. I am only repeating what I hear my father say, though every word seems to irritate me as of late. Especially talks of training."

Jonas stopped to study his friend, as if trying to look beyond his exterior. "You *are* going to train with the Legerdemain, aren't you?"

Edison shook his head.

"You want to be part of the Third Order?!" Jonas cringed when his exclamation ricocheted throughout the corridor and came back at him like a boomerang.

"No, I want to be an archaeologist."

"Oh," Jonas remarked, in lower tones this time. "I suppose that's respectable."

"Not according to my father," Edison divulged. "He always tells me to 'take your choice, you have one option.' I suppose being the consul's son, you don't have much of a choice, either."

"Father and I have a deal," Jonas sighed as they passed vividly painted canvases decorating the stone walls. He paused to admire the colourful spectrums of light cascading over the two-dimensional Etemenanki ziggurat of Babylon. "As long as I go through with my training to become part of the Legerdemain Brotherhood, he promised the Dark Watchers will stay clear of Felix and his family. So that's what I'm going to do." While strength rang with every consonant, an uneasiness darkened Jonas' heart. Yes, it was bribery, but he was desperate.

"You care about him that much?"

Jonas nodded.

His friend simply smiled and patted him on the shoulder. "I should not be surprised. You've always had a heart of gold."

"And you've always had a heart of stone," Jonas said, laughing as Edison took a friendly swipe at him. "Sodalite and agates and—oh! What's that relatively recent one? Hiddenite?"

"Yeah, you poke fun now," Edison remarked, an air of exuberance in his voice. "Wait until I'm a famous scientist with a rock named after me."

"Edisonite?"

"You clown!" Edison aimed another light punch in Jonas' direction, which he easily deflected.

"Anyway, I am dreadfully bored," Edison complained once their humour faded. "What do our fathers even do in Legerdemain Assembly meetings?"

Jonas flashed a mischievous grin at Edison Bellinor. "Well, there's only one way to find out."

In less than a quarter hour, Jonas and Edison had wormed their way into the supposedly impenetrable Assembly Hall.

Reserved for large gatherings and official Legerdemain business, the massive room spanned the length of a rugby pitch. While Jonas expected the auditorium to be reminiscent of the Roman Colosseum, it instead resembled a grand opera house. Multiple rows of seating ascended to daring heights. Three decks of balconies embraced the expanse, clothed in swirls of red velvet curtains. Banners decorated with ancient runes cascaded toward the marble stage, fluttering lightly in a phantom breeze.

Every seat—*there had to be thousands*—contained a member of the Legerdemain Assemblies. While Jonas was well aware the assemblies contained three divisions—the Assembly of Justice, Acquirement, and Quotidian Relations—he knew very little of their actual significance. Every humdrum thing his father said went in one ear and conveniently out the other. But now—

Jonas gulped.

Now the voice of Diederik van der Campe carried into the furthest reaches of his audience, lofty and resilient. Each intonation rang with terror and wonder all at the same time. People listened, leaning forward in their seats. Waiting on bated breath, practically salivating for the next word.

The assemblies revered him. Jonas feared him.

But the transcendent focal point of the space had nothing to do with the construction of the hall or the voice of Consul Diederik van der Campe.

Like a blazing furnace fuelled by eternal flame, a massive pyramid hovered above the stage. The frightening object rotated on an invisible axis, framed by gold. Inside, an emerald eye blinked out at the crowd through wisps of smoke.

"What do you suppose that does?" Edison whispered, transfixed.

Jonas merely shrugged.

Perched atop a catwalk spanning the width of the proscenium, both boys laid flat against the iron grates, surveying the scene below. Jonas' focus eventually drifted from the life-size Legerdemain symbol to his father. Consul Diederik paced the stage, leaning into his ornate cane. Though he walked with a slight limp from a previous carriage accident, his gait exuded vitality, never weakness. Symon stood only metres behind, furiously jotting down notes in a small book.

"The Assembly of Justice recommends a revision of the Dark Watcher Program to enhance our current forces," the Leader of the Legerdemain said, striding back to his podium to refer to a stack of documents. "Of the changes proposed, one of them is to craft our Watchers with the ability to use acts of magic for short timeframes. This would allow our bounty hunters to conjure serpents, birds of prey, and other related items to help them effectively hunt down their targets. We shall put this to a vote in this afternoon's session."

Jonas looked over his shoulder to Edison, who yawned and mouthed the word "boring."

"Also on the agenda for the Assembly of Justice: a request to send a team of Dark Watchers to Lalibela, Ethiopia where a large Chapter of Magi are practicing. Deputy Consul Symon Bellinor and I have formally approved this measure."

"Ugh. Political stuff makes me want to vomit," Edison sighed, tugging on Jonas' shirt sleeve. "Let's go."

"Wait," Jonas insisted. A small, crooked smile sparked his eyes into life. "I want to try something."

Edison watched in curiosity as Jonas cracked his knuckles and stretched out his fingers. He did not know exactly what compelled him to do it; perhaps it was retribution for all the wrongs his father had committed against him. Whatever the cause, his current preoccupation ignited like kerosene. With the meticulous discipline of an apprentice, Jonas withdrew his sunstone wand from his pocket, placed it on the catwalk, and cupped his hands over it. Warmth trickled down his spine and emanated through his fingers. At his command, a sphere of energy sparked into life. He chewed on his lip, concentrating while he moulded the fiery orb into the shape of a palm-sized phoenix.

Thoroughly impressed, Edison applauded.

An excitable ardour bubbled within him as Jonas blew on the firebird. The nebulous creature doubled, tripled, quadrupled in size until its wingspan had grown to at least four metres in length.

That's when he set the phoenix free.

Shouts of alarm circled the Assembly Hall while a palpable trepidation followed in its wake. Jonas' eyes traced the flight pattern of his creation as it swooped, swerved, and frolicked above the Brotherhood.

"Nice one, Jo!" Edison commended him. "Look at that thing go!"

Jonas beamed at his friend, but when he returned his attention to the creature, his eyes grew wide with panic.

All at once, chaos erupted.

The phoenix grazed the long banners hanging from the ceiling and curtains along the box seats, sending fiery fingers crawling over the cloth. Assembly members leapt over chairs and fought their way through the mass exodus streaming toward the exits. Perturbed by the now flaming décor, the enormous eye within the pyramid flitted across the scene in the utmost horror.

"JONAS!"

Consul van der Campe stormed across the stage, glaring up at them through the holes in the catwalk. Symon followed and shielded his eyes to avoid the unforgiving flood lights.

"Go!" Jonas prompted Edison. The two scurried as fast as their hands and knees would take them, but their efforts were no match for Diederik. Within seconds, the consul conjured a radiant lasso from his crystal-topped cane. The tendril of magic wrapped around Jonas' ankle, making it impossible to escape.

"Go, now!" Jonas yelped again, not wanting Edison caught up in whatever punishment he was about to endure. At first, it looked as if his friend wished to stay and attempt to loosen the hold of the magical rope now edging him off the catwalk. But with one look into Jonas' desperate eyes, Edison swiftly made his way to the crevice from which they entered.

Jonas winced as he lost his grip and collided with the dense stage floor.

Consul Diederik yanked Jonas up by the shirt collar and hauled him backstage, away from any wandering eyes still waiting for escape. "Symon! Put out the flames," barked his father. "You can secure your son later."

"Yes, sir."

With Symon aptly distracted, Diederik shoved Jonas against the wall and pressed his cane against his neck. Jonas struggled for freedom.

"What the DEVIL were you thinking?!" Diederik yelled, his hot breath assaulting his face. "What gave you the gall to do something like that?"

"I-I-I'm sorry!" Jonas stammered. His shoes grazed the ground as he flailed for release. "It was a-a lapse of j-judgement!"

Unfortunately, no matter the words of explanation, the wrath of Diederik van der Campe could not be doused. In one wretched motion, Diederik struck Jonas across the face with his cane, causing him to stumble back to the floor.

Lightning shattered his nerves. Pain trickled from his nostrils. He sniffed and summoned what strength remained to hold back tears.

"Get up!" his father commanded. "Right now!"

Jonas' face screwed up in emotion.

"NOW."

Rising to his feet, Jonas stood broken before his father, refusing to make eye contact as he choked for air.

"How DARE you."

It was a threat, not a question.

Jonas gulped shallow breaths. "I said I'm—"

"No," Diederik fumed, striking Jonas again, "because if you were truly sorry, you would not be whimpering like a coward in my presence."

Jonas attempted escape, but his father wrenched him back.

"Stop crying this instant and answer me," he hissed, pinching Jonas' jaw between his thumb and index finger. "What dastardly thing possessed you to *set fire* to our facility?"

Sobs decimated any shred of dignity left. "I—it was an accident," Jonas wept. "I didn't m-mean to—"

Enraged, Diederik shoved him to the floor and slammed his shoe into his gut.

Coughing and sputtering words of apology, Jonas curled his knees to his chest, making himself as small as possible. He squeezed his eyelids together, wishing he had the Gift to disappear. Like a waif in the wind.

His father's presence hovered over him, a vulture about to tear into flesh.

"You are nothing but a disappointment," he said so quietly, Jonas could not be sure if the words were spoken or imagined. "So much for wishing on Stars Everlasting to grant me an exceptional son. I should have known that even the stars fall. How unfortunate the Universe cursed me with you."

That night on the ferry to Amsterdam, Jonas cried himself to sleep, wishing in the fleeting moments of consciousness that Felix was there to hold his shaking hands.

London, 1906

Shielding himself from the frigid rain, Jonas made his way through the quaint urban streets under the protection of his long coat and fedora. Every step fell with purpose as he approached the British Museum. While the fast-paced nature of the city's thoroughfares had never been a favourite of his, tonight, none of that mattered.

Tonight, he did exactly what the Magi Administration expected of him. No matter the ungodly amount of disquietude infiltrating his soul.

As the hour hand of his pocket watch edged closer to midnight, the museum had long since closed its gates to visitors, but Jonas was not here to meander through the exhibits like an average Quotidian. He was here to pay Edison Bellinor a visit.

From the moment Mr. Mears had dictated the orders of the Council, Jonas knew he was not about to waltz directly into the Legerdemain Consulate. Besides the altogether obvious fact he'd be apprehended on the spot, he wasn't sure his heart would be able to withstand such a feat in the first place. Not while his father lived and reigned as consul.

While the doors to the Brotherhood might have been off limits, Edison provided the smallest peephole into his former world. Years had come and gone since Jonas had last received a letter from his childhood friend, and it had been even longer still since he had last spoken to him face-to-face. Through their letters, Jonas deduced Edison had remained truthful to his word, refusing to follow the ways of the Legerdemain Brotherhood or the ways of the Third Order. Instead, he embraced blissful neutrality, despite the heavy persuasion from Symon Bellinor.

Most importantly, Edison had secured his dream job in archaeology at the British Museum. To assist Jonas in his quest, the Administration had secretly gained access to Edison's work schedule, providing Jonas with just the information he needed to swoop in, speak with him, and return to Belfast with the intel the Council requested.

If trouble did not seep like odorous gasses from the *real* London underground first.

Let's hope it does not come to that, Jonas thought.

He crept around the corner to Montague Street, surveying his surroundings to ensure unfriendly eyes had not followed. Approaching the iron gate that guarded the museum's perimeter, Jonas channelled energy into his quartz wand and clunked it against the metal. The bars heated to a glowing orange and parted obediently, leaving just enough of a gap for him to slip through.

Once inside the confines of the museum, Jonas removed his hat and surveyed his dark surroundings.

"The Library of the Royal Anthropology Institute. First floor beneath ground level," he whispered to himself. That was where the Administration said Edison would be waiting.

His steps echoed across the polished floors of Central Hall and reverberated off the decorative tile on the high ceilings. Hasty yet reticent, Jonas navigated to the lower level, finally locating the library and associated study rooms.

Save for a framed portrait here and there, and an impressive amount of shelving for countless books, the library appeared rather humble despite the opulent knowledge it held. While most lights were dimmed, an ornamental tabletop lamp emitted a golden glow from the centre of the space. The lamp's radiant circumference spilled over several open tomes, duster brushes, and ancient tablets atop cushions.

Jonas spotted Edison examining a clay tablet through an illuminated magnifying lens attached to a contraption around his head.

"I always knew you'd end up playing with rocks for a living."

The man jumped and clutched the tablet to his chest. When he turned and realised Jonas stood in the doorway, he set down the artifact to start his approach. "And I always knew I would have a best friend who would disappear into the folds of time, only to spring back into existence like a phoenix in the night."

The two friends embraced. Edison heartily patted him on the back.

"Jonas, it is *so* good to see you!"

"Likewise," Jonas said, pulling back to properly examine him. While Edison now sported a thick beard and spectacles, the boyish charm he remembered from years past still exuded from his aura. "Well, look at you now, Edison Bellinor! When was the last time I saw you in person? 1893?"

"Whatever the year, it was literally last century," Edison chuckled. The light on his headpiece bobbled about as he returned to his workstation. "Though, I must admit your presence is a surprise. What brings you to London at such an outrageous hour?"

Jonas took a seat across the table and examined the array of tablets, analysing the curious marks in the centuries-old clay. "Ancient Sumerian?" he asked, aptly deflecting the question.

Edison dusted off a portion of the fragile artifact with a brush. "Indeed. Written in cuneiform. This one is from the Neo-Babylonian period."

"Mm."

"But you're not here to talk about ancient artifacts," Edison concluded.

"To be quite honest, I don't know why I am here."

Edison delicately placed the tablet on a padded pedestal and adjusted his magnifying glass headpiece so he could read Jonas' intentions. "Is everything all right?"

A discernible heaviness yanked Jonas' sight toward the tabletop. He studied the wandering grains of the wood before swallowing the curious sensation in his throat. "I—er—I need to know something."

"Go on. I am listening."

Jonas folded his hands on the table's surface, running his thumb back and forth over the side of his other hand. "Along with my colleagues at the Magi Administration, I am concerned the Legerdemain Brotherhood is up to something dangerous."

Clearing his throat, Edison abandoned his work and sunk into the chair across from Jonas. "When have they ever *not* been up to something dangerous? After all, didn't that Labynetus fellow dedicate his life to seeking eternal life for King Nebuchadnezzar?"

The beginning of a smile lifted Jonas' demeanour. "So they say."

"Well, I'll have you know that I've completely removed myself from that life," Edison said, a razor-sharp honesty in his remark. "I hardly speak to my father, besides the arbitrary dinner once in a blue moon to satisfy his need to stay updated on his grandchild."

Jonas met his eyes. "Grandchild?"

"Margaret is pregnant with our firstborn," Edison detailed with a grin. "Six months along now."

"Congratulations, old chap!" Jonas exclaimed, unable to contain his excitement. "I knew it was only a matter of time."

"Yes, it has been quite the whirlwind," Edison said. "I cannot tell you how exciting it is to know I'm finally going to be a father."

"You will make a great one."

"And perhaps someday, you will, too," Edison replied. "That is, if you ever settle down and get married."

Jonas arched an eyebrow. "Edison."

"You know I only want you to be happy," his friend said, busying himself with the duster brush once more.

"And marriage is the ultimate path to happiness?"

Edison glanced down at his work and fell into silence.

"If romance has taught me one thing, it is that no matter how much effort you put into making it last, it is as fleeting as time itself." Jonas leaned back in the stiff wooden chair and crossed his arms. "Not to mention everyone wants to stick their nose and opinions in it when the matter is none of their concern."

"Apologies. My intention was not to upset you," Edison answered quietly.

"You do not need to apologise," Jonas responded. "I sincerely appreciate your consideration, but you do not need to worry about my personal affairs."

Edison studied him before returning to the tablet. "So, tell me, after all these years, why are you concerned about the Legerdemain? If memory serves me correctly, they have been rather quiet."

"Times are changing." Reaching inside of his coat, Jonas retrieved a folded newspaper and pushed it across the table toward Edison. "I am concerned the Brotherhood is trying to send the Magi a message."

Edison's eyes surveyed Jonas' anxious features before turning toward the front page of the *Belfast Evening Telegraph*. He frowned while scanning the feature article. "*Quietus*. Good Lord, this is ghastly. And this happened in Belfast?"

"Near Belfast, yes, but it is happening all over the world without signs of ceasing." Jonas retrieved the newspaper. "If you know anything, Edison, anything at all...I need to hear it."

"I—I'm not at liberty to say."

Jonas eyed him. "So, they *are* coordinating something?"

Sighing, Edison set down his tools and pushed the spectacles further up the bridge of his nose. Folding his arms as if debating some internal argument with himself, he finally leaned forward into the lamplight. "There's been a stalemate in the Consulate."

Of course. Legerdemain election season. Jonas scolded himself for not remembering sooner. No wonder he had felt disorder in the stars; ambitions and temperaments were running at all-time highs. "A stalemate? That never happens."

"There's a first time for everything," Edison replied with a shrug. "Our fathers were up for re-election. Though this time, they had stiff competition from an up-and-coming Legerdemain duo promising to make a bigger impact than Consul Diederik has done in all his sixteen years in office. On one side, you have the loyalists, who believe in the vision the consul has for bringing their society into a new age. On the other, you have the next generation of the Brotherhood rallying for radical change. Both wanted to solidify their campaign promises and flaunt their leadership in a new and daring way. For the first time ever, the elections resulted in a tie."

Jonas never once diverted his gaze from his friend. If he had been terrified before, he had become even more horrified in the last minute. Stalemates were not simple deadlocks. They were competitions.

"You know what comes next."

"Unfortunately," Jonas responded. "To gain their seats as head of the Consulate, each party partakes in a Duel of Contingency. A display of power."

"I believe you may be witnessing the displays of power from our fathers' opponents," Edison explained, gesturing toward the newspaper.

"And what is it Diederik and Symon are doing for their act?" Jonas grimaced, afraid of the answer.

Agitated, Edison shifted in his seat. "Seeking the Tablet of Destinies."

"Er—the what?"

"The Tablet of Destinies," Edison repeated. "From Babylonian legend."

"I'm sorry, I don't follow," Jonas admitted. "Is that the same cuneiform tablet mentioned in the papers last month?"

Edison pursed his lips as if contemplating whether Jonas was worthy of the words he was about to speak. After a dreadfully long moment—too long for Jonas' liking—he relented. "No, it is a different one. The ancient Mesopotamian creation story *Enuma Elish* mentions the Tablet of Destinies. Legend says when the god Marduk defeated Quingu, he claimed the Tablet of Destinies from him, thus legitimising his rise to power. To put it simply, anyone who possesses the artifact has the power of a god. And to my father and the consul, it is a sure-fire way to make sure they hold their positions of power."

Jonas nodded as he soaked in the information. "And what happened to the Tablet?"

"It is a symbolic mechanism in a creation myth, not actual fact," Edison reinforced. "Allegorical. Nothing more."

"Yet, *these* tablets exist," Jonas pointed out, his eyes scanning the relics in front of him. "Myths are always rooted in some sort of truth."

"Look, I'll tell you the same thing I told my father: The Tablet of Destinies is like the Ark of the Covenant; even if it is real, it will be impossible to find." He moved his hands in wide gestures as if to enunciate his point even further. "They are on a wild goose chase leading to nothing but disappointment and failure. They'll be forced to concede."

Would that be such a bad thing?

As soon as the thought crossed his mind, a pang of dread gripped his stomach. No matter who claimed victory over the Legerdemain Consulate, one thing was inherently clear: The Legerdemain Brotherhood intended on stealing back a world they thought they'd lost. And the Magi were caught in the middle. If something was not done soon, Jonas feared the worst, be it further violence against Quotidians or the rise of unstoppable power in the hands of his father.

Drained of hope, Jonas placed his elbows on the table and rested his chin against his interlaced fingers. As he looked over top of them at Edison, apprehension swam in his eyes. He forced himself to draw in a deep, calming breath and let it out ever so slowly, but it failed to restore his inner peace.

"I wouldn't be too troubled by it, Jonas," Edison advised. "Once Consul Diederik and my father realise the Tablet of Destinies does not exist, life will fall back into complacency once again."

Maintaining his posture, Jonas closed his eyes as the proverbial weight of the world crashed over his shoulders. "But at what cost?"

Time was ticking for humanity and in Jonas' mind, nothing could slow the ever-advancing minute hand of doomsday.

ℙERDITION IN ႧLYSIUM

A blinding light forced Ezra to squeeze his eyelids shut.

"That's it, young'un. Focus, now!"

"I *am* focusing," Oliver answered Zaire as he cupped his hands around a stubborn mass of energy. The white light pulsed and throbbed as the boy attempted to control its form. "It's just too bloody strong!"

Ezra exchanged a curious glance with Aja, who had perched next to him on the couch of the Irish Chapter's cellar hideout.

"Usually, Quotidians aren't allowed in Elysium at all," she had said on their way over after school. "It's just for Magi. But Jonas said you were always welcome, due to your parents' affiliations."

According to Aja, Jonas had been called away to London for business, so Zaire would conduct their weekend Magi training. Ezra hardly knew anything about the Irish Chapter, but it did not take long before he was introduced to Zaire's flavourful background as an illusionist in New Orleans. The Magus lost no time in showing off his levitation skills and incredible sleight of hand that left Ezra speechless.

"Quite the spectacle, isn't it, dear?" asked Annabelle. She sat in the armchair by the fireplace, concentrating on her knitting.

Ezra smiled, refusing to take his attention away from the training session. "It's baffling, is what it is."

The older woman chuckled. "Oh, honey. Even after all these years as a Magus, the ways of the Universe are still bewildering."

"Are *you* controlling the Lifeforce or is the *Lifeforce* controlling you?" asked Zaire as he circled around Oliver in observation. "The crystal is your conduit, but *you* are ultimately the one who decides how the energy acts once it's brought to earth."

"I still don't understand what the Celestial Lifeforce is," Ezra mentioned to Aja.

"It's the glue of the Universe," Aja answered in all seriousness. "It fuels the stars. In its purest form, it's just a tiny atom. But, when channelled consciously through a crystal or stone, it sparks into brilliant life, creating the energy you see Oliver failing to control."

Ezra snickered.

"It's really a sodding nightmare," Oliver muttered.

Aja made a show of rolling her eyes at her fellow apprentice's remark.

"Oliver, mind your language," Annabelle scolded him in a motherly tone.

"What colour aura do I have right now?"

The energy in Oliver's hands faltered as he stared at Zaire in confusion. "What does that have to do with anything?"

"Auras are perfect indicators of how to strategise your attack," Zaire answered, holding out his hands defensively in front of him. "What aura do I have, kid?"

"You-you're readying for a fight! It's bright scarlet!" Oliver replied, trying his hardest to hold on to the energy. "But the colour is most saturated around your neck and shoulders."

"Excellent!" Zaire praised as he continued to circle the apprentice like a hawk. "My plan was to attack with my upper body, which is why the colours were strongest in that area. That information can help you decide where to block."

Zaire conjured a beam of energy and aimed it toward Oliver, who aptly deflected it with his own energy field.

"Nice work, Little One!"

"Aja! I'm not little," Oliver said, his voice cracking in embarrassment. "Like I keep telling you, I'm going to be fifteen in two months."

"You are still a baby," Aja whispered to herself. "A little Gemini baby."

"That's my boy!" Annabelle exclaimed, lifting her gaze from her needles. "But don't go too lightly on him, Oliver. Zaire needs a good wallop after he broke my bottle of lavender the other day."

"It was an accident," Zaire insisted.

"Ah, an accident," Annabelle murmured with a grin. "I'll bet the Boston Tea Party was an accident, too, right?"

Zaire shrieked with laughter. "Ma, you is kooky."

Ezra hugged his knees to his chest. "Do you all learn this sort of thing to fight off Dark Watchers?"

"Dark Watchers and the Legerdemain Brotherhood," Aja rattled off.

"The Legerdemain Brotherhood?" Ezra asked, his mind convoluted with detail. *Just how intricate was the Magi's world?* "Who are they?"

His magical company fell into uneasy stillness. Their postures stiffened, eyes darting about the room as they silently communicated their nervousness.

"Er—am I not supposed to talk about them?" Ezra asked, awkwardly rubbing the back of his neck. "Sorry, I—"

"No, sweetheart, you are just fine," Annabelle cut in, sparing him from the apology. "I am still surprised your parents never mentioned any of this to you."

"So am I," Ezra mumbled.

"Magi have a complicated past with the Legerdemain Brotherhood," said the elderly woman. "To put it simply, they are the orchestrators of the attack on you and your family."

"So, *they're* the sorcerers," Ezra noted, mostly to himself.

"Sorcerers, traitors, nothing but dirty rotten scoundrels," Zaire growled, crossing his arms as he leaned against the wall. "They done killed my wife and kids five years ago back in the States. I obviously ain't very fond of a society who sees me and my family as someone to snuff out."

Ezra grimaced. "I am really sorry. That is horrible."

"They are horrible people," Oliver confirmed, crossing his arms over his slim middle.

Aja nodded, her eyes wide with agreement.

Ezra frowned. "Why are they so preoccupied with killing people?"

"Well, Jonas would tell you that the Legerdemain Brotherhood sees it a different way," Oliver responded. "To them, killing is justified under the new laws implemented in 560 B.C. during King Nebuchadnezzar's reign. That's when the Order of Babylon came about."

Just hearing the phrase spoken aloud made Ezra cringe. Gulping, he nodded in acknowledgement.

"Jonas says ever since then, the Brotherhood has focused on assisting governments and police establishments across the world to pursue criminals and other dangerous people who require a death sentence," Aja said. "The Celestial Lifeforce does not allow for killing with magical powers, so they use sorcerous magic to kill instead. That's how they get around the limitations."

"And the Dark Watchers help them with that?" Ezra concluded.

"They specifically send their Dark Watchers after Magi," Annabelle clarified, her needles clinking against each other. "While sorcery allows the Legerdemain to kill non-magical people, they still cannot kill Magi lest they risk their abilities being drained. That's why they send their bounty hunters to do the work for them."

"I see," said Ezra. "Just how involved are the Legerdemain with world governments now?"

"I would have hoped you were paying attention in history class, Mr. Newport," came the pleasant voice of Miss Kierra McLarney as she waltzed in through the entrance of Elysium. She winked at him before setting her bag upon a table and approached the stove to begin making tea. "Medieval restrictions on dark magic, rampant witch trials, and even the Witchcraft Act of 1735—still in place in the United Kingdom today, mind you—forbid the use of sorcery. Because of this, the Legerdemain Brotherhood hasn't had the opportunities that Magi have, since our methods meet the current standard of governments and the Church."

By this point, Ezra's mind was spiralling in infinite circles, but he was not about to stop gleaning what information he could about their world. Every insight drew him closer to his parents, closer to the lives they led and why they chose the ways of the Magi in the first place. "And what exactly makes your magic different than theirs?"

Digging for her crystal pendant beneath her uniform, Aja drew out the quartz and held it out for him to see. "How familiar are you with chakras?"

"Er—not much, I guess," Ezra admitted.

She grinned, a mischievous sparkle in her eyes as she bounded from the couch. "Zaire, may I borrow your cards for a moment?"

"Sure thing," he replied in a smooth voice. He levitated his deck and allowed it to fall into her palm.

Aja sifted through the pile and removed seven cards, each representing one of the colours of the rainbow. She held up a violet one and, at first, looked like she was going to hand it to Oliver. Instead, she raised her eyebrows at Zaire, communicating an unspoken request. Somehow, he picked up on the gist of her enquiry and levitated the card until it rested just above Oliver's head.

"Humans have seven primary energy centres associated with the body," Aja began, a stark matter-of-factness ringing in her speech. "The first is the Crown Chakra, represented by this violet card. This is the transcendent connection every Gifted individual uses to pull the energy from the stars to the earth."

"Okay, so magic is summoned through the head. Got it," Ezra noted.

"Next up: Third Eye Chakra," Aja announced and flung an indigo card at Oliver's face. He winced in anticipation of it hitting him, but Zaire slowed its trajectory and held it over his forehead. "This chakra is associated with intuition and direction, so as the Celestial Lifeforce flows through us, it is at this point we decide the most beneficial way of using it.

"Next, we have the Throat and Heart Chakras," Aja continued. The blue card obediently hovered over Oliver's neck while the green one lingered above his chest. "The Throat Chakra is our communication centre. Our pedestal of truth. And the Heart Chakra is where love and acceptance ebb and flow. Everything we do culminates to this one point, this one central mission."

"But that's also where it ends," Miss McLarney stated as she brought a tray of teacups around to everyone. "Our magic is focused on the top four chakras. The Legerdemain Brotherhood rely on the strength of the bottom three chakras."

Aja nodded and flung a yellow card at Oliver's chest. He watched warily as it settled into position over his lower ribcage. "The Solar Plexus. Ambition and power. This chakra is used by the Legerdemain to channel the energy from the Celestial Lifeforce."

"So, they summon the Celestial Lifeforce through their lungs and not their heads?" Ezra enquired, trying to keep up.

Miss McLarney laughed. "It's a bit more complicated than that. Every month during the full moon, the Brotherhood trap magic from the Celestial Lifeforce through a ritual called 'Ascension.' They channel it the same way we do, except that they bring the magic through the body to the lowest chakra so that it is amplified by earth-based energies. They harness this artificially enhanced power within their crystals and then call it back through their Solar Plexus."

"Okay," Ezra murmured into his tea, going cross-eyed with information.

"The Sacral Chakra is another of their energy focuses, dealing with abundance and carnal pleasures," Aja carried on. She allowed Zaire to direct the orange card toward Oliver's navel. "While the last chakra, the Root Chakra, grounds the Brotherhood in their instinctive motive: Security and sense of belonging."

Oliver blanched as the red card hovered several inches below his belt buckle. "Er, maybe we shouldn't focus on the Root Chakra for too long."

Aja made a wide motion with her arms at their young friend. "I present to you: The Seven Chakras!"

Miss McLarney, Annabelle, and Zaire applauded while Aja promptly curtsied.

"Impressive," said Ezra as she joined him back on the couch.

"*Very* impressive," Miss McLarney confirmed. "I'm certain Jonas would say the same."

Oliver breathed a sigh of relief when Zaire retrieved the cards and shuffled them back into their tidy stack.

Just before Ezra had a chance to internalise what he had learned, the door to Elysium swung open again, this time revealing an exhausted young man toting a newspaper. A green Royal Irish Constabulary badge glinted on his waistcoat.

"Oh, hello, Diego," Miss McLarney greeted him cheerfully. "How was your day?"

Annoyance loomed in the dark shadows beneath his eyes. "Oh, you know, the usual: Long and obnoxious. Though not as obnoxious as it could have been since Jonas is away."

Annabelle pursed her lips. "Diego Javier, that is unnecessary."

The young man grumbled inaudible retorts as he removed his hat and raked his fingers through his curly hair. When he noticed Ezra, his attention darted to the others for explanation.

"Diego, this is Ezra Newport," said Miss McLarney, laying her hands on Ezra's shoulders from behind the couch. "He's one of my students and—"

"I know who he is," Diego cut in.

Taken aback, Ezra shrunk into the cushion. Something about this Magus deeply unsettled him, and he was not sure it was his blatant rudeness. Honestly, he had no idea whatsoever.

Aja threw an apologetic glance over her shoulder.

"What's your problem?" Zaire asked.

"None of your goddamn business."

Miss McLarney folded her arms. "Watch your tongue. That is inappropriate—"

"You know what *I* think is inappropriate?" Diego exploded, pointing at Ezra. "*He* gets to be here, and he's not even a Magus. Every time I wish to bring Stella by for a visit, all I hear is 'Another time, Diego!' 'That's not a wise idea, Diego!'"

Perturbed by the outburst, Zaire abandoned his former place against the wall. His towering stature easily overshadowed the young man. "Calm down."

Diego scowled at him.

Following Zaire's lead, Miss McLarney laid a hand on his arm. "What is wrong?"

He shrugged her off. "Don't you dare try to worm your way into my memories, Kierra! I swear to God—"

"Damn, kid. Would you stop acting like a lunatic and talk to us?" remarked Zaire.

"*¡Que te den!*"

"DIEGO JAVIER MONTREAL!" Annabelle scolded, rising from the armchair as fast as the anger in her cheeks. "That is enough! You *do not* speak to people that way!"

Her voice rang with authority, causing the entire company to freeze upon her firm rebuke. Even Ezra cast his gaze toward his shoes.

Drowning in the silence that followed, Diego shifted from foot to foot in agitated exasperation. Finally, with his fiery eyes narrowed, he slammed his newspaper to the floor. "Fine. You know what? Forget it." Without another word, he stomped off down the corridor. A door quaking in its frame shattered the dense atmosphere.

"Okay," Oliver exhaled. "That was weird."

"Yes, quite," agreed Aja.

Ezra smiled weakly. "That was weird for you, too, huh?"

"Never mind him, dear," Annabelle stated as she settled back into the armchair. "Diego has been under a lot of stress lately at the Royal Irish Constabulary."

"That's still no excuse for bad behaviour," said Miss McLarney. She gathered her hat and gloves. "Come, children. We'd best be getting back to the academy."

Trailing behind Aja and Oliver, Ezra inadvertently lost his footing on his exit and steadied himself by clutching a side table. In his path, the newspaper left in the aftermath of Diego's cyclonic tirade unfurled from its former, tightly rolled configuration. As the corners of the pages blossomed outward, *The Belfast Evening Telegraph* offered the slightest glimpse of town happenings: marriages, court cases, and progress on the construction of the new town hall. If printed type held the power to speak, most of it would have consisted of monotonous droning. All except for one seemingly insignificant section, in which the words screamed with the boundless energy of the Shahmaran:

Telegraph Exclusive: New details on the deadly Portadown Train Incident to be released in our upcoming Wednesday edition.

Conscious or subconscious, Ezra? They are not the same. So, which speaks louder?

His heart pounding a frantic rhythm, Ezra scooped up the paper and looked between Zaire and Annabelle.

"Er, would it be all right if I take this?"

"Of course, dear," Annabelle replied. "We always have several copies laying around."

Bowing his head in gratitude, Ezra dashed up the staircase to catch up with the others. No matter how many times he skimmed the sentence, disbelief paralyzed his conscious mind. But an insistent voice—originally entombed beneath fear and scepticism—pierced through the rocky barriers. His subconscious yelled with the same intensity as the print, clearer than ever before.

For the sake of his father, for the sake of his own sanity, Ezra *had* to know whatever details the forthcoming article contained.

And he wasn't waiting until Wednesday.

HAUNTED

Her image was burned in every frame of Diego's memory.

Festive strums from Tío's vihuela *intertwined with Celestina Montreal's laughter. Her brown eyes twinkled in the colourful lamplight, thick black hair framing her face as she twirled in her* Quinceañera *gown.*

"Mi hermano*!" she yelled from across the courtyard. "Come dance!"*

Chewing through an enormous bite of carne asada, Diego glanced over his shoulder at his younger sister. Happiness radiated from Celestina, a star amongst fireflies. She skipped through the throng of family members and their neighbourhood guests, followed closely by a flock of her girlfriends.

"Stop shovelling food down your throat and have some fun!" Celestina encouraged him. "Please?"

"I quite enjoy shovelling food down my throat right now," Diego mumbled with his mouth full. "I'm a growing boy."

"I think you stopped growing two years ago," Celestina joked and nudged him with her shoulder.

"Hey," Diego remarked, swallowing his food. "You're not much taller."

"I'm not eighteen."

The girls behind her giggled.

"Hush, Pequeña.*"*

Celestina grabbed hold of his wrist, urging him to join the light-hearted fun. "Come, Diego!"

"I am a terrible dancer."

"You are not, you liar!"

Diego skirted around his sister, dodging her frantic swipes to catch him. "You cannot make me! Nothing you can say or do could possibly——"

"Lucía wants to dance with you!" Celestina interrupted, folding her arms as if perturbed she had to lay it out so plainly. Even in the fading twilight, Diego could see her young friend flush in embarrassment.

"Well, in that case, let's dance!" Diego proclaimed with a grin. He reached out to take Lucía's hands and whirled her around, moving with the ever-advancing tempo.

Celestina squealed with laughter when Lucía flashed her a look.

Kaleidoscopes of colours and accelerating rhythms spun across his memories until suddenly, they were extinguished by a scream.

Then darkness. Intimidation. Pleading cries for release.

"Let her go!" a voice cried out. For a moment, Diego did not know whether the desperate words erupted from his lips or someone else's entirely. "Please let her go!"

A dark figure moved amongst the shadows, slipping out of his jacket as he towered over Diego.

"Please!" Hot tears flowed until reaching the barrier of a rough hand at his mouth. "Please don't!"

"You know the deal," a cruel voice reminded him. "Have you changed your mind?"

Trembling, Diego attempted to wrangle himself away from the body pinning him down. "N-no!"

"Well, dear boy, as I said, you know the deal."

Diego awoke in a bed soaked in sweat and tears.

Wiping the wetness around his eyes with the sleeve of his nightshirt, he rolled over on his side and clutched his pillow.

She had found her way into his dreams. Again.

He wanted to hold them so close, as if somehow the threads of the dreamworld could conjure Celestina in the flesh. Those very last moments Diego saw his younger sister alive always dissolved into dust and fell through his fingers. At least in Waking Life, his sister's kidnapper could not follow him or force him to relive those horrid memories.

With his stomach tangled in tempestuous knots, Diego rolled out from the bottom level of the bunk beds. He stepped carefully, hoping not to disturb Zaire as he ventured through the Elysium common room, up the staircase, and out into the night. There was no going back to the dream world now.

Not while *he* was watching.

Between the local crimes and terror-filled nightmares, Diego would do just about anything to clear his head. But when tequila lost its charms, another temptation seduced him. Darting across sidewalks and alleyways, he made his way uptown toward Belfast Central Library, practically on instinct. He turned the corner around a brick building and with swift agility, climbed a fire escape to the next level.

He rapped three times with the back of his knuckles over the glass of the second-floor window. Within a few moments, the pane slid upward, revealing his lover in a floral nightdress.

Stella grinned and folded her arms, leaning against the window frame. Diego's mouth went dry at how the silk hugged her curves. "Diego Javier Montreal," she said in a sultry voice. "I wondered when I'd see my favourite police consultant again."

"Stella, *mi querida*," Diego laughed as he swung his legs over the ledge. "You know I cannot stay away."

"Mmm, smart man," Stella replied. She cupped the side of his face in her palm, caressing his cheek with her thumb. "And yet, I cannot help but wonder why you look so upset tonight. Is something the matter, love?"

Diego scrunched up his nose and waved his hand in dismissal. "Nothing for you to concern yourself over."

Stella stared at him incredulously, but her eyes softened when Diego wrapped his arms around her waist and pulled her closer.

She kissed him along his jaw, her lips hovering centimetres away from his. "Oh, but I *do* worry. Chief Constable Norman said you ran into some trouble during one of your recent consultations. The whole experience sounded dreadful; you poor thing," she remarked in a seductive tone as she drew him into the flat by the collar of his nightshirt.

Diego shrugged off his coat and let it fall to the floor. "Ah, is that what he told you?"

Stella draped her arms around his neck. "And you have no idea what that does to a woman—" she pressed her lips against his, "—to hear that her beau courageously faced danger for the good of Belfast, lying injured in the Chief Constable's office—"

"*Ay, Dios mio!* I am fine!" Diego exhaled in annoyance. "You don't need to worry about me, *amada.*"

"I always will, sweetheart." Her fingers tucked a curl behind his ear.

Diego buried his face into the crook of her neck, taking in her sweet scent. Like a fresh breeze in a meadow of lilacs.

"You make me crazy, Diego," Stella exhaled as his lips travelled up her neck, along her cheek and finally met her mouth.

He kissed her deeply. Stella's presence was irresistible, a strong magnetic attraction he could not escape. She always had a way of erasing his worries, his fears, his horrific memories. Everything could be surrendered to her and in exchange, a fresh wave of pleasure renewed his broken spirit.

Seconds turned into minutes and minutes into hours as the two lovers passionately communicated without words. Faces flushed, hair tousled, and bodies tangled in a sea of bedsheets, Diego and Stella held each other so close, their heartbeats were indistinguishable.

Diego stared into the alluring green eyes of the young woman and brushed away strands of hair from her face.

Stella smiled at him and stroked his back. Her fingertips against his skin sent a pleasant warmth circulating throughout his body, a welcome replacement for earlier anxieties.

"Darling, something is bothering you; I can feel it. What's the matter?"

Diego sucked in a breath and held it, hoping the action would stave off his emotions.

"You dreamt about your sister again, didn't you?" Stella asked.

"And *him*," Diego sighed, rubbing his forehead. "What does one do when they are held against a wall? Helpless? Defenceless?"

Stella ran her hand along his cheek. "Do what you can to survive, I suppose," she answered. "Have you confided in Jonas about this?"

"No!" Diego replied a little too quickly. "No, he *cannot* know."

Stella gazed into his eyes. "Why?"

Diego rolled onto his back and stared up at the ceiling, his eyes tracing the designs of the square tiles. "It's a burden I have to bear. Alone."

"You are never alone, Diego," said Stella. Her hand rested delicately on his chest.

Diego laid his hand over top hers and squeezed it. He knew her words were earnest. They always were. But this time, the hurt within himself seemed almost irreparable.

A hurt that even sweet Stella could not fix.

DETAILS ON DEADLINE

"Is there anything I can say to convince you *not* to leave school grounds?"

Ezra did not even lift his head to acknowledge Aja's pleading statement. He could already imagine the tireless expression she wore, the one he'd come to realise frequently creased the skin around her bindi. Instead, he maintained his course, running a feather duster over the busts of former headmasters that guarded the south corridor. Dust caught the light from the late afternoon sun, sparkling like magic in his wake.

"I don't think you understand how important this is," Ezra answered. "I *need* to speak with someone at the *Telegraph*."

Ever since he had laid eyes on the newspaper in Elysium the day prior, Ezra lost no time in mapping out what needed to happen next. Whatever details the journalists at the *Belfast Evening Telegraph* had could be the smoking gun pointing to what really became of his father. As much as he hated to admit it, as much as he tried moving on, desperation for answers had consumed him. Now that it had been a full month since the incident and no whisper of news from the magistrate or authorities, every passing hour solidified the ache that refused to go away.

The longing ache to be reunited with his father.

"Why don't you ask Miss McLarney to accompany you?" Aja stubbornly insisted. "She would go with you, you know."

He shot an incredulous glance over his shoulder. "Just yesterday when we got back to the academy, Miss McLarney told me that while she enjoys seeing me at Elysium, I need to stay on school grounds as much as possible. No more excursions through Belfast. Something about a magical dome or whatever."

"A protective crystal grid," Aja answered before she could process much of his response. "But if you just ask—"

"I appreciate your concern, but I am going whether you and the Irish Chapter like it or not," he firmly replied.

"But—"

Ezra turned to face her, defiance fuelling a fire in his chest. "I'm going, Aja. Right after I finish with my cleaning tasks."

She crossed her arms.

"I don't expect you to understand," he continued, shaking out the feather duster. "But if *your* father were missing, and you had the slightest chance of learning more about the event that sent him running, wouldn't you go out of your way to secure that information?"

Aja did not answer. Instead, she allowed her posture to relax, albeit slightly.

Knowing he had gained the upper hand, Ezra plowed onward. "My father is out there, Aja. I'm going to do everything in my power to find him."

"You weave a compelling argument, Mr. Newport," Aja sighed, mimicking Miss McLarney's Irish accent. "Fine. But Oliver and I are coming with you. Got it?"

"I can agree to that," said Ezra, "as long as you keep it quiet that I defied orders."

With a nod and an ever-expanding grin, Aja watched him as if in complete awe over his response.

Ezra furrowed his eyebrows. "What?"

"You are a Scorpio through-and-through," she laughed. "I wondered when that rebellious nature would come out to play."

Fighting back a smile of his own, Ezra shook his head and pressed on with his duties. The faster he could complete them, the sooner he could get answers.

The setting sun cast a red hue upon the city buildings as Ezra, Aja, and Oliver navigated toward Cathedral Quarter. Unbeknownst to Belfast Royal Academy faculty—or the prefects—the trio had successfully escaped without incident. Ezra was beginning to count himself lucky; twice now he had achieved the impossible.

Just as twice he had slithered out of the grasp of the Watchers.

He was not about to make it a third.

With Aja and Oliver at his side and a driving force behind his steps, Ezra's momentum could not be halted no matter how much his friends urged him to slow down. He kept up his vicious pace until his eyes locked on the target: the reddish-brown stone edifice crowning Royal Avenue. An exquisite clock with golden embellishments jutted out from the façade, prompting Ezra into a mad sprint. He made a mental note to properly examine the bright red trim and arched windows running along the top floor when he wasn't tripping over his feet in a frenzied haste.

"Blimey, Ezra, wait for us!" Oliver called after him.

Throwing open the door, Ezra regretted the intensity behind the motion when the secretary sitting at the front desk spilt her tea in alarm.

"Goodness," she muttered to herself. Eying Ezra with disdain, she withdrew a handkerchief from her skirt pocket and sopped up the mess. "What can I help you with, sir?"

Bolstered by Oliver and Aja's presence now lingering behind him, Ezra straightened his shoulders and pulled out the Sunday paper from his jacket. "Hello. Er, I need to speak with the journalist writing this article."

The secretary's gaze followed his index finger to the newsprint and then met his expectant expressions with a stern look of her own. "I'm not sure you understand how journalism works, Mr.—"

"Ezra Newport," he replied.

"Mr. Newport," she said with a dismissive flourish of her hand. "One does not just burst into a newspaper and demand a preview of an anticipated feature article. We have to make a profit too, you know."

"I understand, but—"

"Mr. Tavin is on a rather tight deadline for other articles, so I suggest you make an appointment and come back when it best suits him," suggested the woman in a rigid manner.

Clenching his jaw, he tried again. He absolutely would not budge until Mr. Tavin would agree to see him. "He's writing about the Portadown Train Disaster, is he not?"

She scrutinised him through narrowed eyes as if trying to see through his intentions. "Yes. Your point?"

"I'm a survivor of that incident," Ezra answered. "If anything, he'd want to speak with me as I have information that could illuminate his piece."

His statement effectively silenced her. After clearing her throat, the secretary smoothed out her skirt and stepped around the desk. "You said your name was Mr. Newport?"

"Yes, ma'am."

"Wait here," she instructed and disappeared through the door on the opposite wall.

Aja giggled. "Nice persuasion tactics, Mr. Scorpio."

Ezra gave her a look. "Aja, come on."

"What?" she said with an innocent shrug. "I'm just stating the facts."

"It's better than being reminded how two-faced you are," Oliver remarked, playfully shoving Aja.

When the secretary returned, her hair appeared legions more frazzled than its original arrangement. "Mr. Newport, er, Mr. Tavin would like to see you right away," she said as if she couldn't believe the words issued from her mouth.

For several blurry seconds, Ezra failed to register his good fortune.

"Well, get a move on," the woman urged, waving him and Oliver and Aja through the door.

Upon crossing the threshold, the atmosphere sparked into palpable vibrance. At least two dozen men ambled about the expanse. Some furiously pounded away at typewriters while others leaned against desks smoking cigars. Others conducted loud conversation laced with profanities, only ceasing when the secretary led the three of them through the madness. Finally, she stopped and gestured to a formal parlour adjacent to the newsroom.

"In you go," she insisted.

Ezra did not need to be told twice. Unable to restrain his inquisitive nature, he took in his surroundings. A magnificent fireplace served as the obvious focal point of the room, paired with an oversized conference table and leather armchairs filling the spaces in between. On another wall, a floor-to-ceiling bookshelf housed hardback editions of everything from encyclopaedias to law books. Electric lamps cast a warm ambiance against the wainscotting. Dying daylight filtered in through grey curtains and illuminated the silhouette of a man with his hands clasped behind his back. When he turned, his thick spectacles caught the light from the nearest lamp, momentarily obscuring his exhausted eyes. His red hair, tousled and unruly, gave Ezra the inkling he rarely had time to comb it. Mr. Tavin nodded in greeting and gestured for the three of them to sit.

"It's a pleasure to meet you, Ezra Newport," Mr. Tavin said, signalling for the secretary to shut the door. "You are what we journalists like to call a 'Deadline Hail Mary.'"

"Er—nice to meet you too, sir," Ezra responded.

Mr. Tavin consulted his pocket watch before turning to a fresh page in his notebook. For a moment, he regarded Aja and Oliver in restrained distaste, most likely ruminating over the fact that his story had gained a premature audience. Much to Ezra's relief, he stopped short of shooing them away. "So, Mr. Newport. I hear you're interested in the story I have brewing for this Wednesday's edition."

"Very much, sir," Ezra answered.

"Good, because I'm very much interested in *you.*"

Ezra ran his sweating palms over his trousers underneath the tabletop. "You are?"

"Of course," he replied, pacing the room with pent-up energy. "Especially now that authorities have given the *Belfast Evening Telegraph* the story of a lifetime!"

Ezra swallowed and broke his attention away to catch Aja and Oliver's reaction. They returned his nervous curiosity in silence.

"*This.* This is wonderful!" stressed Mr. Tavin as he continued his aimless wandering. "Not only do I have the story of a lifetime, but I have *you*, Mr. Newport. Your insight. Memories. Experiences. God, this is wonderful."

"I'm not sure I understand," Ezra said.

Mr. Tavin froze, whirled around, and flashed a brilliant grin at him. "The Portadown train wreck was not an accident."

"Er, yes, I figured as much."

"Let me paint you a picture of what we know," Mr. Tavin stated, almost shivering in anticipation for his own story. "March 2: A passenger train suffers engine failure, and a chain reaction of explosions trigger inevitable derailment. At least one hundred people are dead, including your mother, am I correct?"

Ezra nodded.

"And your father?"

"Missing."

"Right," continued the journalist. "*Perfect.*"

Completely bewildered, Ezra chewed on his lip. "I fail to see how that's—"

"February 28: Mr. and Mrs. Newport, along with their only son—*you*," he winked at Ezra, "leave London behind in a whirlwind of train tickets and immigration papers."

Ezra stared at him. Mr. Tavin sure loved hearing the sound of his own voice.

"February 22: An article on a newly translated Babylonian artifact is published in the *Daily Telegraph.*"

Aja gasped.

"February 21: Ibrahim Newport is thrown out of the *Daily Telegraph* building for harassing employees. According to Scotland Yard, Mr. Newport claimed he was visiting a friend of his who worked at the paper. Apparently, Ibrahim was insistent that the paper abandon their efforts in publishing the translation. When his attempts failed, he became disorderly."

Ezra opened his mouth, but he could not issue a sound.

"So, what we have reads like the plot of an adventure novel," Mr. Tavin persisted. "Man tries to hinder the publishing of an important archaeological article. Man fails and uproots his family from London the next week. Then, his train is attacked. He runs and disappears into the night, without even looking back. To me, this sounds very much like an intentional act. Someone was targeting him."

A heaviness churned in Ezra's stomach as he processed the flurry of information. As much as he tried, he could not imagine his *baba* being so worked up about a simple newspaper article. Unless, it had something to do with—

"I would sacrifice everything for the safety of these two," echoed Ibrahim's words throughout his recollections. *"Life simply would not be worth living without them."*

"I—I can't believe it," Ezra stuttered. He could not manage to say much else.

Aja placed a hand on his arm. "Ezra, I am familiar with that article," she whispered urgently. "I brought it to Jonas' attention—"

"But this is where you come in, kid," Mr. Tavin cut her off. He twirled one of the chairs at the table and straddled the seat so he could lean his elbows atop the chair back. "You know your father better than anyone. Who do you think is behind all of this? A close family friend? A spiteful museum employee? A former boss?"

"I—I don't know," he answered softly.

"A criminal network? Government plot?"

Every syllable dissipated into a low hum, droning within Ezra's ears. He was practically drowning in it. Helpless. Confused.

Baba *couldn't have...he wouldn't have kept such secrets.*

But he already did. His and Anne's affiliation with the Magi had been hidden from me. What other secrets lurked in the deep?

"Any known gang affiliations? What about suspicious activity around the home?"

Remaining silent, Ezra felt his eyes tingle with tears of frustration.

"Okay, that's enough," Aja insisted, standing so abruptly from her chair that it screeched across the floor. She tugged on Ezra's shirt sleeve. "Come on, Ezra. Let's go."

Before he could respond, the entire building trembled from an intense detonation somewhere beyond the walls. Mr. Tavin gripped the table as fragments of dust rained from the ceiling tiles. Shouts of alarm battered the other side of the parlour door, and several loud cracks pierced the air. The lights around them flickered until they went out completely, like candles extinguished by a sigh. Aja clung to both Ezra and Oliver.

"What in the name of God Almighty is going on out there?" Mr. Tavin muttered, throwing open the door. A blast of smoke permeated the parlour, causing the man to cover his nose in the crook of his arm. Without a word of explanation, the journalist plunged into the newsroom, leaving them to fend for themselves.

"We need to get out of here," Oliver prompted in a panic. "I'm picking up on three extremely hostile auras making their way in through the front entry."

"Dark Watchers?" Aja questioned as the three of them backed into the corner by the bookshelf.

"No—they're alive," he answered, squinting through his spectacles. "Just people."

Aja bit her lip. "People with Gifts?"

"Possibly."

"The Legerdemain behind the *Quietus* attacks?"

"Highly probable."

"*Quietus* attacks?" Ezra blurted out. "What is going on?"

"Something we shouldn't stick around to watch," Aja responded, pulling him and Oliver toward the window. Shakily, she ran her fingers over the panes, searching in vain for the latch. "Come on! How do you open this sodding thing?"

A wave of anxiety crept along Ezra's skin and while he desperately wished to run, he couldn't command his feet to move. Only one frantic thought circulated his mind, one that suggested whatever was happening was not a mere coincidence.

"Just bust out the glass, Aja!" yelled Oliver. "We need to go—now!"

"Stand back," she commanded, drawing her pendant out from under her collar. The crystal glowed a brilliant white upon Aja's command. With one fluid motion, she pushed the energy toward the glass. Theoretically, the force of it should have busted the window into tiny shards, providing the exit they needed. Instead, it ricocheted backward, levelling all three of them to the floor.

"What in the name of the Famed Three?!" Aja panted. "The building must have been cursed. That should have worked!"

Smoke wafted into the parlour at an alarming pace, inducing a coughing fit in Ezra's lungs.

"Through the newsroom, then!" Oliver insisted and beckoned them to follow his lead.

By the looks of it, every journalist in the *Belfast Evening Telegraph* had escaped, not even bothering to come back for their guests.

Every man for himself, Ezra assumed, annoyance festering within. *So much for being Mr. Tavin's Deadline Hail Mary.*

They had not made it much further than a few paces before another explosion wracked the building, sending chunks of plaster crashing around them. Dodging the debris, the trio was halfway to the front door when three grey shadows emerged from the smoke.

"Well, who do we have here? Three—no, *two* young Magi and their Quotidian friend?"

Ezra, Aja, and Oliver halted in their tracks. When the cloaked men stepped through the haze, Ezra noticed they wore pyramid-shaped badges at their belts. Each badge triangulated around an Evil Eye. The strangers' ominous footfalls shook the weak floorboards, heavy and foreboding, and within seconds, Ezra found himself with his back against a wall.

"Get back, you filthy Legerdemain!" Aja demanded through her fear. "We're armed!"

"Armed with what, dear girl?" chided one, cruelty dripping like venom as he ran a gloved hand through Aja's hair. She squirmed away, attempting to reach her pendant, but the man effortlessly wrangled her arm behind her. "Celestial Lifeforce magic? You know that hardly works against us."

The other men guffawed at their comrade's remark.

"Oh yeah? Well, this might," Oliver retorted, spitting in the nearest man's eyes.

Hissing in anger, he slammed the boy up against the wall and extracted a dagger out of his cloak. Fire blazing in his expressions, the Legerdemain pressed the blade against Oliver's throat. "Damn kid. You're lucky I cannot kill you right now."

"Conjure a shield, Oliver!" Aja screeched. She fought against her captor's grasp. "A shield!"

The boy struggled to produce anything but tiny sparks from his wand as he writhed against the man's weight.

With all attention on Oliver, Aja kicked her captor between the legs. Temporarily disabled, the man stumbled backward into a desk, giving Aja a chance to aim another attack on the Legerdemain holding Oliver. His hand was too fast for her, catching the heel of her boot and flipping her into a twisted heap on the floor. She cried out, grasping at her ankle.

"Aja!" Oliver yelped.

Anger rising—much like the flames herding them back toward the parlour —Ezra stomped on the toes of the man holding him against the wall. Unfortunately, the action prompted disaster.

In a dizzying scene of black fabric and smoke, the Legerdemain Brotherhood members unleashed hell upon the students. Ezra erratically swung his fists, hoping to land a punch. Some found success. Before he could do much else, he was wrestled into a chokehold.

Aja recovered her composure and aimed an energy field toward Ezra's attacker, narrowly missing his shoulder. It crackled and fizzed as it rushed past his ear, debilitating the man long enough for Ezra to slip out of his possession.

"Thanks," Ezra wheezed.

"Don't mention it," Aja said, breathless as she whirled around to throw another blast of magic at the Legerdemain nearest Oliver.

Raising a gloved hand, the man blocked it and returned the force in her direction. The energy launched Aja backward, slamming her head against the wall.

Ezra watched in horror as she crumpled to the ground, seemingly unconscious. "No!" he screamed, just as he heard Oliver cry out. Glancing over his shoulder, Ezra witnessed one of the Brotherhood pinning the boy against the wall. Twisted glee disfigured the man's expressions. But as he stepped away, even in the dim grey light, Ezra detected a glint of crimson clothing the knife in his hand.

"Oliver!"

Trembling, the fourteen-year-old Magus grasped at the bloody stain on his shirt and collapsed to his knees.

Another tremor rattled the building.

"We need to go," said one of the men, retreating toward the entrance. "It won't be long before the RIC arrives."

"And it won't be much longer before the entire building collapses," replied another.

"Have fun digging out, kids," laughed the last. "Give that bastard Jonas van der Campe our kind regards."

And just as fast as they had materialised, they were gone.

Ezra's breath came in rigid gasps. Fire continued to ravage the scene around him. Smoke choked the life from his body. Looking between Aja and Oliver, Ezra felt panic rising in his throat. He wanted to help. He wanted to scream. He wanted more than anything he could chase down those pigs and hurt them, just as they had hurt his friends.

But it did not matter what he wanted. He needed to actually do something.

Fast.

Ezra skidded to his knees beside Aja, furiously shaking her shoulders.

"Aja? Come on, Aja! Wake up!"

When she did not respond, he crawled through the ash to Oliver, who had curled into the tiniest form on the floor.

"Oliver? Ezra coughed, waving his hand in front of the young Magus' glassy eyes. "Hey! Oliver, look at me."

Oliver let out a sob. "Ezra—"

"How bad is it?" Ezra asked, craning his neck to see if he could get a good glimpse of his wound. He stifled a gasp when he lifted the boy enough to see that the red stain encompassed his entire right side.

"It's bad," Oliver cried. "Ezra, I want—I want Jonas."

"As do I," he sighed, eyes burning.

This could not be happening. Not again. Not so soon after his mother left him. He couldn't lose them, too. Not now. Not ever.

Ezra wiped his face on his sleeve, not certain if the tears were from emotion or the thick fumes enveloping them. "I'm going to try to get you out first, okay?"

Before he could convince his body to move, the ceiling gave in, raining plaster and steel beams from above.

"NO!" Ezra screamed, instinctively reaching out to ward off imminent danger. Just as he did so, a tremendous shockwave of energy engulfed the expanse. Sparking as if electrified, a glimmering shield arched over the three of them, forming an invisible barrier over their heads. The massive debris ceased its descent, effectively held up by the protective enclosure.

Trembling in a mix of shock and bewilderment, Ezra stared at his hands, which gave off an ethereal glow. His mouth gaped, searching for oxygen, answers, anything. Anything at all to describe how it was that he had just conjured something incredibly like the Celestial Lifeforce.

This isn't real. It's just a dream, Ezra surmised. *I must have been knocked unconscious. I'll wake up soon enough and realise none of this ever happened. It is not possible!*

Without warning, the barrier began to fizzle away, melting into the atmosphere around him. But as the shield disintegrated, the rubble teetered on the edge of disaster.

All Ezra could do was cringe and accept the inevitable.

TERROR BEFALLS BELFAST

Diego sucked air between his teeth and allowed his head to thump back against the wall. Pleasure tingled in his abdomen and raced in circles around his navel before plunging into his toes. To be quite honest, the warmth circulating throughout his body felt remarkably like the Celestial Lifeforce. Maybe *that* was why he loved being a Magus so much.

But most importantly, he was enamoured by the unspoken talents of Miss Stella Birch.

And her lips. *Santa Maria*, her lips…

"Mmm. *Mi querida*," Diego groaned, running his hands through her long hair. "I cannot believe I'm saying this, but can we resume this lovely—oh, what do the French say? *Tête-à-tête?*—at your flat? I'm having terrible visions of Chief Constable Norman bursting into this storage closet to fulfill his random urges to clean. And you know how much he loves a spotless off—*ay!*"

Her eyes lifted to meet his, brightening as she grinned. "You are incredibly handsome when you're flustered."

"I am not flustered!" Diego insisted in a much higher voice than anticipated. He gasped when she went back to work. "Okay, maybe I am a little—*Dios!* *¡Ay Dios!*"

"You swear too much, darling," Stella laughed. Her fingers traced his trouser inseams up and down his legs. "Though, I quite enjoy your filthy mouth."

"And I quite enjoy yours," Diego exhaled.

It was not a lie. But it wasn't the full truth, either. He would not dare tell Stella—or Jonas, for that matter—but during times like these, he fantasised only one pair of lips. And they did not belong to Stella. Lips that could simultaneously frustrate and enchant him with nothing more than a simple smile. Conquer him, love him, and leave him wanting more.

Diego allowed his eyelids to fall as he peered through the misty veil of his memories. Burying them six months ago proved ineffective. Prayers to God, Mary, and all the saints to help him move on went unanswered. The more time he spent with Stella, the more he realised their relationship—as shallow and physical as it was—meant nothing more to him than a superficial distraction. A spark to incite jealousy.

And while it was working, Diego was not entirely sure he wanted it to.

"Stella," Diego sighed, his knees weak and worthless. Grunting at the effort of sweet release, he slid down the wall, now eye level with her. Stella leaned over and pressed her delightfully salty lips against his own.

Before he could dwell any longer in his musings, the ground quaked, rattling glass jars of disinfectant and sending mops and brooms crashing to the floor. Frozen, Diego's wide eyes met Stella's just as an alarm wailed throughout the building.

"What do you think—" she began, but Diego was already scrambling to readjust his belt and tuck his shirt underneath his waistband.

"I don't know, but I am getting a really bad feeling about it," Diego noted, offering his hand to help Stella to her feet.

The moment they threw open the storage room door, every constable on duty had suited up and dove headfirst into the carriages stationed outside. Looking considerably perturbed, Chief Constable Norman shuffled along the corridor, stopping briefly to shoot a questioning glare at Diego for why he and Stella had just exited a closet together.

"Sir, what's going on?" Diego asked, catching up to his boss.

"We've reports of a bomb at the *Belfast Evening Telegraph* building," Norman replied, his moustache twitching in anxiety. "All workers made it out alive, but one of the injured claim three kids are still trapped inside."

"Kids, sir?"

"That's what they said."

"*Santa mierda*," Diego groaned, pinching the bridge of his nose. Now he *really* had a bad feeling.

"What, darling?" Stella whispered in concern, following the two of them to an empty carriage.

"You are coming with me," Diego insisted. Grabbing her hand, he hoisted her up into the vehicle after he and Norman had piled in. "Intuition tells me I'll need your assistance."

When the carriage rolled into Cathedral Quarter, Diego leapt to the street before it had even stopped moving. He dashed through the journalists and onlookers congregating in the intersection of Royal and Library. Glass and wooden fragments were strewn across the scene, crunching beneath his shoes as he bolted for the building's entry. But something made him skid to a stop so violently that he almost toppled over in his urgency.

Painted in fresh, red lettering over the curvature of the arched doorway: *Quietus.*

"No!" Diego gasped and whirled around to face the crowd. "I need everyone to back up! The further away you are from here, the better!"

"Listen to the kid!" barked Chief Constable Norman, motioning for Stella and his team to drive them back. Like sheep corralled by dogs, the crowd obeyed.

Without a second thought, Diego plunged inside the Telegraph Building. Ribbons of smoke threatened to strangle him as he fought his way through sparking wires, mountains of plaster, and twisted metal. Using the rush of adrenaline to his advantage, Diego proceeded into what looked to be the remnants of a former newsroom and stopped dead in his tracks.

There, as clear as the devastation around him, Ezra Newport struggled to maintain the largest Celestial Lifeforce shield Diego had ever seen. Trembling in dread, the boy attempted to keep the magic alive. Magic that was dangerously close to petering out and crushing him and the lifeless forms of Oliver and Aja beneath it.

He *was* a Magus after all. A damn strong one.

Diego fell to his knees beside the adolescent. Despondency threatened to take over Ezra's amber eyes, possibly his entire soul. He was giving up. And if he did, all three kids would be killed right before his eyes.

"No! Ezra, keep at it," Diego told him. "You can do it; stay focused!"

"I can't!" Ezra yelled, watching in despair as the barrier continued to fall and with it, the heavy steel beams. "I—I can't!"

"Yes, you can!" Diego urged. "Close your eyes and take deep breaths. I will guide you through it."

Hesitantly, Ezra squeezed his eyes shut, drew in a large dose of oxygen through his nose, and held it within his lungs. Diego watched as the boy tried to steady his shaking hands and drown out the commotion around him, but the aggressive shrieks of the shifting ceiling rubble kept breaking his focus.

"Listen to my voice," Diego spoke, wishing he could get through the barrier to brace Ezra's shaking shoulders. "Pretend the debris above you does not exist."

Ezra nodded and continued to hold out his hands in front of him.

Diego watched as the shield's tattered boundaries began to stitch themselves together again.

"Excellent! You're doing great!" Diego encouraged. "Aja told me you want to be an architect, yes?"

"Yes," Ezra choked. His voice quavered on the verge of tears.

"Good. Imagine the building we are in is simply one of your designs. Sketch the foundation, strong and dependable. You're building on the solid, unshakable ground of the Celestial Lifeforce."

Ezra nodded.

"Next, add in the supports, the components that hold everything together," Diego continued. "The magic flowing through you right now is your reinforcement. Lean on it. Feel how stable it is. Remember to breathe!"

The boy sucked in as much air as he could without sputtering on the smoke.

"You are doing great, Ezra," Diego said, throwing a desperate look back at the entryway. Zaire and the others had to be here soon. Surely, they would be here. They had to. *Dios*, they had to.

"Okay, now fill in all the gaps. Place the walls, the windows, the insulation, everything you need to strengthen the structure. Make it strong, Ezra. Build a fortress."

A deep resonance ebbed and flowed throughout the room, growing more robust by the second. Diego could feel the intensity of the magic's vibrations within his gut. Churning. Impenetrable. Disrupting the very atoms of the air.

"That's it! You have got it!" Diego exclaimed. Despite his positive tone, he knew it was only a matter of minutes before the Celestial Lifeforce battered the inexperienced Magus to the ground. Where once was warmth, bitter cold would deteriorate his senses like an icy spectral knife. Ezra would push himself past the point of mental exhaustion and be killed in the process.

Diego gritted his teeth. Ezra would not fail. He couldn't.

"Kid?! Where are you?"

¡Gracias a los Reyes Magos!

"Zaire! Over here!" Diego called out, beyond thankful for his impeccable timing.

His fellow Magus charged into the newsroom, followed by Kierra. All colour drained from their faces when they recognised what sort of situation they were up against.

"Ah shit!" Zaire swore, grabbing his bowler hat in alarm.

Diego stared at him in surprise. Zaire's devout Christianity hardly ever allowed such language to escape his lips. There was a first time for everything, and this time certainly warranted more than simple swearing.

In fact, Diego wondered just how much swearing Jonas would do once he returned to Belfast. Just the very thought sparked Diego's mouth into a grin. The man was utterly irresistible when he was angry, especially when the Brotherhood was the source of his contempt.

"God be with us," Kierra prayed, kneeling beside Diego. "Ezra, keep going, sweetheart! We are right here."

"I can't hold it any longer, Miss McLarney!" Ezra yelled, still squeezing his eyes shut lest he be distracted by the rubble above him.

"Yes, you can. You are doing a wonderful job," she replied. While her voice sounded even and pleasant, Diego knew Kierra was downright terrified by the lack of colour in her cheeks. "Zaire is going to assist you, all right?"

Channelling the Celestial Lifeforce, Zaire worked to redirect the steel beams away from the children through his telekinetic abilities. But even with his Gifts, it was not an easy feat. Diego chewed on his lower lip while beads of sweat dripped from Zaire's forehead. Painstakingly, the Magus lifted the rubble from Ezra's protective shield and guided it far enough away that the collision with the floor would not maim them in the process.

Finally, the three kids were free.

"Okay, Ezra, let go of the magic," Kierra instructed. "You are safe now."

Dazed and physically drained, the boy lowered his arms and collapsed upon the floor. The twinkling blue magic faded into the smoke around them like it never existed at all.

"Aja and Oliver—hurt," Ezra panted in fragments, looking like he might vomit.

"I'll get Oliver," Diego volunteered. "Zaire, can you assist Aja?"

"On it," he agreed, running to lift the young lady into his arms.

With Kierra now helping Ezra to his feet, Diego scooped up Oliver and made haste toward the doorway.

The six of them emerged from the ravaged Telegraph Building, battling smoke and wicked fears lingering on the evening breeze. Sirens ricocheted across the city, intermingled with congratulatory shouts and dizzying chatter from bystanders.

But the most concerning thing of all was not the fiery building behind them or the hordes of journalists documenting the carnage on notepads. With uneasiness rattling his insides, Diego wondered just how much more violence initiated at the hands of the Legerdemain the world could endure.

Tonight, the Irish Chapter had gotten lucky. But next time—if there indeed *was* a next time—Diego had a feeling their hearts would not withstand the event.

Quietus, indeed.

AFTERMATH

Jonas paced like a caged lion on the ferry deck, glaring at his pocket watch as if the intensity of his gaze could prompt the hands into action.

It had been six hours since he had witnessed the gut-wrenching terror inflicted on Belfast through Ezra's eyes. At that point, Jonas had just boarded the evening train to Liverpool. The very moment the steam engine screamed into life, explosions ignited in his mind. Debris fell like rain. A run-in with the Brotherhood disintegrated into violence. And the shield—God, the shield Ezra had conjured was nothing short of spectacular, confirming everything Jonas had believed about the boy from the start.

But their shared experience ended just as quickly as it had begun, leaving him to wonder if Ezra, Aja, and Oliver were able to escape at all.

And not knowing tore him to pieces.

Every passing second sent Jonas deeper into distress. More than once, he excused himself to the lavatory, where he held his arms against his stomach, fighting off the anger, regret, and other such emotions. Ferocity consumed his soul. Jonas hated the Legerdemain Brotherhood. He hated he had ever been a part of them. Most of all, he despised his father, even if the Quietus ploys were not his direct doing.

The Magi had to be prepared for anything.

The dragon was awake.

When Jonas had finally reached Great Victoria Station at seven the next morning, he hired the first carriage he saw, paying double the driver's usual rate to get to the Emporium as fast as possible. He hardly registered stumbling into his own shop, racing down the spiral stairs to the cellar, and bursting through the threshold of Elysium.

After dropping his suitcase by the coat rack, Aja limped across the common room and tumbled into his arms. She buried her face in his coat, her muffled sobs like newly sharpened blades against his flesh.

He held his apprentice close, not wanting to let her go. Aja was practically a daughter to him in almost every sense of the word, and the very idea of vile Brotherhood members bringing her to tears made him want to do more than just set the Consulate ablaze.

Jonas surveyed the faces of his Magi family. Arms folded, Diego braced himself against the fireplace mantel, fatigue pulling at the skin under his bloodshot eyes. Kierra and Zaire sat at the table, both nursing cups of tea and sullen expressions. Mum perched on the arm of the couch, dabbing a wet cloth over the forehead of an unconscious Oliver. And Ezra, pale and shaken, sat in the armchair with his knees hugged to his chest. No one appeared as if they'd slept much more than a wink.

But at least they were all *alive*, and that was more than he could have asked for.

Jonas nudged several strands of Aja's unkempt hair behind her ear and approached the edge of the couch. He placed his palm against Oliver's face. Bluish bruises circled Oliver's left eye and snaked across his cheekbone and neck. Wrapped in white linen bandages, his chest slowly rose and fell. The boy looked so fragile, so powerless in the light from the gas lamps. Jonas was grateful he had not ended up as mangled as the pair of spectacles that sat on the side table.

"How is he?" Jonas finally found the strength to speak.

"Oliver lost a lot of blood in a short time," Annabelle answered with a frown. "Once the poor dear came to, he went into a fit of shock, so I gave him some of my Frankincense Tea to help him rest. He's been sleeping ever since."

Jonas blinked away the wetness on his eyelashes. "I am so sorry I wasn't—I wasn't here to help."

"That ain't your fault, Mista Jonas," Zaire interjected.

"There was no way you could have known something like this would happen," Kierra agreed, holding her teacup close to her lips. "We barely got to the scene in time as it was."

"As a Magi Master, it is my duty to ensure the safety of my chapter," Jonas responded. "My irrevocable moral obligation."

"My dear, you put way too much blame on yourself for something you had no control over," Mum said, reaching over to grasp his arm. "Besides, you weren't chasing fleeting fancies. You were on assignment as dictated by the Administration."

Despite her words, guilt still churned in the pit of his stomach. After shedding his coat, Jonas knelt beside the armchair. "I saw a great deal of what happened through your eyes, Ezra. How are you feeling?"

At first, he did not respond. The adolescent cradled his knees closer to himself and leaned his chin against them. His eyes swam with fear, doubt, and hesitation. Jonas was certain if he could see inside Ezra's mind, he'd see a compass needle spinning out of control, leaving him lost and directionless.

"I—I'm fine," Ezra managed, though it hardly sounded convincing. "Were it not for Diego, I would not have been able to do what I did. If it weren't for you all, I would be..." he paused, as if the very thought pained him to speak aloud. "I would be dead."

"As would Oliver and I," Aja added.

Jonas met Diego's line of sight and offered his sincerest thanks in the form of an unrestrained smile. The young man nodded in acknowledgment and awkwardly glanced away.

"Ezra, your heroic actions should not be discredited," Kierra chimed in. "Your newfound abilities are really what saved the lives of Aja and Oliver."

"It is the truth," Jonas told Ezra. "And your skills will open a world of opportunities for you as a Magus."

Ezra issued a shaky sigh. He suddenly found great interest in rubbing his thumb over the scuff on one of his leather shoes.

"By the way, why *were* you three at the *Belfast Evening Telegraph*?" Jonas questioned, looking between Aja and Ezra.

"Well, you see—" Aja began as she stumbled through syllables. "We—er—we shouldn't have, but—"

By this time, Ezra had procured a hopelessly wrinkled copy of the *Telegraph* from his interior jacket pocket and held it out for Jonas to see. "I had a feeling this would provide me some answers about the Portadown train wreck. I was right."

Jonas read the text as well as the disbelief in the new Magus' face. "And?"

"A journalist told us that the event was not an accident," Aja broke in.

"Which I figured, due to the Dark Watchers' involvement," Ezra said. "But Mr. Tavin implied that someone might have been retaliating against my father. According to him, my father attempted to persuade the *Daily Telegraph* reporters in London not to publish an article about an artifact translation, just before we left in a mad haste to get to Ireland."

A chill washed down Jonas' spine as he processed the statement. Without delay, he thumbed through past newspapers on the bookshelf and located the copy Aja had brought to his attention what seemed like ages ago. "This? The Babylonian tablet translation?"

Aja nodded.

Words began to click into place, like iron rails materialising for his wicked train of thought. Phrases from Mr. Mears and Edison heaped coal onto the ever-blazing fire, launching the locomotive forward into strange territory. This had to be the reason.

It had to be.

"Christ, this makes so much more sense," Jonas whispered to himself, but it was lost on his company.

"What do you mean?" Annabelle enquired.

With the translation paper rolled in his fist, he paced the length of the room, mulling over the scenario in his mind. For the benefit of the Irish Chapter, he spoke his musings aloud. "When Mr. Edwin Mears came to see me about going to London, he dictated the Administration's fears that the Legerdemain were up to something."

"Well, we know *that*," Diego muttered, "what with the Quietus violence and all."

"But he also said he was concerned about the Portadown incident, because it did not follow what we know about Dark Watchers and the Legerdemain."

"Meaning?" Zaire prodded.

"When the Order of Babylon is invoked, what happens next?" Jonas asked his company.

"If you agree, the Dark Watchers take you to the Legerdemain Consulate to be trained in the ways of the Brotherhood," Aja correctly answered. "If you decline, you are killed."

"Indeed. But they do this only for those with an active connection to the Celestial Lifeforce."

Ezra's quizzical expressions locked on Jonas. "What does that mean?"

Jonas sighed. "It means your parents had their Magi licenses revoked years ago. Not only that, but their connections to the Celestial Lifeforce had also been severed by the Administration due to some past offence against them."

Annabelle and Zaire gasped. Kierra threw a hand over her mouth in shock. Aja uncomfortably hugged her arms close to her body.

Ezra's eyebrows knit together in the centre of his forehead. "Severed? So, they had their abilities taken away?"

Jonas nodded solemnly. "It's an irreversible punishment reserved for the most heinous crimes. Now, I'm not saying whatever your parents did was wrong, because I do not know the circumstances. What I *do* know is that their sentence was why you never saw them perform magic."

"But why would the Legerdemain send Watchers after the Newports if they magic was taken and Ezra's abilities had not shown themselves yet?" Zaire questioned.

"I wondered the very same," Jonas continued, pacing once more. "But now I have an unfortunate inkling, starting with what I learned from my friend Edison at the British Museum. He reminded me it's Legerdemain election season. My father and his father were up for re-election, but they are running against another pair who has proven they have what it takes to run the Brotherhood. Nevertheless, the election resulted in a stalemate, which means both sides must now compete to win the bid."

Diego shifted his position against the fireplace. "Compete? Like a duel?"

"Exactly. Both must prove to the Consulate they are capable. They are assigned tasks and based on the impact those have, the winners are instated as the new leaders. This unknown pair running against my father are most likely the ones behind the Quietus ploys, according to Edison."

"Well, that sheds a light on matters," Kierra replied. "But what are Uncle Diederik and Mr. Bellinor doing for their portion of the duel?"

"They are seeking the Tablet of Destinies," Jonas responded. "A mythical artifact with the supposed ability to grant one the powers of a god."

"Oh, mercy me," Annabelle said.

Jonas hesitated, clutching the newspaper in his hand. Carefully, he unfolded it and after staring at the photograph of the cuneiform tablet, held it up for all to see. "This translation must have something to do with the Tablet of Destinies."

"Could you read it, Mista Jonas?"

Clearing his throat, he grabbed his reading spectacles and shook out the folds of the newspaper.

"When struggles crest
Kings crumble at the tryst
The Roaming Lion shall rise
And the Tribes he'll assist.

Locked within time
Where Destinies are viewed
The Lion's touch opens eyes
Immense power renewed.

Unite the Lion, Dragon, and Bull
At the mouth of Babylon's Gates
A circle of Twelve shall overcome
Hail the victors' celestial fates."

Introspective silence chased Jonas' words as he rolled the publication within his hands once more.

"And Mr. Newport did not want the papers to take that to print?" Diego repeated.

Ezra and Jonas nodded in unison.

"Honestly, it sounds very much like Mr. Newport came to the same conclusion ages before we did," Kierra said, setting down her teacup in its saucer. "He knew the text related to the Tablet of Destinies and did not want it in the wrong hands. But after the article's release, the Legerdemain—namely Uncle Diederik and Mr. Bellinor—found out and sent the Watchers after them."

"But why—" Ezra began, his red-rimmed eyes desperate, searching. "Why would they want to kill us? Wouldn't they *need* us? For information's sake?"

Jonas knelt once again to Ezra's level and put a comforting hand on his forearm. "You will chase your sanity in circles if you try to rationalise the acts of the Brotherhood," he spoke softly. "Chances are that my father wanted you and your family out of the way as not to impede his mission. Simple as that."

But as Jonas watched the boy draw back into himself, he knew the matter would never be that simple. If anything, their theories just exasperated an already complicated situation. And while answers broke the surface, terror still lurked in the depths. Slithering through rocks and growing more powerful by the second.

This was not over yet.

CRESISTANCE

Lounging on a rock, the Shahmaran skimmed her fingertips over the surface of the lake, watching as the ripples expanded outward. She aimed a sideways glance at Ezra, who was sitting cross-legged on a nearby bolder, watching as she toyed with the water.

She grinned when he met her eyes. "I wondered how long it would take you," the Shahmaran's voice bathed his ears in honey, "to realise that you and I are incredibly similar beings."

Ezra sucked in the cavern's damp air and stared out at the lake. "You are not real."

"Sweet boy, I am as real as the magic within your soul."

Ezra laid back on the rock so that he could observe the ceiling in all its opulent magnitude. For some reason, he could not recall if he'd ever realised how the stalactites carried the rock above them, like pillars supporting a grand rotunda.

"That's not real, either."

"Then please do explain to me how you are alive."

"I just—I just am."

The Shahmaran propped her chin upon her hand and angled her body toward him. Portions of her wet hair tumbled across her glistening shoulders like a waterfall spilling over the edge of a cliff. "Do you not believe in the impossible?"

He narrowed his eyes. "I believe that all things happen in accordance with Allah's will. If that so happens to be an impossible thing, then yes."

"But this is not Allah's will for you?"

"I don't know!" he responded a little too loudly. His voice assaulted the deepest rocky crevice and came back at him like a slap across the face. "There was a reason Anne and Baba kept their world hidden. It is what they wanted for me, and I will respect their wishes."

She reached out to grasp his hand, her mouth curling into a dazzling smile. "What do you want, Ezra Newport? What do you really, truly want?"

He bit his lip, hoping the pain would distract him from the tingle in his throat. When he summoned the strength to speak, he abandoned the lake's surface and met her expectant gaze. "I want a clear path."

Drawing herself into a confident posture, she lifted her chin and tilted her head slightly to the side. "Then prepare to move."

The soft orange flame of daybreak illuminated the tiny storage closet.

"In all of the worlds, You are the most praised and the most glorious."

Ezra lingered on his woven prayer mat, his hands resting on his knees. He turned his head to the right, keeping his eyes closed so as not to be distracted by the resident spider spinning its web between two broomsticks.

"May the peace and mercy of *Allah* be upon you."

He turned to his left, repeating the prayer as the *Salat al-fajr* drew to a close.

Ezra slumped forward, burying his head in his hands. No matter how hard he tried, he could not shake the happenings from two nights ago. Nor could he fathom the perplexing details he'd gathered since speaking with Jonas and the Irish Chapter. It was too much to digest. Too much to believe.

Perhaps most frightening of all was the understanding that he—an ordinary immigrant from the Ottoman Empire—used magic from the Celestial Lifeforce, proving his rightful place amongst the Magi. But it wasn't even the first time it had happened. With a sickening lurch in his stomach, he realised his ability to produce a magical shield was the very thing that kept him alive during the Portadown train wreck.

He just did not want to accept the truth.

In fact, the longer Ezra dwelt on the situation, the more insistently the vomit crept into his throat. Besides what he had learned over the course of the past few days, he hardly knew anything of the Magi world. But after the conclusion Jonas and the others came to yesterday, he was not sure he wanted to hear much more. It would just further prove that the existence he lived had never been his own.

Ezra examined his hands. The fading lines on his palms seemed less noticeable since that miraculous moment, almost as if the Celestial Lifeforce had regenerated his cells. According to Miss McLarney, the shield was not even his true Gift. He had simply called upon the power of the Universe, something that he did not know was possible without crystal. However, learning what his real specialty was could take time, as Zaire reinforced. The path of the Magi was not a linear one.

Nor a clear one.

Sitting beside his prayer mat: the Wednesday morning paper. Mr. Tavin's article filled the front page with the same details he'd let on during their visit. This time, though, the story was not confined to the newsroom. Now, everyone would start associating the Portadown disaster with his family. With *him*. And Ezra was not ready for the repercussions.

A sudden blaze of anger bristled within him. Ezra slammed a fist against the floorboards, sending particles of dust into a tempest. Perhaps the magic had awoken more than just his connection to the Universe. More than just releasing an earthquake that shook every foundation holding together his already fragile life.

His parents had *lied* to him.

They lied by omission. By pretending they lived in a world without the existence of magic. Without the Magi and the Legerdemain Brotherhood. Every trace of evidence he had stumbled upon in the past month had been hidden away in hopes that—

As Ezra straightened and leaned back on his heels, he realised he wasn't quite sure his parents' intentions for keeping it mum. They obviously wanted him to be safe. But what was so fear-inducing about a twelve-line quatrain and a Babylonian artifact? What crime could they have committed that was so offensive to the Magi that it warranted the permanent confiscation of their magic?

No matter the reason, they had left him to face the reality of who he was without their guidance. Especially his father. And something about that did not settle well in the pit of Ezra's stomach.

Ezra slipped his hand into his trouser pocket and grasped the crystal quartz wand Jonas had given him. He ran his fingertips along the glacial edges as he reflected on the words Jonas uttered just before accompanying him back to Belfast Royal Academy.

"*You have a tremendous connection with the Celestial Lifeforce, Ezra, and these abilities must be practiced in the proper manner,*" Jonas' voice echoed throughout his mind. "*The Third Order is here to help guide you through the chaos.*"

Ezra was grateful for the Irish Chapter's support but to accept Jonas' call-to-action of training would sign and seal his existence as a Magus. And he was not sure he was ready to tread that path. Not when it had been a death sentence for his mother and gave his father the ability to disappear from his life.

Someday he would be wiser. Someday he would know how to navigate this path. Someday his steps would fall true and sure.

But not today.

IRREVOCABLE MORAL OBLIGATIONS

"I must say, the Council commends you for your success," Mr. Edwin Mears said before shovelling a spoonful of beef stew into his mouth. Midday light spilt through the freshly scrubbed pub windows, streaking gold across the otherwise dark décor. "In fact, they agreed to overlook your recent offences in light of what you learned in London."

Glancing up from his ale, Jonas examined the Administration official, reading the honesty in his features. "So, what happens next? While my own standing is important, I am more concerned over the state of the world."

"Well," Edwin mused. He chewed his lunch like a cow savouring his cud. "The Magi Gendarmerie and the Investigative Division are being briefed by the Council today. From there, we'll assign a task force to combatting further acts of Legerdemain violence. I will be leading a team to look into Consul van der Campe and Deputy Consul Bellinor's activities regarding the Tablet of Destinies."

Jonas nodded and took a sip of his beverage.

"Let me also make something explicitly clear," the official stated, wagging his fork to articulate his point. "Now that we have our heading, please do not muck it up by doing something rash."

"And how would you define 'rash?'" Jonas fought back his amusement at the question. At least Diego would be proud of him for asking.

The plump man lowered his bushy eyebrows. "Stay out of these affairs, as we previously discussed. Not only would it impede the Administration's investigations, but you are too closely tied to the offending parties. I would hate to have to rescue you."

"Who says I'll need rescuing?"

If it weren't for being in public, Mr. Mears looked as if he wanted nothing more than to dump his stew in Jonas' lap. "Just do as we ask, Mr. van der Campe. Stay in Belfast. Keep to your local duties. And that is that."

For some reason, the official's statement felt suspiciously like house arrest.

"Oh, and for the record, we must discuss the Newport boy."

Jonas abandoned his ale. "Yes, we must. Contrary to popular belief, he is indeed a Magus. I thought you said that seemed like an impossibility."

"People make mistakes," Edwin said with the air of someone who never made a mistake. "Besides, you would know all about that."

While he was not positive, Jonas was starting to think this Edwin Mears fellow really enjoyed dangling his past infractions in his face.

"Nevertheless, you are to break your ties with him at once," Edwin commanded, forking more food beneath his moustache. "The Council will be sending an agent to collect him from Belfast Royal Academy within the week so we can bring him to Constantinople for safekeeping. Of course, we'll need to go about all the proper methods through the courts. If the Legerdemain Brotherhood is *truly* after his parents—his father—for his knowledge on the translation and it *truly* has to do with the Tablet of Destinies, he needs the protection of the Third Order more than ever. In a place where we can keep a close eye on him."

Jonas frowned. "But why can't I—"

"Young man, the sooner we can do our jobs and get to the bottom of this, the sooner the world will be out of the Legerdemain Brotherhood's foul grasp. Do you understand me?"

He lowered his gaze to the table, watching the bubbles in his ale rise to the surface, much like his annoyance. "Yes, sir."

"Good man." The official dabbed his mouth with a cloth napkin and placed it alongside his plate. "I trust you understand we are only doing this for your safety."

While Jonas knew Edwin spoke the truth, something reminiscent of disappointment intermingled with the arrogance in his voice.

"Remember, the Council took a chance on you when they granted you this leadership position," Mr. Mears reminded him. "Do not make them regret it."

With his hands deep in his jacket pockets, Jonas strode back toward High Street. On one hand, he felt secure knowing the Administration was on top of the situation but on the other, he was mildly offended that they still did not want him to assist. Especially with Ezra. The boy was exhausted, lost, and while he never admitted it, terrified beyond words. Being chauffeured to the headquarters of a secret society he was only just coming to terms with did not seem like a wise venture. In fact, Jonas could think of three different scenarios better suited to Ezra's needs.

But, as Edwin Mears so often stated, the Administration had it under control. Jonas had his own local, irrevocable moral obligations to focus on.

And, as Edwin would say: "That was that."

Jonas ambled along past the Post Office in a daze, colliding with a body exiting the building.

"Oof! I'm so—" Jonas began, but stopped when he realised it was Diego. "Oh. It's just you."

A twisted expression made its way across the young man's face as he straightened his flat cap. "You know, you could have said, 'Oh, hello, Diego.' 'Good day, Diego.' Nice to see you, Diego.' Not whatever borderline obnoxious thing you just said."

Jonas forced a polite smile, but he was sure it came off as a scowl. "You certainly have a way of making a run-in seem like a personal infringement."

"And *you* certainly have a way of making me feel I was the last person you wanted to run into."

"Apologies," Jonas replied, resuming his trek. "I never wish to make you feel inferior."

"Uh huh," Diego muttered. He fell into stride alongside him. "Yet that happens every time you open your mouth."

Jonas restrained a roll of his eyes. "What were you doing at the Post Office anyway?"

"*Ay, Dios mio!*" Diego threw up his hands in exasperation. "I can't even send a telegram to my *abuelita* without it being an offence?"

"I never said it was."

"You implied it."

Silence. Then,

"Look, Diego, I know this is…*difficult* for both of us. But I am trying. I really am."

More silence.

Clenching his fists within the confines of his pockets, Jonas pressed on. "The Administration is watching me like a hawk. I have to be on my best behaviour right now and that means—"

"Being a prick?"

"No, it—"

"Ah, no, I understand," Diego cut him off. "It means hurting someone who loved you. Leaving him broken and upset. Forcing him to move on even though that was the last thing he wanted."

"God, it's been six months!"

"Six months of wondering what I ever did to you for you to just abandon me like that!"

"Diego," Jonas said warningly, surveying their surroundings to make sure no one had overheard. That was the problem with private conversations. They always seemed to manifest in the most inappropriate places. However, based on the oddly barren streets, it looked like they were in the clear. "You did not do anything *wrong*. Neither of us did. But the government sees it differently. So does the Council. And, in your case, so does the Vatican. We must respect their laws."

Scowling, the young man opened his mouth to retort but nothing made it past his lips. Instead, Diego heaved an aggravated sigh, shot him a vicious glare, and picked up his pace.

"Fine. Good day, *Señor* van der Campe."

With a sinking feeling eradicating any shred of happiness he had left, Jonas watched as Diego disappeared down the street and around the corner. The Magi Administration had given him everything and somehow, they'd simultaneously taken the most important things away: His accomplishments. His responsibility for Ezra's safety. And most excruciating of all, his whole heart.

With the sun beginning its descent in the west, Jonas aimed his steps toward the Emporium of Exotic Trinkets, repeating the same phrase over and over as if that would somehow extinguish the pain:

Do this for Felix.

Do this for Felix.

Do this for Felix.

28

A Future to Stand Behind

The evening sun cast a mosaic of geometric shapes across the corridor. Ezra squinted, reaching as far as he could to trace the grooves of the stained-glass window with a feather duster.

After the harrowing events on Monday, the rest of the week had fallen back into comfortable complacency. Oliver had made his return to school midweek and found himself surrounded by curious students wanting the inside scoop on the explosion. Honestly, he had become somewhat of a hero, even earning a kiss on the cheek from a girl in House Shaw.

Ezra's classes were going exceptionally well, and his latest project in Miss Newton's art class had earned him a top score and glowing praise from both faculty and his fellow classmates. Even his cleaning responsibilities inspired a sense of serenity he could not find elsewhere.

Which was quite ironic due to the fact every centimetre of school property needed to be spotless. An upcoming celebration honouring the 26th anniversary of the academy's current location loomed on the horizon. With this in mind, Headmaster Willigen had increased his demands on the state of cleanliness. And, while Ezra acquiesced, he could not help but wonder if the requirements were just the headmaster's way of reminding him of his lacklustre post-graduation fate.

Graduation. The mere idea seemed more daunting than being a Magus. Three months remained before he would be released into Belfast with a secondary school degree and nowhere to go.

Except—

Ezra sighed as he watched dust particles sparkle in the dwindling daylight. Of course, the open invitation to join the Irish Chapter was still on the table. The more he considered it, the more tempting it became.

But this was *real life.* And real life required he enter the workforce. Not chase potentially dangerous affiliations that made him a moving target.

Or, more of a moving target than usual.

"Mr. Newport."

Ezra started in surprise and whirled around to see an expectant Headmaster Willigen examining the state of his cleaning. "Oh, er, my apologies, Headmaster," he breathlessly replied, attempting to calm his frenzied heart. "I didn't notice you were there."

The man looked more impatient than usual. "Follow me, boy," he demanded. He swivelled on heel and hustled the other direction.

Frowning in confusion, Ezra grasped his duster tighter than was necessary and followed the headmaster on the familiar journey to his office.

When they arrived, the visibly bothered headmaster shoved open the heavy office door and waved him in. "Come on, boy. Don't dawdle," he commanded.

Ezra hurried into the office, feeling the rush of air behind him as Willigen shut the door.

At the front of the headmaster's desk sat a familiar-looking man smoking a pipe. When he heard the door click shut, he turned around in his seat, revealing his identity.

The magistrate.

Ezra had not heard a word from him since he first arrived in Belfast. For one disturbing second, Ezra wondered if perhaps the magistrate had news on his father. The very thought sent his stomach into somersaults.

"Great to see you again, Mr. Newport," said the magistrate as he stood and held out his hand in greeting.

Hesitantly, Ezra shook it. "You as well, sir."

"I do hope you have been getting on well at Belfast Royal Academy."

"As well as I can, sir."

Headmaster Willigen scoffed and attempted to disguise the mockery as clearing his throat.

"Headmaster, I wonder if Mr. Newport and I may speak in private," the magistrate suggested forwardly.

"Er, well, yes, of course," Willigen fumbled, looking a bit pink in the face with embarrassment. He turned to leave the room, glaring at Ezra before shutting the door behind him.

The magistrate gestured for Ezra to sit at his side. He put down his pipe and retrieved a folder of some type of paperwork from his briefcase.

"Is this about my father?" Ezra blurted out.

"What? Oh. No," answered the magistrate. "Your father remains missing."

"Oh," Ezra sighed in disappointment.

"No, this conversation is on a much happier note," said the magistrate. "According to my records, you turn eighteen this October, correct?"

"Yes, sir," Ezra replied. "The thirty-first of October."

The Irish official glanced up briefly, a smile playing at the corner of his lips. "Ah. An All Hallows Eve boy."

Ezra just stared back at him in confusion.

"Never mind," the man chuckled. He seemed to be in a much more light-hearted mood than the day they had first met in the magistrate's court office.

"Have you thought about which trade you would like to pursue after your graduation from the academy?"

Ezra cast his gaze toward his leather shoes. "Architecture and engineering have always been a dream of mine, sir."

"Ah, well. Then this conversation should intrigue you," replied the magistrate, laying a paper down on the desk in front of Ezra.

He immediately recognised it as his recent art project: the pencil-etched recreation of the Hagia Sophia mosque. Ezra studied the magistrate in curiosity.

"You are quite talented," he said in all honesty.

"Oh, er," Ezra mumbled, recalling the last conversation he had with his mother on the train. He swallowed the lump in his throat. "Thank you."

"Your art teacher, Miss Newton, is a friend of mine," the magistrate explained. "I recently had tea with her, and we got on the topic of how you were doing at the academy. One thing led to another, telegrams were sent, meetings arranged, and an exciting opportunity came about in the process." He paused, a wild grin conquering his face. "The city of Belfast would like to offer you an opportunity of employment with Harland and Wolff following completion of the term. Are you familiar with the company?"

Ezra shook his head, a motion which was reciprocated by another sheet being thrust before him. But this one was embellished with bold lettering, reading "BUILDING THE FUTURE OF THE HIGH SEAS" and littered with illustrations of ocean liners and cargo vessels.

"The Harland and Wolff shipbuilding company is a thriving business here in our local harbour," the magistrate explained. "They were recently awarded with several major contracts and are needing to expand their operations in Belfast, which includes hiring additional personnel. If accepted, you would be employed as an apprentice in the labour and assembly sectors. You would not only gain valuable experience with a renowned company but also be compensated two pounds per workday. Is that something in which you would be interested?"

"I—I don't know what to say," Ezra stammered, overwhelmed with gratitude. "That is very kind of you."

"Don't thank me, thank the good men at Harland and Wolff," the magistrate remarked with a grin. "I can absolutely let you think on it, but please be prompt in getting me a response. Telegraph my office at your earliest convenience," he said, handing Ezra a calling card with his information and a Harland and Wolff brochure. "The company would love to have you join them."

Speechless, dazed, and head swimming with possibilities, Ezra left the headmaster's office in deep reverie.

Finally. *This* was a future he could stand behind.

SOUVENIRS FROM THE PAST

For the longest time, Diego could do nothing but stare at the underside of the bunk bed. He had memorised every winding grain of the wooden slats, every placement of the steel bolts, and every weakness of Zaire's mattress, creaking whenever he would shift positions. The harder he tried to enter the dream world, the thicker the barrier grew in his mind. No matter what he did, or how heavily he came at it, the Gates of Sleep would not allow him through.

Instead, recent memories blurred together in his mind's eye: threatening red letters, Ezra's status as a Magus, the terrifying predicament with the Legerdemain, and the harsh sentiment from Jonas. All of it threatened to spiral Diego into madness.

He turned onto his side, tucking his duvet under his chin to initiate at least some comfort. At first, he thought the change in scenery finally did the trick, but then came the onslaught of conversation from Chief Constable Norman.

After the attack on the *Telegraph* Building, Norman had filed the proper reports with the Magi Gendarmerie but not without spewing his growing annoyance for the organisation.

"This has got to stop," Chief Constable Norman had muttered to Diego whilst signing the documents. "The Magi are sinking further into a cesspool of chaos that I don't believe they can crawl out from. They either get their act together and apprehend these criminals or governmental authorities may have to take matters into our own hands."

Diego did not fear losing his job. However, he *did* worry over the Third Order's reputation. They couldn't risk being dragged onto the world stage, exposed and blamed for just about everything in history. And if that happened, their society would not survive.

Huffing in exasperation, Diego rolled onto his other side.

"Kid, would you go to sleep?"

Diego narrowed his eyes at Zaire's voice. "I am trying."

"Not hard enough."

"Wow. Thanks for your overwhelming voice of concern."

Zaire shifted in the bunk above him. A weighty sigh filled the silence. Diego could almost picture him rubbing the bridge of his nose in exhausted indignation. "Go make yourself some of Ma's Frankincense Tea. The one with chamomile in it. It works wonders, you know."

"I hate that tea."

"You liked it whenever Mista Jonas made it for you."

"Yes, because he used the perfect ratio of tea to honey."

"Mmm-hmm."

Grumbling, Diego threw the covers back, swung his legs out from underneath them, and crossed the room to open his trunk. Using the light from his glowing quartz crystal, his fingers scrounged amongst his collection of Souvenirs. From Aztec coins to postcards from France and a recovered necklace from a Spanish ship lost at sea, Diego's time pieces spanned centuries. Millennia, even. He'd collected rock fragments, trinkets from traveling museum exhibits, and essentially, anything he could get his hands on to serve him in his Time Excursions.

But buried deep within the trunk—past the old books and arrowheads— were some of Diego's most prized Souvenirs. Portions of rope from Jonas' *cenotes* explorations. Old coins from the Netherlands. Handwritten letters.

Everything that would lead him back to the beautiful adventures the two of them had shared over the last three years.

His hand closed around a party noisemaker and tiptoed back to the bunk, confiscating his pocket watch from the bedside table on the way back under the covers.

"I hope you're not planning on blowing that thing when I'm just falling back into the dream world," Zaire mumbled.

"Don't worry about it," Diego whispered, as he summoned the Celestial Lifeforce into his crystal. "If I cannot sleep, the least I can do is relive pleasant memories."

Belfast, April 1905

When Diego opened his eyes again, he found himself leaning against the bookshelf in the Elysium common room. Not his astral projection, of course. His past self. The one with the goofiest grin, utterly bewitched by the sight in front of him.

Swallowing an unexpected surge of emotion, Diego turned to watch as Jonas wobbled on a step stool to affix a celebratory banner to the wall above the mantel. He had rolled up his shirt sleeves to the elbow, exposing his forearms in a way that made Diego lightheaded.

"This will not be a successful birthday party unless someone's face ends up in cake," stated Past Time Diego.

Once Jonas verified the cloth had been properly secured, he threw a puzzled glance over his shoulder. "Truly, the number of peculiar things you say on a daily basis is unmatchable."

Past Time Diego surveyed Jonas' work. "It looks a tad crooked to me."

"Everything looks a tad crooked to you."

Making his way to Jonas, Past Time Diego eased him off the stool and pulled him into an embrace. They pressed their foreheads together, smiles broad and eyes bright with happiness. Holding one another in blissful silence, they slowly rocked from foot to foot in their own sort of dance.

"Make way for the Queen of Cakes!" sang Annabelle as she waltzed into the Elysium common room. She gingerly placed the decadent multi-layered dessert upon the table and slowly, almost comedically, swivelled on heel to face Jonas and Diego. "Oh, I do hope I did not interrupt anything."

"Not at all," Jonas replied, ruffling Past Time Diego's hair after he stepped out of his arms. "Can I help you with anything, Mum?"

"I think we are all set," she exhaled in satisfaction. "Kierra and the children should be here soon; hopefully they get in before Zaire arrives. You know how he's always early to every engagement."

Within minutes, the entirety of the Irish Chapter crowded around the common room table, the celebratory nucleus of Elysium, each with their faces aglow from the candlelight.

Diego kept his eyes trained on Jonas, who kept glancing at his pocket watch in anticipation for Zaire's approaching footsteps. Any moment now, the guest of honour would arrive, heralding the official beginning of the festivities.

"I think we should all hide and turn out the lights," suggested Oliver. "Birthday surprises make the best memories."

Diego could not argue with that logic.

"Oh, excellent idea!" Aja replied, clapping in excitement.

"You would probably give the old man a fright," Past Time Diego said just before he swiped his finger across the top of the cake. "He is a Taurus, after all."

Kierra slapped his hand away from the cake. "Diego!"

"Kierra!" he mocked her and smeared frosting across her nose.

"Shhh!" Jonas insisted, motioning for everyone to quiet down. "He's coming downstairs."

The group's excitement muted to silence just as the door swung open, revealing an unsuspecting Zaire.

"Surprise!" Aja yelled.

"*Mazel tov!*" Oliver declared.

"Happy birthday!" Kierra said in a sing-song voice after blowing into a noisemaker.

"Congratulations on forty years of life, you old codger," Past Time Diego remarked, giving Zaire a light punch on the shoulder. "*Feliz cumpleaños!*"

"*Gefeliciteerd*, my friend," Jonas said reverently.

"Wow!" Zaire exclaimed, observing the vibrant decor. He wiped a tear from the corner of his eye. "Y'all didn't have to do this."

"Oh yes, we absolutely did, Mr. Jameson," Annabelle remarked. "Every year lived is a year to be celebrated."

"Even if you *are* ancient," whispered Past Time Diego out of the corner of his mouth.

Diego chuckled at his own antics.

"And this cake!" Zaire said, admiring the intricate confectionary swirls. "Ma, did you make this?"

"Red cocoa, your favourite," Annabelle happily confirmed.

"Y'all too kind," Zaire responded. He shook his head in disbelief.

"Hey, let's sing that facetious song you all like," suggested Past Time Diego with a shrug.

Kierra playfully rolled her eyes at his comment. "*For he's a jolly good fellow,*" she began.

The rest of the Magi joined her in song.

"*...for he's a jolly good fellow, for he's a jolly good fellooowww, and so says all of us!*"

The entire room erupted into cheers. Joy filled Diego's heart as he watched his Magi family congregate around Zaire. He grinned, taking in their abundant enthusiasm as Annabelle dished out pieces of cake. Diego was grateful he had the ability to relive times like these. Who needed an expensive camera when every beautiful moment could be frozen within Time and cherished forever?

"Zaire, tell us about your birthdays in America," Oliver mumbled, his mouth full of cake.

"Oliver, mind your manners, please," Annabelle scolded him.

Aja snickered at Oliver and continued his train of thought seeing as he was still chewing through the massive bite. "Yes, how did you celebrate when you lived in New Orleans?"

"Much like this," Zaire replied. "Back when I was a young'un, Pa would take me to watch street performers in the French Quarter while Ma cooked up jambalaya and cornbread. We'd end the night sitting out on the porch swing, just staring up at the stars. We wasn't rich, but I could-a sworn I owned the world."

"That is beautiful," Aja sighed.

"But one of my most favourite traditions started when I turned sixteen," Zaire continued. "My younger brother, Arnie, was upset after dealing with some bullies at school, and I really wanted to make him laugh. So, I took my piece of birthday cake and done smashed it in my face."

Oliver and Aja howled in laughter. Kierra rolled her eyes. Diego applauded.

"I think we need a demonstration," eagerly replied Past Time Diego.

Diego smiled. This was his favourite part.

"Oh, yeah, of course," Zaire agreed, turning toward Annabelle. "Ma, mind if I sneak another piece?"

"Anything for the Birthday Boy," Annabelle said, pursing her lips into a smile as she supplied him the second helping.

Zaire took the plate and looked down into the sugary depths of the frosting. He cracked his neck and shook out his shoulders as he comedically prepared himself for impact. "All right, somebody count me down."

"Five!" Aja screeched, bursting with exhilaration.

"Four…three," Oliver, Diego, and Jonas joined in, "…two…ONE!"

Zaire lifted the plate toward himself but at the last moment, changed its trajectory and smashed the dessert in Past Time Diego's face.

Oliver gasped. Aja opened her mouth in surprise. The entirety of the room fell into silent expectation for his imminent reaction.

At first, Past Time Diego just stood there, trying his best to hold in laughter as chunks of cake fell from his chin. "Oh, you did *not* just do that!" he finally exclaimed. He wiped the frosting from around his eyes and rushed at Zaire with handfuls of cake.

Zaire yelped and dodged the couch to avoid Diego's enthusiastic wrath. "Ma, the kid is chasing me again," he jokingly complained to Annabelle.

"In Mexico, we have our *own* traditions," Past Time Diego said, knocking over the Moroccan side table in his haste. "And it is called 'beating a *piñata* with a stick.'"

Jonas laughed and pushed up his sleeves even further. "Now, I think you both are forgetting something."

Past Time Diego slowed his chase, staring back at Jonas in confusion. To anyone else, they wouldn't be able to see much more than smeared cake remnants.

"You're forgetting that despite my lack of dance skills, I have impeccable hand-eye coordination," Jonas responded, striding over to the table to grab a fistful of dessert. "And I could never pass up an impromptu cake ambush." He pitched the cake across the room, hitting Zaire square in the nose.

"Get 'em, Jonas!" cheered Oliver.

"Go, go, go!" shouted Aja.

"Oh my," breathed Kierra.

Past Time Diego nodded in appreciation toward his counterpart in cake-throwing crime. "*Muy impresionante.*"

"Why, thank you," Jonas said, taking a bow.

Zaire used the moment to his advantage and scooped up the remains of Jonas' ammunition only to toss it back at him.

"Argh, I'm hit!" Jonas groaned. He clutched his arm and crumpled theatrically to the floor. "The agony! Oh!"

Kierra placed her hands on her hips. "You buffoons are wasting perfectly good cake."

"Cake never goes to waste when it is in your face!" Past Time Diego replied as his shoes slid over a slippery spot on the floor. He lost his footing and tripped over the corner of the rug, flailing before landing on Jonas.

Diego remembered it as clear as daylight. The light-hearted lurch in his abdomen. The thrilling spark, warm, yet fleeting. Swimming in his vast ocean blue eyes. Jonas was not merely his inamorato. He was his anchor. His reason for living. His *everything*.

Jonas reached up to wipe frosting from Past Time Diego's cheek. "You have got a little something on your face," he teased.

"You are just jealous you don't have any on *your* face," Past Time Diego replied. "But that can be arranged."

Their eyes locked on each other for a moment before Past Time Diego closed the space between their lips.

For some reason, Diego could not bear to watch. He turned, chewing on the inside of his cheek, anything to distract him from the wildly content version of himself only metres away. He was a stranger. And so was the man beneath him.

"All right, that's two down. Who else wants to crumble at the hands of the Cake King?" Zaire roared in a mighty—yet altogether hilarious—voice. He wrestled Oliver into a headlock, rubbing his knuckles over the boy's head. "How about you, young'un?"

"Argh, I surrender, Cake King!" Oliver laughed, waving his cloth napkin. "I surrender!"

While the joyous party continued, Diego clutched the noisemaker in his palm and his pocket watch in the other. The hour hands began their forward progression on his familiar journey back to the Present.

Some things were meant to be left in the Past.

30

HARLAND AND WOLFF

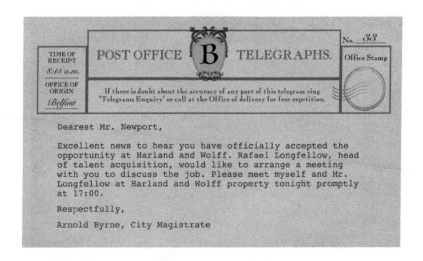

| TIME OF RECEIPT *8:15 a.m.* | POST OFFICE **B** TELEGRAPHS. | No. *33* Office Stamp |
| OFFICE OF ORIGIN *Belfast* | If there is doubt about the accuracy of any part of this telegram ring "Telegrams Enquiry" or call at the Office of delivery for free repetition. | |

Dearest Mr. Newport,

Excellent news to hear you have officially accepted the opportunity at Harland and Wolff. Rafael Longfellow, head of talent acquisition, would like to arrange a meeting with you to discuss the job. Please meet myself and Mr. Longfellow at Harland and Wolff property tonight promptly at 17:00.

Respectfully,

Arnold Byrne, City Magistrate

For the entire second half of the school day, Ezra found himself engrossed in the contents of the telegram he had received earlier that morning. He could not stop thinking about the meeting with the Harland and Wolff recruiter. In fact, it preoccupied so much of his awareness that his teachers spent substantial efforts reeling in his attention.

During arithmetic, an irritated Mr. Cotton smacked Ezra upside the head with a ruler, much to his classmates' entertainment. And in grammar class, Ms. O'Flannigan's beady little eyes burned in ferocity behind her spectacles when she discovered him staring idly out the window. Infuriated, she made him sit in the corner and wear the most ridiculous looking dunce cap until the final bell.

Stumbling through the daze of recent events, Ezra realised he hadn't even told Aja and Oliver the news of his interview. While he imagined they would be excited for his opportunity, he had a sneaking suspicion Aja would make it clear that focusing on his newfound abilities was a much better decision.

It's all for the best, he repeated to himself. *My parents would want this for me. I want this for me.*

When the last session had concluded, Ezra rushed toward the iron gates separating Belfast Royal Academy from the rest of the city. As it was not after dinner hours just yet, he knew they would still be open, granting him full access to the outside world. The soles of his shoes skidded across the loose gravel in the drive, but that did not deter him from picking up his pace.

Forward, ever forward. He could not slow down and neither would his corybantic thoughts. Opportunity awaited just beyond the bend.

By the time Ezra reached the Harland and Wolff shipyard, the sun slouched in the evening sky, shedding a pinkish hue over Queen's Island. Massive cranes and metallic gantries glinted in the dying daylight. Ezra scanned the vicinity for the magistrate, but he only saw merchants loading crates into their vessels and a man fishing at the end of one of the piers. Commercial ships hauling freight in the direction of the North Atlantic blasted their horns, echoing across the sound. Smaller boats drifted into their appointed docks. Seagulls dove in and out of marine traffic, eager to snag a bite of dinner from the fishermen's hauls.

Ezra did a second sweep of the property. No sign whatsoever of the magistrate.

He said to be here promptly at seventeen hundred hours, thought Ezra in a moment of panic. He double checked his telegram and next, his pocket watch.

17:07.

Seeing no other immediate option, Ezra wandered toward one of the benches overlooking the inlet. His heart pounded a steady drumbeat, rhythm hastening as the minutes pressed on. Swallowing his anxieties, Ezra decided his time was better served mentally rehearsing his prepared discourse for the recruiters.

Why yes, sir, I have demonstrated excellence in all my classes at Belfast Royal Academy while being employed by the institution, he imagined himself confidently stating. *Put simply, I apply a firm dedication to any task before me. I believe you will find my devoted work ethic an asset to your already thriving company.*

"Ah, Mr. Newport, there you are."

Ezra broke out of his reverie as the magistrate approached the bench and patted away the perspiration from his brow with a handkerchief.

"I apologise for my tardiness; the tram was running a bit behind this evening," Magistrate Byrne explained, smoothing over his curly auburn hair. "Are you ready?"

"As ready as I'll ever be," Ezra replied.

"Good man," he commended and clapped Ezra heartily on the back. "Now, let's find our contact...er, Raphael, I believe he said his name was."

The two of them journeyed toward the main corporate building, a fortress built of brick and grandeur. Completely awestruck, Ezra's eyes gazed at the striking lettering spelling out "Harland & Wolff" above the rows of arched windows. Everything about Queen's Island was drenched in industrialism and reeked of hard work and prosperity.

Here, dreams were built as tall as the smokestacks.

A middle-aged man with dark hair and even darker eyes sat casually upon the steps leading up to the entrance. A pipe drooped from his mouth, with smoke permeating through cracked lips. Bits of grey ash flecked over his worn cotton shirt and tweed trousers, the unofficial uniform of the blue-collar working class.

The man stood, brushed off his trousers, and nodded in greeting toward the magistrate and next to Ezra. "This must be our new talent, eh? Mr. Ezra Newport?"

"Yes, sir, hello," Ezra spoke nervously, shaking his hand.

"I am Raphael Longfellow, head of talent acquisition at Harland and Wolff," said the man. "Shall we take a tour of the facility before speaking on job specifics?"

"Uh, yes, sir, that sounds wonderful," Ezra agreed. He looked to the magistrate for affirmation, which was echoed in the Irish official's smiling eyes.

"Excellent. Follow me," instructed Raphael.

At once, Raphael guided them toward the shipyard. Ezra could barely keep pace; the man's long legs covered almost twice the distance in a single stride.

"Here at Harland and Wolff, we take great pride in building the best maritime vessels in the industry," said Raphael monotonously, almost as if he were quoting a brochure from memory. "We have several ships in various stages of production. In fact, the SS Ortega just commenced construction. We are looking to start on several other contracts in the next few years, including some ambitious orders from the White Star Line."

"Fascinating!" commented the magistrate.

"If you find that fascinating, wait until you see our drawing room," Raphael remarked as he drew from his pipe.

They approached the pier that overlooked the grand ship platform. Ezra stepped closer to the railing and scanned the vast shipyard in quiet admiration. Daylight had faded into twilight, drawing a grey curtain over the iron plates, wooden frames, and other building material. All employees had left for the evening, leaving the area silent and void of all life, save for the sporadic call of seagulls.

Suddenly, the sound of a gurgled cry snapped Ezra out of his observations. He whirled around and watched helplessly as the magistrate collapsed to his knees.

Cool and collected, Raphael swiped a long dagger across his handkerchief, leaving a trail of red on the white fibres.

The Irish official grasped at his throat, a look of pure dread clouding his eyes just before he fell forward into the gravel. Motionless. Bleeding. *Dead.*

A heavy cold sank to the bottom of Ezra's gut, like a lump of ice plunked forcefully into a cup of hot tea. Mouth gaping in horror, his breath came in rigid gasps as he tried to make sense of the scene before him.

"Wh-what...what is going on?" Ezra managed. He attempted to force his feet—or anything—to move, but his body refused to cooperate.

Not again.

Raphael tucked away his dagger and fished around in his vest pockets. He withdrew a small glass bottle and emptied its liquid contents onto another cloth.

Before Ezra could react, the man rushed at him, forcing the rag over his nose and mouth. He squirmed, trying to gain freedom from his death grip.

"Help!" he yelled, but the cry was stifled before it could reach much further.

"Shhh!" Raphael hissed. "Don't want the whole town to hear, now, do we?"

Ezra fought for air. He struggled, choking and gasping. But with every passing second, his strength deteriorated.

"Sorry I had to off your case worker, but he was a liability," muttered Raphael, a biting cruelty in his voice. "Besides, *you* are the one my boss needs. My *real* boss. Not some namby-pamby Harland and Wolff idiot. But I was fairly convincing, eh, kid?"

Once again, Ezra tried shouting for help, but the rag muffled any hope of anyone overhearing his cries. Coughing and panting, he wrestled against the man's hold. Instead of breaking loose, however, Ezra's knees buckled, and he crumpled to the ground.

"Fighting is useless," spat Raphael as he smothered him with the sickly-sweet cloth. "The quicker I can get you to Consul Diederik, the better."

Ezra's mind spun in a whirlpool of confusion. The next few minutes melted into an obscure scene of dull colour and indistinct noises. He fought for freedom, but his tingling arms and legs betrayed him. Not long after, his vision tunnelled, sending him to a place he knew all too well.

ANDROMEDA ERIDIAN

"Ezra?"

Calm and melodic, the voice of the Shahmaran saturated his subconscious. It rippled like water, gently nudging him awake.

"Ezra, darling?"

"What!?" His response fractured the dark serenity draped over him like a blanket. Despite the Shahmaran's insistent beckoning, Ezra refused to open his eyes. "Do not bother me."

"Would you rather I sing to you instead?"

"No."

"You're awfully churlish, aren't you?"

He cracked an eyelid, jumping in surprise at the proximity of the creature laying in the shallows. Her brilliant smile basked in the water's reflection while long strands of dark hair flicked about like snakes on the surface. Purple light glimmered in the deep, causing everything around them to radiate with a vibrance Ezra couldn't put into words.

"I'm only churlish because I've found myself in trouble again," Ezra muttered. "Will I ever be able to just...just exist like I used to?"

"I have asked myself that same question," the Shahmaran answered, propping herself up on an elbow. "You will come to find when you hold such power, everyone wants their share when it was not theirs to begin with."

"I suppose," sighed Ezra, recalling the legends. Mangled by countless retellings over the decades, the tales of the Shahmaran had twisted into unrecognisable forms. But every iteration ended the same: The Shahmaran was hunted for her magic. Captured. Tortured. Killed. All in the name of lust and greed. "How do you escape?"

Her eyes searched him. "Sometimes, you don't."

"I can't let them get away with this," Ezra replied, lifting himself out of the shallow water. "Besides, I don't know what they want from me. I am still unsure where my father is, I don't know anything about the artifact translation, and I can't even begin to describe how it is that I'm a Magus."

"Well, I assume the Brotherhood wants something with the Tablet of—"

"I know," Ezra interjected. "But I don't have any answers to give them and when they realise that, they…"

The eyes of the Shahmaran softened as he choked on his words. She reached out and caressed his cheek. "It's okay to be scared."

"I'm not scared. I'm petrified."

"Sweet boy," said the Shahmaran, bracing herself as a sudden tremor quaked through the cavern. "You have survived more daunting things than this. You can do it again."

The world swayed in a topsy-turvy dance as Ezra returned to consciousness. Before he could even open his eyes, his nose was assaulted by a crude mix of salt and exhaust. He struggled to crack an eyelid amidst the raging headache sending streaks of lightning throughout his skull. Somehow, he managed.

After his sight adjusted to the shadows, Ezra's eyes roamed his new surroundings. A shallow pool of ocean water enveloped him, springing from some undetectable fissure in the craft. Rope, life jackets, various tools, and wooden crates littered the space around him. A lantern swung above a sitting bench like a demented pendulum. The dreary, cramped quarters were hardly suitable for the items in it, let alone a human being.

And yet, here he was.

All at once, flashes of what had happened in the shipyard sent panic crashing through him like an icy wave. The magistrate had been killed in front of his very eyes. Because of *him*. In the midst of it all, he had been taken against his will.

Ezra propped himself up with his elbow but groaned in frustration when he realised his wrists and ankles had been bound with bulky iron shackles, consequently limiting his mobility. He huffed and laid back on the floor, staring at the ceiling. When the rocking of his surroundings became too much, he swallowed his nausea and shut his eyes. He silently cursed himself for not taking Jonas up on the offer to sharpen his abilities. For if he had listened, if he had stayed, perhaps he would be able to conjure some type of magic to sever his binds and escape from the mysterious prison.

No matter how hard he tried, Ezra could not summon the Celestial Lifeforce to do much of anything, besides aggravate him further. Perhaps if he held his new crystal—

Ezra's heart pounded when his fingers scrounged for the quartz in his trouser pockets but turned up empty handed. It must have been confiscated.

Muffled voices disrupted his thoughts. The inaudible conversation journeyed across the topside of the ceiling in tandem with creaking footsteps. Shocking yellow light spilled down a stairwell as a hatch flew open and with it, a curtain of rain.

"Yes, Mr. Ackerly," shouted a woman over the deluge. "Leave it to me."

The woman slammed the hatch behind her. She flipped the switch of an electric torch and shone the beam directly into Ezra's face.

"Ah, looks like someone is finally awake," observed the woman in a throaty Greek accent. She lowered the hood of her cape, revealing bountiful brunette hair cascading over her shoulders. Her sharp cheekbones and the elegant slope of her nose invoked a sense of familiarity, but Ezra had no idea where he might have seen her before. Perhaps Budapest? Despite this, Ezra marvelled at how the wisdom in her eyes seemed incongruent with the youth in her features. "I started to wonder if Mr. Ackerly accidentally killed you."

Mr. Ackerly?

A dark glimmer rippled through her golden eyes. "My colleague can be quite convincing. I assume the real Raphael does not have a clue as to what transpired in the shipyard this evening."

Ezra glared at her. "Why don't you finish me off, then?"

"That will not be necessary," she replied coolly, sitting on the bench underneath the lantern. "Consul Diederik and Deputy Consul Symon want you alive."

A shudder tingled through his body.

"Why?"

"Oh, but where are my manners?" she said, ignoring his question. "Hello, Mr. Newport. You can call me Andromeda Eridian." The woman offered her gloved hand in greeting and almost immediately retracted it. "My apologies, I forgot you cannot use yours."

He did not answer but narrowed his eyes in response.

Andromeda removed her cape, revealing a dress that looked like it cost more than his boat prison. The golden buttons on the bodice of the garnet material glistened under the lantern, stars in their own right. Setting the dripping outerwear aside, the corner of her mouth twinged with some sort of sadistic pleasure.

Ezra struggled against his binds, but the iron cut off circulation to his hands. "What do you want with me?" he spat. "Where am I?"

Andromeda laughed. She stood and brushed the wrinkles out of her dress before pacing the length of the lower hold. "Last I enquired, we were somewhere due west of the Isle of Man."

Ezra gulped.

"We are on a boat if you have not quite figured that out yet," came the woman's condescending reply.

"I know," he countered. "I am not stupid."

"Hmm," Andromeda remarked with a slight grin. "No. Just naive."

Ezra shook his head in disbelief.

"Hmm."

Andromeda knelt to his level. He instinctively edged away but the woman grasped his chin and forced his head in her direction. She reeked of wine and perfume. Her attention sank to his scarf, fingers following only seconds behind. "What a curious print. The Shahmaran, yes? I suppose her legend is practically a national treasure in the Ottoman Empire."

Ezra refused to answer.

"Personally, I have always believed the Shahmaran inspired my ancestors to weave the tales of Medusa," Andromeda speculated. "After all, both legends feature two alluring beings with powerful abilities." She stroked Ezra's cheek with the back of her hand. "Much like you."

Straining, he attempted to move out of her reach. "You don't know anything about me."

"Mmm, on the contrary, darling," she answered, returning to her feet. Andromeda observed him in hushed calculation, like a wildcat scrutinising its prey before the kill. "You and your family have become quite the talk around Legerdemain Headquarters."

"What do you mean?"

"And it seems you do not even know," Andromeda said, as if making a humorous observation. "Fascinating."

Ezra's quickened breath formed clouds in front of his face, obscuring the scene around him. "What do Diederik and Symon want with me?"

Andromeda found interest in staring beyond the walls of the vessel for a moment before turning to face him. "You want to find your father, don't you?"

Ezra hesitated a moment, then nodded.

"Well, so do they."

"I still don't under—"

"Leverage," she interrupted. "They want to draw your father out of hiding with the one thing they know will work without fail. *You.*"

Anger burned in Ezra's tear ducts. He sniffed and wiped his face on the shoulder of his school jacket. "He hasn't come for me yet; what makes you think he will come for me now?"

Andromeda smirked. "If Ibrahim loves you, he will not be able to stay away."

"I've nearly been killed three times since I last saw him, yet he never did anything to help," Ezra said, his voice trembling. "This time won't be any different."

"Aww, you poor boy," Andromeda cooed mockingly. Again, she knelt to his level, her index finger tracing the embroidered insignia of Belfast Royal Academy on his jacket. "I am sure the consul will make the offer extra enticing."

Ezra fought against his shackles. "Let me go!" he yelled. "Take me back to Belfast!"

"Sorry, darling, I cannot do that."

"Take me back to Belfast," he commanded through clenched teeth. "*Now.*"

"Oh, hush, you," Andromeda answered, returning to her feet. "Your tone is really starting to annoy."

"So is yours!"

Without warning, Andromeda smacked him across the face with a surprisingly powerful backhand.

"Do not *ever* talk to a lady like that again," she growled. The woman plunged her fist into her skirt pocket, drew out a handkerchief, and stuffed it so far into his mouth that he gagged. "You had better watch yourself around Consul Diederik and Deputy Consul Symon. They won't be as forgiving as I am."

Ezra's eyes burned concurrently with the stinging pain in his cheek. He turned his face away so the stranger would not see the confusion and despair now consuming him from the inside out.

As much as he wished for his father to come to his rescue, that frail longing seemed as impossible as his mother returning from the grave. Just as elusive: the hope of getting out of the situation alive, if rumours were true about the consuls of the Legerdemain Brotherhood.

With tears now streaming over his cheeks, he bowed his head, defeated.

Somewhere on a distant shoreline, a melancholy cry of an owl echoed into the night.

ℰMERGENCY

"I thought we had an understanding, Mr. van der Campe."

At the sound of Mr. Edwin Mears' voice, Jonas begrudgingly tore his attention away from restocking the Emporium shelves. The Administration official, looking more haggard than usual, was flanked by two members of the Magi Gendarmerie. *Presumably to take Ezra to headquarters,* Jonas recalled from the last conversation with him. He stood, dusted off his trousers, and folded his arms.

"On which account?"

Mr. Mears could not resist rolling his eyes. "That you do not interfere with the Newport boy."

"I assure you, I haven't," Jonas insisted, his eyes flicking back and forth between the three of them. "What could possibly make you think that I—"

"Ezra is missing," Mr. Mears cut in. "I spoke with the headmaster, various faculty, including your cousin, and even the mess hall staff. No one has seen the boy since the end of classes yesterday afternoon."

Jonas tried to speak but for once, finding the right combination of syllables was a struggle. He searched Edwin Mears' expressions for a shred of deceit but found nothing except truth in his features.

"I—I don't know what to say."

"How about you start with what you might know about Mr. Newport's whereabouts," the Administration official suggested impatiently.

Jonas ran his fingers through his hair. "I haven't the slightest idea, sir. If he's missing, he must be in trouble."

"The Administration does not have time for this sort of thing, Mr. van der Campe. If you know anything—"

"Sir, I already told you I do not!"

An abrupt clamour of the shop bell doused the tension in the air.

"Jonas, we've got a problem," Diego asserted, breathless. He shot a questioning glance at Mr. Edwin Mears before thrusting a newspaper and Ezra's crystal quartz wand into Jonas' hands. "Ezra is in trouble."

"So I've heard," Jonas sighed. Bracing himself for the worst, he unfurled the paper, his eyes growing in horror at the sight of the front-page article.

"The Royal Irish Constabulary is investigating a death at the Harland and Wolff shipyard," Diego summarised for the benefit of all in the room. "The body of City Magistrate Arnold Byrne was discovered this morning at the start of first shift. Supposedly, he had accompanied Ezra to a job interview last night, but no such meeting ever took place. And with Ezra now missing, the RIC is naming him as a suspect."

"Christ," Jonas whispered in disbelief. "What happened when you went back in time to view the events?"

"Well, ever since the Legerdemain started using Time Blemishes to cover their tracks during recent events, I was not able to gather any evidence whatsoever," Diego muttered, folding his arms. "So, while that leads me to believe that by default the Brotherhood is involved, it is not enough for Chief Constable Norman or anyone else, for that matter. We would be incredibly lucky if the RIC still trust the Third Order right now."

Edwin Mears frowned and directed his aversion at Jonas. "This is absolutely what we did *not* want to happen."

A defensive fire prickled within Jonas' being at the official's statement. Despite this, the matter of Ezra being in the hands of the Brotherhood made his skin crawl. His surroundings spun around him, a disorderly waltz between nausea and dread. It took everything within him to remain upright.

While the strange mental connection Jonas shared with Ezra had been enlightening on several occasions—especially when Ezra's fear was insuppressible—he hadn't seen anything in the last day to even know anything was wrong. The absence of whatever element connected them stirred up a frustration within Jonas he could not quite understand. And it was time the Administration needed to know.

"Sir, sometimes I can see glimpses of Ezra's memories as if through his eyes," Jonas found himself saying before he could stop the words from tumbling from his mouth. "It's a strange connection I can't quite explain. I don't believe it is a Gift. I'm not sure what this is. But ever since the Portadown train wreck, I—"

Edwin studied him. "A connection, you say? Has this been disclosed to the Administration?"

"As of ten seconds ago."

"Mm. And you've seen nothing recently that would allude to his current whereabouts?"

"None whatsoever, sir. That's what bothers me."

Edwin jotted something down in a pocket-sized notebook before returning his attention to Jonas. "Well, if you do happen to see anything, contact my office at once. Until then—"

"What do we do?" asked Jonas. He hoped his words wouldn't betray the fear in his chest. Unfortunately, the question came out as a strangled plea.

With a demulcent sparkle in his eyes, Diego laid a hand on his shoulder. Jonas flinched at the contact but did not pull away. "We will find him," Diego said with confidence. "And by God above, we are going to make those Legerdemain pay."

"You sure as hell *will not*," Mr. Mears growled, stepping forward with an unyielding intensity in his aura. "This situation falls under the

Administration's jurisdiction. You and the entirety of the Irish Chapter will stay here and not move a muscle; do you understand me?"

"I understand English easily enough," Diego replied with an apathetic wave of his hand. "But what you just said does not translate. Ezra is one of us, and you cannot believe that we will just sit around and—"

"Mr. Montreal, one more word from you and my colleagues and I will not hesitate to arrest you for interfering with an official investigation." Heat radiated from Edwin like an imploding star. "Is *that* understood?"

"Yes, sir," Diego sighed, defeated.

Edwin looked to Jonas next. "And you, Mr. van der Campe?"

"Yes, I understand."

But as the Administration officials departed the Emporium of Exotic Trinkets, Jonas could not help but wonder if the figurative wall they were up against was something more than a simple obstacle. This wall was a target through a scope, just seconds from a barrage of bullets.

According to Diego, maps were simultaneously the best and worst things to ever exist.

While they were immensely helpful during travel—and a beneficial distraction from the earlier conversation with Edwin Mears—the two-dimensional landscapes did nothing but torment him now. Especially when the flame of action had been ignited and showed no signs of wearing off. Nevertheless, Diego sank deeper into the comforts of his favourite atlas, trying his hardest to redirect his thoughts from the bleak circumstances.

There was nothing the Irish Chapter could do for Ezra. Their hands were tied.

As Diego lazed on the common room couch, his feet propped upon the furniture's armrest, he studied the eastern coastline of Australia. However, Kierra's persistent pacing in front of the fireplace had become increasingly annoying. Fulgurating flames in the hearth illuminated her exhausted scowl. Sections of light red hair fell from their original pinned position atop her head, making her appear frazzled and disheartened.

"If you keep pacing like that, you're going to wear a hole in the ground," Diego murmured without looking up from the vast regions of Australia's outback.

Kierra huffed, blowing the hair away from her forehead. "I just don't understand how everyone can sleep right now, knowing that poor boy is out there. He's probably frightened. Upset. What if he's hurt?"

"I guarantee you Jonas is not sleeping," Diego said, peering over the top of the atlas. "He's probably tossing and turning thinking of how to strangle Edwin Mears without the Council knowing."

"This isn't funny, Diego!" Kierra exclaimed, hugging her arms close to herself.

"I never said it was."

"Then what do we do?"

"What *can* we do? The Administration made it clear they've got it under control."

"But they have said that before and look how that turned out," Kierra fought back, gesturing vaguely around her as if to further annunciate her point. "Ezra needs us."

"I agree," Diego replied, setting the atlas on his lap. "But we don't have a choice right now."

"We always have a choice."

"You wouldn't be saying that if you saw the savage look Mr. Mears gave Jonas and me earlier. That man has it out for us. Well, more Jonas than anything, but I guess when you are the enemy's son, that's…"

He allowed his voice to trail off when he realised tears now flowed freely over Kierra's cheeks.

"*Dios*," he muttered to himself before getting up to draw her into his arms. "It's going to be all right."

"How can you say that?" Kierra cried, leaning her head against his shoulder.

"Because if I don't say it, who will?"

She sniffed as she pulled back, tears glistening on her eyelashes. "I want to believe you. I really do. But—"

Just then, the Magi transponder chimed into life on the mantel.

"Attention all chapters of the Third Order of the Magi," transmitted a voice that sounded on the verge of breaking. "The Administration has issued an urgent warning for all Magi to seek shelter at once. We repeat: The Magi Council has declared a Triple Star emergency—"

"¡*Santa mierda!*" Diego exclaimed, sharing a look of pure dread with Kierra.

Before Kierra could say anything in response, Diego bolted down the corridor, pounding his fists over Zaire and Annabelle's rooms. "Wake up, Zaire! *Mamá!*"

He proceeded through Jonas' doorway and leapt onto his mattress, shaking him into consciousness.

"Good Lord, Diego," fussed Jonas in a hoarse voice. He hoisted himself into a seated position. "What is all this madness about?"

Diego frantically yanked on his arm. "The Administration is transmitting! And they said something about a Triple Star emergency!"

Jonas swore under his breath and swung his long legs out from underneath his quilt.

Hustling back into the Elysium common room, the five Magi gathered around the flashing transponder.

"... details are still arriving as we speak. For those just joining us, we find ourselves in the midst of terror this evening. With rising violence in and around our twelve Magi Chapter jurisdictions, the Magi Council has initiated a Triple Star Emergency. We have confirmed the Legerdemain Brotherhood is behind the attacks as part of an internal political ploy. While these heinous acts have been targeting Quotidians, the Magi Gendarmerie confirms at least one hundred Magi worldwide have been killed while attempting to rescue those involved."

"God be with them," Annabelle whispered as she pulled her robe tighter around her shoulders. Diego laid a comforting hand on her arm, and she grasped it in hers.

"As we work in cooperation with international authorities, the Magi Council advises all Chapters to shelter within a safe area until further notice. Travel outside of local municipalities is not advised and will be punished by the fullest extent of the Magi Code."

Kierra's glistening eyes met Diego's.

"For the safety of our couriers, the Magi Administration will also be suspending our courier service. As always, we encourage open communication between our Chapters and the Council. Telegrams and telephone messages are highly recommended during this time.

"May the Famed Three and the Yonder Star protect you now and into the future as we rise above the folly of our foes."

The transmission fizzled, leaving a bitter silence settling over the room.

"Christ," mumbled Jonas as he massaged his forehead.

"I can't believe it has come to this," said Zaire.

"This is awful," Annabelle agreed. "In my entire life, I have never witnessed such international atrocities at the hands of the Brotherhood." She approached Jonas and rubbed his upper arm in consolation. "I believe your interpretation of the night sky at the turn of the year is starting to make sense, my dear. But remember, as Magi, our hope in the future is as everlasting as the stars."

Jonas collapsed into the armchair. After running frustrated fingers through his bedraggled hair, his shoulders sank in dejection, and he turned his glassy stare to the fireplace. "Someone once told me that even the stars fall."

Diego crouched beside the chair to confront the ocean storm within Jonas' eyes. "What do we do now?"

Chewing on his thumbnail, with disquietude weighing down his facial features, Jonas broke his silence. "I'll tell you what we're going to do: We're going to listen to the Administration and do exactly as they say."

Diego searched his expressions for a hint of cynicism, but every fibre of his being emanated sincerity.

"I know this is going to be difficult with Ezra missing," Jonas remarked. "But until the Administration says it is safe again, none of us are to leave Elysium. As they have made it quite clear, they have got everything under control." With exhaustion and the slightest glimmer of doubt in his face, Jonas made eye contact with his cousin. "Kierra, will you bring Aja and Oliver over first thing tomorrow morning? You will need to take a leave of absence from the academy, if possible."

Kierra nodded without a word of objection.

Crossing his arms over his chest, Diego struggled to process what had just transpired. In a month's time, his happy-go-lucky existence had crumbled beneath him, leaving doubt, disappointment, and perturbation in the rubble. Diego fully expected his dreams to haunt him, but not waking life. Waking life was the only place he could find redemption. Healing. Justice.

But the more he thought about it, the more he realised the anxieties of waking life had always been there, crouching like a predator in the dark.

And the darkness would not be letting up anytime soon.

FINAL PIECE OF THE TRAP

For two days, restless waves tossed the small vessel from the North Atlantic to the Irish Sea and into the English Channel. By the time it had docked—based on the exchange between Ezra's captors, somewhere on the River Thames outside of London—he could hardly stand from the horrible concoction of dehydration and sea legs. Much to Mr. Ackerly and Andromeda's dismay, both adults had to physically lift him from the lower hold and haul him to a carriage parked just off the marina.

Still bound at the wrists, Ezra collapsed in exhaustion on the transport's seat cushions while his captors spoke in hushed tones with the coachman.

"What took so long?" said an unfamiliar voice in an accent that Ezra guessed was Egyptian.

"You have to understand, Rami, that we were transporting an adolescent in rough seas," snarled Mr. Ackerly. "That's about as impossible as speeding up time."

"Especially a young man who cannot stomach sailing to begin with," Andromeda grumbled.

"Well, let us get a move on; the consul is expecting you," Rami explained in a stern tone. The carriage swayed on its chassis as he climbed into the coach box. His two captors followed suit, hoisting themselves up into the transport with Ezra.

Ezra moaned miserably. His gut churned in retaliation for denying it food, water, and stable ground for so long. Each shallow breath seemed harder to inhale than the last, and his head felt as if someone had taken an axe to the back of his skull.

After what seemed like hours of fading in and out of consciousness, Ezra found himself being unloaded from the carriage amid an all-too-familiar city. Led by the man called Rami, Andromeda and Mr. Ackerly ushered Ezra into an upscale building and up a winding staircase, flanked by marble railing. Every step forward felt like an ironic step backward, and even further into a nightmare from which he desperately wanted to wake.

Once they had arrived at the top landing, Rami rapped his knuckles over the polished door. A flurry of commotion on the other side sounded just before the door flew open, revealing at least a dozen people gaping in astonishment. Whispers circulated amongst the lot but were expeditiously silenced by Rami's commanding voice.

"Out of the way! Alert Consul Diederik and Deputy Consul Symon that we have arrived with Ibrahim's son."

"Most impressive," said a smooth voice from somewhere behind the horde. "Most impressive, indeed."

The group parted down the middle, allowing Andromeda and Mr. Ackerly to drag Ezra forward into the penthouse and deposit him onto the marble floors. Ezra fell to his hands and knees. Too weary to raise his head, he slumped forward in front of two pairs of feet he assumed belonged to the leaders of the Legerdemain Brotherhood.

"Hmm," mused one of the men, using his cane to lift Ezra's chin.

While his sight was unfocused, Ezra could see the man looked to be in his fifties, with dark brown hair tinged with streaks of silver and clear, blue eyes. He looked so much like Jonas. Or rather, Jonas looked so much like him. But Ezra knew the person behind the façade was nothing like the Magi Master.

Ezra shivered to the point he had to hold himself to get the tremors to stop. But his overwhelming nausea won. Falling forward onto his hands, he coughed violently, heaving nothing but air. He had nothing left.

The other man—Ezra assumed through process of elimination had to be Symon—knelt in front of him and placed two fingers on the side of his neck. Symon shook his head at the consul, communicating unspoken fear.

"I told you to bring him to me *unharmed*," the consul articulated in a biting voice, "not with his life hanging by a thread. He is no use to us dead."

"I—I figured he was just seasick," Andromeda answered, a faint trace of panic in her voice.

"And how long were you at sea?"

"Two days, more or less," replied Mr. Ackerly, glancing at his partner in crime for confirmation. "We ran into some rough weather past St. George's Channel; our boat got turned around for a time."

Consul Diederik scoffed. "I would like to see how you feel when you are dangerously close to dying of severe dehydration."

The whole room fell into uneasy silence, as if every one of its occupants had turned to stone.

"Well? Don't just stand around like imbeciles; someone bring me a Restorative Potion!" commanded Diederik. "Rami, Symon, help me get him to the study."

Every onlooker exploded into action. After being lifted to his feet, the pattering of footsteps rushed around him in a furious pandemonium. Moments later, Ezra stumbled face first into a leather couch as the world around him spun out of control. He shut his eyes, praying for it to stop.

"Come now, boy, you need to stay conscious," Diederik instructed as he lifted him up into a seated position. He patted him on the cheek. "Look at me."

Ezra's eyelids fluttered. Staying awake was a losing fight.

"Tell me your name," the man demanded as a servant rushed into the room with a crystal vial. "Your full name."

"Ez-Ezra…N-Newport," he struggled to speak. His parched lips could barely form words.

Diederik snatched the vial and uncorked it. Cupping one hand under Ezra's chin, he gingerly poured the elixir into his mouth.

At first, the simple action of swallowing felt like a foreign concept as Ezra choked on the liquid. But after a few moments of reacquainting himself with hydration, he allowed the potion to chart a smoother course down his oesophagus.

"That's it, Ezra," Diederik encouraged, tipping the vial until every drop had been drained. "Drink up."

He exhaled as he laid back and let the strange, unfamiliar world around him fade away.

Lurching into consciousness, Ezra found himself lying under a heavy quilt in an unfamiliar room. Moonlight seeped through the penthouse flat's windows, illuminating the muslin curtains framing them. He blinked several times, as if it would clarify his convoluted mind.

"Welcome back to London, Mr. Newport."

Starting at the unexpected voice, Ezra launched himself into a seated position. One wary glance across the study proved he had an audience watching him.

Consul Diederik perched on the edge of a writing desk, leaning both hands against his cane. His piercing, hawk-like eyes bored into him. Across the room, Symon hovered over a beverage cart, fixing himself a drink. The ice clunked against its glass enclosure when he swirled the liquid, sloshing amber waves over perfectly square icebergs.

Ezra clenched his jaw at the two of them.

"You once called this city home, am I correct?"

He hesitated before answering the consul. "What's it to you?"

Diederik's mouth curled into a sneer. "Quite the feisty one, aren't you, boy? Of course, I would expect nothing less from the son of Ibrahim Newport."

Ezra remained silent, trying to maintain a brave front.

"You are most welcome, by the way," Symon added, raising his glass at Ezra, "for saving your life."

Something about the way the men held themselves, self-righteous and smug, made Ezra physically ill. Here they were, sharing vicious grins with one another as if everything that had transpired over the past few days was some sort of joke. As if now, they not only owned him but the entire world.

But Ezra could see right through them. They were liars. Kidnappers. Murders.

These men were the reason his friends had been hurt. The reason his mother was dead. The reason his father had disappeared and hadn't come back. The very reason he was here now, filled with a hatred Ezra had no idea he even possessed.

"Feisty and unmannered, apparently," the consul responded.

"Why am I here?" Ezra growled. "What do you want from me?"

"Actually, nothing at all," Diederik said with a lazy flourish of his wrist. "We just wanted to invite you to tea."

Symon snorted into his liquor glass.

Unamused, Ezra never once let his attention deviate from their faces. "You have destroyed my life."

"My boy," the consul chuckled, sliding off the desk to his feet. "I believe we have *saved* it."

Ezra gritted his teeth. "And how is that?"

With an unabashed smile, the leader of the Legerdemain Brotherhood strode forward, moonlight glinting off the triangle badge at his waist. His cane clunked heavily onto the wooden floor; resounding with finality as he came to a halt only centimetres from Ezra.

Ezra shrunk back against the cushions.

"You Newports have become quite the hot commodity ever since you left London," said Consul Diederik. "Personally, I would hate to have you end up in the wrong hands."

Ezra narrowed his eyes. "Like now?"

The consul laughed but it did not reach his eyes. "You might think you're clever, boy, but what you do *not* know is the level of danger you and your father are in right now."

"Yes, from *you*."

"No, not from me," Consul Diederik said as if trying to restrain irritation. His white knuckles closed around his cane. "From others in my organisation. From treasure-seeking Quotidians. Even the Magi. You have stumbled upon the world stage if you like it or not. And now, all eyes are on you."

Ezra gulped but attempted to disguise his panic as stubborn confidence. "This is because of the Tablet of Destinies, isn't it? An artifact that may or may not exist? That stupid translation that has everyone all worked up?"

Diederik retreated behind his desk and settled comfortably into the leather chair. "And what do you know of the translation?"

Ezra held his gaze but said nothing.

"Come now, Ezra, do not make me force it out of you."

"I don't know anything!" he yelled, a sting of frustration blinding him. "Whatever my parents knew was never passed to me. I'm just as much in the dark about this as you are."

The consul cocked his head, a grin twisting along his mouth. "My boy, I may not have the answers I'm looking for, but don't for one second think I am in the dark."

Exhausted from their conversation, Ezra allowed his gaze to flutter toward the floor.

"What do you know about the translation?"

"All I know is that it somehow relates to the Tablet of Destinies," Ezra caved with a shaky exhalation. "There's something about a Roaming Lion and Babylon's gates and immense power. That's it. That's all I know."

Consul Diederik leaned back in his chair, folding his hands atop his belly. He exchanged a humoured look with Symon before turning back to Ezra. "You are correct in that much. The translation is a guide, providing instructions on how to find the Tablet of Destinies. It speaks of a Roaming Lion—in this context, the person who will uncover the artifact and unlock its power. Unfortunately, we are missing some key information, information we were hoping your dear father would help us with."

A prickling sensation bloomed across Ezra's palms and travelled up his arms. The weight of both Consul Diederik and Symon's attention bore heavily upon him, so much so that he could barely breathe. He balled his fists, his nails digging into the skin.

"And you are using me as bait to lure him in," Ezra spat bitterly, a darkness returning to his expressions. "I am nothing but a bargaining chip."

"Ah, seems like the little brat is catching on," Symon noted to Diederik. He threw back the rest of his liquor before depositing the glass on the beverage trolley.

"Yes, I'm catching on that for some absurd reason, you think my father is going to willingly give up information about this Roaming Lion person,"

Ezra fumed. "Even if he does know their identity, he will never tell you. He has fought hard so far to keep whatever secrets he knows quiet."

Consul Diederik shared another glance with Symon before regarding Ezra as if he were simultaneously astounded and amused by his outburst. Rising to his feet, the consul leisurely ventured to a picture window, observing the foggy London streets below.

"You misunderstand me, Mr. Newport," the consul said without even turning to address him. "The information I'm looking for has to do with the *location* of the artifact, not the identity of the Roaming Lion. According to the translation, the Roaming Lion is the key to finding the tablet because he has seen it before. *'Locked within time, where Destinies are viewed,'* it's all there, you see?"

Ezra's heart rammed against his ribs. "But I—I don't—"

"We do not need the identity of the Roaming Lion because we already know who he is," Consul Diederik clarified. "And right now, Ibrahim Newport's memories are more precious to us than all the treasure in the world."

LATE NIGHT CALLER

"All right, now, Oliver. I need you to pay close attention." Jonas readied an orb of energy between his palms, sparking with vibrant intensity.

"Why do you and Zaire always assume that's the last thing I'm doing while training?" Oliver retorted, grimacing when he twisted too sharply at the waist.

"Because the second a Magus breaks focus is the moment they open themselves up for attack," said Jonas as he side stepped around the boy. "And right now, I sense your thoughts are everywhere but this cellar."

Oliver set his jaw in concentration, guiding the Celestial Lifeforce into his fingertips. "Well, of course they are! I cannot stop thinking about Ezra."

Aja, who had been waiting patiently for her sparring session, sank back against the couch in dejection and folded her arms. "Me too."

Jonas looked between his apprentices and allowed the magic to dissolve into the air. He motioned for Oliver to take a seat next to Aja. Crouching in front of them, Jonas rested his elbows against his knees and surveyed their downcast expressions. "I know you are concerned for our friend," he started. The effort of keeping his voice steady was surprisingly harder than he anticipated. "But the Magi Administration is taking care of the situation."

"You know how you always tell us to trust our intuition?" Aja said. "Well, my intuition says that's not good enough."

"Yeah, mine says the same," Oliver replied. "But my intuition isn't saying it. It's shouting it."

Allowing his sightline to fall, Jonas sighed and rubbed his forehead. "I know, I know. But there is nothing we can do while we are under a No Travel Order. Is that clear?"

His apprentices shared a disappointed look with one another before nodding in understanding.

The wild swinging of Elysium's red door shattered the stoic atmosphere. Visibly shaken, Zaire's eyes communicated disbelief as he grasped the doorframe for support. "Mista Jonas! You're gonna want to see this!"

Jonas frowned in concern, standing to his full height. "What? Is someone trying to break into the shop again?"

"No! No, it's…" Zaire panted. "A man claiming to be Ezra's father is here!"

A shocked stillness overtook the room. Oliver and Aja gaped at Zaire. Even Jonas struggled to process the information and wondered if he had even heard him correctly in the first place.

"Say again—Ezra's father is here? In the Emporium?"

"Yes!"

"Okay, the both of you stay put," Jonas commanded his apprentices. "Neither of you move a muscle while I assess the situation first. Anyone could be up there trying to deceive us. Zaire?"

"Yeah?"

"Go fetch Kierra."

"On it," he responded and dashed up the spiral staircase toward the second level.

With his heart pounding in anticipation, Jonas followed suit. He barely registered the clanging of his own footfalls as he climbed toward the ground level of the building. Absolutely anyone—a member of the Legerdemain, a clever Watcher—could be waiting around the corner, and Jonas was not about to take chances with the visitor's intentions. He reached into his pocket, withdrew his quartz crystal, and held it at the ready.

A man with untidy dark hair stood with his back to Jonas, showing great interest in the crystal display case.

"Good evening," Jonas called out, cautiously approaching his guest. "What can I help you with, sir?"

The man looked over his shoulder. His unkempt beard framed weathered skin and brown eyes. Fraying trousers and a tattered suit jacket hung upon his tall frame and his toes peeked out from a hole in his left shoe. The Middle Eastern gentleman appeared to be in his late thirties, but concern and exhaustion cut deep creases around his eyes, making him seem much older.

"Greetings," the man responded in a thick Turkish accent. "Are you Jonas? Jonas van der Campe?"

"That depends. With whom am I speaking?" Jonas asked, attempting to convey a calm exterior by placing his hands in his pockets. He gripped his crystal until the edges pressed into his palm.

The man reached into his jacket.

Jonas' muscles twitched defensively. However, he relaxed as the man retrieved a calling card, much like the one Jonas had given Ezra after their first meeting.

"My name is Ibrahim Newport," responded the man, brandishing the card, "and if you are Jonas van der Campe, I desperately need your help."

Skirts rustling with intensity, Kierra rushed into the Emporium with Zaire at her heels. Once she reached Jonas, she made momentary eye contact with him before examining the stranger.

"Mr. Newport, may I introduce you to my cousin, Miss Kierra McLarney," Jonas replied, gesturing toward her. "I hope you understand that we take every precaution necessary these days, and that includes what is about to happen."

"Er, yes, of course," Ibrahim said. He nervously shifted his weight from foot to foot.

"While I am inclined to believe you are who you say you are, I will allow Kierra to be the judge of that," Jonas stated, gently guiding her forward. "Kierra, would you kindly take a look inside this man's memories?"

Kierra approached the individual claiming to be Ibrahim. "I apologise, sir, but this may cause some distress," she warned.

Hesitantly, the late-night caller nodded in consent.

The young woman extended her hand and held it over the man's forehead.

Jonas watched intently as his cousin closed her eyes and began her work. Kierra's furrowed eyebrows accompanied the man's pained facial features, which only grew in magnitude over the next few seconds. Jonas grimaced when the scene became exceedingly uncomfortable, especially when the stranger struggled to hold back tears of anguish. He deflected his attention toward Zaire, who returned Jonas' silent wonderings.

Kierra withdrew her hand, breaking the connection. Her eyes grew wide as she stumbled backward in amazement.

"He…he is indeed Ibrahim Newport," she whispered in disbelief.

Completely bewildered, Jonas cleared his throat and held out his hand in greeting. "Anything you need, Mr. Newport, I would be more than happy to assist."

Ibrahim shook Jonas' hand and brushed away the remnants of emotion. "Thank you, Mr. van der Campe. I've run out of options and am afraid you might be my very last hope."

He sat before them, a broken mirage shrouded in steam from recently brewed tea.

After all this time, he lived.

Jonas perched atop the armrest of the couch, watching in astonished silence as Ibrahim Newport sipped his beverage. An hour had passed since Kierra confirmed his identity, yet a profusion of thoughts, questions, and harsh emotions battered Jonas' internal reasoning.

And, judging by the dumbfounded looks on everyone's faces, the entirety of the Irish Chapter could wholeheartedly relate.

"Mr. Newport, this might sound somewhat crass, but I must know: Why now? Why did it take so long for you to seek us out?" Jonas asked.

Ibrahim stared into the depths of his cup. "I wanted to come sooner. I did. But after the train wreck, after the murder of my wife, I knew I needed to stay hidden for as long as possible. But now," he paused, meeting the eyes of his company. "Now, the future of our society rests on a cliff's edge."

Jonas exchanged a baffled look with his cousin when the man paused to wipe tears from his cheeks.

"My son has been taken, and it is all my fault."

"You said *our* society," Jonas emphasised. "The Magi Administration told us you and your late wife had your licenses revoked. Not to mention your connection to the Universe was severed."

The ashy remnants of a once vicious blaze stirred in the man's eyes. "That does not mean I turned my back on the Magi."

"Well, as my boss so often says, you had better start at the beginning, Mr. Newport," Diego insisted. "We have got all day with literally nowhere to go."

Ibrahim clutched his teacup. "By now, you will have seen the papers talking about a Babylonian cuneiform artifact's translation. I'm sure you think it is innocent enough, but—"

"We already know it has to do with the Tablet of Destinies," Diego interrupted. "And we already know that the Legerdemain Brotherhood is after you because of it."

Zaire elbowed him in the ribs. "Let him speak, kid."

"You are correct on all accounts," Ibrahim said without batting an eye. "But do you know *why?*"

Silence reigned over the Elysium common room. Diego looked as if he wanted to open his mouth again but a stern glance from Zaire made him freeze mid-breath.

"From the moment I was born, my Seer mother had recurring dreams of a lion cub roaming the wilderness," Ibrahim explained, pausing only to take a sip of tea. "While her visions did not give clarity as to its importance, she knew inherently that the lion represented me. She would often call me 'Roaming Lion' throughout my childhood. Even on her deathbed, her last words were 'May *Allah* bless the wandering path of the Roaming Lion.' It was not until I began working for the Magi Administration after Ezra was born that I fully understood what that meant."

"The translation speaks of *you,*" Jonas concluded. For some reason, hearing the words spoken out loud sent goosebumps over his arms. Next to him, Aja and Oliver whispered to each other at the revelation.

"There is a room—a massive vault within Magi Headquarters—where the Administration keeps all records of prophetic texts, dreams, and visions," Ibrahim continued. "You might know it as the off-limits wing just down from the historical vaults."

"Ah, yes," Jonas replied. "I am familiar. As part of my Magi Master training, I spent many hours reading the texts of Balasi in those vaults."

Ibrahim nodded. "I worked as a nightguard alongside my good friend Taylan, protecting the secrets within."

"Wait, wait, wait," Diego said, throwing up a hand to keep the conversation from progressing. "At the impenetrable fortress that is Magi Headquarters? How on earth would anyone even get in and succeed in accessing the vaults in the first place?"

"The Administration was quite clear when I was hired that I wasn't necessarily protecting it from outside threats," Ibrahim answered. "Believe it or not, the highest areas of concern were *internal* threats."

"Mm. That doesn't surprise me," Jonas noted. "So, you made sure no one made it past those gates. But something tells me you didn't keep *everyone* out."

"No, I did not," Ibrahim sighed. "A heist occurred one night while Taylan and I were on duty."

A chill rushed down Jonas' spine.

"And I was the one who led it."

"Pardon me?" Jonas almost toppled off the couch in utter astonishment.

Ibrahim cringed when the reticence had become deafening. "Taylan's wife, Kiraz, worked as a Knowledge Keeper and mentioned a prophetic text having to do with a 'Roaming Lion.' Intrigue got the best of me, so I arranged for Taylan to cover me while I infiltrated the vaults during our shift. I found the prophecy easily enough but when I read its contents, I was shocked. According to the text, this Roaming Lion was meant to uncover an artifact of great and terrible power: The Tablet of Destinies."

"But the Magi Gendarmerie arrested you before you could do much else?" Oliver theorised.

"No. They had no idea," Ibrahim replied. "As I looked further into the text, I realised just how dangerous this Tablet of Destinies could be for our world. Even though the text claims the Roaming Lion would one day assist the Kings—the Magi—with the magic, something still did not resonate well in my soul. So, I made it my duty to wipe any mention of it from the earth in hopes that I could take the secret to my grave. Throw away the key, as it were. And that would be the end of it.

"In the days following, Taylan and I devised a fool proof plan: We would break into the vaults again to destroy any record of the prophecy. But we had to cover our tracks—especially from Time Manipulators—so together, we invented something called a 'Time Blemish' to erase history at the very moment we set fire to the prophecy."

Diego blanched a sickly white. "A—a Time Blemish? *You* created those?"

Ibrahim stared at the young man a moment before nodding. "I assume you're familiar with them?"

"Too familiar," Diego replied, "but only at the hands of the Legerdemain Brotherhood."

"I figured it was a matter of time before they confiscated it for their own uses," said Ibrahim with a disappointed sigh. "Ultimately, I succeeded. I destroyed the prophecy and any trace that it had even existed. Or so I *thought*. However, it wasn't long until the Magi Council discovered I'd tampered with the vaults and not only fired me and my wife but took our licenses and magic as well."

"That is extremely harsh," noted Kierra.

"Well, it would not be the first time they've been known to be harsh," Jonas said, sharing a knowing look with Diego.

"Well, I suppose if a prophecy says you will one day assist them with that power, no Magi would be very happy about that," Ibrahim replied.

"Did the Magi Administration ever find out which prophecy you tampered with?" Annabelle questioned.

"Not to my knowledge," Mr. Newport responded. "If they knew, they didn't let on."

"So, when the recent cuneiform translation spoke of the very prophecy you tried to destroy, you wanted to do anything you could to stop the publication," Jonas gathered.

Ibrahim bowed his head. "Indeed. But I failed. And now, the Legerdemain Brotherhood knows. Just days after the translation went to press, a team of Dark Watchers combed through our borough looking for us. I did the only thing I knew how to do: Pick up everything and move my family to safety. But I failed at that, too. My wife is dead, and my son has been taken by Consul van der Campe and Deputy Consul Bellinor."

"Are you positive they have him?" Jonas asked.

"Unfortunately," Ibrahim exhaled. The phrase left his mouth like a curse.

"But how did they find you?" Zaire questioned.

Jonas swallowed a tightness swelling in his throat. "Symon Bellinor is a Dream Speaker."

Ibrahim nodded. "He came to me in a dream requesting I come to London—alone—and turn myself in. Only then would he allow my son to go free."

Every ounce of life in Elysium faded as the group of Magi considered the predicament. Apprehension sullied Aja's rosy cheeks. Oliver nervously turned his crystal wand over in his hands. Zaire crossed his arms, while Kierra pursed her lips together. Diego chewed on his thumbnail.

"Did Symon tell you *where* you needed to meet him in London, dear?" enquired Annabelle.

Ibrahim drew out a folded train ticket on which he had scribbled words. "He said to meet him at the Royal Observatory in Greenwich. He stressed I come alone, but—" He hesitated, staring at his handwriting. "Isn't that the location of—"

"The Legerdemain Consulate," Jonas finished for him. "Their underground facility spans that entire area."

"That's why I was hoping you would come with me, Jonas," said Ibrahim, his eyes pleading. "With your connections, your knowledge about the Brotherhood, you could help me get Ezra back."

Any shred of hope that remained bled from Jonas' body as he considered the mission. Not only was it audacious, but the chances of success were slim to none. Jonas could not bear the thought of Ezra in his father's clutches, but he equally could not stomach the inevitable confrontation with the consul. He had spent the last twelve years avoiding him. The last thing he wanted to do was go to battle with a man who would crush him, both in will and power.

"We will *all* come with you," Kierra answered before Jonas could get a word out. "Ezra is just as much a part of our family as he is yours."

Jonas cast a worried look at his cousin. "Kierra, I *cannot* risk any of you getting hurt. You will all stay in Elysium where we have been commanded to stay."

"The hell we won't," Diego retorted. "I am coming."

"So am I," Zaire said.

"Me too!" Aja and Oliver exclaimed simultaneously.

"And you sure aren't leaving me behind!" Annabelle piped up. "Knitting is becoming awfully mundane."

Jonas stared at them, disconcerted. "No! This is not some holiday excursion! We are talking about an *extremely dangerous* rescue operation—"

"Which is *why* we need to come with you," Zaire answered respectfully. "You and Mista Ibrahim ain't doing this alone. You need us."

"I don't think you understand," Jonas remarked, getting to his feet. "I am *not* going. This isn't a matter of right or wrong. This is a matter of logic and reasoning. The second I step foot out of this building, the Magi Gendarmerie will be scrambling to arrest me, and then I won't be able to help anyone." He turned toward Ibrahim, hoping the look in his eyes adequately communicated his apologetic brokenness. "Mr. Newport, I care about your situation, but I cannot risk it. You may stay as long as you'd like, but as for me, I will be staying where the Administration wants me. Right here in Elysium."

At that, Jonas shoved his hands in his trouser pockets and strode toward his bedroom, with overwhelming despair blurring his vision.

BEYOND OUR UNDERSTANDING

Domburg, the Netherlands, 1893

Eighteen-year-old Jonas van der Campe walked in stride beside his father as the first pinpricks of stars dotted the skies over Westhove Castle. Exhausted from the lengthy train ride from Amsterdam to Domburg, Jonas found it difficult to be excited for his first Ascension Ceremony. From what he had heard from his peers trained in the ways of the Legerdemain, the ritual served as one of the most momentous rites of the Brotherhood. Every month, under the power of the full moon, members of the Legerdemain would gather in temples, monuments, or other ancient structures. Strung together along invisible lines of energy, like a web across the world, each site connected the Brotherhood in an unbreakable universal bond. Only then would their crystals be charged to their full strength, allowing them to enhance the power of the Celestial Lifeforce and give them the sorcerous advantage that the Magi could never wield.

Jonas apprehensively grasped the sunstone wand in his pocket. Smooth to the touch, the talisman had seen him through every day of his training, from his fifteenth birthday until now. Though he admired the beauty of the polished orange point, it seemed to emanate pretension, something his father could readily appreciate. But the folded parchment next to it nudged his shaking fingers, inspiring just the slightest serenity over his nerves. He grinned to himself as a warmth caressed his cheeks.

Though the letter had been hidden away within the fabric of his trousers, Jonas had kept the words close to his heart, where they sang like the breeze through a springtime tulip field. He could practically quote them from memory:

Dearest Jonas,

I hope this note finds you well. Every waking moment, I pray for your safety amongst the Brotherhood. I understand that at this point, it is a matter of upholding family legacy, but please remember there is still time to pledge your ways to the Third Order of the Magi instead. We would welcome you with open arms.

My Magi Master just informed me he will be relocating to Stockholm to help build up a local Chapter there, and I am considering joining him. Jonas, let's run away to Stockholm. We can leave your father and the Legerdemain behind. We can start a new life. A better life. Together.

When you return from Domburg, meet me in our spot. I cannot wait to see you again.

Forever yours,

Felix

"Are you feeling all right?"

Jonas snapped out of his daydreams and met his father's expectant gaze. Honestly, he felt like retching on his shoes, but he was not quite sure how to eloquently state that fact. His father would die of embarrassment. Especially since Diederik's entire Division (as well as reporters from the *Daily Ascendant*) would be studying Jonas like some sort of science experiment. The son of the consul never strayed too far from the Legerdemain Consulate's attention.

"Yes, fine."

"Excellent," his father responded in his confident manner. He adjusted his tie and smoothed out the folds in his tailored jacket. "This is not just any Ascension Ceremony, Jonas. This is your initiation into the Brotherhood. Tonight, you officially become one of us."

While his peers had divulged all about the crystal charging ceremony, they flagrantly left out details of the *actual* initiation. After successful completion of a range of trials, Legerdemain recruits knew they would face their final challenge during initiation but as for what that entailed remained an abstract anxiety. Those who completed the Last Act were sworn to strict secrecy.

Jonas chewed on his lip as they approached at least a hundred men congregating on the expansive grassy field. Torches staked in the ground shed a lambent glow across the trees and carved grim shadows on the faces closest to them. Meanwhile, Westhove Castle loomed in the background, a shadowy reminder of the incredible magic about to take place.

"Ah, Consul Diederik, there you are!" shouted Symon Bellinor from the throng. "We halfway wondered if the boy decided to delay his initiation."

Diederik laughed and blithely shook the hand of the deputy consul. "Not at all, dear friend. Jonas is as ready as he'll ever be. Isn't that right, son?"

Jonas attempted a smile. "Of course."

"Good man," Symon replied, patting him on the upper arm. "Now, if only you can convince Edison to follow your lead. We need more bright young men like you to join our ranks."

Diederik glanced up at the northeastern sky, the light from the full moon glimmering in his irises. "It is time."

Jonas swallowed uneasily as his father stepped up on a makeshift platform in the centre of the crowd. The man did not even have to raise his hand to silence his Brotherhood; their voices fell into quietness at his mere presence.

"Welcome, my Brothers, to the ninth Ascension Ceremony in the 1893rd year of our Lord," spoke Diederik, elegance and prestige carrying every syllable into the night. "Tonight, we gather as we have for millennia, since the very days of Labynetus. For in Babylon, our great society rose from the dust, taking us into a new era. Tonight, we celebrate the incredible power we possess as the Legerdemain Brotherhood.

"Let us also celebrate the induction of our newest recruit: my son, Jonas van der Campe!"

Cheers from the crowd practically burst Jonas' eardrums. Several hands reached out and slapped him heartily on the back.

"Jonas, would you join me?"

Dazed and distracted by the racket from the men, Jonas obeyed and stumbled up the stairs to the platform. His cheeks burned in awkwardness as all eyes focused in his direction.

"As you know, in order to become an official member of the Brotherhood, one must complete one last trial on the night of their consecration," Diederik continued, laying a hand on his son's shoulder. "This Last Act demonstrates unadulterated devotion to the Brotherhood. It proves to us you are not only capable of carrying out the duties associated with the Legerdemain, but also that you wield the strength to make difficult decisions. Are you ready, son?"

Jonas inhaled sharply through his nose and balled his fists. "Yes."

"Magnificent." Orange flames cavorted across his father's face. "Let the Watchers come forward."

Jonas readied for action as two Dark Watchers approached the stage, dragging an undefinable shadow between them. As they clunked up the staircase, he could just make out the sight of a body being hauled by his arms. A cloth sack had been draped over the person's head, concealing his identity. The Watchers deposited their prisoner and grunted with laughter as the man fell to his knees.

"As every Legerdemain is aware, we are forbidden by the Celestial Lifeforce to take the life of another Gifted individual, be they friend or foe," Diederik spoke, his words becoming as dark as the landscape around them. "If we do, our powers wane. Sometimes, they never return. That is why we work with Dark Watchers, so that they may do our bidding for us. They carry out the Order of Babylon in our place and work to recruit the next generation of Legerdemain, ensuring our numbers stay strong."

No! No, no, no, Jonas screamed internally. His gut churned. His brain ran a million kilometres an hour. The world around him faded into a dizzying blur.

He knew *exactly* what came next.

"Therefore, one of the most crucial things we must do as Legerdemain is make difficult—yet necessary—decisions. Especially when Magi refuse to cooperate." His father crouched down and with a wide, theatrical gesture, yanked the sack away from the prisoner's head.

Felix.

Jonas' heart leapt in horror. He instinctively ran forward, dropping to his knees at the Magus' side.

"Felix!" Jonas exclaimed, cupping the young man's face in his hands. His own eyes watered at the sight of dried blood and tears trailing across his freckled cheeks. "Are you hurt?"

"Jonas," the adolescent croaked. His voice lacked the abundant life it normally contained. "You need to get away from them. *Now.*"

Fire ignited within Jonas' chest. He aimed a dangerous stare at his father. "What have you done to him?"

"You know what you must do," his father sneered. "Order his execution, and your training comes to an end. Consider his death a sacrifice."

"No!"

After a solid minute of stunned silence, shouts of disdain and cruel heckling echoed across the field.

"Come on, kid," Symon jeered from the crowd. "Do not throw away your training for this dirty bastard."

"Kill him!"

"Spill his blood!"

"NO!" Jonas screamed. He leapt into a protective stance over Felix. "I will not! I refuse!"

The volume of the crowd grew to a horrifying magnitude but tapered into hushed silence when Diederik took slow, menacing steps toward his son. A brief moment of panic played across his father's features as he stood face-to-face with him.

"Jonas, complete what you were trained to do. *Finish it.*"

Jonas squared his shoulders, standing tall and resolute. "If being a member of the Legerdemain means murdering innocent people, then I do not want any part of it."

Before Jonas could react, his father backhanded him across the face. He stumbled backward as Diederik kept on his advance.

"How *dare* you defy me in front of them?" he growled, striking him again. "How *dare* you embarrass me in front of my family?"

"I *am* your family," Jonas cried, shrinking away from him.

"Not anymore."

A snap of his father's fingers shocked him back into reality. The twang of a Watcher's crossbow resounded throughout the night while the thud of an arrow sent a shockwave of chills throughout his being. Every motion slowed to a crawl as Jonas turned to see Felix clutching at his chest as if that alone would stop the blood from seeping across his shirt.

"NO!"

Collapsing upon the platform, Jonas cradled Felix in his arms.

"Jonas—" the young man moaned.

Uncontrollable sobs wracked Jonas' entire body. "I am…I am so sorry," he replied. "I never meant for this to happen."

Felix looked up at him, the light of his hazel eyes flickering in and out of existence. "Promise me something."

"Anything," Jonas said, wiping away the tears from Felix's face with his thumb. "Anything for you."

"Promise me you'll take up the ways of the Magi," Felix spoke, each raspy breath becoming shallower than the last. He clasped Jonas' trembling hand. "Promise me you will always fight for what is right. Follow the ways of the Light. Become the force your father fears."

Jonas nodded his head in firm agreement. "Until my dying breath, I swear to you that I will."

Satisfied with his answer, Felix smiled and squeezed Jonas' hand before his aura faded into darkness.

Belfast, Ireland, 1906

For once, the stars were silent.

Jonas sat under the trellis, absorbing the stillness of the night. A delicate wind rippled his hair and the foliage of the Emporium's urban rooftop garden. Despite the serene evening, he never got too far in his meditations before the last few hours crept back into focus.

Ibrahim's timely appearance was both a blessing and a curse. On one hand, just the confidence that he was alive sparked a renewed hope in Jonas' heart. But along with Mr. Newport's revelations and claims about his identity, uneasiness once again took the reins.

A deadlock had risen with the moon.

With Ezra in the custody of his father and Symon Bellinor, as well as the desperate warning of the Magi Council to stay put, Jonas fought to understand where to go next.

The reckless one would say there was no debate. That above all else, Ezra must be rescued. But the careful one would tread guardedly, notifying the Magi Administration in the hopes that action would be taken.

Jonas leaned his forehead against his folded hands. Time was not on their side. And every time he leaned toward alerting the Administration, something would jerk him back in the other direction. The tug and pull threatened to tear apart the very fibres of his mind.

"I thought I might find you up here."

Jonas forced a smile as Annabelle drifted in his direction. She gathered her skirts and perched upon the swinging bench beside him.

"My dear, you look as if you have been run over by a train."

He chuckled absently and turned his attention to the heavens. "That's putting it mildly."

Jonas felt the heat of Annabelle's gaze examining his downtrodden body language. "I know you made your stance firm, dear, but something tells me you wouldn't look so upset right now if that was the end of the argument."

Sighing in defeat, he rubbed circles into his temples. "I need to contact Mr. Edwin Mears about this first thing tomorrow morning."

"That's what your conscious says. What does your heart tell you?"

"That we must accompany Ibrahim to get Ezra back," Jonas answered. "My father will not hesitate to kill that boy after he gets what he wants. I would never...I would never forgive myself if that happened."

The elderly woman made a small noise of approval in her throat.

"If Ibrahim is who he says he is, we cannot let him journey into Legerdemain territory alone. That would be ludicrous."

"So, what is stopping you, my dear?"

Jonas picked at his thumbnail as if the distraction would somehow erase the fears lingering on his tongue. "The Administration was very clear with the No Travel Order. I'm not about to get my whole Chapter imprisoned—or worse, permanently stripped of their licenses—for a foolhardy attempt at foiling a Legerdemain plot."

"Mm. What else?"

Confused, Jonas searched her face. "What do you mean?"

"There's got to be something else holding you back," Annabelle responded in her soft, yet poignant way. "You went against orders before saving Ezra from the Dark Watchers. What makes this any different?"

"Because this time," Jonas began, but an unpleasant constriction in his airways strangled his words. He cleared his throat and tried again when realisation struck a chord. "Because this time, the Council will be less forgiving. They won't just take my license away, Mum. They'll sever my connection to the Celestial Lifeforce. My vow to Felix will be null and void. I will have failed him. I will have failed *everyone*."

Annabelle wiped away a tear from his cheek with her thumb. "Look at me, Jonas."

Hesitantly, he lifted his eyes to meet her fervent gaze.

"Felix wanted you to do what was right. He wished for you to follow an honourable life like he had witnessed in his Magi Master. But dear," she paused, reaching to hold his face in her palm, "even if the Magi

Administration took everything away: your position, your license to practice, even your Gifts, they cannot take away your spirit. And that spirit is what gives you the power to do wondrous things, not the Celestial Lifeforce."

"I appreciate your sentiment," Jonas whispered, bowing his heavy head. "But if that is true, then why is it that no matter what I do, everything seems to fall apart? In the end, I will only ever be the screw-up son of the Legerdemain Brotherhood consul."

"You are a genuine, kind-hearted being with the desire to do good in a dark world," Annabelle corrected him. "You are *not* your father. Is that clear, young man?"

An authentic smile tugged at his cheeks. "Lucidly."

"Good," Annabelle remarked as she folded her gloved hands together, "because trying to thrive under someone else's shadow isn't any way to live."

"You say that like it's the simplest thing in the world."

"Simple? No. Necessary? Absolutely." Annabelle grasped Jonas' hand firmly in hers. "No one said you have to be the person your parents tried to raise. No one said you had to carry the weight of the world alone. The Irish Chapter is your family, and we are not going to let you fall. It does not matter who your father is, where you have travelled, or what you have done. We respect you for the man that you are. And that man is an admirable, talented young Magus with a spark of greatness just waiting to ignite."

"Thanks, Mum," Jonas replied. "What would we do without you?"

"Oh, somehow you would manage," Annabelle laughed. "Although, I'm not entirely certain about Diego. That lad is a handful."

Jonas joined in her laughter and nodded in agreement. "Yes. Yes, he is."

Annabelle patted him on the knee and rose to her feet. "You're a good man, Jonas van der Campe. Just remember to give yourself grace and a wee bit of room to breathe."

Annabelle gave him one last smile before disappearing inside the building, leaving Jonas to savour the warmth of her words.

Turning his sight skyward once more, Jonas drew in the night air through his nostrils, breathing in a new life into his body. His eyes scanned the heavens. Racing along their appointed courses, the stars graced the celestial tapestry in breathtaking arcs of light.

This may go wrong in every way possible, but I'm not about to let you down, Felix Jonas spoke into the night.

Somewhere in the brilliance, Felix beamed his approval.

And, despite the restlessness threatening to tear him apart, tomorrow, they would be on the first train out of Belfast.

ARCHITECT OF DREAMS

An entire day had come and gone without any sign of deliverance.

Ezra stared longingly out the rain-streaked window of his palatial prison. Every anxious breath clouded the glass panes, hazing over the view of the posh London streets that served as his only access to the outside world.

Between the penthouse's proximity to Hyde Park and the direction of the rising sun, Ezra had deduced Symon Bellinor—the actual owner of the flat—lived somewhere in the Knightsbridge neighbourhood. The quaint streets, opulent foliage, and pristine buildings were a mere stone's throw away from Buckingham Palace and King Edward VII himself. One thing was abundantly clear: Money and prestige were practically dinner companions to Mr. Bellinor. And if the deputy consul could afford such luxury, Ezra could only imagine what Consul Diederik had at his fingertips.

Despite his unfortunate status as a hostage, Ezra was bewildered by his excellent treatment. The day of his arrival, Symon had gifted him an expensive set of clothes: fine trousers, a crisp oxford shirt, leather belt and shoes, and even a dinner jacket fresh from the retail windows of Harrods. Symon's staff had also held to a rigorous timetable of refreshments, carting in round after round of chef-prepared cuisine. While Ezra appreciated the gestures, something just beyond the surface felt suspiciously like a twisted retelling of

Hansel and Gretel. And it was only a matter of time before the elegant façade faded, exposing the macabre framework within.

Ambling across the drawing room, Ezra's attention wandered to an oversized oil painting commanding dominance over the wall on which it rested. Framed in gold and streaked with hues of bronze, the artwork depicted a man peering out from under the hood of his cloak. While his features portrayed a man in his mid-twenties, his striking green eyes told a different tale, one that portrayed centuries of life in his irises. He cradled a glass bottle to his chest, tendrils of mist pouring from the opening. Underneath the portrait, a golden nameplate heralded an engraving of the words *"Vita Perpetua."*

Ezra started in astonishment when the door creaked open, revealing a servant manoeuvring a tea trolley through the threshold. Ezra recognised her as Tina, one of Symon's primary staff members. Bright-eyed, short-statured, and stunningly beautiful, the young woman could not have been much older than Ezra.

"Good afternoon, sir," Tina greeted him in her foreign accent. "Care for some afternoon tea?"

Ezra lingered by the painting. "Of course. And you can call me Ezra."

A friendly smile accentuated the maid's dimples as she parked the tea trolley perpendicular to the settee. Tina's manicured fingers uncovered a tray of tarts while she simultaneously poured steaming liquid into a porcelain cup.

"Who is in this painting?"

Tina met his eyes and swiftly refocused them on the trolley. "Labynetus of Babylon. The founder of the Legerdemain Brotherhood."

"Oh," Ezra answered, examining the artwork's painstaking realism.

"Mr. Bellinor quite enjoys the old tales," Tina expounded, offering the tea to Ezra, "especially the one that tells of Labynetus' quest to find Eternal Life."

"Vita Perpetua," Ezra whispered in understanding. "Did he ever find it?"

Tina grinned, almost as if she regarded Ezra's words as a joke. "No. But the Brotherhood like to paint him as a god nonetheless."

"So, do you like working for Symon?" Ezra asked abruptly, curious to see how she would respond.

Tina blinked, thrown off by the question. Wisps from her short, silky black hair fell into her face as she found interest in rearranging the milk and sugar tray. "Oh, ah, yes. Well enough. He pays decent wages and provides us room and board."

Ezra added a splash of milk into his tea and swirled the beverage with a small spoon. "Where are you from originally?"

The young lady forced a smile, but her brown eyes communicated brokenness. "A long way from here."

"Same with me," Ezra sighed. "Although, I most recently lived here in London."

"Oh, yes?" Tina replied, genuinely interested. "Whereabouts?"

"Haringey," Ezra answered after taking a sip of tea. "There is a large Turkish community in that borough. Living there made London feel a bit more like home."

"That's lovely," Tina said. "And when life withholds any familiarity, I suppose one always carries a piece of home in their heart."

"Mmm, yes," Ezra remarked, a tinge of sadness returning to his voice. He stared into the brown abyss of his teacup. "Though even that can fade."

The young lady awkwardly cleared her throat. "Well, sir, I best get back to my rounds. Please do let me know if you require anything at all."

"Thank you, miss," said Ezra as Tina curtsied and went on her way.

Setting his teacup on the serving cart, Ezra rubbed his hands over his face and exhaled. Sleepless nights had led to dismal thoughts. And dismal thoughts had disintegrated any fragment of hope he had left. Despite the temporary solace in conversing with the servants, the heaviness of his situation built up like bricks upon his chest. He was not sure how much longer he could wait for his father to whisk him away to safety. With every chime of the golden grandfather clock in the foyer, Ezra's faith in his father deteriorated more into nothingness.

That, and a noticeable lack of Brotherhood members somehow unnerved Ezra. The day he arrived, Symon's penthouse had been abuzz with activity. Now, save for the doorman who patrolled the entry, the residence had fallen into an unusual stillness. Silent and unwavering, the guard's watchful eyes never deviated beyond the boundaries of the front foyer, giving Ezra the freedom to roam. To observe. To figure out how in the world he might escape.

Rising, Ezra excused himself from the drawing room and journeyed toward the closest toilet down the way from Symon's study. The Legerdemain leader had been locked behind closed doors for hours. Muted conversation between Symon and Diederik seeped underneath the study door, along with the dancing rotation of light and shadow.

Consumed by curiosity, Ezra slowed his walk to the lavatory and lingered beside the study door. Carefully, he pressed his ear against the polished oak.

"Time is not infinite, Symon!" Diederik's voice urged, drowning in the pattering of rain on the rooftop. "Every day Ibrahim hesitates is another day our opponents have to secure their bids for consul."

"Ibrahim will come," Symon calmly answered, "and when he does, we shall be one step closer to the Tablet."

"Did he receive your message?"

"Oh, he received it all right," Symon responded. "I instructed him to come alone. I made it clear that if he tries otherwise, I cannot guarantee the safety of his son."

Shock caused Ezra's heart to skip a beat. His father was *alive*, after all this time…

"You don't think he would be daft enough to recruit help from the Magi, do you?"

A stark stillness followed the question until groaning floorboards suggested Diederik's pacing had resumed. "If they do, I will personally see to it that they suffer."

The words froze the molecules in the air. Every breath, every heartbeat sent vibrations throughout the wood panelling. His nerves were electrified. Ezra was convinced it would be only a matter of seconds before Symon and Diederik would hear him lurking.

"Once Ibrahim arrives, what shall we do with his son?" Symon wondered.

A heavy pause lingered as Diederik considered his response. "When Ibrahim arrives, Ezra is no longer of use to us. I sense a connection to the Celestial Lifeforce in the boy, so it would be unwise for us to kill him."

Ezra held his breath.

"Instead, instruct the Watchers to kill him and dump his body where no one will find it."

Ezra's mouth went dry. His legs buckled beneath him, and he crumpled against the wall. Diederik and Symon had saved his life without a second thought. But just as quickly, they could take it away.

"*How do you escape?*" his voice resounded in the deep.

"*Sometimes you don't.*"

Perhaps he wasn't so different from the Shahmaran after all. The longer Ezra hesitated in this lair of imminent doom, the less likely he was to escape with his life.

He had to get out of here. *Now.*

Mustering the strength to move, Ezra scrambled down the corridor to the south side lavatory and latched the door behind him. Moving swiftly toward the window, Ezra slid the pane upward, but an unexpected obstruction in the track halted his escape.

"Come on!" he growled, struggling against the jam. "Open!"

He had become so intent on loosening the window that a sudden banging on the lavatory entrance made him clutch the pane in pure terror.

"Ezra, are you in there?" The consul's voice oozed through the crack beneath the door. "Be a good lad and unlock this door for me."

Raindrops splattered over Ezra's cheeks as he urged the window upward. Every jolt of physical persuasion resulted in nothing but growing trepidation and smarting fingers.

"Come now, Ezra," threatened Diederik, now pounding the butt of his cane against the entrance. "Open this door, or so help me, God, I will open it for you."

"Move!" Ezra commanded through gritted teeth. He was so close; he could practically taste freedom. With his heart pounding in his ears, Ezra finally convinced the window to ascend. But at that very same moment, the lavatory door blew off its hinges, skidding into irreparable pieces over the tiles.

"Get over here!" the consul roared, grabbing hold of Ezra's shirt collar. "You're not going anywhere!"

Ezra choked at the constriction of his shirt as Diederik wrenched him from the lavatory back to Symon's study. Stumbling over his own feet, he dug his fingernails into the consul's hand, hoping it would prompt a premature release. But all it did was enrage the man to the point that he shoved Ezra to the floor before slamming the door behind them.

Ezra's chest rose and fell as he vied for control over his breath. Rainwater dripped from his hair into his face. Hesitantly, he met the eyes of his captors. They glared at him, examining him like an amoeba under a microscope.

"This little bastard decided he wanted to go for a stroll by means of the toilet window," the consul spat, leaning heavily against his cane.

Symon squatted to Ezra's level. "Is that true, Ezra? Were you trying to run away?"

Ezra hung his head to avoid the man's judgement, but Symon grabbed his chin and forced it upward.

"Oh, no, no. That won't do," the deputy consul whispered dangerously. "Let me make something clear, boy: While you're a guest in my home, you follow my rules."

"I am not a guest," Ezra retorted. "I'm a *hostage*. There is a world of difference."

Symon tightened his pinching grasp on Ezra's chin. "Another thing you must learn: Do *not* talk back to your superiors."

Swallowing his fear, Ezra set his jaw in determination and kept eye contact with the men. There *had* to be a way out. And he would find it, even if it killed him.

Mentally scanning the layout of the penthouse, he searched for the route of least resistance. The south lavatory was out of the question. So was the drawing room, knowing the proximity of guard stationed at the entrance. Perhaps the servants' quarters? That corridor did have a secondary entry, including a stairwell to the first-floor lobby. Maybe he could have Tina cause a distraction so he could test the waters. Though, in his current position, there was no possibility of making it to that side of the flat without first being apprehended by Diederik and Symon.

Nevertheless, he had to act before time ran out.

An unrelenting vigour flooded his veins, spurring him into momentum. Before Ezra knew it, he had darted for the study entrance. But when the door flew open on its own accord, he skidded to a standstill, mouth gaping in astonishment.

Right before his unbelieving eyes, the walls became fluid and bendable, fluttering like a Union Jack in a spring breeze. The floorboards squealed as they folded over one another into new configurations. Doorways and windows slithered across walls. Rooms retracted into themselves. Others burgeoned into colossal halls, tugging at the corridors between them. A symphony of grinding and clanging resounded throughout the penthouse and just when Ezra thought it was over, an ear-splitting groan vibrated in his teeth as everything settled into place.

Impossible…

The turbulent world fell into silence. A chandelier swayed above him, golden light swirling over his feet in luminous encouragement. Ezra rubbed his eyes. The very staircase he'd deemed an unlikely contender for escape materialised before him. Open. Accessible. Waiting.

Trembling, Ezra threw a glance over his shoulder to catch Symon and Diederik's expressions, but they were nowhere in sight. Perhaps they, too, were caught in the shuffle, still imprisoned in Symon's study, wherever that now existed.

Ezra bolted down the staircase. He took two and three steps at a time, aghast by the miraculous events that had just transpired. Was it another manifestation of the Celestial Lifeforce? Perhaps even his Gift? Whatever it was—be it power from *Allah* or another timely use of magic—the act had granted him freedom to the drenched London streets.

Go, go, go! Ezra urged himself, his body propelling into a sprint. *Just keep going until you physically can't anymore. Run first, plan later.*

As he crossed into Hyde Park, a tree root caught his ankle. Teetering on the edge of balance and the ground, Ezra fought to keep moving, but the tendril wrapped itself tighter around his leg. Frantically, he squirmed to free himself and realised far too late that it was not a root at all.

Instead, a vibrant, crimson rope sparkling with magic snaked around his foot. At its other end: the cane of Consul Diederik van der Campe.

Before Ezra could process much else, Symon and Diederik wrestled him into iron cuffs. He flinched as the metal pricked against his wrists, as if it were angered by confining hands that had just wielded the Celestial Lifeforce.

"Thought you were being clever, boy?" Symon growled, fire burning in his eyes. He yanked Ezra to his feet. "You're a slippery one, aren't you?"

The consul stabbed his cane into the mud. Silver raindrops cascaded from the brim of his top hat while rigid lines carved their way across his face. "Your little show back there just earned you a trip to the Legerdemain Consulate," he spat in a low tone. "Maybe there, you will rethink your foolishness."

Flanked by monsters, Ezra unwillingly trudged along, wondering if he had bought himself more time or if death was one second closer.

WE ARE THE STARS

Nothing soothed Jonas' soul like a hearty dose of travel, even if the matters spurring it were grim at best.

Electrified by the mission before them, the entirety of the Irish Chapter—along with Mr. Newport—had departed Great Victoria Street Station the next day at noon. Bags and travel cases in tow, a palpable energy fuelled their determination, even as the train took them on the lengthy stretch from Belfast to Dublin.

Jonas shifted in his train seat but somehow, the agitated stirring in his soul dissipated with every click-clack of the locomotive. Despite defying orders from the Magi Administration, every step into recklessness felt strangely invigorating.

With kilometres of track behind them, the eight Magi soon found themselves waiting for their overnight ferry in the Dublin Port terminal. Jonas smiled to himself as he glanced around at his company. Aja and Oliver had borrowed a deck of playing cards from Zaire and became immersed in a game of Irish Switch. Kierra's eyes devoured her favourite romance novel. Zaire chatted pleasantries with the lady at the ticket podium while Ibrahim thumbed through the latest edition of *The Irish Times*. Despite complaining that knitting was "what stodgy old folk did when they had nothing better to do," Annabelle had taken up her needles and diligently worked away at her scarf. And, weary from the train travel, Diego leaned against Jonas' shoulder for a snooze.

"It's nice to see you two getting along for once," noted Kierra, grinning over her novel at Jonas.

Wordlessly, Jonas gestured at Diego and then at himself. "What? Us? Kierra, he's not even conscious."

"Well, be that as it may, I wish I had a camera right now. The expressions on his face as he clings to your arm are quite adorable."

"He is not clinging to my arm," Jonas muttered as he looked down at Diego clinging to his arm. "Oh, God. I think he might be drooling on my jacket."

His cousin tried hiding her laughter behind the pages of her book. "That is even more adorable."

"It is *not*."

Zaire returned to the benches and draped his arms casually over his knees. Humour built in his expressions as he glanced between him and Diego.

"Aw, now ain't that something?" Zaire chuckled.

"Quiet, the both of you," Jonas mumbled under his breath, hoping the warmth in his cheeks was not as evident as his annoyance. Thankfully, he was spared any more embarrassing discourse by an announcement over the loudspeakers.

"Passengers boarding the nineteen hundred ferry to Liverpool, please gather your belongings and queue at the departure dock," instructed the smooth voice of a woman. "To speed up the boarding process, have your tickets at the ready."

Diego lurched himself awake.

"*Ay ay ay*, already?" he groaned and wiped his mouth on his sleeve.

Once Diego had stood, Jonas exhaled a breath he hadn't even realised he had been holding. He proceeded to smooth out the wrinkles—and the unfortunate wet dribbles—on his jacket before anyone would notice.

Kierra retrieved the ferry tickets from her handbag. "All right, everyone, we have two four-berth cabins. Men in one room, women in the other." She paused when she got to Oliver. "You'll have to stay with the women, Oliver." He sighed and begrudgingly took his ticket while Aja giggled at him.

"Excellent, because I need more time with my little Ollie," Annabelle stated. She drew the boy into a tight embrace.

"Argh, Mum," Oliver complained, flushing pink in the cheeks. "I'll never get to sleep with that bright yellow aura of yours."

Within no time, the Irish Chapter had boarded the ferry and retired to their respective rooms. But with all the travel activity and the unsteady rocking of their transportation, Jonas decided shut eye would not come easily. Instead, he donned a jacket and made his way up to the outlook deck.

Muted lights faded as the boat left the hazy Dublin Port harbour behind. The crisp night air blended with the salty breeze and tickled Jonas' nostrils. Overcast skies blanketed the stars, but the Magi Master knew if the heavenly bodies could shine through, he'd see the moon rising with Libra in the east.

Perhaps the scales of justice were tipping in their favour.

As he strolled starboard side, he caught sight of Aja leaning against the edge of the ferry. She had been so immersed with the surrounding seascape that she only turned her head once she sensed Jonas at her side.

"I couldn't sleep," explained his apprentice.

Jonas smiled. "Neither could I."

The sea breeze rippled Aja's coat as she held fast to the railing. "I miss Ezra so much."

"As do we all. But we shall see him again very soon."

Aja nodded as if trying to convince herself the words he spoke were the truth. She wiped her face with the palm of her hand and gazed out at the Irish Sea. "But what if we don't? What if we are stopped by the Magi Gendarmerie? What if the Legerdemain consuls kill him before we arrive? What if—" She allowed the waves lapping against the vessel to swallow her voice. "I'm scared for him."

"My intuition tells me Ezra is capable of things we can't even imagine," Jonas replied. "He can hold his own until we arrive."

"What made you change your mind?"

"Mm?"

"About saving Ezra," she prompted. "What made you switch gears?"

Jonas turned his sight skyward. While wisps of clouds obscured most of the celestial canopy, brilliant specs still managed to shine through the early April gloom. And Arcturus—now pulsing a vivid orange—bewitched the southern sky. Onward, it moved with purpose in its course across the galaxy. Its undetermined, diametric course.

There it was – the soft whisperings of guidance. The stars never failed to give him inspiration when he lacked it. And now, he appreciated it even more.

Bracing himself against the railing, Jonas leaned forward and clasped his hands together. "Tell me, Aja, what do you know of Arcturus?"

Aja turned to read Jonas' expressions while her eyebrows knit together in confusion at the abrupt shift in conversation. "Er. Well, it's the fourth brightest star in the night sky."

"Good. What else?"

"I can locate it easily because it sits beside the constellation of Virgo."

"Mmm-hmm," Jonas answered. "Anything else?"

"Arcturus in my culture is called *Swati*, which means 'very beneficent,'" Aja added.

"All excellent points," Jonas commended her, "but did you know Arcturus is just one of a multitude of stars that moves differently than others in our sky? Instead of moving with them, it orbits in another plane altogether. And quite quickly, at that. Essentially, it travels with its unconventional group *against* the stream."

Aja attempted a smile, but it lacked the life needed to sustain it. "That is very intriguing and all, but what does that have to do with our current situation?"

"We *are* the stars," Jonas said with an encouraging smile. "We are a menagerie of radiant beings traversing through this life. As Magi, our path is not the same as our neighbours. It is in our very nature to travel against the stream, just like Arcturus. But sometimes, it becomes evident that even within our own Order, even within our own stream, we must take an entirely different route."

"What are you saying?" enquired his apprentice. "That we should disregard the Administration's mandates?"

"We should always respect those in authority," Jonas answered. "But that does not mean we need to blindly follow a decree if it means abandoning what we have been put on this earth to do. And right now, there is a boy out there who needs our help."

A chill conquered the space around them, causing the flame of the oil lamp on the deck to ripple with a transient restlessness. In the quiet, a determined stirring prodded at Jonas from within his core. A thirst to prove himself. A desperation to ensure the safety of a young Magus. And a longing to fulfil every promise he made before Felix joined the stars, for as long as the Administration would allow him.

Jonas lifted his eyes again to the heavens, fixating on Arcturus. For a moment, it looked as if the clouds would overtake the star in favour of smudging the Irish skyscape with the promise of rain. But the star, as tenacious as ever, sparkled through. Burning bright, as brief as a sigh. Insignificant, yet grander than anything that Jonas could ever dream of...

That was hope.

UNDER THE WATCHFUL EYE

An eerie fog had descended upon London as Ezra and the Legerdemain consuls made their way across the grounds of the Royal Observatory.

The trek to Greenwich had been almost as dreadful as the journey to Symon's penthouse flat. Every time his captors would glare in his direction, Ezra's nerves sparked into a frenzy. Nevertheless, Diederik and Symon remained tight-lipped, causing Ezra's imagination to run rampant with the dastardly plans brewing behind their skulls.

From the moment he was apprehended in Hyde Park, Ezra scrambled to devise another getaway. Anything to lessen the chances of the inevitable. Twisting against his shackles, Ezra realised escape was nothing but a dream on the verge of waking life. Fragile and intangible. And if the devilish glint in Diederik's eyes had weight, Ezra knew he'd be beaten to the ground several times over. He made Dennis look like a saint.

Diederik *van der Campe*.

The mere idea that someone like Jonas had been raised by someone like Diederik baffled Ezra. From darkness, light. From ashes, fire. An angel nurtured by a demon. Whatever the case, he made a mental note to discuss it in further detail with Jonas when he saw him again.

If he saw him again.

The three of them strode across the expansive lawn of Greenwich Park. Diederik's hand never strayed too far from Ezra's elbow. He grit his teeth as the consuls urged him along the walking paths toward the central structures. White accents on one building—the Flamsteed House, according to signposts—clashed against the grey-tinted landscape. Meanwhile, brownish brick culminated in domed towers atop the edifice, disrupted only by black birds returning to their roosts.

When they arrived at the entrance to Flamsteed, Symon yanked on the door handle and ushered Ezra inside. The antique atmosphere of the building overwhelmed Ezra's senses. A faint buzzing festered in his eardrums while an array of brass instruments on tabletops whirred in a chaotic symphony. In fact, he had become so enamoured by the astronomical apparatuses that he did not even notice a woman had appeared before them.

"Nice to see you again, Mr. Newport," came her pleasant Greek accent.

Ezra's heart sank when he recognised the woman from the fishing vessel that brought him back to London.

"Ezra, you remember Miss Eridian, don't you?" Diederik asked.

It took everything in his power not to glare daggers at her.

She grinned, holding out her hand. "Assistant to Astronomer Royal Frederik Ackerly and Receptionist for the Legerdemain Consulate, at your service, Mr. Newport."

Ezra refused to take her hand. While he couldn't be certain, he had a distasteful feeling Miss Eridian was more than just an astronomer's assistant and receptionist working for the Legerdemain. Something cruel danced behind her eyes; something wicked tugged at her tongue. Her precise, elegant movements mimicked that of an arachnid, spinning a beautiful—yet deadly—guise.

Resentment prickled in the air like electricity as Diederik directed a warning glare at Ezra. "Well, boy? Don't be rude. Say hello."

"It is no matter," Andromeda laughed with a dismissive wave of her spindly fingers. "I am sure we'll become great friends. Won't we, Mr. Newport?"

A chill tingled down Ezra's spine as she stroked his cheek.

Andromeda's fingers grazed his cuffs and her eyes flicked upward at Diederik. "Out for a little stroll, are you?"

"What makes you think that?" Symon asked, dumbfounded.

"Why else would you keep your pet on a leash?" the woman replied, holding up Ezra's wrists.

"Unfortunately, Miss Eridian, we are in need of your services," Consul Diederik announced with a scowl. "I'm afraid our guest here has outgrown his welcome in Symon's home."

The woman folded her arms over the gemstone pendant on a long, silver chain around her neck. "I assume the both of you forgot what it was like to watch over an adolescent?"

"Not at all," Symon snapped. Ezra expected him to say more in defence of himself, but Diederik held up a gloved hand.

"Adolescents I can manage," Diederik responded. "Ones who rearrange the interior features of a penthouse are a different matter altogether."

"Ah, we have an Architect in our midst," Miss Eridian said, winking at Ezra. "I suppose you want me to take him to the Dousing Chambers for safe keeping?"

Gulping in terror, Ezra fought to keep his expressions neutral.

"If it wouldn't be much trouble," Diederik confirmed. "Only until his father comes to collect."

"Certainly," said Andromeda. Her long hair seemed to grow frizzier by the second. "But I'll have you know the extent of my involvement is taking him to Julien. The Legerdemain Consulate is not a nursery, and I am not a nanny. Besides, you two should know the dangers of letting boys run loose in the Consulate."

"Correct as always, Miss Eridian," Symon murmured. He shared a dark look with Diederik that Ezra could not decipher.

The consul pushed Ezra forward into Miss Eridian's clutches. "See to it he is properly watched. I do not want him slithering out of our grasp like the little serpent that he is."

Ezra glowered at him.

"Be a good boy," Symon chided with a tip of his bowler hat. "Let's hope daddy shows up soon, eh?"

Andromeda secured a blindfold around Ezra's eyes, plunging his world into darkness.

The British Museum

Physically, Diego had never been to London. But through time manipulation, he had seen it all.

From the construction of Big Ben to the coronation of Queen Elizabeth, Diego's exploration of the city spanned centuries. Who needed maps or travel agency consultations when one could witness a place through historic milestones? Every expedition into the past taught him more than he could have ever learned otherwise. And the knowledge he had brought back shed a fresh light on his incredible new surroundings.

Diego watched in awe as the buildings whirred past them in a dazzling blur. Fresh off the morning train from Liverpool, the Irish Chapter had hired two horse-drawn carriages, with Zaire, Ibrahim, Annabelle, and Kierra in one and Jonas, Oliver, Aja, and himself in another. According to Jonas, they were bound for the British Museum, where his friend Edison Bellinor would be waiting.

Over the past three years, Jonas had hardy breathed a word about Edison. All Diego knew was that they were close during adolescence but inevitably drifted once Jonas left Amsterdam. And, other than the fact that Edison had declared neutrality between the Magi and the Legerdemain (he must have been a Libra), Diego did not know much else.

But it was enough for Diego to know he did not trust Edison. No one was *truly* neutral. Even neutral parties had their preferences.

By the time they'd reached the British Museum, raindrops flecked the carriage windows. As quickly as they could manage, the Magi unloaded from their transports and, with their travel bags in hand, followed Jonas onto the grounds of the museum. Visitors queued within the entryway, their voices casting lively echoes off the polished floors. Parents walked hand-in-hand with their children while scores of secondary school students followed their teachers like ducklings seeing the world for the first time.

Hungry for the knowledge that only history could offer, Diego lingered near a glass display case protecting centuries-old Roman gladiator armour. Reverberations of the Past sparked his imagination as he pictured courageous victors donning the armour before battle. He made a mental note to visit the opening of the Roman Coliseum on one of his next adventures through Time.

"Keep up, Diego!" beckoned Oliver as the group moved onward.

The sensory experience left Diego dizzy with excitement. Before he knew it, he and the others had found themselves in the museum's lower levels, away from the hubbub of the crowds and the lure of ancient artifacts.

Jonas guided them through a maze of corridors past a "Staff Only" sign. He rapped his knuckles over the door and waited in nervous impatience during the silence that followed.

A man in his early thirties with a neatly trimmed beard poked his face through the door opening.

"Jonas!" Edison welcomed him with a smile. "Come in, come in."

Diego cringed. Edison Bellinor in the flesh. Diego was not expecting the sudden distress squirming in his stomach at the sight of him.

"It's good to see you again so soon, Edison," said Jonas as he led them into what looked to be an expansive artifact storage area. "Though I wish we were visiting on brighter circumstances."

"Indeed," Edison replied. He made a grand gesture into the room behind him. "Well, on that note, welcome to the inner sanctum of the British Museum!"

Between the remnants of exhaustion from the journey and the lingering irritability with Jonas, Diego had kept to himself for the remainder of the evening. He did not speak a word as the Irish Chapter unloaded their travel bags. Nor did he offer much in the way of assistance as they devised a plan to rescue Ezra.

Besides, they've got everything handled, Diego thought while Oliver worked with Annabelle to create the ultimate cloaking potion, the Aura Eradicator. *They don't need me to muck anything up.*

While the Irish Chapter erupted into lively conversation with their host over dinner, Diego chased his peas around his plate with a fork and downed several rounds of liquor in silence. For some reason, the light-hearted reminiscing between Jonas and Edison had become almost too much to bear.

"Jonas, remember when you accidentally set fire to that tulip field?" Edison chuckled, holding his drink to his lips until he could get control over his laughter. "I don't think Farmer Seegers ever forgave you for that."

"No, but he and my parents did make me replant it," Jonas replied. "And at seventeen years old, I decided a career in flower farming would never be in my future."

"Of course, I could never forget when you set the Legerdemain Consulate ablaze," Edison continued, shoving Jonas with his shoulder. "That was impressive, to say the least."

"You set the Consulate on fire?" Aja asked in surprise.

Oliver giggled until he nearly fell out of his chair. "Wow. That is quite the accomplishment!"

"They had it coming," Jonas responded with a wink at his apprentices.

Diego chewed on his fork, thinking about the collection of items Jonas had set ablaze during the time he had known him. He had lost count of the bedding and curtains Jonas incinerated during their private moments. Certainly, Edison had no idea about *those.*

"Oh, Jonas, you are quite the fellow," Edison remarked.

"Why, thank you, Edisonite," said Jonas.

Both men dissolved into raucous laughter.

The more Edison spoke, the more Diego wished to disappear. Their friendship seemed so pure, so utterly perfect. Jonas and Edison had not conversed in over a decade, yet they were able to pick up right where they left off.

All Diego had with Jonas was an acquaintanceship barely holding on by a thread.

But perhaps, it was better that way.

Itching to steer away from his annoyances, Diego excused himself from the pub and began the solitary journey back to the British Museum. At least the comforts of sleep would be excited to greet him.

Unfinished Reports

A tremor shook Ezra awake.

Uncurling from his uncomfortable position on the boulder, he hoisted himself to his feet and surveyed the caverns. A mysterious bioluminescence illuminated pillars that rose like giants from the lake. Each pillar, crowned with Corinthian capitals, supported arches of stone along the ceilings. Ghostly ripples danced along the architectural wonders, prompting Ezra to marvel at how an underground world like this even existed.

"Beautiful, isn't it?"

Glancing over his shoulder, he located the Shahmaran lounging on a rock. Drenched in violet light, she twisted her wet hair into intricate braids.

"It is," Ezra answered, "but I don't remember this place being so—so breathtaking."

The Shahmaran's laughter tickled his ears. "It is amazing how time erases even the most vivid things."

Ezra frowned. "But it hasn't. All of this," he gestured at the pillars and carved ceilings, "never existed until now."

Her mouth curled into a smirk. "Is that your conscious or subconscious speaking?"

"You are impossible."

"So are you."

Ezra scoffed and returned his gaze to the ceiling.

"Would you believe me if I said it has been here all along? Just waiting for you to open your eyes?"

"I don't know what to believe anymore."

"Sweet boy," she sighed, slipping into the water. When she reached his boulder, she crested and used her forearms to hold her in place. A smile bloomed across her cheeks as she rested her chin atop her arms and cocked her head to the side. *"Confusion is just a part of the process. In time, you will find the things that baffled you were the things that shaped you into the person you became."*

Ezra pulled his knees into his chest. For some reason, the injury in his thigh twinged unpleasantly at the shift in motion. *"I am still scared."*

"Good," said the Shahmaran. *"Strength without fear is but folly."*

"It's just," Ezra began, not even sure he knew how to voice his thoughts. *"If I had some inkling this world existed earlier, perhaps it wouldn't be such a shock for me now. Shouldn't I have had some clue about my identity as a Magus in my childhood?"*

"If you did, would you have even noticed?"

"Of course!" Ezra retorted, almost in hysteria. *"I would remember shooting magical shields out of my hands and rearranging interior walls. That's not something you easily forget."*

"Hmm," she replied. *"You baffle me, Ezra Newport."*

"I baffle you?"

"For such an intelligent boy, you have a strange memory."

"What is that supposed to mean?" he asked just as the ground beneath them trembled. *"Unless…are you a memory?"*

The Shahmaran laughed again. The very intonations of her lighthearted joy sent pebbles and dust raining from the ceiling. *"I am not a memory. I am an illusion."*

When his awareness shifted back into reality, Ezra jerked his head around in a sudden terror when his surroundings failed to spark familiarity. Beneath him, a rocky floor. Around him, a cell of some kind. Three of the walls were carved from stone, but the front had been barred with iron. At least, Ezra *thought* it was iron. The metal bars glowed a scorching blood orange and electrocuted the elements of the air that dared caress its surface.

It's got to be some type of magical entrapment, Ezra theorised. *That or a torture device.*

Carefully, he got to his knees and pulled himself as close as he could to the bars without touching them. From what he could see, he had to be in a prison somewhere...

Of course. The Dousing Chambers.

After Miss Eridian had blindfolded him, Ezra remembered being shoved through the twisting corridors of the Flamsteed House. The slam of a door and shifting air pressure popping in his eardrums followed afterward. A rush of damp, mildewy air wafted under the cloth, the only hint that he'd entered some subterranean realm. From there, the needle of his internal compass spun in the maze of darkness until he had been thrust onto a rough floor.

He vaguely recalled being injected with something before losing consciousness. Remnants of pain still twinged in his upper arm from the forced entry of a sharp instrument. While he wasn't sure, Ezra figured it was the only way to keep him from fighting back whilst Andromeda prepared his cell. Or maybe it was to stop him from using his Gifts? Whatever the reason, he was imprisoned with not a plan nor a hope in sight.

A gruff cough startled him out of his recollections. Edging closer to the bars, Ezra squinted in the dim light, trying to get a view of the corridor beyond the shadows. A young man—early twenties, by the looks of it—sauntered closer. One hand gripped a radiant yellow stone and the other, an oversized mug. Under his armpit, he carried a file folder and a fountain pen poked out from behind his ear. His hair was slicked back against his head except for one wavy section at the front that tapered into a curl. Beady eyes peered through spectacles, but they narrowed as soon as he came to a stop in front of Ezra's cell.

"I see you're awake," he said. For some reason, it sounded like an accusation. "Welcome to the Dousing Chambers, Magus."

The young man waved his crystal in front of the bars until the motion dampened the fervent glow to a mild glimmer. He shoved the mug through the slats and plunked it down on the ground.

Ezra did not say a word.

"Well, go on then. Drink," the man commanded as if he were wasting precious daylight.

Or rather, nightlight? For all he knew, it could have been evening. The caverns made it impossible to be certain.

Ezra retrieved the mug and sniffed its contents. It smelled suspiciously of water straight from the Thames. But as his throat felt like he had inhaled a bucket of sand, he drank it without a word of argument.

When he had finished, he returned the mug and scooted until he reached the back of the cell. The stranger's clear blue eyes trailed after him like a hunting dog.

"Who are you?" Ezra asked, shattering the stiff silence.

"My name is Julien," growled the young man, "and that's all you need to know."

"Are you some sort of prison warden?"

"No."

"Where am I?"

"The Dousing Chambers. Did you not hear me before?"

Ezra scowled at him. "What exactly *are* the Dousing Chambers?"

"You ask too many questions," Julien grumbled. He propped himself against the wall as if already exhausted from interacting with him. "The Dousing Chambers are where we keep our most high security prisoners. If you're in a cell, you cannot use magic. Simple as that."

Drawing his knees into his chest, Ezra never once let his eyeline fall away from the young man. Something about him seemed so familiar, yet so dreadfully unnerving. His grating personality provoked Ezra's irritation closer to the surface. "You Legerdemain Brotherhood members are obnoxious."

"And you Magi are full of yourselves," Julien shot back.

Ezra let his gaze fall. "I—I am not part of the Third Order."

Julien studied him a moment before drawing the folder out from under his arm. He uncapped the pen with his teeth and scribbled a note. "You are still a Magus without affiliation. It's basically the same thing in my mind. It's a pity the Watchers did not kill you when they had a chance."

Rubbing his nose on his sleeve, Ezra sighed and rested his chin on his knees. "I suppose everything would have been better if that had happened," he whispered, disheartened.

"And here, Carpenter said we'd never get a hold of you Newports," Julien laughed, continuing to make notes in his paperwork. "That's another bet he owes me. Your presence made me five hundred pounds richer, kid." He smiled to himself and proudly patted the lump in his trouser pocket. "Although, I still find it fascinating the Watchers were on your case so early when even Consul Diederik did not know of your significance yet."

Ezra lifted his head. "What do you mean?"

A disgusted scowl crested over the top of his file, but his attention soon fell back toward its contents. "I guess I should be thanking my lucky stars for that *Belfast Evening Telegraph* piece on the Portadown incident. Ultimately, that article tipped off the consul about your father's connection to the Babylonian translation."

The blood drained from Ezra's face. "That—that's *impossible*."

"And why's that, Magus?"

"Because," Ezra began, fighting an unnerving pressure rising in his chest. "He had to have known sooner. The Dark Watchers followed my family from London at the beginning of March. They attacked us on the train in Portadown. They—they chased me through the streets of Belfast."

"Your point?" Julien murmured. His severe glare never once wavered in intensity.

"The timing is all wrong," Ezra mumbled. His heart thumped against his ribs and his breath caught in his throat. Trembling, he ran his hand over his face as he desperately tried to make sense of the information. Somewhere along the line, an error must have been made. How else would the Watchers known about his family? Why else would they be so intent on killing his Magi parents? On killing him? "Then, the Dark Watchers must have gone rogue."

"Dark Watchers always answer to the Legerdemain Brotherhood. All requests begin in the Assembly and are signed off by the consul," Julien snapped. "Dark Watchers have never acted on their own accord."

"Well, someone authorised it!" Ezra fought back. "They must have known!"

"Unless…" Julien whispered to himself, on the verge of some sort of hypothesis. He thumbed through the pages of the file and scanned the contents until a grin carved across his cheeks. "Nah. That'd be ludicrous."

"If the consuls didn't authorise it, who did?"

Julien rolled his eyes. "Honestly, kid, you need to stop talking."

Ezra approached the bars, keeping a safe distance from the crackling static. It was a long shot, but he needed to know. "If your mother were killed by Dark Watchers, wouldn't you want to know why? Wouldn't you do anything to learn more about the person who authorised it?"

"Look, the fact is that we don't have records of an authorisation," Julien divulged. "More than likely, an Assembly intern lost the paperwork, or it was a bold move by Diederik and Symon's opponents. Based on how this election season has played out, I would place my bets on the latter."

Massaging his forehead, Ezra considered the explanation. But without understanding Legerdemain Brotherhood politics, he really had no idea what to make of it. "Why would they even care about my family?"

"Perhaps they knew of your significance before the consuls did. *I don't know*," Julien growled. "Who knows what goes through Taylan and Kiraz's heads half the time? Personally, I side with Consul Diederik's interpretation of Brotherhood politics, but—"

Ezra had to remind himself to keep breathing. "Wh-what did you say?"

"I'm a Loyalist."

"No, about—about Taylan and Kiraz?"

"They are running against Diederik and Symon for the consul positions of the Legerdemain Brotherhood."

Drowning in a torrent of details, Ezra stumbled backward and slid down the wall.

Taylan and Kiraz. The very people he'd spent celebrating Ramadan with year after year—

They were responsible for sending the Dark Watchers?

They were responsible for the Legerdemain attacks on the world?

It had to be a mistake…a misunderstanding…

"Darling, are you down here?"

Bewitched by the female voice, Julien's demeanour perked up. He spent an unholy amount of time brushing off nonexistent particles from his shirt until Andromeda Eridian blessed them both with her appearance.

Apparently, not all magic was off limits in the Dousing Chambers.

Ezra did not even look up when Andromeda and Julien shared a kiss.

"Well, don't you look dashing tonight," she complimented Julien, cupping his face in her hands. "I see you're getting to know our newest prisoner?"

"The kid is an absolute nutter," he replied. "I do hope you are here to get him out of my presence."

"It's your lucky day, love," Andromeda responded. "Mr. Newport? Stop sulking in there and get up. Symon will be here to collect you shortly."

Still lost in his thoughts, Ezra raised his head and glowered at the woman. "Why? Did he miss me?"

The woman put her hands on her hips. "No. Apparently, you both have company. Ibrahim Newport has arrived in London."

A DANGEROUS NIGHT

Under the darkness of night, the horse-drawn carriage drew to a stop on the edge of Charlton's Way. Diego glanced out into the evening, surveying grey obscurity just beyond the windowpane. His stomach squirmed in dread. If everything went according to plan, the night would go down in history as a successful rescue by the Irish Chapter. If not, then...

Diego refused to dwell too much on the alternative.

Discreetly, he and Zaire stepped out of the carriage, their shoes treading lightly against the gravel. Diego cringed at the unseasonably cold temperatures. Even for the United Kingdom, the frozen air felt much too heavy against his chest. Condensation from his breath shrouded the scene as Jonas and Ibrahim also climbed out of the transport.

"We gotta be fast," Zaire instructed. He dug into his jacket pocket and dispersed vials of teal liquid to Diego and Jonas. "Ma's concoction will only render our auras invisible for a short time. We got an hour tops, got it?"

"*Ay ay ay,*" Diego sighed resolutely and grabbed a vial. Even though Aja and Oliver had tested the idea before they departed the British Museum, that still did not calm the storm ravaging his insides. "Here goes nothing."

"Bottoms up," Jonas agreed, tipping back the liquid into his mouth.

Instead of the elixir, Ibrahim took in a cleansing gulp of oxygen and nodded solemnly. "*Allah*, be with me," he prayed.

"We will get your son back," Jonas reassured him, placing a hand on the man's shoulder. "I promise you that."

Kierra leaned over the coachman's seat. "All right, men. Get a move on," she commanded. "I'll be waiting right here for your return. Bring him back safely."

Jonas tilted his head in the direction of a grove of trees and underbrush meandering across the south end of Greenwich Park. Diego, Zaire, and Ibrahim trailed him, hunching behind the natural cover.

"Diego and Zaire: Remember, your mission will be getting Ezra out of there," Jonas directed, "and I'll distract the consuls so Ibrahim can make his escape." His voice quaked in uneasiness, though Diego knew he was trying his hardest to disguise it. He could see it in the maelstrom of Jonas' blue eyes.

For a fleeting moment, a twinge of an old—almost unfamiliar—emotion churned within his abdomen. Diego wished he could stop everything just to embrace Jonas. To hold him close and tell him everything would be okay. To confide in him like he once did. But that seemed as impossible as the objective before them, and the reasons outnumbered the stars.

The four Magi crept along the hedge line, peering out amongst the gaps in the branches to inspect the scene. Jonas squatted behind one of the bushes, motioning for Diego, Zaire, and Ibrahim to do the same.

Approximately twelve paces away, four shadowy human outlines—two of them presumably Symon and Ezra—lingered in the open, grassy area. At least a dozen taller figures congregated around them. Lurid and macabre, each nightmarish silhouette stood atop eight spider-like legs and brandished crossbows glinting in the moonlight.

"What *are* those?" Diego cringed at how squeaky his question sounded.

"Dark Sentinels, guards of the Legerdemain Consulate," Jonas replied, his eyes darting about in frenzied distraction. "They're similar to the Dark Watchers we are familiar with but are much stronger."

"Creepy buggers," Zaire commented. "I ain't never seen something so frightening in my entire life."

Breaking his focus away from the scene before them, Diego watched as Jonas sank deeper into his internal anxieties. The wand clasped within his shaking hands emitted vibrations of despair. Sweat beaded across his forehead, despite the temperature of the air hovering near the freezing mark.

Of course, he's afraid, Diego internalised. *He's in Legerdemain territory. He is practically on his father's doorstep.*

Unable to refrain, Diego grasped Jonas' hand. "Hey."

Tranquillity quelled the storm in Jonas' eyes but only for a moment. Still trembling, he squeezed Diego's fingers.

"It is going to be all right," Diego encouraged, a tender honesty in his voice. "We can do this."

Regaining his composure, Jonas nodded wordlessly. At one point, Diego thought he detected a faint smile, but oppressive darkness shrouded it.

"You know the signal, Ibrahim," said Zaire, shocking Diego back into reality. "Once we see it, we'll be right behind you."

Ibrahim squared his shoulders in determination.

Still holding onto Jonas, Diego attempted to quiet his frantic heart as Ibrahim stood, straightened his suit jacket, and strode confidently into the open.

Ezra struggled against the grasp of Andromeda and Mr. Ackerly as they stood in the empty expanse of Greenwich Park. He glared at Symon, who paced the field with his hands clasped behind his back.

"Do you think Ibrahim will show?" asked Mr. Ackerly.

Symon smirked. "Oh, he will come. Won't he, Ezra?"

Ezra said nothing but hoped the dark look brewing in his eyes communicated what words could not.

"It's a pity Consul Diederik could not be here for this," Andromeda noted. "I'm surprised he trusted you to carry out the exchange on your own, Deputy Consul."

Symon scoffed. "You speak much too boldly, Miss Eridian."

Her lips pursed into a grin.

Movement out of the corner of Ezra's vision seized his attention. The shadow of a man moved across the grass. At first, Ezra figured another member of the Legerdemain Brotherhood had decided to join Symon's night-time assembly. But that confident gait, the way the man held his shoulders straight and steady…Ezra's heart leapt in hopeful anticipation.

Symon drew out an electric torch and directed the beam toward the approaching stranger.

That was no stranger.

Ezra could not believe his eyes.

Tears of joy clouded his vision as Ibrahim Newport closed the space in between them. "*Baba!*" he cried in disbelief. "*Baba,* you are *alive!*"

"Ezra, my son!" Ibrahim exclaimed, rushing toward him.

Symon nodded to Andromeda and Mr. Ackerly, who let go of Ezra long enough for him to run into his father's arms.

Ezra buried his face into the warmth of his father's chest and wept in relief. Every painful memory, every bitter thought he had once harboured toward his father faded like fog in the Constantinople harbours. "I didn't think I would ever see you again!"

Ibrahim held him close and stroked his hair. He pressed his bearded cheek against Ezra's tear stained one and whispered softly, almost ominously, "Get ready to *run*."

Ezra pulled backward, reading the desperate look clouding Ibrahim's face. Instead of communicating anything more, his father leaned in and kissed both of his cheeks.

In a dizzying explosion of action, three men tore from the hedges. Ezra recognised Jonas van der Campe—and next, Diego and Zaire—and immediately understood.

This was not a reunion. This was a *rescue*.

"GO!" his father screamed as he shoved Ezra forward.

As Symon, Andromeda, and Mr. Ackerly leapt into action, Ezra tore into a sprint, throwing a hasty look over his shoulder to see two sets of hands restrain his father.

"*Baba!*" Ezra yelled.

"Ah, you decided to play dirty," Symon chided as he readied for the eminent collision between the two forces. His palms glowed in red hot barbarity; every atom in the air erupted into static electricity. "But so did we."

"Ezra, you need to come with me," Diego beckoned, waving him closer. "*Vamos!*"

"Diego, get the kid outta here!" directed Zaire. The Magus manifested energy between his hands and launched it at Andromeda and Mr. Ackerly, effectively releasing Ibrahim. "Get him to safety! Ibrahim – go! Go with them! I will cover Mista Jonas!"

"These fists can still throw a punch," Ibrahim insisted. "I'm not leaving you!"

Not wanting to leave his father behind, Ezra hesitated as a concussive explosion cracked open the night air, making it bleed ribbons of mystifying colours. Out of instinct, he cowered and tripped over a clump of earth in the confusion.

"Come on!" Diego commanded, grabbing Ezra by the wrist.

Their footfalls pounded the path in a delirious rhythm as they rushed toward a black carriage.

While Zaire and Ibrahim attempted to narrow their odds with the other two Legerdemain, Jonas had one objective: crippling Symon Bellinor. Thankfully, the absence of his father was both a relief and an anxiety. Who knew just where that Wretched Snake lurked, preparing to strike?

Harnessing an orb of blue-green energy between his palms, Jonas glared at Symon as they stepped toward each other, like great beasts preparing for a brawl.

"Jonas," Symon laughed as he readied energy of his own. "Now, isn't this a pleasure?"

Jonas narrowed his eyes. "Unfortunately, I cannot say the same."

"I see the cavalier attitude you had as a child hasn't faded in your thirties," Symon replied with a smirk. "How are things? How's the family?"

"Do *not* bring them into this," Jonas growled through clenched teeth as he aimed the energy at Symon's face.

Symon effortlessly deflected the energy into the earth. "It's a pity your father had another engagement tonight, but I daresay he would have enjoyed this little reunion."

Anger bristling throughout his core, Jonas held his palms out in front of him. An invisible wave of momentum radiated from his hands and through the already fragile air, spiralling Symon into a tumble.

"You were such a peculiar boy," Symon sneered as he got to his feet. "I hardly understood why Edison befriended you in the first place."

"Because Edison is honourable," Jonas retorted, rolling out of the way of Symon's fireballs. "Much unlike his father."

Jonas was only partially cognizant of the fierce power struggle between Zaire and his Legerdemain opponents. No matter what the two individuals threw at him, he was able to block with extraordinary precision. But Jonas knew it wouldn't be long before Zaire's defences would be shaken. By the looks of things, Ibrahim had managed to physically hold off the Sentinels by wielding a massive tree branch but without any magic to shield himself, he, too, would find himself amidst an uphill battle.

"Jonas!" Diego yelled as he dashed across the green toward him and Symon.

"Help Zaire and Ibrahim!" Jonas called out to him.

Before he could advance any further, one of the Legerdemain conjured a pulsing rope of electrified matter. The energy transformed into a whip, tripping Diego right off his feet.

"No!" Jonas gasped.

Symon lunged at Jonas while his attention was displaced. He cringed as he collided against the frigid ground and struggled when Symon pinned him with his knees. The deputy consul fished out iron shackles from his overcoat. Making haste, he clamped them around Jonas' wrists just before he attempted to blast him backward with his lifeforce.

Jonas' eyes grew wide in shock when he realised any effort to emit energy had been rendered completely useless. He stared blankly at his hands.

What had Symon done?

"You like these?" Symon asked, flicking the enchanted iron with the nail of his index finger. "You left us just before the Legerdemain started working on them. They're designed to temporarily keep a Magus' innate powers at bay. Makes you feel rather helpless, don't they?"

Jonas wriggled against Symon's weight. Upon hearing Diego yelp in pain, Jonas craned his neck to locate him. Just meters away, the young man had curled into a foetal position as one of the Sentinels slammed its pointed feet into his gut.

"DIEGO!" Jonas screamed.

"I think it is rather adorable how much you care for him," Symon remarked as he placed his elbow against Jonas' windpipe. "Promise me you won't cry like a fool if his story ends just like that Felix boy."

He panted for air. Panic crippled him, making his limbs feel as though they swam through mud and mire.

"That's the problem with you, kid. You open your heart too readily," Symon sneered. The man threw a nonchalant glance over his shoulder, watching along with Jonas as the Sentinel tossed Diego through the air like a toy. He landed with a sickening thud upon the ground.

"No, stop!" Jonas pleaded. "*Please*! Please don't—"

"You should know by now that loving anyone puts them in grave danger," Symon interjected with a grin. "Especially your precious Ganymede you brought home from Mexico. Well, Zeus, remember that even the apple of your eye can rot away whilst separated from its tree."

Diego's body laid motionless in the grass but that did not stop the Dark Sentinel from lifting the injured young man and disposing of him in a nearby pond.

Terror strangled Jonas' insides. "No! No, *please*!"

"Pathetic. One of the most promising Magi on this earth reduced to tears while he begs for his lover's life. *Again*," Symon continued, pressing harder against his throat. "You disgust me, you insufferable sodomite."

"STOP THIS AT ONCE!" shouted a woman in the vicinity.

Kierra.

"Kierra, get out of here!" Jonas struggled to say, but his warning came out no louder than a raspy whisper.

Before anyone could react, Kierra reached up into the night sky with both hands, channelling a fearsome column of energy that disrupted the atmosphere around them. Without hesitation, she forced the Celestial Lifeforce into the ground, causing the land beneath them to tremble. Her red hair whipped wildly over her shoulders while her eyes burned in a terrifying rage, as deadly as the surface of the sun.

The mystical cyclonic force caused Symon, the other two Legerdemain, and the Sentinels to tumble head over feet. Using the dizzying moment to his advantage, Jonas propped himself up with his elbow and frantically attempted to free himself from the binds.

His cousin dropped to her knees at his side. "Jonas, are you all right?"

He nodded and held up his wrists for her to undo the shackles. Kierra waved her quartz crystal pendant over them, causing the enchanted iron to crumble into a pile of grey ashes.

"Diego needs help," Jonas coughed, scrambling to his feet. "He's hurt."

But when Jonas and Kierra reached the edge of the reeds, they froze in pure dread. Waist deep in pond water, Zaire solemnly emerged, carrying a lifeless Diego in his arms.

The Great Escape

"Back to the carriage! Now!" Jonas instructed.

Zaire, Ibrahim, Kierra, and Jonas left the battered and confused Dark Sentinels in their wake as they rushed toward the transport. Within moments, the crew had loaded in.

"Go, go!" she yelled at the horse, who obediently lurched into action upon her insistent tugging of its reins.

Inside the carriage, Zaire placed Diego on a seat cushion. Jonas crouched beside him and pressed his ear against the young man's chest to check for any signs of life. Ezra and Ibrahim sat across the way, clinging to each other as they looked on in worry.

He was breathing. After all the hell he had endured, Diego still had life left in him.

Thank the stars above...the planets...the Universe.

Placing his palm on the side of Diego's bruised face, Jonas fought against the emotion that bubbled like a hot spring under immense pressure. A feeling of complete helplessness quaked through him while watching Diego shiver from his soaked clothing.

Zaire slipped off his jacket to lay overtop the young man.

"I am so sorry," Jonas whispered, tears dripping from his nose as he gently pulled Diego into an embrace. "Christ. I'm sorry for *everything*. For bringing you to Ireland, for bringing you here, for allowing you to get caught up in all this mess."

Zaire gripped Jonas' shoulder as he returned his injured comrade to the seat cushion. "He's gonna be all right, Mista Jonas. Diego's a strong kid. You know that."

"I cannot lose him, Zaire!" Jonas wiped his eyes. "I can't—I can't do this again! It would break me."

"You ain't gonna lose him," Zaire insisted. "Now stop talking madness, y'hear me?"

By the time they had returned to the British Museum, Jonas could barely process anything. All around him, life blurred into a hectic assortment of sounds and faded pigments. He hardly noticed when Ezra and Ibrahim lingered in the corridor outside the storage room. He did not even bat an eyelid when Annabelle, Zaire, and Edison worked to create a makeshift bed for Diego amongst the artifacts. And his mind continued to swirl in a tempest of confusion while Kierra shepherded Aja and Oliver away from the hysteria.

"Edison, could you gather all the sheets and insulating materials you can find?" Annabelle requested, throwing open her case of oils and crystals. "The thicker, the better."

"Yes, ma'am," he responded and dashed off without another word.

"Kierra, my dear?"

"Yes, Mum?" she said, rushing over.

"Would you raise a protective crystal grid over the museum?" Annabelle requisitioned. "I won't take any chances of having those idiot Legerdemain attempt to infiltrate the premises."

The young woman nodded and departed to retrieve her protective crystals from the luggage.

"Zaire, would you get the poor dear up here?" Annabelle asked, gesturing to the line of wooden crates pushed together. "Also, we'll need to make this area as private as possible."

"You got it," Zaire agreed. He lifted Diego through telekinesis, laying him delicately on the platform.

"Oh, Diego, my darling," said Annabelle as she pushed his wet hair back from his forehead. "What did I tell you about catching cold?" She frowned when his shivering became even more pronounced.

"Jonas, could you help me get his clothes off?"

"Wh-what?" he sputtered in an awkward, high-pitched tone.

"Good grief, you know what I mean," Annabelle sighed as she undid Diego's shirt buttons. "Unless you'd rather have Zaire—"

"N-no, I can assist," Jonas replied, moving to the opposite side of the platform. His fingers shakily unclasped Diego's suspenders from his waistband.

Annabelle studied him through sceptical eyes. "Don't go too far after this, my dear, because you are my next patient. You're in shock."

"I am not—"

"Do not question me, Jonas van der Campe."

As Jonas and Annabelle worked to remove the last of Diego's drenched attire, Edison returned with an armful of sheets.

"We had these in a storage closet from our last exhibit opening," Edison explained as he offered the fabric to the Magi. "They worked well to keep the artifacts under wraps, but I think they'll work even better to get him warm."

Jonas forced a weak smile. "Thanks, Edison."

Annabelle draped the multiple layers over Diego and tucked the edges close to his body. "Jonas, what happened out there?"

He crossed his arms. "Exactly what I thought would happen."

Without warning, Diego's eyelids shot open. He gasped for oxygen and promptly grimaced.

"Argh!" he yelled, clutching his ribs. "*Dios!*"

"Try to stay as still as possible," Annabelle instructed him, holding his shoulders down.

With every strained breath, tears of pain built in Diego's eyes. "I—I cannot breathe, *Mamá*," he cried.

"Shhh, I know, sweetheart," Annabelle answered in a motherly tone.

Methodically, she positioned an open palm a few centimetres above his forehead, closed her eyes, and began her mental assessment of his injuries. As her hand progressed past his ribs and abdomen, her facial expressions became increasingly concerned. While Jonas had watched her conduct energy healing many times before, this moment seemed almost unbearable to observe, especially when she remained silent for several excruciating minutes following her evaluation.

"*Mamá?*"

"Yes, my dear?"

"Am I dying?"

"No, you are not dying," Annabelle insisted as she rummaged through her case for the appropriate crystals.

"Jonas?" Diego croaked.

Jonas scrambled to grasp Diego's clammy hand. "I am right here."

"Are you okay?"

"Am I…" Jonas laughed uneasily. "Am *I* okay? Yes, I'm all right. Are you?"

Diego squeezed his eyes shut. "*Jesucristo*. Everything hurts."

"Hmm, well, it should," Annabelle remarked, now rummaging through her medicine case. "You have got two fractured ribs, bruising, mild hypothermia, and a concussion. From now on, you do not leave my sight without encasing yourself in a balloon full of cotton, feathers, and kittens. Is that clear, young man?"

"*Mamá*," Diego whined.

"Here, drink this," Annabelle said, holding a small glass of dark liquid to his lips. "It will help the pain."

Diego took in a mouthful of the medicine only to promptly spit it back out again. "Ugh, this is *muy horrible*."

"It is either that or you writhe in agony all night," Annabelle stated in a matter-of-fact tone. "Take your pick."

"Please take it," Jonas urged him. His gut churned with every shallow gasp Diego inhaled. Seeing him in his current state slashed Jonas like a sword, and he was not sure he would be able to stomach the torture he would inevitably undergo without Annabelle's healing concoctions.

"Fine," Diego complied, tipping back the contents of the cup. He shuddered and handed the glass back to Annabelle.

"At any rate, you will need to rest for some time," Annabelle responded as she mixed oils and herbs into a thick salve. She pulled back the coverings long enough to apply the mixture over the left side of Diego's chest. "No gallivanting across the continent or fraternizing with Miss Stella until you are all healed up, understood?"

Diego narrowed his eyes while Jonas rolled his.

Annabelle caught both of their expressions. "You two are an everlasting enigma. You *do* realise that, right?"

But Jonas had not heard her, for he had already given himself over to his anxious mind. Flashes of what had just transpired at the Royal Observatory flickered through his memory like an out-of-control film projector. And with every jolting visual came the sound of a voice Jonas hoped to never hear again. Symon's words tore through him, brutal and fierce. If there was one thing Symon Bellinor excelled at, it was ripping open old wounds.

"Jonas?"

"Hmm?" he murmured, his vision refocusing on the scene before him.

Annabelle shook her head as she navigated around the makeshift bed. She placed her hand on his arm and guided him away from Diego.

"Let him rest, my dear. He is going to be just fine. Right now, we need to get you back to your chipper old self."

COMING TO PEACE

While Jonas and the Irish Chapter ran amuck to revive their fallen comrade, Ezra lingered in the museum corridor away from the madness. The longer he stared at his father, the more convinced he was that he had somehow been trapped in a dream realm. No other explanation for Ibrahim's timely reappearance in his life made any sense.

Ibrahim sank into a seated position in the corridor alcove. The weary man motioned for Ezra to sit next to him on the polished floors.

"My son, I am *so* sorry," Ibrahim began, cupping Ezra's face in his hands. "I should have told you sooner about all this. I should have known that one day, our world would inevitably find you."

Ezra chewed on his lip, reading the sincerity in his father's eyes.

"Your *anne* and I debated many times whether to tell you we were once Magi," Ibrahim continued. "We thought that by keeping our former identities secret, you would be safe. But I see now that that could not be further from the truth." Ibrahim dabbed away a stray tear from under his own eye. "And our mistake has undoubtedly put you in deeper danger."

Ezra lowered his gaze to the floor. He traced the silver swirls of the marble with his fingertip as he waded through the information. Every arc, every wandering flourish of the tile seemed just as twisted as his thoughts. But at the forefront, the lingering shock of Taylan and Kiraz's affiliation with the Legerdemain Brotherhood crippled him.

And his father needed to know. Or perhaps, he already did.

"*Baba*," Ezra started, but his father hushed him.

"I owe you so many apologies," said Ibrahim. "So many words of explanation—"

"*Baba—*"

"No, Ezra. Listen to me. Every move across Europe was not only because of who I am, but because of what I did while working for the Magi Administration—"

"*Baba*, please," Ezra begged, his sight blurring with tears. Several hours had passed, but the revelation had festered within him for far too long. Holding it inside only scorched what sanity remained. "While I was at the consulate, I learned that Taylan and Kiraz are running against Diederik and Symon for the consul positions."

Life drained from his father's face. Ibrahim put a hand to his forehead, processing the information through the filters of disbelief, sadness, and horror. He opened his mouth, but nothing came out besides broken exhalations. "They—they *are*? Are you certain?"

"Positive."

"No. No," Ibrahim murmured. "No, this cannot be."

"It is," Ezra sighed. "I was young when we left Constantinople, but I always got a good feeling from them and Yonca. I never thought they were affiliated with the Legerdemain."

"Because they never were," Ibrahim answered. "Both Taylan and his wife were part of the Third Order. They served by my side." He bowed his head and raked his fingers through his untidy hair. "At some point after we left, they must have given in to the Order of Babylon."

"I think they might have been the ones to order the Dark Watchers after us," Ezra struggled to say through the emotions gripping his heart. "But why would our friends want us dead?"

"Oh, *Allah*, be with us." His father drew Ezra into an embrace and held him against his chest. "I never thought I would live to see a day as treacherous as this."

Ezra pulled away, anticipating some sort of explanation.

After arming himself with a cleansing breath, Ibrahim wove an incredibly detailed account of his *babaanne's* visions, his association with an ancient prophetic text, and his valiant attempts to erase it from history by inventing Time Blemishes. Ezra's mind spun with dizzying details of his parents' dishonourable ousting from the Magi and confiscation of their Gifts. He listened with intrigue as Ibrahim traced the reasons for their travels across Europe, every relocation relating to hiding his identity and keeping them all safe. But the Portadown train incident had been the defining moment, with fears as fervent as the flames.

As the words tumbled from his father's lips, a rising anguish drowned Ezra's thoughts as he pictured his mother's last breath.

"*Baba*, why—" Tears dripped from Ezra's eyelashes. "—why didn't you come find me after the train accident? Why did you leave me?"

"I never intentionally left you," Ibrahim insisted, pushing back Ezra's hair from his forehead. "That night, I counted at least six Dark Watchers scouring the train for our family. In the calamity that followed, we became separated. I searched for you but stumbled into two Dark Watchers instead. I was able to get away but by that time, the entire train was in flames. I thought for sure you and your *anne* were dead." Ibrahim paused a moment, his face contorting with emotion. He pinched the bridge of his nose before continuing. "For weeks, I hid amongst the Irish countryside, finding solace in barns or caverns. Weeks later, I discovered you were alive and had been taken to Belfast Royal Academy. I kept watch over you from the shadows, as best I could. But I lost track of you. That's when Symon came to me in a dream saying I needed to turn myself in to him if I wanted you to live."

Ezra laid his head on his father's shoulder. "*Baba*, I missed you so much."

Ibrahim drew Ezra into a tight embrace. "You cannot imagine the horrible thoughts gripping my heart and mind on the journey here. I already thought I had lost you once. I could not bear to confront those fears again. But now I am overwhelmed with gratitude to *Allah* for Jonas and his group of Magi. Without them, I would not have been able to get you back."

"They are good people," Ezra concurred.

"They are, indeed," Ibrahim said. His father rummaged through his interior jacket pockets and held out a crystal quartz wand, the same one Jonas had given him after discovering his powers. "And they tell me you have stumbled across abilities of your own?"

Ezra retrieved his wand, his eyes skirting away from his father. "I have. Though I do not understand them quite yet."

"Not to worry, son," Ibrahim said. "I can help you with that."

After several minutes of contemplation, Ezra swallowed the lump in his throat. "What if I don't want to use them, *Baba*? After seeing what you and *Anne* and the Irish Chapter have gone through, I do not think I am ready for something like this."

"No one is ever completely ready," Ibrahim replied. "Yet, that's how the Celestial Lifeforce knows we are worthy to wield its power."

In one precipitous moment, the heaviness of recent events crashed through every flimsy fibre of strength he had left. Ezra's shoulders shook with overwhelming grief as he wept into his father's shirt. "But I'm *not* worthy," he cried. "I couldn't save *Anne* that night on the train. I couldn't—"

"That was not your fault, *canım*," Ibrahim replied, using his thumb to brush the wetness from his face.

"Do you think," Ezra began, his eyes heavy and lifeless, "do you think *Anne* is in *cennet*?"

His father held him close and kissed the top of his head. "She is in Paradise. And she is watching from above, beaming with pride upon seeing who you have become. She may be gone now, but she lives on within you."

Ezra closed his eyes. As much as he wished all three of them could be here in this moment, having Ibrahim once again by his side was more than he could have ever imagined. Relaxing in the arms of his father, Ezra surrendered to sleep.

Theories

Standing on a precipice, Ezra glanced out over the vast underground world. The City of Pillars boasted indescribable grandeur. The resonating hum he'd first heard in the caverns had returned, festering in his ears like an insatiable memory on the edge of remembrance.

But the Shahmaran was nowhere in sight.

Her absence sent a bitter chill through his veins and prompted his feet into motion. Climbing down toward the lake's illuminated surface, Ezra searched the cave for the creature, but to no avail. Everything had fallen into stillness. Even the continuous dripping of water from stalactites had ceased, giving his beating heart a chance to inundate his surroundings.

"Shahmaran?" Ezra called out, wincing at the volume of his question. "Where are you?"

"I am here," her weak voice sounded through the darkness.

Ezra followed the reverberations into the lake, trudging through the shallow water until he reached the base of a massive pillar. He gasped when he caught sight of the chains around her body, effectively binding her against the pillar.

"Who did this to you?" Ezra asked, his fingers trailing over the iron links.

The Shahmaran writhed against her restraints but let out a defeated breath when the action did nothing but press them deeper into her torso. "Someone I once thought was an ally."

He met her golden eyes. They had lost so much of their life, their original glow. Her limp hair hung over her pale shoulders. Everything about her seemed to be wilting.

"My magic is fading," the Shahmaran confessed, as if reading his mind. "Soon, I will have nothing left."

"But why?"

A single tear trickled down the Shahmaran's beautiful face. With great effort, she urged her tail to the water's surface, exposing a broad laceration across her reptilian skin. "Greed. As long as humanity gives in to their covetous desires, I will continue to fade."

Ezra brushed his fingers along her tail. "They are using you for your magic."

She nodded.

"I won't let them."

The Shahmaran allowed an exhausted chuckle to escape from her lips. "Sweet boy, you are incredibly brave. But you cannot stop what has already been put into motion."

He squared his jaw in determination. "Yes, I can. If—if people were to live like that, nothing would ever be accomplished."

Sighing, the Shahmaran met his gaze as if she pitied his optimism. Before she could answer, another powerful tremor shook the caverns. This time, however, the quake commandeered their entire surroundings, sending boulders toppling from the heights. They crashed all around them, causing the lake to churn in agitation.

Ezra grasped onto the pillar to steady himself. "What's happening?"

"It is time," said the Shahmaran. Her eyes became strangely unfocused, her muscular limbs slack.

"Time for what?" asked Ezra. But he never heard her reply, for a boulder crashed into the waters between them. Knocked prostrate by the force, Ezra attempted to pull himself back up but screamed when he realised his ankle was caught under the rock.

"Leave this place!" the Shahmaran's voice commanded him. "Go now!"

Trying to keep his head above water, Ezra fought to move the heavy stone, but his strength was fading fast, along with the creature's magic.

"Help!" he hollered. "Help me!"

"Go, Ezra!" For some reason, the image of the Shahmaran coruscated, replaced by a translucent likeness of his mother. Her long, dark hair dripped with blood. Her cheeks had lost all colour. And a cobra, fierce and deadly, hung around her neck like a scarf. Hungrily, its eyes turned on him, its jaw opening in anticipation for his flesh.

"NO!" Ezra yelled. He closed his eyes, praying that would douse the images from his mind. But every time he opened them, the scenery would flash between the cavern and the train. The juxtaposition stimulated nausea, especially when Ezra noticed the red-tinged water bleeding from beneath the toppled boulder. He fought for freedom as the cobra advanced, but no matter how hard he tried, he couldn't get loose.

A piercing white light swallowed the scene.

"Rise and shine, sleepyhead."

With his dreams dissolving into ashes, Ezra's eyelids fluttered open, greeted by dusty museum surroundings. Groaning, he pushed himself up and stretched his arms above his head. Something about Aja's melodic voice so early in the day seemed unnatural. But as abrupt and brazen as it was, her cheerfulness inspired relief. Relief that for once, he woke up to something other than captivity and incertitude. Though he would never have the boldness to admit it, Ezra found her bubbly persona comforting yet astounding all the same. "How are you so chipper in the mornings?"

The young lady giggled and twirled amidst suitcases and travel bags. The long fabric of her floral embellished dress blossomed in a dazzling dance, wrapping upon itself as her pirouette ended. Aja's braid fell over her shoulder when she dipped into a curtsy. "Because morning is the perfect time to celebrate another day of life. As well as another day I have to be thankful you are safe."

Warmth flushed Ezra's cheeks. Hours ago, after his father had woken him to find a more comfortable place to sleep, Aja had smothered Ezra with the longest embrace he could ever recall having with someone. Even now, she looked as if she wanted to throw her arms around him again. Ezra hoped she would refrain, not because he did not want her close, but because he was not sure he would be able to control his face from flushing even more of an obnoxious red.

And yet, in the sweet promises of the new day, the world began to transform into something resembling normalcy. Edison and Jonas had returned from a local café with a smorgasbord of breakfast items: tea, scones, fine cheese, smoked sausages, breads, and an assortment of jams. Still bleary from exhaustion, Ezra joined the Magi and sat cross-legged beside his father. They gratefully tucked in, their bellies ravenous for anything passing for order and routine.

Only several bites into his scone, Oliver broke the silence. "What happens now?"

Shifting his back against a wooden crate, Jonas returned his teacup to its saucer. "We accomplished what we set out to do," he said, his body posture emanating a more relaxed demeanour. "With Diego's injuries as they are, I want nothing more than to get you all back to Belfast. Safely and without delay."

Something stirred behind Miss McLarney's eyes. "But Jonas, what about the Tablet of Destinies? You know Uncle Diederik is going to still be after Mr. Newport. Just because we succeeded in getting Ezra back does not mean they have suddenly instated a truce."

"Miss Kierra is right," Zaire said. "Yes, we have gained the upper hand, but for how long?"

"Have you heard any updates from the Magi Administration?" Aja enquired.

"None whatsoever."

"That is hardly encouraging," muttered Diego.

Setting his tea atop the crate, Jonas slipped his hands into his trouser pockets. "Okay. I'm listening."

"If I may," Ibrahim cut in. "Last night, Ezra revealed a bit of troubling information about your father's opponents, Mr. van der Campe. They are none other than Taylan and Kiraz, my good friends."

Jonas blinked. "What?"

Ibrahim nodded. "I can only believe this is some sort of personal agenda now that they've pledged allegiance to the Brotherhood. Both know of my connection to the prophecy."

"Yes, but remember, they are also competing for the bid for consul," Jonas answered swiftly, sharing a look with Edison. "By sending Dark Watchers after you and your family, it would erase you from the picture and set Consul Diederik and Deputy Consul Symon up for failure, basically ensuring their win."

"Oh, this is getting more dreadful by the second," Annabelle sighed.

"So, what do we do?" asked Diego in a hoarse whisper.

"Er—well, when I was being held captive, Consul Diederik mentioned something about *Baba* being the Roaming Lion from that Babylonian text," Ezra said as he finished his tea. "According to him, the text suggests the Roaming Lion has seen the Tablet of Destinies before, which is how he knows where to find it." He studied his father. "Do you know where it is?"

Ibrahim lowered his eyebrows in worry. "I—I cannot be certain. I have seen many things in my life. And memories are such fleeting things; I would not know where to begin."

A confident grin edged its way across Miss McLarney's cheeks. "Everything you've ever seen is stored within your hippocampus. It might be risky knowing the length of time it will take to review, but I could try—"

"Kierra, I don't want you getting hurt, too," Jonas interrupted. "You have never attempted something on this scale."

"I can do it, Jonas."

"Even if you could, it is not wise—"

"Are you suggesting I am not capable?" she retorted, folding her arms. Her hair appeared frazzled, her cheeks a scorched red to match.

An abrupt trepidity washed through Ezra at his teacher's fury. He could not tell if he was more surprised at her hellbent rebuttals or curious to see her Gifts in action.

"No, that is absolutely not what—"

"I'll have you know that women are much more resilient than you menfolk give us credit for," the young woman fervently responded. "I could face a hundred Time Blemishes and emerge stronger than ever." She paused, throwing an awkward glance over her shoulder at Diego. "I mean no offence, Diego."

"None taken. It is the truth," he laughed, clutching his ribs at the sudden movement. Annabelle rested a hand on his shoulder, signalling he needed to take it easy.

"Still, the Celestial Lifeforce can overcome even the strongest Magus if you use it long enough," Jonas reminded her. "Multitudes of Magi have lost their lives in audacious attempts to undergo its power for extended periods."

"What other choice do we have?" she fought. "I know you are just trying to protect me, but damn it all, Jonas, there's an opportunity sitting right in front of us!"

The fire in her voice engulfed the room. Ezra shared a surprised glance with Aja and Oliver, both of whom returned his wide-eyed reaction.

"I am sorry, but our hands are tied."

"But they don't have to be," Ibrahim spoke, a spark of optimism igniting the silence. "We were always meant to do impossible things, Mr. van der Campe. The odds may be stacked against us, but how can one rise without something on which to climb? We are Magi. And *inshallah*, we shall prevail."

Ezra surveyed his company as their faces radiated new inspiration. While he still did not know them all that well, he could not help but wonder if maybe—just maybe—this new reality could be something worth fighting for.

Jonas exhaled and ran a hand over his tired facial expressions. "Very well. We shall do this Kierra's way. But the moment the either of you exhibit any pain, I'm breaking the connection."

Miss McLarney nodded in agreement and motioned for Ibrahim to sit beside her on a smaller wooden crate. Rising, Ibrahim grasped Ezra's shoulder before taking his seat. She placed her palm over Ibrahim's forehead and, after drawing in a deep breath to ground herself, closed her eyes.

Every passing minute made Ezra squirm with discomfort. While he knew Miss McLarney and his father were strong individuals, the warnings dictated by Jonas made him wonder just how deadly the Celestial Lifeforce could be when used beyond its recommended length. Ezra snuck a look at the Magi Master, who observed them with crossed arms and an unreadable expression. Annabelle wrung her hands together in worry, while Diego, Zaire, and Oliver watched in anticipation. Scooting to his side, Aja gave Ezra an encouraging smile before reaching for his hand. Ezra held on for dear life.

Ten minutes went by without much fanfare.

Thirty minutes progressed with mounting restlessness.

But after nearly an hour, everyone in Ezra's company shared in his distress. Ibrahim had been reduced to silent tears, clinging to Miss McLarney's other hand in anguish. Miss McLarney's fair skin had turned a terrifying shade of grey. The only colour in her face was the blood that trickled from her lip as she held back cries of pain.

"Okay, that's enough," Jonas commanded, retrieving his crystal from his pocket. In one authoritative movement, he sliced the air above and between them with the wand, shattering the invisible connection with the Universe.

Ibrahim doubled over, cradling his head in his hands. Miss McLarney let out a sob while her cousin drew her into his arms.

"Kierra, are you all right?"

"I am fine," she assured him. The young woman pulled a handkerchief from her skirt pocket and dabbed at her lips. "But I—" She shared a meaningful glance with Ibrahim before turning back to Jonas. "I could not find anything."

"Nothing at all?" pried Diego.

Miss McLarney shook her head. "If Ibrahim has seen the artifact in his lifetime, it is very well hidden."

Ezra's shoulders sagged in disappointment, and he untangled his fingers from Aja's. The fragile hope that they were on to something shattered upon the jagged rocks of reality. Perhaps the prophecy had got it wrong. Perhaps the Roaming Lion hadn't seen the artifact *at all*.

But if that were the case, what hope did they have against the consul of the Legerdemain Brotherhood? What hope did they have against the traitorous Taylan and Kiraz? When all else failed, what kept *him* from being caught in the crossfire between two secret societies grappling for dominance?

Like the Shahmaran's magic, his hope was draining.

Without another word, Ezra excused himself from their temporary hideout, trusting the ambiance of the British Museum would steady the tremors in his heart.

The Last Location

Early afternoon sunlight streamed through the café windows, casting shadows across the inky black waters of Jonas' cup. Usually, he preferred brewed herbs for midday tea but today, he needed something stronger. He brought the cup to his lips, taking in the tantalising aroma of the coffee before allowing the liquid to envelop his mouth in warmth.

While the rest of the Irish Chapter and the Newports waited at the museum for clarity on their next steps, Jonas slipped away to clear his own head. After the disappointment of not finding any usable evidence in Ibrahim's memories, they had gone back to the drawing board. If they could even call it that when they were at a complete loss for where to go next.

Jonas took another gulp of his coffee.

"I thought I would find you here."

He glanced up at Edison, who slid into the booth across the table from him.

"Coffee this afternoon?" his friend enquired.

"Mmm, yes," Jonas responded half-heartedly. "My mind has been running like mad."

"Understandably so," Edison said, crossing his arms. "How are you holding up after that wretched run-in with my father?"

"As good as one can after being humiliated and called a sodomite to their face."

"Good Lord," Edison exhaled. "I am terribly sorry, Jonas. I know you will never get an apology from him, so please accept mine."

"Thank you," Jonas replied. He cringed as he swirled a silver spoon within his coffee cup. "But perhaps someone with transgressions like mine does not deserve an apology."

His friend looked him directly in the eyes. "The integrity of a man stems from his unadulterated desire to do good, not from the path he treads or the stones that cause him to stumble."

Jonas set down his spoon. "Why are you doing this for us?" he suddenly asked, the words tumbling from his mouth before he could stop them. "You have always been firm on your neutral stance. Why help the Magi now?"

Caught off guard, Edison considered Jonas' question in silence. His eyes cautiously darted out the window, almost as if he were watching for someone. On his breath, a weighty sigh and mixed emotions. Even deeper confliction simmered behind his expressions. "Because it is the right thing to do," Edison relented. "Though I never admitted it at the time, I was quite moved by an eighteen-year-old Legerdemain who denounced his ways all because he wished to be honourable."

A faint smile began its journey across Jonas' face. "Thank you, Edison. For everything."

"Thank me later," Edison replied as he took his notebook out of his pocket. "As for right now, we have an artifact to locate."

Jonas shifted in the booth, the heavy leather creaking in resistance to his sudden movement.

Edison glanced up from his notes scattered across the surface of the tabletop. "What?"

"Edison," Jonas began, refusing to make eye contact. A nervous energy fuelled the whirlpool of coffee swirling around in his porcelain mug. "I don't even know if I want to pursue that wretched artifact right now. After everything that has happened, all I want to do is get my Chapter back to Belfast. Safe and sound."

"What if I told you I am on to something?" Edison admitted. "What would you say then?"

Considering his words, Jonas allowed an anxious breath to escape from his lips before answering. "And by on to something, you mean—"

"—I might have figured something out, yes."

"And again, I would ask why you are providing this information to me and not your father."

Edison grinned, almost as if he were expecting the rejoinder. "Because you have a Time Manipulator in your group. And he's the only one who can validate if my hypothesis is correct."

"Yes, and my Time Manipulator is also suffering a brain injury preventing him from utilising his Gifts," Jonas rebutted.

"Nevertheless, I think you should know. After Kierra couldn't find anything within Mr. Newport's memories this morning, I tore through volume after volume of texts, notes, anything I could find on *this*." Edison stressed the last syllable, sliding one note across the table.

Curiosity creased the lines in Jonas' forehead as he digested the information. "The Library of Alexandria?"

"Of all the texts I came across, the Library was the only place to strike a chord," Edison replied, shuffling through the notebook pages. "In the third century B.C., an extensive call for scrolls, artifacts, and any item of higher learning was issued by Ptolemy II Philadelphus in Egypt. The entire Ptolemy line had been dedicated to the establishment of the Musaeum Institution of Alexandria, of which the Library served as one part."

"Ah," Jonas thought aloud. "Temple of the Muses."

Edison nodded. "The Musaeum of Alexandria would have been the place where men of all walks of life studied under the greatest intellectuals of their time. I have a feeling many Magi studied here and if you were alive in those times, you would have beaten down the doors to be accepted as a scholar."

Jonas laughed and took a sip of his coffee. "Incredible."

"At any rate, under Ptolemy II Philadelphus, the Library of Alexandria saw its golden age," Edison continued, sifting through his notes. "It is estimated over a half a million articles of learning were stored in the Library and at one point, an additional storage facility had to be built to house the overflow of items. It would not have been a stretch of the imagination to think that perhaps, the Tablet of Destinies was transferred from the Library of Ashurbanipal in ancient Nineveh. As a matter of fact, that's where most of the British Museum's collection of Babylonian tablets come from; they were excavated from the dig site in Mosul."

"You really think the Tablet of Destinies was kept at the Library of Alexandria?" Jonas asked.

"I do," said Edison. "That is, until the fire."

"Mmm, yes," Jonas mused. "48 B.C., was it?"

"Precisely," Edison replied. "When Julius Caesar set the ships ablaze in the Alexandrian harbour, the Library of Alexandria incurred damage as well. But think about it: When faced with imminent danger, what is the first thing you do? You look toward what you value most and attempt to preserve it."

Jonas cleared his throat and diverted his gaze out the cafe window. Echoes of the conflict at the Royal Observatory reverberated throughout his memory. He shivered when he remembered Diego's pained cries while he fought for his life.

"My hypothesis is that the moment the flames began, scholars rushed to relocate the Tablet of Destinies," Edison said. "But of course, we will never know that for certain, unless—"

"Unless Diego goes back to that moment in time," Jonas concluded.

While silence overtook the two of them, the rest of the cafe buzzed in a cacophony of lively chatter, clanking of dishware, and resonance of the entrance bell. The activity all around them continued in its usual fashion and to Jonas, that was just as unsettling as the mission before them. If the consuls got their hands on that powerful relic, the world would not survive whatever cruelty they had up their sleeves. Hundreds of millions of innocent lives were at stake, each one blissfully unaware that danger lurked just beyond the horizon.

The time was now. This was their last chance.

Jonas swallowed his fear. "Let's just hope Diego is strong enough to attempt the venture."

§WEET ÐREAMS

For once, Diego's dreams had drawn him into the comforting warmth of his memories. He sat atop La Casa de Montreal, *staring up at the stars. The open rooftop of the two-story abode served as the perfect vantage point, not only of the Guadalajara skyline but of the pinpricks of light in the celestial canopy. This year, the June sky looked rather dull, with only Venus, Mars, and the Moon set like diamonds amongst the blackness. But throughout the centuries, Mexico's skies had seemed more alive. In Junes past, Venus, Mars, Jupiter, Saturn, and Uranus all raced across the southern quadrant, while the milky band of stars arced across the great expanse. Diego loved scrolling back through Time, watching the skies transform in front of his very eyes as the years flew by at breakneck speeds. It seemed more magical that way.*

"Looking at the stars again, mi hermano?*"*

Diego looked over his shoulder at his younger sister as she joined him on the rooftop perch. "Of course. What else would I be doing?"

"Toying with that pocket watch of yours," Celestina said with a smile. She gathered her colourful skirt and sat beside him. "And doing whatever Magi do."

He grinned. "Someday, you may find you also have Gifts."

"Abuelita says the very same," Celestina said with a hopeful sparkle in her eyes. "She says sometimes it takes a while to wake them."

Diego laid a hand on her shoulder and squeezed it. "Patience, Pequeña. They will come."

Celestina ran her fingers through her long, black hair. "Diego, what is my sun sign?"

"Tina, Tina, Tina," Diego scolded her in jest. "How do you not know one of the most important aspects of your identity?"

The adolescent girl sheepishly shrugged.

"You are a Capricorn, an Earth sign. Fiercely ambitious, intelligent, and stubborn."

"Hey," Celestina said, punching her brother in the shoulder.

"It is what the stars say, Pequeña.*"*

Silence consumed the Montreal siblings for several moments.

"Diego?"

"Hmm?"

"Abuelita has said before that Sagittarians and Capricorns do not get along."

Diego smiled and put his arm around his sister's shoulders. "Impossible. I would climb the highest mountain, swim the deepest ocean, and traverse the most dangerous forests for you, Pequeña. *Until the very end of Time."*

"Diego, wake up."

Diego stirred, groaning as he transitioned to waking life. "Go away."

"Unfortunately, this cannot wait."

His eyelids fluttered open. Diego jerked awake when he noticed the entirety of the Irish Chapter had gathered around, staring at him with unwavering focus. He clutched his blanket protectively around his chest.

"*Ay, Dios mio!*" he exclaimed, glaring sharply at all of them. "Can't a man get some privacy while he sleeps?"

"It is quite fascinating to watch you," Aja readily admitted as she played with her braid. "You make the funniest faces."

"That is horrifying, Aja," Diego replied dryly.

"Never mind that," Jonas said, sitting beside him. "How are you feeling?"

Diego winced as he shifted his body to the side. "Like I was beaten by Dark Sentinels."

Jonas grimaced but nevertheless, continued. "Edison believes he has

323

uncovered the last known location of the Tablet of Destinies. We were hoping—" he threw a sideways glance at Annabelle, "—that you would be up for the task of navigating through Time to the destruction of the Library of Alexandria."

Diego met Jonas' eyes. "*Sí.* I have been there before. And for your information, the library was not destroyed, only slightly damaged."

"Did you ever notice anything that might suggest any items were relocated at the time of the blaze?" asked Edison as he stepped into the circle of Magi.

"Not that I can recall," Diego answered. "I would need to return to be certain."

"You do not have to do that, my dear," Annabelle countered. "We can wait for you to heal, no matter how much Jonas and Edison cry and plead like children."

Jonas crossed his arms. Edison struggled to contain a humoured grin.

"*Mamá,* if Jonas thinks it is okay, then—"

"Hush," Annabelle cut him off. "If Jonas thought it would be okay for you to jump off a bridge, would you?"

Diego shared a brief look with the Magi Master. "Probably."

"Well, I am asking you not to do anything rash," Annabelle requested.

"No, I can do it," Diego insisted, mustering the strength to lift himself to a seated position. He dug through his knapsack for his quartz crystal and pocket watch and laid them on his lap. "48 B.C., correct?"

"Are you absolutely certain about this?" Kierra asked in concern, laying her hand on Diego's shoulder. "Please do not try to put on a strong front for us. We already know you are brave."

"I'm not doing this because I am brave," Diego said. A smirk carved itself across his cheeks. "I'm doing this because—well, have you *seen* the wrath of Jonas van der Campe when he is angry? I have. And I would rather not be mauled by a vicious lion."

Annabelle sighed. Jonas chuckled. Kierra suppressed a smile and smacked her cousin on the arm.

Diego looked to Edison. "Do you have a Souvenir for me?"

"Ah, yes," the museum employee replied, offering him the glossy black box in his hands. "Jonas told me you'd need them to navigate the Past. I included artifacts from Alexandria circa 48 B.C. as well as some relics from the Middle East and Northern Africa that will take you through the Crusades to the thirteenth century. I took the liberty of labelling them with their years and locations."

Diego received the box, almost dropping it when he realised it carried a much heavier burden than he was anticipating. Nevertheless, he set out the range of artifacts, retrieved his timepiece and held his crystal wand to the clock face after tracing the Star of David in the air. "I will see you all again in the future," he yawned and without another word, dove headfirst into Past Time.

A City Burning

Alexandria, Egypt, 48 B.C.

When Diego opened his eyes again, the world was ablaze.

Smoke billowed from the ships in the Portus Magnus, leaving smears of black across the Egyptian sky. Terrified shouts, in both Greek and Egyptian, resounded across the coastline, while several groups of men attempted to douse the flames with urns of seawater.

A city burning. Not just with flame, but a less obvious destruction: a bitter civil war between two royal siblings.

Diego shielded his nose in the crook of his arm and dashed into the commotion, weaving his way amongst frightened onlookers. By this time, the fire had crept across the embankment fortifying the city and sauntered along the promenade toward several nearby residences. Daunting and unrelenting, the blaze continued its journey of devastation in the direction of a massive limestone building.

The Great Library of Alexandria.

Taking in as much air as he could without choking on ash, Diego rushed toward the library. Scholars tore from the arched entry, tripping down the staircase in their haste. Others lingered behind the granite columns, barking orders in Greek. While Diego had much to learn in the way of linguistics, he prided himself on knowing just enough Greek to form rough translations. Certainly, the skill would serve him well now that he had a precious artifact to track down in Hellenistic Egypt.

Once Diego crossed the library's threshold, the pandemonium from outside faded. In fact, an eerie silence permeated the once lively building. A thin grey veil of smoke entwined around statues of the great philosophers, the only indication something was amiss. He darted from room to room, not seeing much more than dust refracting in the late afternoon sunlight amongst a backdrop of scrolls and tomes.

Diego exhaled in frustration when every floor following the first yielded the same results. *Nothing. Absolutely nothing.*

"If I were an all-powerful tablet, where would I be?" Diego asked aloud, circling the top floor one last time before descending the poorly lit staircase. "The sneaky artifact is just as elusive in history as it is in modern life."

Just then, a clamour from somewhere below ricocheted throughout the stairwell. Diego dashed down the stairs, taking two and three at a time as he navigated toward the source of the noise.

"Make haste! We haven't much time!"

Despite the volume of the frantic order, Diego found it impossible to pinpoint the source. Every shout of warning, every clatter of falling shelves seemed to emanate from everywhere at once. It did not matter that he had been to this very scene several times before. The library corridors still had an uncanny ability to contort themselves into unfamiliar territory.

Diego had almost given up hope when moments later, his astral projection nearly barrelled through three men in scholar's robes. The men manoeuvred a wooden crate from what looked to be one of the library's learning rooms. Diego stood on the balls of his feet to get a better view of its contents, but all he could see were heaps of fabric.

"What is our destination?" asked one of the scholars.

"We need to get these to Queen Cleopatra," commanded another. "She can protect them better than we can here."

Diego frowned. *Them?*

"Did you get the lot?" asked a fourth man, scuttling down the hall.

"Pandora's Box, the Shield of Achilles, and the Ring of Gyges," recounted one of the men. "The Book of Thoth, the ancient Ankh, David's Harp, and remnants of the Ark of the Covenant."

Diego's mouth hung open in disbelief.

"Imbeciles! You forgot the Tablet of Destinies!" exclaimed the fourth man. "Keep going; I shall retrieve it and meet up with you."

Leaving the three scholars and their crate behind, Diego trailed after the fourth individual down another winding corridor. At its end, an arched doorway gave way to a grand hall. Supported by rows of columns and floor-to-ceiling shelving, the expanse served as another of the Library's many study rooms. Yet in this one, golden beams from the sun streamed through an open skylight, illuminating a two-meter pedestal in the centre of the space and upon it—

The Tablet of Destinies.

"*Santa María,*" Diego whispered, initiating the sign of the cross over his chest.

Standing at a height of approximately three decimetres, the Tablet of Destinies exuded an air of authority. Unlike the reddish-brown artifacts Diego had seen in many excavations through Time, this rectangular tablet appeared silver with faint light radiating from within. Engraved across the stone were the familiar cuneiform markings, along with an imprint from a cylindrical Babylonian seal. Even the surrounding atmosphere pulsed and vibrated, as if the object commanded sovereignty over the electromagnetic spectrum.

Diego watched as the scholar removed his outer layer of robes and wrapped the artifact within the textiles. Tucking it under his arm, the man dashed from the room, with Diego at his heels.

The pursuit led them away from the Library of Alexandria through a maze of paved streets and across manicured lawns. With each footfall, Diego's head screamed for respite. At one point, he almost lost the scholar entirely as he braced himself against a building, fighting the debilitating agony tearing through his brain. Groaning, he forced himself to continue. He had to. This *had* to work.

Finally, the scholar slowed as he reached the entrance of the palace. The Alexandrian man took one frightened look over his shoulder in the direction of the burning marina before darting up the marble staircase. Gripping his timepiece within his sweaty palms, Diego followed until both he and the Tablet's carrier had arrived at the inner sanctum of the royal building.

Surrounded by her advisors, Queen Cleopatra hugged her arms against her middle as urgent whispers swirled around the room. Her dark eyes communicated a strange longing as she turned her head in the direction of a window overlooking the destruction.

Diego swallowed and diverted his eyes from the authoritative woman. Not only was the Greek-born a lovely sight, but she ruled with power and grace. And even though Cleopatra would never see him in his current state, Diego lowered his head respectfully in her presence.

"My Queen," panted the scholar. He carved his way through her court and sunk into a reverent bow. "The Library of Alexandria is in danger. We were able to extract our most important treasures, but I fear the worst…"

The queen regained her focus. "You got them all, you said?"

He nodded. "My colleagues should be here with the rest, but until then—" he handed her the bundle of robes, "—please protect the Tablet of Destinies."

"I shall," Cleopatra answered, her voice radiating strength as she accepted the relic. "If Ptolemy thinks he is going to gain the upper hand this time, he is sorely mistaken."

"With all due respect, my Queen," began one of her advisors, "the fires were not started by your brother but by Julius Caesar."

"Sometimes, in order to get one's attention, desolation must speak instead of complacency," she answered, her faraway gaze returning as she placed a hand protectively against her belly.

Of course, Diego reminded himself as Queen Cleopatra held the artifact close to her chest. *Not only was she dealing with the betrayal of her brother, but her Roman lover had unleashed hell upon her city. That and—*

Diego doubted many in the room realised she was carrying a child, a child he knew would one day grow up to be Caesarion, future co-ruler of Egypt and supposed son of Julius Caesar himself. And perhaps—

Diego raised his pocket watch and readied his quartz crystal.

Future holder of the Tablet.

Diego took one last look at the conflicted features of the Queen of Egypt and urged the hour hand forward through history. Days and nights flickered like a faulty lightbulb. Blurs of human outlines buzzed across his palatial surroundings as months faded into years. The hum of activity around him slowed as he retracted the crystal from the clock face.

30 B.C.

When the relentless ache in his head dissipated enough to see his surroundings, Diego could feel the negative energy tearing apart the very atoms in the air.

Tonight, a queen would be slain.

Seventeen-year-old Caesarion looked at his mother with pleading eyes. The depths of despair in his face echoed that of Cleopatra. Diego thought the young prince resembled Ezra, with his sad eyes and unkempt black hair.

"You must promise me you will not look back," instructed a worn and weary Cleopatra. "Go with Rhodan. He will accompany you to Port Djibouti on the Ethiopian coast. That's where you will find a ship to take you to India—"

"Mother, I cannot just leave you here," answered Caesarion, fear brimming in his tear ducts. "Please—"

"Listen to me," Cleopatra interrupted in a choked whisper. Smudged makeup beneath her eyes completed her semblance of unmitigated exhaustion. "There is nothing for you here. Not anymore."

Caesarion sniffed.

"Let me take care of what will become of Alexandria," the queen said, bringing her son into her arms. "Your safety is most important to me, *leventi mou*. I love you more than life itself."

The mother and son clung to each other for several precious minutes. Wishing not to intrude on the private moment, Diego turned away and spotted a dark-skinned man hurrying into the throne room. He toted a travel pack on his back and carried yet another bulky bag in his arms.

Cleopatra withdrew from her son and dabbed the tears around her eyes. "Rhodan, have you everything you need for the journey?"

"Yes, my Queen," Caesarion's tutor responded. "The camels are ready and waiting just outside. We should depart at once."

The woman nodded and retrieved a rectangular item wrapped in fine linens. "There is one more thing I need you to take, and I want both of you to guard it with your lives." Carefully, she unwrapped the exterior, exposing the glow of the Tablet of Destinies. "Once you've reached India, aim your travels northwest and seek out the Persian Magi. They will know what to do."

Caesarion stared at the Tablet curiously. "What is this?"

"A treasure that belongs to them," stated Queen Cleopatra.

"It shall be done," promised Rhodan. He took the Tablet and tucked it away in his pack. "Come, Prince Caesarion. We must hurry."

"Fly with the winds of Aeolus at your back," whispered the queen.

After one last tearful embrace, the young prince and his tutor fled, leaving Cleopatra in the silence of her last moments.

"Okay, next destination: Port Djibouti, Ethiopia," Diego spoke aloud. Using his crystal, he made an arcing motion in the air before him, creating an opaque circle with the ghostly representations of the Souvenirs Edison had provided. He scrolled through them, analysing each one for time and location. There were coins from Egypt, funeral amulets from the Giza plateau, a scroll from Jerusalem, sword fragments from the Crusades and—

¡Ah, sí! Diego's heart leapt in excitement.

Pottery from Port Djibouti.

Edison, I could kiss you, Diego exclaimed as he pressed his index finger against the projection.

All at once, his surroundings faded again, spinning like mad in a whirlwind of colours and smells. Envisioning a map of the world, he redirected his awareness across the African continent. Like a spirit navigating amongst the living, Diego soared through time and space. He had always likened the feeling to what a bird might experience during flight.

But this time, something was wrong.

As he pushed forward through the Past, he realised the relative ease of Time Travel had evaporated, leaving his journey rather turbulent and haphazard. With every lurch forward—even though the Time landscape consisted of weeks, not years—dizziness festered within Diego's brain, nearly breaking the connection with his Gifts altogether. He swallowed a wave of nausea as the sun and moon slowed their unrelenting race across the sky.

Once he could focus again, Diego reviewed his knowledge of the events about to transpire. He knew that within mere weeks after leaving Alexandria, Caesarion would turn back, lured into a trap set by Roman conqueror Octavian. And, with a heaviness in the pit of his stomach, Diego knew the young prince would be executed by Octavian, joining his mother in death.

But did Caesarion bring the Tablet back to Alexandria with him only to let it fall into Roman hands? Or did his tutor claim it, playing into Octavian's schemes so that he could benefit from the relic's power? As Diego's surroundings morphed into the Ethiopian port city, the answer quickly became clear.

Rhodan made his way amongst the bustle of activity along the piers in Port Djibouti. Evening approached, casting long shadows across the docks. The man halted and shifted the weight of the bag over his shoulder. Prince Caesarion was nowhere in sight, but the Tablet of Destinies was in full view.

A smile played on Rhodan's lips as he held the linen-wrapped package in his arms. Whatever plot brewed behind his eyes only thickened as he waited for a ship in the gulf to make port. While he could not be positive, Diego had an intuitive feeling Rhodan was hardly focused on carrying out Queen Cleopatra's last wishes. Instead, the man looked as if he were on the brink of making a clean getaway, with the ancient Tablet in tow.

Impatient, Diego sped up the events of history again, only to re-enter the scene amid a brutal scuffle. A group of black-clad men had beaten the Alexandrian man until he lay lifeless in a pool of his own blood. Snatching his belongings, the robbers fled into an alley across from the harbour.

Diego sighed in frustration and followed them. While Aja would have called what had just happened 'a prime example of karma,' the Tablet's constant change of hands wore thin on Diego's nerves. In fact, as Diego hopped from location to location over the course of the next several centuries, the Tablet had been passed between owners like a rampant virus.

After being stolen from Rhodan in 30 B.C., the artifact was lost along the banks of the Awash River. Flood waters during the rainy season took it even further downstream until, decades later, it reached the town of Addis Ababa.

From there, the Tablet found its way into the hands of a shaman, who travelled across the Ethiopian highlands using it in healing rituals. But greed showed its face once more, and the Tablet of Destinies earned a new host: a former leper who had been supposedly cured by touching the relic. Instead of using it for its power, the man sold it to the highest bidder, taking the money to feed his family. That highest bidder happened to be a Magus advisor of the King of Aksum, who brought it to the ruler as a treasure for the royal palace.

And there it stayed for six uneventful centuries, hidden away with other treasures of the Ethiopian ruler. But like other kingdoms before it, Aksum disintegrated into history. Sparks of conflict rose in the north and with growing unrest between the Muslims and Christians, eventually resulting in the crusades, the Tablet was carried north to Jerusalem.

The boundaries of Time had been stretched to the point of collapse. Physically and mentally exhausted, Diego forced his forward venture. His entire body ached; he could barely stand upright. The hands of his pocket watch spun in a sickening spiral, prompting the scenery around him to explode into stripes of pigment. Yet, he pressed on, more determined than ever to verify the final resting place of the Tablet of Destinies.

Just as he coasted into the Middle Ages, a violent jolt in his brain brought him to his knees. Time swam around him. His eyes flicked back and forth, refusing to steady themselves. Diego braced himself against the pain, the twisting of his stomach, the excruciating burning in his head. Every nerve twitched in agony.

"Come on," he urged, clutching his pocket watch until he was sure it'd crumble into dust. "Come on!"

History had dissolved into shadows. A heaviness pressed him to the ground, while familiar laughter rang throughout his mind.

"Dear boy, you know the deal."

"No! No, no, no—"

Cold fingers stroked his cheek. Diego cringed, fighting for escape.

Not now! Please, not now…

Lips grazed his ear. "Have you made up your mind?"

"Go away!"

The voice laughed again, a bitter cruelty echoing like thunder. "No matter where you go, no matter what you do, you will always be mine. Do you hear me?"

"No," Diego sobbed. An oppressive dampness closed in around him.

"Please—"

"Always, dear boy. *Always.*"

Swallowed by a sea of darkness, Diego collapsed under the weight of the Past.

London, 1906 A.D.

Diego inhaled deeply. At first, his ears rang with conversations from the past, ebbing and flowing with the river of Time. His chest burned. His throat ached. Finally, after a minute of fighting the pain, his consciousness transitioned to the familiar surroundings of the British Museum.

He placed a hand over his forehead. A brutal ache clobbered his brain and every time he tried to open his eyes, flashes of light corrupted the boundaries of his vision. Drowning in nausea, he rolled onto his side and vomited. The spasms in his abdomen tore at his already smarting ribs, causing him to whimper and curl in on himself.

"Oh, I knew it," Annabelle's disappointed voice reverberated through his mind. "I knew this was a terrible idea from the start!"

"Diego," whispered Jonas in concern. Diego felt him sink to his knees at his side and run a warm hand over his arm. "Talk to me. Are you all right?"

"Look at the poor dear! Of course, he's not all right," Annabelle said critically, patting Diego's chin with a handkerchief. "Just a moment, sweetheart. Let me get you some tonic."

"I—I am fine," Diego insisted, struggling to sit up.

Jonas gently pushed his shoulders back to his bedding. "No. You need to rest. No sudden movements."

"Well?" Oliver asked. "What did you learn?"

Aja elbowed him. "Oh, for the love of the Famed Three! Give him a chance to breathe."

"I couldn't—I couldn't do it," Diego cried. "I couldn't—"

"Shh, it is okay," said Jonas, tenderly brushing the curls away from his forehead. "Rest. Mum is getting you some medicine right now."

"I failed," Diego continued. "I found it, but I failed—Just like Kierra. I couldn't do it."

"It's okay," Jonas repeated. He felt his hands slip into his, grasping them with comforting fortitude. "You are okay."

Closing his eyes, he allowed Annabelle to pour liquid into his mouth and before he knew it, he had given in to blissful, dreamless sleep.

The Shahmaran's Revelation

Now *two* had failed.

First Miss McLarney, then Diego. Both in the same day.

With every loop around the British Museum's exhibit halls, Ezra found his steps falling progressively heavier. Both opportunities to track the relic had ended in miserable failure. They had been *so close*. But an impasse had backed them into a corner, and of all in his company, Ezra could not bear looking Jonas in the eyes.

Quick to forgive but even quicker to apprehension, the Magi Master had instructed the crew to gather their belongings. At dawn, they would board the first train out of London. Once safe in Belfast, they would shelter in Elysium until given the all-clear from the Magi Administration.

"After all," Jonas had reiterated, "the Administration has a task force on the Legerdemain situation as we speak. Our confidence should lie with them in finishing the job."

But Ezra could detect the subtle uncertainty in his voice.

Since he lacked any belongings to pack, Ezra allowed the rest to assemble their things while he did one last rotation around the museum. One last moment to allow the worries of the world to fall away amongst the exhibits. Erased by comforts of knowledge.

Ezra wove a path through the throng of families and schoolchildren, hesitating only to admire the mummies of ancient Egypt and the Rosetta Stone. Not far from this, a nostalgia-inducing display of Ottoman relics urged him closer.

Ezra sighed and leaned against the exhibit's brass railing. The cacophony of visitors had softened, bathing him in sweet serenity. Every sketch of the Hagia Sophia, every piece of pottery and tools of Turkish origin sparked an aching desire to return home.

To where it all began.

His eyes skimmed across a painting of the Shahmaran, prompting a flutter in his heart.

That hadn't been there before.

Had it?

Eyes widening, Ezra shifted his attention to the picture beside it and gripped the railing lest he fall over in shock. There, as vivid as the morning sun: A glossy photograph of a cavern held up by rocky pillars.

The world of his dreams.

A low hum simmered in his ears, luring him away from the discovery. Annoyed, Ezra shook his head, hoping the motion would rid him of the sound. But no matter how much he rubbed his ears, no matter how hard he tried to redirect his focus, it continued. Relentless and aching.

Unsteady feet guided him in his search for a place to sit down, even for a moment. He had to rest. He had to get a hold of himself before he went completely mad. Ezra stumbled to a bench and bent forward, grasping at his hair.

What was going on?

Prickling white sparks ate away at the scene around him, leaving him grappling for consciousness.

The adhan echoed across the courtyard.

338

Gripping Ezra's young hand in his, Ibrahim pulled him along in his sprint toward the mosque.

"Come, canım,*" he said. "The Call to Prayer has begun."*

But five-year-old Ezra's attention was everywhere but his father. Or prayer, for that matter. Instead, his eyes traced the grand heights of the Hagia Sophia's minarets, its layered domes, and the way the entire edifice sparkled in the midday summer sun.

"Baba, I don't want to go inside," young Ezra complained. He dragged his feet in retaliation. "I want to stay out here."

When they reached the entry, Ibrahim knelt to Ezra's level and held him firmly by the shoulders. "If you stay, you must not move from this spot," he instructed, gesturing inside the threshold of the sacred building. "Do you understand?"

"Yes, Baba,*" Ezra answered.*

"Good boy." He ruffled Ezra's hair before disappearing inside.

For what seemed like an eternity, Ezra kept his promise. But restlessness was a difficult beast to tame, and he found himself on a trek across the courtyard. He chased every whim: first a songbird, then a blowing newspaper on the breeze, and next a stray cat.

"Come here, kitty," Ezra commanded. His little voice hadn't the power to instill obedience in the animal, so he dashed after it. "Kitty! Stop!"

The lithe creature raced over the cobblestones with young Ezra in pursuit. After bounding over barriers and zigzagging through a quaint garden, Ezra stood face to face with a sign he couldn't read and a shack that appeared all too inviting.

Ezra snuck a glance over his shoulder at the mosque. Satisfied with the reassuring proximity of the building, he pried open the wooden door and descended into darkness.

A faint, purple glow lured him further along the rocky corridors. Damp, stale air made him scrunch up his nose in disgust; he'd never been one for peculiar smells. Or snakes. He prayed to Allah that he would not stumble across one.

The cat had long since vanished, but Ezra's sense of adventure grew with every step into the unknown. It was not long before the corridor gave way to a world of wonder.

Ezra gasped. Colossal pillars extended as far as his eyes could see, illuminated by the source of the mysterious light. He found himself wading through knee-high water, disregarding the bitter chill.

Veering to the left, young Ezra examined a curious pillar, this one boasting a base unlike any other. He cocked his head sideways, giggling when he realised the pillar had been propped upon the stone likeness of a woman with snakes for hair.

"Merhaba, snake lady," Ezra said in Turkish, running his fingers over the contours of the carving.

Hello, sweet boy.

A fierce tremble beneath his feet sent ripples through the water. He clutched the stone, wondering if the whole cave were about to collapse. Rocks fell from the arches in the ceiling and plunked into the water all around him. Fear seized his heart. Perhaps Allah did not want him to be here. Perhaps he was angry at his disobedience.

The world around him shuddered and groaned. Terrified, young Ezra trudged through the water toward the corridor but before he could make it, a boulder crashed down upon him.

He cried out in pain and fought to keep his head above water. No matter how furiously he pulled at his leg, all attempts at freeing himself from the boulder became more impossible by the second.

"Baba!" Ezra screamed. He sputtered on a mouthful of water. "Baba, help me!"

Almost as soon as it had begun, the shaking stopped. The water had become unbearably cold and still. Somewhere above the surface, sirens blared. Voices yelled. Terror reigned.

Not knowing what else to do, Ezra sobbed. Through the veil of tears, an amethyst glimmer sparkled in the Snake Lady's eyes. A deep, throbbing pulsation caressed the atmosphere, lulling him to sleep.

He was only half conscious when they found him. Murmurs of conversation swirled about in his ears, but he couldn't make sense of any of it.

"Ezra! My son! I am here."

"Is the boy all right?"

"He is hurt, but he is alive. Praise be to Allah!"

"What was he doing in the cisterns?"

"That does not matter now. All that matters is that he is safe."

"Unlike so many others. We've heard reports that many are dead because of that quake."

Silence. Blackness. But this time, a woman's voice rose from the depths, words tripping over one another in chaotic urgency:

"Sweet boy, you have survived more daunting things than this. You can do it again."

"It is amazing how time erases even the most vivid things."

"I think you already know the truth."

"I am not a memory. I am an illusion."

An illusion.

Ezra's eyes snapped open. A wave of goosebumps washed over his clammy skin. Once the roaring in his ears had faded to a more manageable level, he bolted from the exhibit hall, sprinted down the staff corridor, and burst through the doors of the museum storage room.

"The Basilica Cisterns!" he yelled.

The Irish Chapter collectively halted their packing and stared at him in alarm.

"Er—what?" Oliver croaked in uncertainty.

Without answering, Ezra approached his father and grasped his shoulders. "The Basilica Cisterns. The 1894 Constantinople earthquake," he explained, breathless and eager. "You were there; you must have seen it."

"What are you talking about, son?" Ibrahim responded.

"I was five years old," Ezra replied. "You found me in the cisterns near the Hagia Sophia after the quake. Don't you remember?"

Reminiscence swam in his father's eyes. "I do, *canım*. But what does that have to do with—"

"The Tablet of Destinies is there."

Everyone froze in stunned silence.

"Are—are you certain?" Jonas managed.

"Call it an educated hunch," Ezra answered the Magi Master. "*Baba*, tell me everything you remember from that day."

"Well, I—" Ibrahim began. He exhaled and put a hand to his forehead. "I remember the heaviness of guilt for allowing you to traipse around by yourself."

"Besides that."

"It had to have been an hour after the earthquake when Taylan, a few men from the mosque, and I found you," said Ibrahim. "I remember wondering how you found your way into the cisterns and our incredible luck locating you when we did."

"How *did* you find me?" Ezra wondered.

"I want to say it was a miracle from *Allah*, but—"

"What does your subconscious say?"

Jonas flashed an approving grin at Ezra.

Ibrahim frowned and closed his eyes, searching his memories. "I remember a humming noise. The closer we got, the louder it became. The instinct to follow it was overwhelming. It must have drawn me to you."

"I heard it, too," Ezra confirmed. "What else?"

"To this day, I've wondered where the light came from," his father replied. "There was no electricity in the cisterns at that time, and I don't recall seeing any lanterns or torches."

Ezra nodded. "And the eyes?"

"Oh, Lord," Miss McLarney gasped. "The eyes of Medusa."

Ibrahim met her gaze.

"I saw that in your memories," she explained. "But I thought it was a trick of the light, or—"

"An illusion," Ezra finished for her. "I believe the artifact is in that pillar."

"But what if it ain't?" Zaire broke in. "What if all those things have a scientific explanation?"

"All I know is that something of immense power resides in that cistern," Ezra responded. "Something that can generate light and sound. Something that can disrupt the atmosphere, much like what the Celestial Lifeforce can do. Something that could possibly distort memories. And if it is not the Tablet of Destinies, perhaps it's something even stronger."

Possibility stirred beneath the expressions in his company. Sideways glances communicated conflicting emotions of fear and hope. Of foreboding and opportunity.

"And you're confident in this, Ezra?" asked Jonas, placing his hands in his trouser pockets.

In his mind's eye, Ezra pictured a smile edging over the weary face of the Shahmaran. He had never been so sure of something in his entire life.

"Someone wise once told me to never discredit my intuition," Ezra remarked, recalling his first meeting with the Magi Master. "And in this moment, my defences have never felt so strong."

Jonas returned his eager assurance with a twinkle in his eyes. "Very well. Tomorrow morning, we shall be en route to Constantinople."

AN ALTERED COURSE

Jonas thought it ironic that to secure an artifact of historical wonder, they had to *leave* the very place that housed thousands of them.

After issuing warm-hearted thanks to Edison for his hospitality, Jonas and the Irish Chapter—along with the Newports—left London behind. The dreary skies had given way to rare April sunshine, which lightened the mood of his traveling companions. Despite this, his nerves still prickled when he reviewed the scenario in his mind.

The plan was straightforward enough: Now that they had a strong inkling of the Tablet's location, they would retrieve it from the Basilica Cisterns and deliver it to the Magi Administration, where it could be placed in the Council's hands for safekeeping. It sounded so simple. So effortless. But the gravity of his heart spoke where words could not.

Of course, the Administration's disapproval on the bold approach weighed on his mind, but they were racing against time and tragedy. As long as Edison stayed quiet about their travel plans, as long as Diederik and Symon did not force the information out of him, their quest would succeed. The Magi would prevail. At this point, they *had* to.

With every transfer, the bustle of passengers and frequent exchange of boarding passes distracted Jonas from even the simplest things. He could not remember the last time he ate. Several times, he almost left his luggage on the train. If it had not been for Mum and Kierra keeping tabs on everyone and their belongings, he would have been lost to the whims of his mind.

While waiting to board in Brussels, Jonas looked on as Aja, Oliver, Zaire, and Ezra played a round of cards over the platform tile. Kierra had buried her attention in her book again, and Ibrahim and Annabelle chatted about his former life in Constantinople. After a quick headcount, Jonas' heart fluttered when he realised they were missing one.

Diego.

"Have any of you seen Diego?" Jonas asked.

"Darling, he just told you he was going to the station's telegraph office," Mum answered. "Are you feeling all right?"

"Yes, fine," said Jonas hastily. "Why the devil does he need to do that?"

"Oh, *you know*," Aja said with a wink. "Young love." The way she drew out the vowels grated on his nerves.

"Good Lord," Jonas grumbled. "How many telegrams has he sent to Stella since we left London?"

"Why is it any of your business?" Kierra asked from behind the pages of her novel.

Jonas scoffed and found interest in examining his pocket watch.

For some reason, Zaire thought it appropriate to chuckle at his perturbation. "Well, I think he's going on three telegrams now?"

"One in London, one in Dunkirk, now here," Oliver listed off, jabbing his cards in the air for dramatic effect. "Oh wait! And Dover, too. That makes four."

When Diego reappeared, Jonas avoided eye contact at all costs. He bit his tongue, holding back the words he so desperately wished to release. Words of disdain for Diego's flippant stance on their situation. Words of caution, to not be traipsing around the station alone with a head injury. Words tinged in bitterness. Begrudging, pharisaic words.

Curse love. And curse the dreadful repercussions of it.

Thankfully, the train whistle cut through the absolute monstrosity of his inner dialogue. The conductor's call over the station loudspeaker had never sounded so inviting.

After several exhausting days of non-stop clacking of the train rattling his ear drums, Jonas lost himself in a daze of ever-changing scenery. From France to Belgium and Germany to Austria, their surroundings transformed before his eyes. Flowers and wild pasture grasses waved in the wind, mountains rose to glorious heights from sky blue lakes, and quaint European towns dotted the countryside in flecks of luminance and painted colour. But his surroundings could only deter his thoughts for so long.

As they got closer to Constantinople, disguising the inconceivable dread in his expressions became more difficult than ever. He knew the others felt it, too, but at least they were more tactful in hiding it. Kierra, especially. He envied how she took everything life threw at her with such grace and composure. Curious creatures, Cancerians.

Even frivolous distractions morphed into fodder for his anxiety. Every newspaper article transfigured into visions of what could become of the world if Diederik got his hands on the artifact. Every morsel of food seemed slimy and tasteless, slithering down his oesophagus like sludge. And whenever he'd skim a razor over his face for a much-needed trim, he could not go long without acknowledging the man in the dust-streaked mirror. He shared the same trembling fingers as the boy beaten by his father. The same eyes as the grief-stricken adolescent who fled Amsterdam. The same frown as the young man who hid in the shadows, hoping he'd never have to face his father ever again.

While fire was his specialty, the flame he fooled with would not be tamed so easily. If Diederik caught on to them, then—

Then *what?*

Exhaling, Jonas placed the razor on the sink's edge and patted his face with a towel. He kept his sight trained on his reflection, clenching his jaw in defiance.

If Diederik catches on to what we know about the Tablet of Destinies, I will stand up to the despicable human that he is, Jonas thought to himself, confident and sure. *Yes, he hurt me. Yes, he killed Felix. But I will go to hell and back before he kills our chances.*

This was going to work.

50

My Story Without You

Later that evening, after transferring to their final train bound for Constantinople, the weary crew retired to their appointed rooms. Diego found himself a soldier in a fruitless battle for comfort with his bunk mattress. Every tick of his pocket watch sharpened his already electrified senses. Even the slightest movements sent bolts of pain tearing through his body. Running low on patience and medical ammunition, he decided to abandon sleep altogether.

Pocketing a pamphlet he had nicked from the British Museum, Diego tiptoed down the narrow corridor toward the outlook carriage. Ever since his mental escapade through Africa, Annabelle warned him not to push his luck again with his abilities. If he could not adventure through his dreams or through Time, then perhaps he could allow his mind to wander through the promise of learning instead.

Just as Diego manoeuvred through the sliding doorway of the carriage, he collided with Jonas.

"AHH!" Diego's exclamation prompted stern looks from a band of grumpy gentlemen playing cards. He tried again, this time in a strained whisper. "*Santa Madre de Dios*, Jonas! That hurt!"

"Good God, I am *so* sorry," Jonas apologised, ushering Diego to an empty seat. "Are you all right?"

Diego gritted his teeth and braced himself against the cushion. "I will be. Give me five minutes." He closed his eyes and allowed the scent of Jonas' after shave to tantalise his nostrils.

And his fancy.

Jonas frowned. "Did you take your medicine this evening?"

"Who are you, the Medicine Gendarmerie?" Diego groaned, not even bothering to open his eyes. "You try drinking that stuff. It is awful." When the rumble of the locomotive served as the only response, Diego cracked open an eyelid to witness a smile had exploded across Jonas' face.

"It's refreshing to see your sarcastic spirit has returned."

Diego flashed a sly grin. "You missed it, didn't you?"

"One could say that."

"One could also ask what *you* are doing up, aimlessly roaming a passenger train?"

"I could not sleep." Jonas' tired eyes, laced with red, wandered the carriage's elegant interior, across the sconces, velvet curtains, and intricately carved woodwork. "I cannot seem to silence my brain."

"Neither can I," answered Diego. He reached for the pamphlet in his pocket and unfolded it, diving into the glorious illustrations of the Rosetta Stone exhibit. Even in its fragmented state, the magnificent relic commandeered dominance over the pages. Housed in dark granodiorite, dusty white script flowed in distinct sections. Three written languages. One remarkable piece of history.

Diego smiled to himself. *They cleaned it up nicely*, he thought as he recalled his 1799 Time Expedition through Egypt. The last time he saw the Rosetta Stone, it was being pulled out of the earth by French soldiers. Witnessing that incredible moment provided valuable historical context that simple museum brochures could never achieve.

"Brilliant, isn't it?"

Diego glanced at Jonas who had joined him in admiring the pamphlet's contents. "*Absolutamente*. It is fascinating to think we could not understand Egyptian hieroglyphics until this stone unlocked the secret."

Jonas nodded and crossed one leg over the other. "And I imagine the Tablet of Destinies will have much the same effect. It shall be a key unlocking a world beyond our current understanding."

"Mmm."

"Diego, may I ask you something?"

"*Sí.*"

Jonas avoided eye contact. "Do you...do you ever miss Mexico?"

Diego leaned his head back against the seat cushion and turned to study Jonas' face, wondering what had fuelled his curiosity. "From time to time. I miss my *mamá* and my *abuelita*. I miss the heat of summertime and the warmth of the people. I miss the way the afternoon sun streams through the stained-glass windows of the Guadalajara Cathedral." Diego hesitated, his gaze unfocused as he pictured his former home. "What I left behind is only one chapter in the story of my life. I can always revisit it. But right now, I am in the process of writing a new one."

"Beautifully said," noted Jonas. "So, you do not regret coming to the United Kingdom?"

"Why are you asking me this?"

"Because," Jonas exhaled, massaging his hands together as if that could help him better craft his thoughts. "Ah. It is nothing. Just a—a passing thought."

"I doubt that."

Jonas tried to smile but it fell flat. "You know me too well."

"Uh huh," Diego replied and placed his hand on Jonas' forearm. "I came with you to Ireland because I could not bear the thought of my story without you in it."

Jonas swallowed, tears brimming in his eyes.

"Now, do not get all emotional on me, *Señor* van der Campe," Diego joked, lightly shaking Jonas' arm. "Then I will start crying and those old codgers playing cards will start crying, and that would be a rather awkward situation, so I would probably cry even more."

Jonas laughed. "Diego, sometimes you are utterly ludicrous, and I am quite fond of it."

"*Bueno*," Diego said. He playfully shoved Jonas with his shoulder. "Because despite the happenings at the Royal Observatory, you are not getting rid of me that easily."

The longing to tell him was so overwhelming, Jonas doubted he could put his introspection into anything comprehendible.

With Diego's previous sentiment absorbing deeper into his soul, he cleared his throat and tried his hardest.

"Diego, can I be candid with you?"

The young man's features immediately fell into confusion. "Uh—isn't that what we are doing?"

"Well, yes," Jonas responded. His attention faltered when the men playing cards wrapped up their game, collected their winnings, and issued farewells for the evening. A sense of relief at their departure slightly calmed his nerves, but he trudged onward. "This—this is different."

"Here you are acting strange again," Diego responded with a smirk.

"Dammit, Diego, just listen to me!" The insistence in his tone surprised even himself. "I have spent countless hours thinking of all the ways I'd be able to tactfully communicate this but every time, it just seems hopeless. Especially now that you are courting Stella."

Understanding sparked in Diego's eyes—or was it panic?

"After my hearing in September, after my sentence was given, the Council took me aside and insisted that we parted ways," Jonas confided, not even daring to meet Diego's eyes. "Not doing so jeopardised my status in the Third Order, not to mention every Quotidian law I had already defied. I couldn't—I couldn't risk going to prison. I couldn't risk losing my role as part of the Magi. It would ruin me."

Diego folded his arms, a scowl crossing his expressions. "You did not have to end it. I would have kept our secret."

"I did what I had to do. There is no argument about it," Jonas stated. "But you must know—" He swallowed the constriction in his throat. "I had no idea that losing you in the process would ruin me even more. And that night at the Royal Observatory—I thought I was going to lose you for good. Surrender you to the stars, just like I had to do with Felix. One thought kept circling my mind the entire time, one dreadful little truth that I hadn't the courage to face until now: After all this time, I never stopped caring about you. Not for a second."

Diego sucked in a sharp breath, stung by the admission.

Jonas wiped his sweating palms on his trousers before continuing. "Every night you left to be with Stella, every love note you wrote her, every telegram you continue to send, all of that gnaws at me until there's nothing left but a gaping void."

Diego remained silent.

"I am sorry," Jonas sighed, the sting of tears making its presence known. "I shouldn't have—" He glanced up when Diego's hand enclosed around his.

"Perhaps this would not be so difficult in another world, another life," Diego whispered. "But this is the world we live in. This is the life we endure."

Nodding through the pain, Jonas sniffed when Diego squeezed his hand.

"I appreciate your honesty," Diego said. "It might make me want to murder you in your sleep sometimes, but I appreciate it nonetheless."

Jonas laughed, but it sounded more like a sob. "I cannot imagine my story without you, either, Diego Montreal. I refuse to see it any other way."

A brokenness washed over Diego. It corrupted the sparkle in his eyes, dimming his aura until there was hardly any light at all. Bridging the space between them, Jonas placed his palm against the young man's face and ran his thumb across the ridge of his cheekbone. The Adam's apple bobbed in Diego's throat. He closed his eyes, fighting emotion beginning its ascent to the surface.

Jonas brushed his fingers across Diego's forehead, pushing back his hair so he could properly see him. He shuddered, knowing he could so easily drown in those eyes. Every arc of gold in the earthy browns of his irises mesmerised him. In that moment, Jonas wanted nothing more than to take away whatever hurt lurked beneath, to protect him, to hold him close until morning light. By the time Jonas realised mere centimetres separated them, every quickened breath converged between their mouths like wind in a sandstorm. His heart erupted into a dangerous rhythm. His pulse pounded in his ears, edging ever closer—

"No. I can't," Diego remarked, tearing away from Jonas as if his proximity scorched him. "I can't. I—I am sorry."

The young man stood abruptly and without another word or even looking back, he fled the carriage.

CONSTANTINOPLE

Ezra awoke to vigorous shaking of his shoulder.

Squinting through the haze of sleep, Ezra rolled over in the train bunk and surveyed his father's brilliant smile.

"What, *Baba?*"

"Come, *canım*. There is something you must see."

After tugging on a pair of trousers and a collared shirt, Ezra followed Ibrahim through the overnight rooms to the outlook carriage.

Golden sunlight streamed through the wide windows. Several passengers sheltered from the glare behind newspapers or exquisite fans. Others sipped their morning coffee, enjoying the ever-changing scenery.

Ezra stopped in his tracks when he caught sight of a familiar city glimmering on the horizon.

Constantinople.

Nostalgia caught in his throat as he drew toward the window like a moth to flame. He sank into an empty seat cushion, his eyes hungrily scanning the city skyline.

Home.

"Looks just as beautiful as the day we left."

Ezra sighed, running his fingertips over the glass. "I miss it, *Baba.*"

Ibrahim sat across from him. He smiled and gazed out into the dazzling daylight. "As do I."

"Will we ever go back? To live?"

Ibrahim folded his hands together in contemplation. "Perhaps when everything settles down again, we will."

Ezra stared longingly at the magnificent mosques, the minarets of Hagia Sophia, and the cluster of buildings reaching toward the heavens. For so long, the Constantinople skyline had consisted of blurry images painted within his memory. Even now, its presence felt almost dreamlike. Being in such proximity to the city filled in every detail he had forgotten. But the most curious detail of them all was that the port city radiated a golden magic that Ezra had never noticed before, almost as if it were welcoming the group of Magi to its shores.

"You never told me what your Gift is," Ibrahim spoke in genuine interest. "Jonas told me about your impressive shield during an attack by the Legerdemain Brotherhood, but I did not hear any other specifics."

Ezra's attention departed from the glorious view. "At the time, I didn't know, either. But after I was taken from Belfast, I experienced something…" He paused, not knowing how to adequately describe the miraculous event. "Er, well, I—I moved parts of a building to reconfigure it into a new layout."

Ibrahim could not supress his wide smile. "Ah, an Architect! I should have known. Very impressive."

Ezra tried to smile but it fell short of his father's excitement. "What were yours and *Anne's* powers? Before the Magi Administration took them away, that is."

The man's expressions transformed from proud to sentimental. "Mm. Well, I could control weather phenomena. I could conjure sunshine, rain, wind…anything. But your *anne* could communicate with animals."

"What?" Ezra sputtered. "Really?"

"Yes, really," Ibrahim chuckled at the enthusiasm in his response. "Leyla worked for the Magi Administration for many years in the Department of Transmissions. During her tenure, the Magi Courier Service consisted almost entirely of birds, instructed by Leyla to carry messages to Chapters across the world. While she would work with ravens and pigeons, she preferred her favourite avian creature: owls."

Ezra's unblinking stare made his father laugh.

"That is peculiar."

"No more peculiar than rearranging the interior of a building," Ibrahim answered.

"Do you miss them?"

"Miss what, son?"

"Your powers."

Ibrahim opened his mouth to respond but stitched his lips back together and redirected his focus beyond the window. A contemplation brewed behind his expressions, lost in the blur of scenery whirring past. "Every day. But Leyla and I knew the risks. I knowingly went against the rules, and the Administration had every right to enforce them."

"But you did that for the good of the world," Ezra continued. "Shouldn't that selfless nature be rewarded?"

"By *Allah*, perhaps. But the Magi are quite curious in that regard," said Ibrahim. "While my efforts were premeditated, their reasons for those rules outweighed my actions. I do not regret what I did, nor do I harbour any ill will toward the Administration. They are not bad people for taking away my Gifts."

Ezra considered his words, not knowing how close to hold them.

"In fact, it is my fervent hope that you will go through formal training to become part of the Third Order," Ibrahim said. "Jonas would be an excellent teacher for you."

Their conversation disintegrated into silence. Ezra fidgeted with the hem of his sleeve, not daring to look his father in the eyes. After everything they had been through on the account of the Magi or their sorcerous counterparts, why would he willingly open his life to that world? One step across the threshold had erased his mother's life as well as all concepts of his former reality. Of course, he wanted to help the Magi in their quest to stop the Legerdemain Brotherhood. But that was where he drew the line. After the doors were closed, after the Magi were safe, Ezra hoped to take one step back. Away from the pain. The grief.

Far from the Great Unknown.

Now reunited with his father, a normal existence sparked just beyond his fingertips.

"I—I don't know if I want to, *Baba*."

"And why is that?"

Ezra ran his thumb over the edge of the seat cushion. "Why would I do something to further put myself in danger?"

"My son, the moment you were born, you entered a life destined for danger," Ibrahim replied, a frank seriousness deepening the lines around his mouth. "Even if you decide not to train, you are still putting yourself at risk. A Magus without affiliation is a Magus in desperate limbo with the Universe."

Ezra allowed his eyes to wander beyond the window. "I know."

"Whatever you decide, I will put my full support behind you," said his father. "But what a blessing it would be to see you shine amongst the shadows of this life."

Another glimmer of hope saturated the space around them with beautiful optimism. But Ezra never quite gathered his thoughts for the ear-splitting call of the train screamed over the clattering of the tracks.

"Ah, we must be close," Ibrahim noted. "You had better gather your things; this is our station."

Sighing, Ezra stole another glance at the splendour of his former home before disappearing toward the sleeping rooms.

They crafted their steps and moved amongst the night.

The sun sank below the western horizon, yet Constantinople still buzzed in contagious wonder. Now that they had deposited their luggage at the Istanbul Hotel, their steps were lighter, more urgent. Ibrahim led the way, explaining their timing meant everything upon their approach. Halfway between *Akşam* and *Yatsı*—mostly to avoid the crowds attending for worship—the crew would wait in the Hagia Sophia while Ezra would guide Ibrahim and Jonas into the depths of the Basilica Cisterns. Diego was assigned to keep watch at the mouth of the passage, ensuring no unfriendly eyes strayed in their direction.

The nine of them navigated on foot toward the Hagia Sophia, but to Ezra, every footfall was a nostalgic journey through his childhood. Every detail, preserved within time, beckoned a past that did not seem so far away. Fragrant food in the marketplaces tantalized his nostrils. City dwellers waved to each other across alleys, chirping enthusiastic greetings. Fresh laundry draped over clothes lines served as veins that branched from one building to another, billowing in the evening breeze.

Despite the beauty around him, traipsing back into the world he had buried within his memories issued a terror he could not put into words. Yet, a lingering resonance of the Shahmaran strengthened him, even as the domes of the mosque came into sight:

"Sweet boy, you have survived more daunting things than this. You can do it again."

Feet aching and nerves prickling with anticipation, Ezra and the others found themselves in the expansive courtyard of the Hagia Sophia. Orange lamplight inset within the central arch was partially obscured by the flanking supports. The minarets flickered like candles in the wind. While darkness threatened to consume the city, energetic life radiated from the structure, singing of something ancient. Something secret. Something lurking beneath the shadows of its grandeur. A wistful sigh mingled with the breeze as Ezra surveyed the grand mosque.

He had missed it so much it *hurt*.

"All right, everyone, you know the plan," Jonas stated, rattling Ezra from his internal musings. "This is where we part. Rendezvous within the Hagia Sophia at twenty-one hundred. Not a second longer, otherwise Zaire and Kierra will come after us. Does everyone understand?"

Murmurs of agreement and sharp nods made their way around his company.

"God be with y'all," Zaire said, giving Jonas' shoulder a reassuring pat.

"Good luck," Aja whispered to Ezra. She opened her mouth again, but nothing came out. Her eyes flitted away. Her cheeks flushed a rosy pink.

But as both groups made for their assigned posts, Ezra had a harrowing feeling they would need more than luck to make it through the night.

ᴇNTER THE ᴄAVE OF THE ᴤHAHMARAN

Guided by the radiant orb of fire in Jonas' palms, Ezra, Ibrahim, and Diego moved amongst the foliage toward the mouth of the Basilica Cisterns. When they had reached the wooden shed, Ezra found himself clinging to his father's arm.

"Son, it is going to be all right," said Ibrahim, lifting Ezra's chin toward him. "Besides your mother—may she rest in *Allah's* arms—you are the bravest person I know."

His words still did not squelch the fear. It was as if at any moment, Ezra would be shaken right off his feet, swallowed by the earth in one gulp.

"Your father is right," Jonas replied, putting his hand on Ezra's shoulder. "And we will be with you the entire time."

"Be careful down there," Diego instructed them. He stationed himself at the entrance, retrieving his crystal wand out of his back pocket for a source of light. "I will be here if you need anything."

After a firm nod in Diego's direction, Jonas led Ezra and Ibrahim beneath the surface of the earth. The boundaries of light from his hands rippled outward, illuminating a sloping, rocky trail snaking deeper into the cisterns. Beyond this, the scene plummeted into the unknown.

And so did Ezra's heart.

The closer they inched toward the heart of the Basilica Cisterns, the more a mouldy dampness permeated the air. Something familiar buzzed within Ezra's brain, something timeworn and foreboding. With every step, a pulsating energy sparked the atmosphere. The throbbing power circulated amongst their surroundings, following the curves of the ornate ceiling arches.

Jonas had been right about one thing: A world of wonder had *indeed* been around the bend. It had been within the very confines of Ezra's mind, leading him and his father back to this place all along.

Just as the Babylonian text had written.

Finally, the claustrophobic tunnels opened to the cisterns, revealing the grandeur of the historic site. Just like in his visions, the Corinthian pillars sprang from the depths. Amethyst waters swirled around their bases. Everything was bathed in an ethereal glow, prompting Jonas to douse the fiery orb in his palms. Beads of water dripped from unseen fissures. The coolness of the cave sent chills over Ezra's skin, and he hugged his coat closer to himself.

Ibrahim navigated around the columns until he came to the one resting upon the sideways head of Medusa. He knelt before her, tracing his fingers along the curls of her snake-like hair.

"This is it," he whispered.

Ezra sank beside his father and pressed his palm against the statue's cheek. A mixture of energies tickled his senses. So many memories were stored within the stone. So many dreams and aspirations. And perhaps, just as many tears and heartaches.

"Just like in my dreams," Ezra breathed.

Jonas smiled at him. "Wondrous things, dreams."

Ezra could have sworn in that moment the statue winked at him in her playful manner. The spirit of the Shahmaran sang in the depth of her omniscient eyes.

"So, how do we get to the Tablet?" Jonas broke the silence.

After examining every centimetre of the pillar's base, Ibrahim rose and stroked his beard. "I am not entirely sure, but I do have an inkling. Do you feel the magic in the air?"

Jonas nodded. "The area must be protected by a crystal grid."

"We must remove that before proceeding," Ibrahim insisted. "If we do not, who knows what harm will befall us?"

"I agree. We'll need to survey the area to find the stones," suggested Jonas. "You cover the West and South walls, and I'll get the North and East."

While Jonas ventured to the opposite side of the cisterns, Ezra followed his father over the boulders along the outer edges. His shoes slipped on the uneven surfaces, but he managed to maintain his balance.

"What are we looking for?" Ezra questioned once he caught up with Ibrahim.

"Gemstones," his father answered. "Crystal grids are immensely strong enchantments. They must be dismantled in the proper manner. One false move and—well, let's just say that even some Magi Adepts training to become Masters had their arms blown off in my day."

Ezra gulped.

"Unfortunately, *canım*, I cannot disable the grid. You are the one with the connection to the Universe."

"What?! You want me to get my arms blown off?"

Ibrahim attempted a smile, but the motion made him look weary and weak. "You will be fine. Jonas will guide you."

Ezra watched as Ibrahim crouched into the shallows and pointed out a submerged stone. To him, it simply resembled a rock amongst the natural topography of the cavern. But as Ibrahim guided Ezra's hand through the glacial water and his fingertips brushed over its resting place, a violet glow burst into life. One by one, other points of luminance were triggered into existence, from the perimeters converging inward. Like the spokes of a gigantic carriage wheel, the grid came together at a single hub at the centre of the expanse. The unspoken authority commanded by the grid only increased the buzzing in his eardrums as the seconds ticked on.

"We need to dismantle it in a counter-clockwise manner from the outside in," Jonas's voice echoed against the pillars. "Ezra, are you with me?"

"I'm with you," Ezra called out. Every syllable accentuated the palpitations of his pulse.

"Good. Now, take out your wand and hold tight. I am going to start on my end and make my way toward you."

Gripping his quartz wand in nervous anticipation, Ezra nodded despite Jonas not being able to see him. But Ezra could see *him* or rather, the outline of his shadow as he touched the point of his crystal wand to the lustrous stones. Every time he did so, the gemstones' illumination faded to extinction, and little by little, so did the resonance in the atmosphere. With scrupulous precision, Jonas collected the gemstones in his arms on his journey until finally, he reunited with Ezra and Ibrahim.

"Ezra, I need you to take your wand and touch the point to the gemstone," Jonas instructed. "Visualise yourself calling the stone's strength into your crystal. Allow it to flow through your being and offer it back to the Universe."

"R-right," said Ezra, attempting to supress the queasy feeling in his gut. Carefully, he did as Jonas had advised. One stone after another, Ezra disabled the remaining crystals in the outer perimeter. And each time, his entire body tingled with otherworldly power until he released it to the Celestial Lifeforce, its rightful owner.

"You're doing great," Jonas encouraged. He had made his way back to where he first began, waiting to start with the next rotation of stones. "Once you finish here, I shall begin the second layer."

On they went for another painstaking quarter of an hour. With every passing minute, Ezra's heart fluttered in a mixture of nerves and excitement. And with every deactivated stone, clarity and peace flooded through his veins. Ibrahim collected the dimmed crystals and laid them at the base of the Medusa head column like a ritual sacrifice before a god.

"And now, the Activator Stone," Jonas said once they had dismantled the rest. "The very last step. And often, the deadliest."

All Ezra could do was stare at Jonas in wide-eyed horror.

"You may want to stand back, Ezra," the Magi Master urged.

"Oh, right." He edged away and grit his teeth together, not knowing what to anticipate. Nevertheless, he braced himself against a pillar and watched in wonder while Jonas summoned the energy from the stone. Unlike the others, this feat drained the life from him. He could see it in every crease between Jonas' brows, every bead of sweat along his forehead. Ezra's breath caught in his chest when Jonas swayed on his feet before recovering his balance.

Nearly five minutes had passed before the stone gave up the ghost. All at once, the cistern fell into a silence that seemed even louder than its former ambiance. Jonas collapsed, panting from the exertion.

"Are you all right?" Ibrahim asked, helping him back to his feet.

"Do not worry about me," Jonas assured him and shook out the water from his shirt sleeves. "What comes next?"

"Ever since Ezra mentioned the eyes of Medusa, I've been thinking about the mechanisms that must exist to extract the artifact from the column," Ibrahim explained as they gathered before the sideways likeness of the mythic Greek creature. "I have not been able to locate such contraptions. But without a button or latch or other means of activation, I am at a loss for an answer."

While Jonas and Ibrahim investigated the pillar, Ezra allowed his attention to wander. His eyes skirted the ceiling and darted amongst the pillars. He shifted from foot to foot in the water, realising then the numbness in his toes. In the silence, he could almost hear a woman whispering into the night:

"Would you believe me if I said it has been here all along? Just waiting for you to open your eyes?"

Ezra frowned, remembering his answer. *"I don't know what to believe anymore."*

"Confusion is just a part of the process. In time, you will find the things that baffled you were the things that shaped you into the person you became."

Nothing had baffled him more than this world. This world of the Magi and the Legerdemain Brotherhood. This world where prophecies had changed the lives of his family forever. If it had not been for those words from the past, he wouldn't even be standing in confusion in a world he thought he'd left behind.

If only he'd done what the Shahmaran had commanded he do from the very start. If only he had opened his eyes sooner to the—

Opened his eyes.

Locked within time, where Destinies are viewed, the Lion's touch opens eyes, immense power renewed.

"What do you want, Ezra Newport? What do you really, truly want?"

"I want a clear path."

The Shahmaran lifted her chin and tilted her head slightly to the side. "Then prepare to move."

Her image burned into his retinas. Her snakelike image, cocking her head to the side...

"...just waiting to open your eyes?"

"Where Destinies are viewed," Ezra said under his breath and then blurted out, "What if you have to look into her eyes?"

Ibrahim regarded him as if he had just spoken a foreign language. "Do what, *canım*?"

"Of course! Just like the myths," Jonas replied. "Those who looked into the eyes of Medusa turned to stone."

"And since *she* is the one who is stone, perhaps now it is the other way around," Ezra concluded. "We need to look at Medusa to bring her back to life." Coming alongside his father, he got to his knees and tilted his head sideways, lining up his eyes with the blank stare of the Snake Goddess. "Like this."

Ibrahim sank into the water beside him and replicated his stance. When nothing happened, his father's disappointment dampened his hopeful expressions. Ezra grasped his hand.

"The Lion's touch opens eyes," he quoted. "Together?"

"Together," Ibrahim agreed.

The two of them extended their arms until their fingerprints pressed into the stone. An explosion of white light made Ezra retract his hand to shield his eyes from the brilliance. But once their surroundings disintegrated into darkness, one side of the moulding atop the statue's cheek had retracted into itself, revealing an open compartment.

Ibrahim sprang to his feet and extracted a linen-wrapped rectangle from the base. "In the name of *Allah*, most gracious, most merciful," said Ibrahim, breathless.

"The Tablet of Destinies," Ezra murmured in disbelief. He met Jonas' gaze and burst into an astonished grin. "We actually found it!"

Jonas beamed his approval beneath the brim of his fedora. "I am proud of you, Ezra Newport. As will the Magi Council once we get it in their hands."

"On that note, let us make haste," Ibrahim said, tucking the artifact under his arm. "Administration headquarters are still an hour's journey north."

Guided by the fire in Jonas' palms, the three of them stumbled up the pathway toward the entrance of the cisterns. This time, every step felt lighter than before. In fact, if Ezra hadn't tripped over his own feet in his excitement, he would have sworn he was walking on air. The humid evening greeted them upon their exit, as well as an expectant Diego.

"Well? Did you find it?"

"I hope so," Ibrahim replied, holding out the relic before the young man. "I suppose you're the only one here who has actually seen it, so you will need to verify its authenticity."

With a strange expression tugging at the skin beneath his eyes, Diego received the artifact. He folded back the cloth just enough for the purple radiance to pierce the evening gloom and nodded in affirmation. "It is the Tablet of Destinies."

"Good, because if it wasn't, I'd have to kill a man for false information."

Ezra gasped as a figure emerged from the blackness. Arrogant and resolute, the man approached, a faint glimmer reflecting from the silver embellishments of his cane. His shoes scuffed to a stop over the loose gravel. Ezra detected a wicked grin flickering into life in the shadows of his top hat.

The silhouette of a monster.

BETRAYED

Jonas whirled around and instinctively held out his arms to shield Diego, Ibrahim, and Ezra.

"Don't you dare take another step!" he hissed through clenched teeth. "I swear to you I will not hesitate to stand my ground!"

The consul of the Legerdemain Brotherhood smirked, resting both of his gloved hands atop his cane. While he looked every bit the same as Jonas last remembered, flecks of silver permeated his dark hair and beard. Wrinkles tugged at the skin underneath his eyes, weighed down by years of malevolence, no doubt.

Edison must have given in, Jonas thought, his heart sinking in disappointment.

"Twelve years of hiding must get dreadfully tedious, does it not?"

Jonas narrowed his eyes at the ingratiating voice of his father. "Not when I'm avoiding *you*."

"Hmm. 'Tis a pity you didn't finish your training," Diederik replied, adjusting the fingers of his leather gloves. "And to think we could have basked in this moment together, on the same side. Leading the Brotherhood as an unstoppable father and son duo."

"You know nothing about leadership," Jonas spat. "All you know how to do is manipulate people to do your dirty work. That's all you and the Brotherhood have *ever* done."

"Now, is that any way to speak to your father?" rebuked Diederik. "Especially when he has the lives of your entire Chapter at the tip of a Watcher's arrow?"

No.

Jonas cringed upon seeing a line of shadows emerge from the darkness, each one followed by the looming form of a Dark Watcher. Symon Bellinor led the way, the beam from his electric torch sweeping the ground at his shoes.

"Ah, why hello, Mr. van der Campe and friends," laughed Symon, holding out his arms in welcome. "Lovely to see you all again."

Just the sight of his Magi family in the same enchanted shackles he'd been fitted with at Greenwich Park made his stomach turn. "Let them go, or you shall face my wrath," Jonas threatened, fire burning in his palms. "You *do not* want to do this right now."

"Oh, actually, I really do," Diederik responded. Symon's electric torch cast ghastly shadows across his cruel smile. "Tell him how much that would make my night, Diego."

Gulping for air that would not come, Jonas turned to face him. "What is he talking about?"

Tears welled in Diego's eyes as he held the Tablet protectively against his chest.

"Your precious Ganymede decided his loyalties lie elsewhere," Symon said, revelling in the horrendous tension that violated the night air.

"No. No, that's—"

"Oh, Jonas, don't be so naïve," Diederik chastised. "For weeks, Diego Montreal has served as my undercover informant, feeding me all the information I needed about your activities as well as the Tablet's location. In fact, he was quite helpful on your journey here. All those telegrams kept us briefed on how to coordinate this little rendezvous."

Jonas gaped at his father and then at Diego. He struggled to process the onslaught of pain that threatened to tear apart the very filaments of his heart. The very pieces that had once loved without hesitation. Without fear. "That's not possible!"

Without a word, Diego brushed past him and willingly handed the artifact over to Diederik.

Every member of the Irish Chapter choked in astonishment.

"No!" Oliver sobbed.

"Diego Javier, how dare you!" Annabelle admonished.

"Kid, what're you doing?!" exclaimed Zaire.

Amidst the tears, a wave of panic avalanched through Jonas' torso. Shaking from the escalating discomfort in his chest, he barely noticed when Dark Watchers seized him and the Newports.

"Diego, how—how could you?" Jonas cried. "What *on earth* possessed you to do something like this?!"

"You would not understand," Diego muttered, avoiding eye contact while he held his arms close to his stomach.

"No, apparently I *don't* understand!" Jonas yelled, temper flaring. He struggled against the Watchers restraining him. "After everything we have been through together, after everything I have done for you—"

"That's just it, Jonas," Diego replied, his face flushed in aggravation. "I am fully capable of living my own life and making my own decisions! I—I am not your puppet for you to control!"

"No, it seems only Diederik has that power!"

"Now isn't that charming," his father chided, entertained by the argument. "Like father, like son."

Jonas glowered at him. "I am nothing like you."

"Oh, and you do not have to worry about your confidant here," Diederik continued, ruffling Diego's hair. "Symon will take excellent care of him."

Diego flinched when Symon patted him on the cheek.

Jonas dug his fingernails into his palms. If it had not been for the Watchers restraining him and the newly fitted binds around his wrists, he would have unleashed hell on Diederik and Symon in that very moment.

Diederik flashed a devilish grin and snapped his fingers. The Dark Watchers flanking Jonas shoved him to his knees, causing him to yelp in discomfort. Sauntering forward, he erected his cane and lifted Jonas' chin with it.

"Jonas, Jonas, Jonas. You certainly haven't lost your defiance. I can see why it was so difficult for Mr. Montreal to lure you into a false sense of security."

Jonas struggled against his binds, his airways constricting in anger. "How dare you," he growled.

"You know, this has really shaped up to be an excellent evening," Diederik bragged, walking in a cocky gait toward the captive members of the Irish Chapter. He toyed with Aja's braid before lifting her chin to meet his eyes. "What do you think, Beautiful? Do you think I have a chance at keeping my title now that I am in possession of the Tablet of Destinies?"

Aja whimpered, trying to pull away.

"Don't you *dare* touch her!" Jonas warned, attempting with all his might to break out of his shackles. "Don't you dare touch any of them!"

"Mmm," Diederik muttered, casting a glance in Diego's direction and next, a knowing look at Symon. He sneered at his son. "Too late."

"Uncle Diederik, please stop this!"

"Ah, and as for you, Miss Kierra," Diederik spun on his heels, marching toward her. "Much like your cousin, you are also a disappointment to the family. Do not think my wife has forgiven your mother for all the hurt she has caused by foolishly following the path of the Magi."

Fire blazing in her eyes, she spat at his feet.

"Impudent bitch," he growled at her, striking her across the face.

Jonas ground his teeth together.

"You know, I think it's time you all learned a valuable lesson this evening, starting with what happens when you refuse to cooperate."

At that, Diederik snapped his fingers. The Dark Watchers shoved Jonas against the ground and violently descended upon him.

"No!" Kierra gasped. "Stop!"

Jonas cringed as they assaulted him from every direction. With each blow, any shred of strength that remained bled into nonexistence. He positioned his bound hands in front of his face, attempting to shield himself from the Watchers' wrath. But the creatures continued to beat him with increasing force.

"Please, stop!" shouted Diego at the consuls. "This was not a part of the deal!"

"Maybe not," sighed Diederik. "But it *is* entertaining."

Battered and bruised, Jonas curled his knees into his chest as if that could somehow quell the torment. A salty concoction of blood and tears pooled beneath him. He fought for every breath. When he attempted to get to his knees, Diederik kicked him to the dirt. The jarring motion knocked the oxygen out of his aching lungs. Disregarding his audience and the pain that threatened to bleed him dry, Jonas lifted his swollen eyes to Diego.

For a moment, their gazes collided. But just as quickly, they fell apart.

Diego, how could you do this to me?

Trembling, Jonas tried to control his overwhelming emotions. Diederik crouched at his side, surveying him in callous distaste.

"You sealed your fate the moment you walked away from the Brotherhood," he seethed.

"Do not listen to him, Mista Jonas!" Zaire yelled. "He playing games with your mind!"

"Consider the stars," Diederik continued, abandoning Jonas in favour of a new target. A dastardly smile distorted his face as he approached Ibrahim and Ezra. "The Magi see warmth, a source of light. But the Legerdemain

Brotherhood see a powerhouse of kinetic energy, ripe for the taking."

Diederik tore the fabric from the artifact, unleashing its luminance into the night. "Mr. Newport," he said with a tip of his hat. "It's an honour to be in the presence of the Roaming Lion."

"Though I cannot say the same for you," Ibrahim spoke darkly.

The consul scoffed. "Despite your affinity for disrespect, I need you to unlock the magic you were always meant to set free. *Now.*"

Ibrahim stood firm. "I refuse."

"You refuse?" Diederik responded, finding hilarity in the bold statement. "You *refuse?* You sound dreadfully like Jonas when he was eighteen."

Jonas swallowed the metallic taste swimming in his mouth. He had seen that fire in his father's irises before; they blazed with the same intensity as the moment Felix's spirit left the earth. Whatever hideous idea lurked behind those eyes would not end well for any of them.

"Then I am honoured to be like him," Ibrahim answered, steeling himself.

"Very well," Diederik said, running his tongue along his teeth. He raised his hand to signal a Watcher to nock a black arrow into his crossbow. With the arrow in position, the mechanical human hybrid aimed the weapon directly at Ezra. "Then your son dies."

The cruel vibration of a bowstring shattered the remnants of Jonas' heart.

Unlock a New Magic

The foundations of Ezra's world had never felt so fragile.

In a blink of an eye, the avalanche of events had petrified him, so much so that his brain could hardly process what had just unfolded. Hope faded. Trust crumbled into ashes. The most powerful Magi Master he knew lay on the ground, beaten and frail. And Ibrahim—who had somehow wormed his way from his captor's grasp to shield him—struggled against the Dark Watcher's poisoned arrow, something Ezra knew all too well. With tears streaming down his cheeks, Ezra collapsed beside his father, whispering desperate prayers while grasping his hand.

"*Baba*," Ezra cried, examining the extent of the damage. A ring of darkness soaked through his white shirt and spread across the fibres.

"All right, Roaming Lion," chastised Diederik van der Campe. He squatted to their level and held out the Tablet. "You do not have much time left, so show me what happens once a lock is united with its key."

"Stay away from him!" Ezra shouted as a wild anger electrified his insides.

The consul challenged him with the same hellbent fury. "I *will* see the prophecy come to fruition. Tonight."

"If you take one step closer, you will regret it."

"Ezra," Ibrahim muttered weakly. Still bound at the wrists, he conjured just enough energy to pull at his son's hand. "Please back down. I do not want to see you hurt."

"Listen to your father, boy," Diederik demanded. In one fluid motion, he waved his cane over their shackles, causing them to crumble into dust at their feet. He thrust the artifact toward Ibrahim. "Activate it. *Now.*"

"Don't do it, Ibrahim!" Jonas managed, his voice shaking in weakness. "Please!"

The Watcher closest to Jonas kicked him in the gut, effectively silencing him.

Exhaling, Ibrahim lifted his hands, trembling with the effort. His fingers edged ever closer, grazing the stone. But before his father could reach it, his arm gave out and fell back to his wounded side. He grasped at his injury, gritting his teeth in pain.

"Help him," Diederik barked at Ezra. "Do it right now, unless you want to see your friends pierced with arrows alongside your father."

Crossbow strings taut, the Dark Watchers aimed their weapons toward the Irish Chapter. Frightened, Ezra's eyes connected with each of them. Aja chewed on her lip. Tears trickled down Oliver's face. Miss McLarney's blue eyes pleaded with him to make the right decision. And while Annabelle and Zaire seemed stoic, Ezra had a feeling they were both running scenarios through the cogs of their minds. Symon's electric torch illuminated the terror in all their expressions, fuelling an unspeakable panic within him. Quaking in dread, Ezra met his father's gaze.

"It's all right, *camm*," whispered Ibrahim. "You may proceed. Ask *Allah* to be with you."

Nodding, wishing he could wake from the nightmarish scene before him, Ezra lifted Ibrahim's hand toward the Tablet. Hand atop his, their fingers pressed against the stone. Warmth radiated from his father, saturating Ezra's skin, while a familiar prickling sensation sparked beneath his palm.

A grey mist seeped from the relic, swirling around their hands and enveloping the immediate vicinity in a supernatural radiance. He reeled against the physical pain in his stomach. A quick glance at his father revealed he also grappled with the anguish.

"*Allah*, most gracious, most merciful. Be with us," Ezra prayed aloud, but his voice was drowned out by the turbulent activity all around them. "We seek refuge in you!"

Diederik rose to his feet, his face illuminated by the violet glow. "Finally," he proclaimed, holding out his hands to touch the cyclonic mist that thickened at an alarming pace. Wind cascaded in vicious torrents throughout the area, rippling his dark cloak. "The power of the gods is within my grasp."

An intense shockwave of energy blasted across the scene, throwing everyone against the ground. The air fizzled with electricity and, all at once, collapsed into a vacuum of silence. As the dust settled, Ezra propped himself up on his elbows. What he saw next nearly stopped his heart.

Rising from the obscurity, a silhouette unfurled. Clothed in amethyst flame, the figure curiously examined its hands, turning them over as if it were simultaneously confused and delighted at their sight. The being stepped forward through the smoky veil and the definition of his features solidified.

Ibrahim gasped and grabbed hold of Ezra. "Son, leave this place. *Now*."

Horrified and lost for words, Ezra gaped at him. "What? What's going on?"

Even Consul Diederik stumbled backward, his mouth hanging open in surprise as if he had just seen a ghost.

And perhaps, he had. Perhaps they all had.

The mysterious figure surveyed his audience. "Tell me, what is the year?"

Symon was the first to recover his soundness, though he clutched Diego's arm for dear life. "1906, sir."

"1906," repeated the stranger, his fiery eyes continuing to scan his company. He examined the outline of the Hagia Sophia against the sky and circled a nearby Dark Watcher in wonder.

"Are—are you the Babylonian god Marduk?" enquired Diederik.

"Marduk? No," said the man, a strange glint sparkling in his green eyes. "I am Labynetus of Babylon."

A ghastly stillness strangled the Irish Chapter. Ezra clung to his father, who—despite the pain—had gained enough strength to pull Ezra closer. A dangerous scowl tugged on his eyebrows.

"I need you to listen," Ibrahim instructed into his ear. "On my mark, you need to get the Irish Chapter out of here. Flee as fast as your legs can take you."

"*Baba*, I'm not leaving you," Ezra insisted.

"You must," he hissed, as an incomprehensible magic pulsed through the night air. "Every moment we remain here puts us in a danger I am not sure we can overcome."

"But I—"

"Ezra, promise me," Ibrahim begged. Tears brimmed along his eyelashes. "Promise me you will take up the ways of the Magi."

His pleading eyes lingered on his father for several moments until finally, he nodded.

"Ezra," Ibrahim said, caressing his cheek. "I love you more than life itself."

"Don't leave me, too," Ezra wept. "Please, don't leave me!"

"Go!"

Forcing himself into obedience, Ezra ran and dodged arrow fire on his way to Jonas. He skidded across the dirt, reaching for Jonas' wrists to free him of his binds.

"How do I—" Ezra began.

"Your wand," Jonas croaked. "Ask the Universe to release me."

Despite his father's warnings, Ezra threw a glance over his shoulder to see Ibrahim hoist himself up, jerk the arrow from his flesh, and lunge at Labynetus, wielding the arrow like a knife.

"Ezra, now!"

Withdrawing the wand from his pocket, Ezra held the crystal point against the shackles.

Please, Universe. Please free Jonas. Please help my father. Please let everything be all right…

The iron clanked to the ground, and Ezra helped Jonas to his feet. All around them, pandemonium ensued. Dark Watchers rushed at Ibrahim to restrain him. Consul Diederik wrenched the arrow from his hand. Symon held Diego steady, undeterred by the young man's insistent attempts at escape.

"Enough!" commanded Labynetus. A savage repugnance tainted his expressions as he regarded Ibrahim at his feet. "Kill the Magus."

In unison, the Watchers reloaded their weapons.

Ezra met his father's eyes. Once so strong and passionate, the flame inside had dwindled to a lifeless spark. His will wavered in the wind. Nearly extinguished. Completely broken.

Ibrahim forced a smile. "I am proud of you, *canım*," he mouthed, just before a barrage of arrows met their mark.

Ezra stumbled backward, bitter sobs decimating his lungs.

"Ezra, come," Jonas beckoned, guiding him away from the scene. "Don't look back."

But as he and the Irish Chapter fled the grounds, leaving disaster in their wake, it took every fibre of Ezra's heart to keep beating.

ONE BRAVE STEP

Golden daylight filtered through the curtains, but all Jonas could see were shades of dismal grey.

He stared blankly at the hotel room walls, tears obscuring the floral wallpaper print until it blurred together in a multicoloured haze. Redness from earlier emotional release irritated his eyes. While the swelling on his face had retreated, he knew the bruises remained, remnants of the horrors from mere hours ago. He wiped his face with his palm, prickled by the stubble framing his jawline. Deprived of energy and answers, Jonas held his arms close to himself, rocking gently on the bed's edge, begging the Universe to keep him from falling apart. But every time Diego's face appeared in the dreary landscape of his mind, Jonas squeezed his eyelids shut and choked back the sobs he desperately wished to release.

Betrayed by someone he held so dear. Family heartache, revisited. And an artifact, an unspeakable red herring containing the power to bring back a force of evil from Magi history. Amidst it all, the untimely death of Ibrahim Newport. But wasn't Ibrahim meant to assist the Magi? Wasn't he meant to turn the tides in their favour? With him gone, how could any of that hold true? Nevertheless, Jonas knew he had to report back with the Administration and give his account of what had happened. How he could not stop the treachery of his father. How Ibrahim was forced to unlock the power of the artifact and murdered thereafter. It served him right that the Magi Gendarmerie would take him into custody for the hurt he had inadvertently unleashed on the world.

This was the final straw. It was over. Every promise. Every hour of training. Every good deed. Lost in a futile attempt to save the world.

Every chaotic blow knocked Jonas' spirit further into misery.

The only thing left to do was to pen his resignation letter. After all, he deserved nothing less, and the Council would hastily accept. He had not only let his own Chapter down, but he had let the Administration down. He'd let the entire Third Order of the Magi down. And Felix.

He had *failed* them all.

An insistent knock sounded at the door.

"Jonas?"

He groaned and buried his face in his pillow.

Kierra's voice sounded weak, hesitant. "Jonas, may I come in?"

"If you must."

Before he even realised the door had clicked back into place, he felt Kierra sink onto the bed beside him. She squeezed his shoulder. "Cousin, speak to me."

Drawing in a shaky breath, Jonas rolled onto his back. "Kierra."

Kierra bit her lip; heaviness dampened her expressions. She took his hands in hers, tears obscuring her blue eyes. "Oh, Jonas. I am so sorry."

He swallowed his pain and tightened his hold on her hands.

"I am so sorry you had to go through everything with your father and Symon and Diego. I know how much Diego meant to you," Kierra continued, her eyes darkening at the mention of his name. "You loved him. And when people we love do unspeakable things, it shatters our already fragile notion of the human bond."

"I just—" Jonas began, blinking away his own tears. "I cannot believe Diego would do something like that to us. To *me*."

Kierra placed her hand on his cheek. "I know. I am just as baffled. But maybe—" she paused, perhaps uncertain if she should continue on the path of her thoughts. "—maybe he had a legitimate reason."

Jonas scoffed. "What other reasons could exist besides selfish intentions?"

"Only God knows."

Fighting back another wave of sadness, Jonas' emotions caught in his throat. He opened his mouth to speak but stopped, dissolving into sobs.

"It is okay to be upset," Kierra consoled him. She gathered him in her arms, wrapping them around his trembling shoulders. "Emotion is how we know we are still alive."

"It is almost too much to bear," he wept.

"Of course, it is," Kierra whispered, running her fingertips up and down his back. "Diego broke your trust. Trust is one of the most sacred elements that connects us to another person. When that bind is severed, our whole world spins out of orbit. It is entirely acceptable for you to feel hurt right now. We all feel it."

Jonas pulled away from Kierra, fishing for a handkerchief on the bedside table. After dabbing his face with it, he cleared his throat and attempted to pull himself together. Along with Diego's betrayal and his father's vengeful actions, the release of unknown tyranny from the Tablet nagged at his conscious. Their enemies' actions had ultimately smeared a black mark of death on both the Third Order of the Magi and potentially the entire world.

A true quietus.

"You are not still thinking about submitting your resignation, are you?"

He sighed. "It is for the best."

"Jonas van der Campe, don't you *dare* say that!" Kierra answered, a tinge of disappointment in her voice. "The Third Order *needs* you right now. The Legerdemain Brotherhood just unleashed danger into the world. They need you more than ever. *We* need you."

"If I do not, the Council will see to it that I am removed," Jonas replied, despondent. "I've failed them one too many times."

"And that gives you permission to give up?" Kierra continued. By this time, she was nearly in hysterics. "If I were to give up on fighting for women's right to vote, do you really think I could live with myself when lawmakers drop the issue altogether? Do you think I could tell the generation of women after me that the reason their voice isn't heard is because I gave up? No. When you fight, you fight until the end."

"Then where do we go from here?" Jonas asked, his voice wavering with brokenness.

"This is not over. Not yet," Kierra answered optimistically. "So, we do what we were always called to do: We move forward, one brave step at a time."

56

ᵁNSTOPPABLE ꟾORCES

Rain streaked across the train windows, falling in time with Ezra's tears.

No matter how hard Ezra tried to suppress it, the events from the night prior kept replaying in his mind like a broken gramophone. He still did not want to believe any of it happened. He *couldn't*. He still did not want to accept that his father was gone. He *wouldn't*.

He was alone.

While Jonas and Miss McLarney had stayed behind in Constantinople to brief the Magi Administration on the happenings, Annabelle and Zaire accompanied him and Aja and Oliver on the journey back to Belfast. Besides the occasional trip to the lavatory, Ezra avoided leaving his solitary compartment in the hopes that he'd be left alone by the rest of his traveling party. Especially now, when anytime he would pass through the outlook carriage, the downtrodden faces of Aja and Oliver caused his own vision to become bleary.

During those excursions, Ezra would catch sight of Ms. Chicory as she drew out her lacy handkerchief and patted away the tears from Aja's face. After attending to the young lady, Annabelle would cup Oliver's cheeks in her hands, brushing the wetness from his eyes with her thumb.

"Keep your chins up, dears," Annabelle would encourage them. "We will get through this."

Completely defeated, Ezra sat alone in his train compartment and leaned his forehead against the window. His unfocused gaze stared through the condensation collecting on the glass. Only a week ago, the opportunity of a fresh start seemed more attainable than ever. Promising, even. But now—

Now, the Universe had once again left him empty handed. Broken. Lost.

Ezra chewed angrily on his lip. *The Universe.* The very phrase left a sour taste on his tongue. For something allegedly a source of strength and power, the Universe had a knack for dealing out the worst of destiny's cards to Ezra.

The compartment door slid open, revealing a weary Annabelle Chicory. She offered a kind smile and took a seat on the cushion across from him.

"I thought you could use some company, my dear," Annabelle said, patting his knee.

Ezra frowned and turned his attention out the window.

"Sweetheart, I know this is difficult for you," Annabelle replied, "but I want you to know that no matter what, the Irish Chapter will always be here. You will always be a part of our family, and we will protect you from whatever the Legerdemain Brotherhood has brewing behind closed doors."

Ezra attempted a polite smile, but it did not possess the vitality to reach his eyes.

The elderly woman reached over and grasped both of his hands. "Do not let hopelessness consume you."

Ezra choked in disbelief. "With all due respect, ma'am, I cannot see the positive in *anything* that has happened in the last month," he said, acridity souring his tone. "How do you and the others honestly think things will get better? It—it is *impossible.*"

"A wise man once said that Magi were always meant to do impossible things," Annabelle said. "Never let those words go, Ezra. Your father meant them."

His face screwed up with emotion.

Annabelle tightened her grip on his hands. A sudden sadness glittered in her blue eyes, with a redness flushing her nose. "Ezra, if anyone knows grief and heartache as much as yourself, it is me."

Ezra waited in silence for her to explain.

"Thirty years ago, I lived happily with my husband and three young children in Canterbury," Annabelle began, her voice trembling. "I had everything a young woman could ever dream of having: a lovely home, a supportive spouse, and the most beautiful, Gifted children. But one day as I was returning home from the market, a dark smoke obscured the horizon. With a terrible ache in my chest, I rushed like mad to get to them but by the time I arrived, it was too late. In less than a few hours, my entire life had gone up in flames. My husband, my children, and my home—my reasons for living—were all taken away from me."

"I—I am sorry," Ezra whispered. "I had no idea."

"For years, I doubted if any decency existed in the Universe," Annabelle continued, "for if there were an atom of goodness, if there were truly a higher power, how could such dreadful things happen to innocent people?

"Eventually, after a long career working as a nurse in England, I relocated to Belfast and, by complete happenstance, met Jonas and Kierra. They were celebrating the purchase of the High Street building at a pub. After chatting with them, I finally understood my calling.

"My whole life, I had this ideal picture of what I thought I needed when all along, my purpose was to serve the community through my Gifts and care for my new family."

Annabelle paused, squeezing Ezra's hands once more. "From the beginning of time, Magi and Quotidians alike have stared up at the stars, begging for them to somehow shed light on the meaning of this life. And when things go wrong, we see no other choice but to blame the very Power that gave us life to begin with."

Ezra sniffed and pulled his hand out of Annabelle's grasp so he could wipe the sadness away from his eyes.

"We might not understand the ways of the Universe, but that is just the mystery of how it works," Annabelle said, a hopeful glint sparkling in her eyes. "The Light is on our side. Events in our lives are merely lessons we must face along the way. Lessons that make us stronger. Lessons that make us the unstoppable forces we were always meant to become."

Ezra glanced up from his teacup, meeting the eyes of the newly appointed magistrate.

The clock on the wall ticked the same, insistent rhythm. The crystal ashtray on the desk refracted a spectrum of colour over the same mahogany desk. A familiar collection of fountain pens occupied the same cylindrical container, now accompanying Harland and Wolff materials splayed across the desktop.

While the elements were frozen in time from his last visit to the magistrate's office a month and a half ago, the Ezra Newport sitting in front of the Irish official was an entirely different person.

Ezra examined his reflection on the surface of his tea. His unkempt hair fell across his forehead, a perfect companion to his dark eyebrows and tanned complexion. A wistfulness saturated his amber eyes. His strong jawline was set in fervent determination. Yes, he certainly looked the same. But deep inside, he had lived a thousand years. Seen a million things. Embarked on a lifetime of adventures.

"Congratulations are in order for winning the attention of the Harland and Wolff recruiters," said the new magistrate. A man in his mid-twenties, the young official held his tall, skinny frame in a confident stature. His eyes skimmed over the contents of the papers before him through golden spectacles.

Ezra stared absently at the brass nameplate on his desk that announced him as "Associate Magistrate James Murphy" and fell back into the cadence of his mental musings. Once he and the Irish Chapter had returned to Belfast, everything shifted back into a semi-familiar existence. His lessons and responsibilities at the academy resumed as if they had never ceased. Interviews with the real staff at Harland and Wolff had come and gone in a frenzy of colour and fleeting emotions. While he still had another two months to go before finishing the term, the opportunity at the company beckoned louder than ever before. A promise of new life. And in the midst of the madness, the mid-April winds blew late spring into Northern Ireland, a striking contradiction to the scene in which he had first arrived.

"Mr. Newport?"

"Oh—er, thank you, Mr. Murphy," Ezra replied, jolting out of his thoughts.

Associate Magistrate James Murphy stared at him over his spectacles for a few moments before returning to his paperwork. "During your short absence from Ireland, the Royal Irish Constabulary wanted your head for Mr. Arnold Byrne's murder," stated the magistrate. "But a fisherman spoke up about seeing the real criminal on Queen's Island that evening, so you are now off the hook." The man spent a quarter of a minute laughing at his own joke. "Fisherman. Off the hook. Oh my."

Ezra raised an eyebrow, unamused.

"Anyway, the fact of the matter is this: The man who kidnapped you might have been posing as a Harland and Wolff employee, but as you know, the job offer was—and still is—entirely authentic. Should you accept, the company is willing to begin training you once you graduate from the academy," said the associate magistrate, pushing a document and fountain pen across his desk. "All we need is your signature."

Ezra brushed his fingertips across the paper, excitement tingling in his hands. The typewritten lettering, along with the official logo of Harland and Wolff, resolutely declared his future. Ezra's heart fluttered an anxious rhythm as he picked up the pen.

If only Anne *and* Baba *were here to see this,* Ezra reflected gloomily. He imagined his mother's smiling eyes encouraging him onward and his father's strong hand resting on his shoulder.

Ezra swallowed, gripped the fountain pen, and scrawled out his name above the bold, black line.

"Excellent," approved the magistrate. He accepted the paperwork from him and issued a curt smile. "Welcome to the Belfast workforce, Ezra Newport."

Dear Jonas,

After everything that happened in Constantinople, it's been difficult to form any coherent thought or word. So, I hope this makes sense.

I wanted to let you know that I accepted a shipbuilding apprenticeship with Harland and Wolff, set to start after term ends. While I'm grateful to have this opportunity, Aja so often reminds me that my Magus abilities will not disappear if I ignore them. Therefore, I have decided to pursue both.

Would you be willing to train me in the ways of the Magi? I'm eager to know more about the Celestial Lifeforce and carry on the legacy of my parents. You are incredibly admirable, and I would be honoured to learn from you.

Ezra Newport

The darkened shop windows of the Emporium of Exotic Trinkets greeted Ezra as he lingered on the sidewalk. The closed sign had not budged. With Miss McLarney's continued absence from Belfast Royal Academy, he knew she and Jonas must have still been caught up in affairs at Magi headquarters. No one knew when they would return. But Ezra could not ignore the restlessness in his soul any longer.

Scrounging in his coat pocket, Ezra retrieved the letter he had written earlier that morning. He nodded in determination and slipped the letter through the post slot, hearing it flutter over the wooden floors.

He had made his father a promise. And *inshallah*, he would see it through to the end.

A GRAVE MISTAKE

Every centimetre of Jonas van der Campe's aura had once shimmered with unexplainable magic. But now, that magic had faded, and so had the usual sparkle in his eyes.

Jonas straightened his waistcoat while observing himself in the hotel room mirror. Fading bruises edged along his cheekbones and jawline. Sleepless nights saturated the skin beneath his eyes. Despite the depths of depression, he'd managed to put a comb through his hair and a razor to his unkempt beard. He had to look presentable for the Council when he delivered the news.

Swallowing the lump in his throat, Jonas picked up the hotel stationary from the stately writing desk. He had committed it to memory after reading it over so many times:

ISTANBUL HOTEL

Dear Magi Council,

After due consideration, I have made the unfortunate decision to resign from my duties as a Magi Master. This decision did not come lightly, but with painstaking deliberation. I am only endangering our society by my reckless actions, for which I take full responsibility.

Recent events have prompted me to take a step back and examine my life as a whole. I cannot be the leader you expect of me. I cannot be the Magus the Third Order needs.

Please instruct me on steps necessary to turn in my badge and license.

Respectfully,

Jonas van der Campe

For some reason, the loops of his urgent handwriting seemed almost unfamiliar. The black ink shone in a different light. A light that painted him as a failure. A fraud.

The happenings at the Basilica Cisterns haunted him, like a never-ending nightmare on a relentless loop. With every remembrance of his father's words, inadequacy slashed through him. His Magi family had gotten hurt because of him. His closest companion had betrayed him only to join forces with his worst enemy. Everything that used to make all the sense in the world had deliquesced into utter chaos.

And that was why he had to go through with this.

Folding the letter into a crisp envelope, Jonas allowed the silence of the room to comfort his piercing anxieties. Yet, his fingers still trembled when he unclasped the Magi pin from his jacket lapel and dropped it into the envelope. And tears still pricked the corners of his eyes when he clutched the communication close to his heart.

Behind him, the hotel room door creaked open.

"Are you ready? The carriage is waiting."

Without turning to acknowledge Kierra's presence, he sniffed and ran a hand over his face. His cousin's encouraging touch grazed his shoulder, which somehow made him feel even weaker than he already was.

"Jonas, you do not have to do this."

"I do," he sighed, tucking the envelope inside his jacket. "There is nothing more I can do to salvage this broken commitment. Besides, it is what they would expect of me."

"Exactly," Kierra responded, grabbing his shoulders so he would not find interest in some other distraction. "It is what *they* would expect. But you are not the Magi Council. I am not sure if you have realised this yet, but you already do not fit the mould of the average man."

Jonas allowed the slightest grin to brighten his expressions.

"This level of perfection you are holding yourself to is unachievable."

"I know," he replied, pinching the bridge of his nose. Just as he opened his mouth to speak again, an insistent pounding shook the door.

Both cousins leapt in astonishment. Kierra recovered first, cautiously approaching to greet whoever stood on the other side. When the door swung open, a short, dark-skinned woman draped in a cloak traipsed into the room with terrifying intensity. Her golden Magi pin—alongside the silver seal of the Administration—sparkled on the left side of her outerwear.

Jonas opened his mouth, but nothing came out.

The Administration official looked between the two of them, her sight finally resting on Jonas.

"Jonas van der Campe?"

He shrunk backward, caught off guard by her gruff, Australian accent. "I am Jonas. With whom am I speaking? Are you from the Sydney Chapter?"

"Formally, yes, but now I lend my talents to the Investigative Division," she answered without blinking. "Edwin Mears tells me you have an affinity for breaking the rules."

"Wh—who are you?" Jonas asked.

After sweeping away bouncy black ringlets from her face, she held out a confident hand in greeting. "My name is Atlantis Townsend, and I *also* have an affinity for breaking the rules."

"Er, aren't you my probation officer?"

"Technically."

"Are you here to arrest me?"

The woman stared at him through an odd expression. "Do you want me to arrest you?"

"Not particularly."

"Good, because I don't have time for that paperwork," Atlantis admitted.

Baffled by the statement, Kierra stifled a dumbstruck laugh behind her hand.

"See, Mr. van der Campe, we have a problem on our hands," said

Atlantis. Striding with purpose to the hotel window, she surveyed the streets below as if expecting someone to be watching. "The Administration does not want our communities to know, lest we have a worldwide panic. However, against my better judgement and against the wishes of the Council, I am coming to you with the interpretation of the prophecy and the identity of the Roaming Lion. After all, among our twelve Chapters, you were the first to enquire about it."

Jonas shared a bewildered look with Kierra before turning his attention to his probation officer. He fought the urge to explode into raucous, disbelieving laughter. After all this time, after everything that happened, *now* the Magi Administration wished to communicate? "Er—I beg your pardon, Miss Townsend, but you are much too late. We have already determined the identity of the Roaming Lion. And Ibrahim Newport is dead."

Atlantis furrowed her eyebrows, standing within mere centimetres of Jonas. Her gaze locked onto his; he could practically feel the electricity of her aura sparking and fizzling like firecrackers.

Jonas gulped, backing into the writing desk.

"Did you know Dark Watchers were ordered to hunt down his family?"

"Of course, I did," Jonas responded. "The Legerdemain Brotherhood was on to them before—"

"No," interrupted Atlantis. Her stormy, silver eyes softened for a fraction of a second. "My department ordered those attacks."

"Oh, God above," Kierra gasped, clutching her heart. "The Magi Administration was behind the Portadown train wreck? All the attempts on the Newports' lives? But why? The prophecy said that Ibrahim—"

"Whatever you think the prophecy said, you were wrong."

"But the Legerdemain Brotherhood came to the same conclu—"

"You *both* got it wrong," sighed the woman. She folded her arms in impatience. "Typical, coming from the minds of men and Quotidians without formal training on ancient Akkadian."

"So, if our understanding of the prophecy is wrong, what does it really say?" Jonas questioned.

Drawing a folded piece of paper from her trousers, the young woman glared silver daggers at Jonas to silence him. "The prophecy was misinterpreted, both in our original records and in the newspapers. But when we obtained the cuneiform tablet from the British Museum, our language experts were able to ascertain the *actual* message." She cleared her throat.

"When struggles crest
Kings crumble at the Alliance
A Roaming Lion seizes the throne
And the Tribes he'll control.

Locked within time
Where Destinies are viewed
His memories unlock magic
And together, great power shall they wield.

Bring forth the Lion, Dragon, and Bull
In the city where it all began
A circle of Twelve shall overcome
Or bow to the Queen's celestial fate."

Bitter silence felled what meagre expectations Jonas had left. It couldn't be true. Not after all that had happened.

"And before you make a snide remark about how that doesn't rhyme or that the metering is off, ancient Babylonians weren't as fond as phonetics as Europeans," Atlantis remarked.

"So, you are saying Ibrahim Newport is not the saviour of the Magi?"

"The Roaming Lion is *not* Ibrahim Newport."

Grappling for words that stumbled over each other in his mouth, Jonas' jaw fell open in shock. "Wh-what? But that's not possible!"

The young woman's eyes danced from Jonas to Kierra and then returned to their original target.

"When the Prophetic Translation Case was reopened in February, the Investigative Division unearthed another excerpt from the same Babylonian author," the young woman explained. "But that segment went into greater detail of the identity of the Roaming Lion. He is someone much stronger than Ibrahim Newport. Someone possessing magic so advanced that he has not once, not twice, but multiple times cheated death."

Confused, Jonas met Kierra's gaze. She pursed her lips and crossed her arms. But even through wordless communication, he could tell they were thinking the very same: *Could the Roaming Lion really have been alluding to Labynetus all this time?* If only they had known sooner, before his reincarnation had been unleashed into the world.

"The fact is, Jonas, we have known who he was all along," she continued. "But you kept mucking up all our efforts."

Anticipation for her next words seared the air. Jonas swallowed, terror blazing in his chest.

"*Ezra* Newport is the Roaming Lion," she said. Her words clattered like iron against the marble floors. "And he was never meant to save the Magi."

"H-he isn't?" Jonas asked, his knees becoming weaker by the second.

Atlantis sauntered forward, her features grim and ghastly. "He is meant to destroy us."

Author Acknowledgements

When I started writing *The Magi Menagerie*, I knew I was on the cusp of something remarkable. Every word written became a testament to the strength an individual must possess while conquering periods of depression, creative droughts, global pandemics, and societal injustice. I could not have made it through this journey without the following people:

To the incredible women who first taught me how to write: Ms. Cheryl Monks and Ms. Carol Chasteen Green. I imagine if you were both alive today, you would be proud of the personal and professional growth you helped cultivate within me.

To Sarah Collins, I honestly cannot thank you enough for the guidance you provided with editing, story structure, and character development after the first draft. Your expertise helped me craft this story into an unforgettable adventure.

To my editor, Quinn Nichols, your insight took this story to the next level. I sincerely appreciate your notes and suggestions (I took them, ran, and never looked back!) Thank you for the time you spent helping me put the final polish on this gem.

To Natalie Fee and Jennifer Parr, thanks for letting me sob about my characters and their life choices to you on the phone. You are literal saints.

To my parents, a million thanks for being my first fans, from the moment I could pick up a pencil. Your support for my writing means so much to me. I've come a long way from penning tales about monster flies, right? Maybe not that far.

About the Author

Since the early age of 6, Kale Lawrence knew she either wanted to be an astronaut or an author. Obviously, the astronaut gig didn't work out, so instead, Kale turned to fantastic fictional worlds. When Kale is not writing creatively, she works as a Marketing Manager at a pet product company, and pretends she's an Olympic swimmer at the gym. She has also served as a board member for the South Dakota Writes organization.

In addition to books, Kale's writing has been featured on nationwide PBS television programming, NBC newscasts, ABC newscasts, and the Travel Channel.

Kale currently lives in Sioux Falls, South Dakota with her feisty tortoiseshell calico cat, Emma Bug and sassy Siamese, Seattle Bean.

Connect with Kale Lawrence

Instagram
@kalelawrence

TikTok
@authorkalelawrence

Facebook
@authorkalelawrence